THE SECRETS OF STRANGERS

CHARITY NORMAN was born in Uganda and brought up in successive draughty vicarages in Yorkshire and Birmingham. After several years' travel she became a barrister, specialising in crime and family law in the north-east of England. Also a mediator and telephone crisis line listener, she's passionate about the power of communication to slice through the knots. In 2002, realising that her three children had barely met her, she took a break from the law and moved with her family to New Zealand. Her first novel, *Freeing Grace*, was published in 2010. *After the Fall* was a Richard and Judy Book Club choice and World Book Night title. *See You in September*, her last book, was shortlisted for Best Crime Novel in the 2018 Ngaio Marsh Awards for Crime Fiction. *The Secrets of Strangers* is her sixth book.

THE SECRETS OF STRANGERS

Charity Norman

First published in Australia and New Zealand in 2020 by Allen & Unwin

First published in Great Britain in 2020 by Allen & Unwin, an imprint of Atlantic Books Ltd

Allen & Unwin, an imprint of Atlantic Books Ltd
Ormond House
26–27 Boswell Street
London WC1N 3JZ

Phone: 020 7269 1610
Fax: 020 7430 0916

Email: UK@allenandunwin.com
Web: www.allenandunwin.com/uk

A CIP catalogue record for this book
is available from the British Library.

Paperback ISBN: 978 1 91163 041 8
E-Book ISBN: 978 1 76087 200 7

Printed and bound by CPI Group (UK) Ltd, Croydon CR0 4YY

10 9 8 7 6 5 4 3 2

For Barnaby Norman
(Pluffy)
1998–2018

'I shall not look upon his like again.'
William Shakespeare, *Hamlet*

ONE

Neil

It's the rattle of coins dropping into his cup that wakes him. That, and his friend the one-legged pigeon with his happy-bird crooning. That, and the stream of arctic air invading his sleeping bag. That, and the whole bench shuddering as a bus wheezes down the High Road.

Thirty seconds ago he was comfy in his old bed, his arms around Heather, his nose in her hair. Shampoo and laundry powder. But there must have been a door open somewhere because ice was seeping in. He'd have to get up and shut that bloody thing. Anyway—dammit—he needed a pee.

Then the clatter in his tin mug. Heather's beautiful warmth is going, going, gone as reality pours back in all its disastrous glory. Mind you, it's a relief to wake up at all. Always good to know you've made it through another night. He opens his eyes just in time to register the squeak of rubber soles and glimpse a sturdy silhouette marching off across the church car park. Buddy pokes his head out from his blanket, ears pricked, sniffing.

There's four quid in the cup: a lucky birthday present from someone who doesn't even know it's his birthday. *Many happy returns, you useless sod.* He mouths it, not quite aloud. Tries not to talk to himself. Losing battle. Soon he'll be one of those shambolic wrecks who mutter and curse under their breaths, the kind he used to feel sorry for. To be honest, he doesn't want many returns of this kind of day.

Buddy heaves a sigh, and his greying muzzle sinks back onto his paws. He's old. He just wants to sleep. Neil watches the one-legged pigeon pecking at a hefty crust of bread. His bladder's becoming insistent but he's putting off the moment when he has to face the cold and find out the hard way which bit of him aches the most. His dodgy knee. Maybe his creaking hip. Maybe his back.

He lowers his feet to the ground just as a pair of fire engines come bellowing past, sirens dropping and slowing. Doppler effect. He used to teach kids about that. He even had a video clip of a passing ambulance he used to play in the classroom, once upon a time when he was a clean-shaven know-all with a family and friends and a home and a sofa to sit on at night to watch telly.

His daily routines are different these days: rolling the sleeping bag and Buddy's blanket with raw fingers, folding the cardboard box he uses as a mattress, shoving everything into his trusty back-pack. It's been on Duke of Edinburgh tramps, this pack. He's carried it all over Exmoor with sixth-formers hanging on his every word. Mr Cunningham, the fount of all knowledge—how are the mighty fallen! The pack's decrepit now, straps broken, open-mouthed tears all along the seams, more hole than it is nylon. He's done his best to plug the gaps with plastic bags but the end is surely nigh for his old friend.

Jeepers, this wind. Might as well be in bloody Siberia. He's wearing the warmest clothes he's ever owned: gloves, anorak and what's left of his blue-and-red bobble cap. He never takes it off in winter. Sleeps in his boots too. It's safer. He keeps everything else he owns in three plastic shopping bags. These, along with the backpack, he stashes under the hedge at the church's boundary, getting down on hands and knees to push them out of sight. His worldly goods blend in. They look like all the other rubbish.

Foxes live under this hedge. It's one of the few joys of rough sleeping, watching those wild creatures up close and personal under the sickly streetlights. He feeds them when he can. Buddy's stopped growling at them, and one of the vixens is getting bold. He's almost touched her.

He has a pitch selling the *Big Issue* outside Sainsbury's but his slot doesn't start until the afternoon rush hour. Sometimes he whiles away a few hours in the bookie, or sneaks into the library to read newspapers. Often he has to beg if he wants to eat. Not today. Four pounds in his cup, another three-and-a-bit in his pocket. Seven quid. Luxury. By rights he ought to put the whole lot on Westerly Boy in the first race at Haydock. He's got a very good feeling about Westerly Boy.

There again, the bookie won't be open until eight o'clock, and Neil's shivering *now*. His stomach is gnawing itself. Hunger hurts. Cold hurts. Everything hurts. He'd murder for a cup of tea and a bit of human company, and Tuckbox do giant mugs for one pound eighty. They've got big radiators, a toilet with fluffy towels, even a bowl of water outside for dogs. Last week the barista gave him some leftover pies. Buddy and he and the foxes shared them.

'Tuckbox it is, then,' he says, passing a frayed piece of string under the dog's collar. 'C'mon, Buddy.'

The streetlights are still glowing along Balham High Road, orange halos in the murk. A rind of ice coats the gutters. Skeins of hurrying commuters flow around him as though he's a slow-moving branch in their river. Some are smoking, some talking nonsense into phones, their shiny shoes crunching in the grit. Buddy's a good scavenger. He finds half a burger by the side of the road and scoffs the lot without changing pace.

Neil begins to whistle quietly. He's picturing himself jammed right up close to one of those heavy old radiators in Tuckbox, a mug between his hands, tea with lots of sugar. Newspaper to read. Marvellous. And when the bookie's shop opens he'll get himself straight in there and keep his fingers crossed for birthday luck.

Today's the day! The tide is on the turn, and his ship is coming in.

TWO

Abi

She felt his kiss as he crept out at six, heard his hopeful whisper—*Let me know, won't you? Even if it's not good news?*—and nodded without opening her eyes. She couldn't bring herself to tell him. Better to wait for the phone call to make her latest failure official.

Sleep's overrated. After all, you're a long time dead. Charlie left a mug of coffee for her on the bedside cabinet, and it's still hot when she hauls herself into the shower. By seven-fifteen she's dressed, blow-dried, has sent off several urgent emails and is slamming the front door closed behind her. Turn left at the gate, head for the station, double-quick. So much to do, so little time.

Monday. Results day. That all-important piece of paper will already be on someone's desk. For some reason, Charlie's been extra optimistic about this round. He keeps rubbing his hands, muttering, *Fifth time lucky, eh? It's our turn, isn't it, Abi?* Poor guy. He's going to be crushed again.

She's due at St Albans Crown Court this morning to defend a woman accused of shaking her nine-week-old baby, causing catastrophic brain injury. The brief only arrived in Abi's pigeonhole on Friday, after her fraud trial was adjourned. She met the mother an hour later. Kelly Bradshaw: young, gaunt, dissolving. *I love Carla. I know you never ever shake a baby.* It all hangs on the timing of the injury, but there's a glimmer of hope there, because the prosecution expert doesn't seem quite sure.

Abi speeds up, towing her case on its wheels. The next train is due in twelve minutes and she intends to be on it. She's mentally running through the week: lists, decisions, things-to-remember—organised, compartmentalised and flagged for action. She's planning her cross-examination of the prosecution's neurologist. She's conjuring excuses to avoid Christmas lunch at her parents' place: Dad being Dad in all his dickish glory; her sister Lottie like the Madonna, beatifically breastfeeding. She's thinking about results day.

Heartburn is raging in her solar plexus. Without breaking her stride she checks her bag, looking for antacids. Bugger, she's out. Better get some more.

The judge in *Bradshaw* has zero empathy. He's going to be a total bastard when Abi starts making last-minute applications—which she fully intends to do because the defence case is a shambles. She needs social services records, and she plans to challenge the admissibility of Kelly's disastrous police interviews. Abi is going to be public enemy number one this morning.

She's nipping into Boots when her phone rings. It's early for the clinic to be calling, and it's not from their usual number, but she feels a lurch of anxiety as she answers.

Not the clinic. It's Henry, her instructing solicitor in today's trial. He's losing his cool.

'Slight problem,' he says. 'The prosecution served an addendum report from their neurologist.'

'And?'

'It plugs the gap. He puts the time of injury squarely during the hours when Mum was alone with the baby.'

'When did they serve this?'

Henry sounds mortified, and well he might. 'Actually, two weeks ago. It got misfiled at our end. Luckily I came in early, I was checking the file. An intern . . .'

'Bloody hell.' Abi's thinking fast as she grabs a packet of antacids from the shelf. 'Look, can you get in touch with our expert, email him that report, try to get his response immediately? Email it to me too. I'll read it on the train.'

'Okay.'

'I should be with you by nine.'

The self-service tills aren't working. She and two other customers have to wait for a guy to amble across, chewing the cud. Bloody hell, would he hurry up? Seconds tick by and are lost forever—time, the most valuable commodity in her life. She can feel drips of acid burning her oesophagus as she finds Tuckbox Café on her phone and texts in her order. They don't faff about. That's why she's so loyal to the place. It takes Sofia, the barista, an average of ninety seconds to exchange staccato pleasantries and produce an espresso-to-go.

She's out. Six minutes to the train. Three dogs are waiting on the pavement outside Tuckbox, their leads attached to bike racks. A rangy old boy sits a little apart from the others with his ears pressed forwards, gaze fixed on the door, obviously determined not to move until his human reappears. His lead consists of a piece of blue twine. The other two know Abi and are tail-waggingly delighted to see her.

'Hi, gals,' she mutters, patting them as she passes by. Dixie and Bella: an anorexic greyhound and a creamy teddy bear, both dolled up in twee tartan coats. Abi's got a soft spot for these two, although she avoids their owners like the plague. Renata, Rory and their twin baby boys live next door, at number 96. Their smugness knows no bounds.

Fifty per cent chance, the quacks say. *Fifty per cent.* Seemed like reasonable odds the first time, even the second. Don't seem so good now that she and Charlie are enduring their fifth round, rapidly using up their precious frozen embryos, their savings, their hope. It's an endless marathon: running and running, hearts and lungs screaming while the finishing line keeps moving further away. Yet all this time they've been brazening it out. They commute, they work, they laugh, they go to other people's children's christenings, they redecorate their home, they radiate success and control, they feverishly pretend their childlessness is a lifestyle choice. They watch one another grieve.

The clinic will be calling this morning, probably at about eight. She knows the drill. She also knows exactly what they're going to tell her and she doesn't want to hear it.

She reaches for the door of Tuckbox Café. Five minutes to the train.

THREE

Mutesi

Mrs Dulcie Brown died in the early hours of the morning. She drifted over the bar from sleep to death, no fuss or fanfare, her heart finally still after almost a hundred years of life. Three in the morning is a popular departure time from the Prince Albert wing: the peaceful hour, when night staff move quietly through their routines and the cooks haven't yet begun to clatter.

Her family began to arrive just after the doctor who certified the death. Mutesi brought them a tray with tea and biscuits. She found them chuckling over their memories, making up for all those years when memory was lost. Mrs Brown had been absent for a decade, wandering through that homesick hinterland where all faces look alike and nowhere is home, clinging to a stubborn straw of dignity. Mutesi had pinned photos up in her bedroom as a reminder of who this shadow really was: *Dulcie Agnes Brown*. Mother, grandmother, great-grandmother. A Land Girl in the war, a magistrate. A tiny girl in a white dress and socks, staring solemnly out at her descendants.

Mutesi's shift ends at six, though she lingers to write up her notes before stepping out of the tropical heat of the nursing home into an icy pre-dawn. She catches the bus to Balham, lumbering across the frosty savannah of Tooting Common before hopping off at the stop beside St Jude's church. It's still dark—at least, the air glows in that constant twilight that passes for dark in London—but the city is already awake. You can hear it; you can feel it. Mutesi loves the sense that a giant is stirring and opening its eyes.

The homeless man is sleeping on the bench again. She can just make out his bobble cap and his dog's white-speckled muzzle peeking out from under a ragged blanket, both of them looking far too old for this kind of life. A tin mug sits on the ground nearby. Perhaps he's left it there in hope of donations, or maybe it's his bedside cup of water. After all, why wouldn't homeless people have bedside cups of water like everyone else?

The bench is a popular spot for rough sleepers. It's set into an alcove in the church wall, sheltered from the worst of the weather. There was a fuss about it at the last parish council meeting. It's true that some of the sleepers leave bottles, cigarette butts and a pervading smell of urine behind them, but not this one. The curate offered to contact an emergency shelter for him but he'd politely refused, saying it was a revolving door and, anyway, he needed to keep his dog. Mutesi fears they'll find the pair of them dead one day, frozen stiff in the church grounds. It can't be right.

St Jude's is locked up like Fort Knox, but she's on the cleaning rota and has keys to the side door. She flicks on a minimum of lights, strolling peaceably among the frozen shadows of the nave, her footsteps startling saints in their stained-glass windows. The echoing space smells of polish and dust and plasticine from Sunday school, and now the pine of the enormous Christmas tree. Some people won't venture in alone at night—*spooky*, they say, shivering. Mutesi likes it. She can certainly feel the spirits all around, but they're kindly. Well, most of them are.

She stops under the ornate carving of the pulpit, beside the tea-light stand with its wooden box for donations, and lights a candle for Mrs Brown. This is her private ritual whenever a resident dies. After a minute has passed she lights another for all the beloved souls she lost long ago, back home. Just one small flame must represent them all: it would take all the tea-lights in the basket if she were to light one for each. She leaves the candles burning, two tiny tongues of fire in the darkness.

It's only as she is stepping out into the dissolving night that she remembers the donation box. It's not compulsory, but to light candles without paying feels like stealing. She has a couple of two-pound coins ready in her pocket. Ah, well, never mind. She'll settle up on Wednesday when she goes in for choir practice.

The one-legged pigeon flutters to land at her feet. He lives on one of the gargoyles and he knows her very well. *Clever bird!* She rummages in her bag for her plastic sandwich box.

'Yes, yes,' she murmurs, tipping it upside down. 'You're in luck, Hoppy.'

The pigeon is already pecking as crusts cascade onto the asphalt. Yawning, Mutesi holds her watch close to her eyes. Five past seven. She'd dearly like to go home and make tea in the *Grandma* mug Emmanuel gave her. She longs to curl up under heavy blankets with her eyes closed. *That* is a luxury—drifting away while the rest of the city suffocates on trains and buses. But it's Monday, and she has to meet Brigitte and Emmanuel at Tuckbox. Mutesi's job is to give her grandson breakfast before walking him to school. They will share a cheese toastie and a pot of tea. He will talk and talk, and she will smile and smile. Mutesi counts her blessings every day. The blessings keep the horrors at bay.

She stoops to check the man's tin mug is empty before sliding her coins into it. *There.* Her gift has been delivered straight to a place where it's needed, with no middleman. She's never quite sure whether this is true of the donation box.

It takes a little over ten minutes to walk along the High Road, past the GP surgery—cheeky young locum she saw last time tried to put her on a weight-loss program, as though she's anything but healthy and fit for her age!—under the railway bridge. Fire engines scream past, scattering a queue of cars, and she spares a thought for whoever's life is being turned upside today.

Tuckbox is another world again: humid and neon-lit, cheerfully noisy with the hiss and gurgle of the coffee machine, the rumble of conversation, music from a radio station. The front counter faces the door, with cabinets forming an L-shaped border around a busy kitchen. Customers queue at the counter, or hang about as they wait for their takeaway orders. Most seem fixated on phones or newspapers. A young man and woman stand gazing into one another's eyes. A trio of teenagers in school uniform has just ordered. One of them sees something on her phone and holds it out to the others, who double up with laughter.

The café's owner is polishing his glass-fronted cabinets. He's a tall, handsome figure, always upbeat, though Mutesi knows the poor man buried his wife about a week ago. Tragic thing. Cancer, and so quick. Brave of him to be back at work already.

'How are you today, Robert?' she asks.

He lights up at the sight of her. 'Keeping on keeping on,' he says. 'Lucky to have customers like you.'

'You won't take some time off?'

'Nah. Helps to keep busy. If I think about Harriet too much I'll turn to mush.' He's still smiling, but his voice is fraying. 'The thing is, she was my life, you know? Home isn't home without her.'

'I know.'

'I wake up and she's not there.'

A timer beeps loudly in the kitchen.

'No rest for the wicked,' Robert mutters, and he winks at Mutesi before skidding behind the counter to take trays of golden-brown pastries out of the big oven. Next he's helping the new runner at the back service counter. He's a hands-on boss, always ready to pile in himself.

Mutesi orders tea and a cheese toastie before looking for a table.

Ah! Good! Emmanuel's favourite spot in the window corner is free. She sits and waits, takes delivery of a pot of tea from a girl in a black T-shirt with TUCKBOX in white letters across the front. Snatches of conversation reach her from the booth nearby. *Did one-ninety, dead lift, made it look easy . . .* Apparently someone missed leg day last week and is suffering for it.

Brigitte and Emmanuel are late. Never mind. Mutesi is just taking that first heavenly sip of tea when they come scurrying in from the street. Her grandson looks smart in his green school uniform, a satchel slung across his chest. She feels her heart swell at the sight of those bright eyes, the broad forehead and sticking-out ears. His lashes flick upwards like sunbeams. She knows her survival has been worth something, because this beautiful child is the result.

At five foot nothing, Brigitte is several inches shorter than her mother-in-law. So clever, so loving—Mutesi can't imagine anyone else who might be good enough for Isaac. Emmanuel gets his enormous eyes from her, and his white teeth and lovable grin. She's wearing a beret over short, braided hair, her mouth muffled by a scarf. She feels the cold.

'Late again,' she gasps, shivering. 'I'm so sorry.'

'Don't worry!' Mutesi stretches her arms wide so that both mother and son can fit into her embrace. 'You have a lot on your plate. And how is the handsomest and most brilliant schoolboy in the world?'

The most brilliant schoolboy has his mittened hand stuck high up in the air. The rule at his smart school is not to speak until the teacher says you may, and he's taken to doing the same at home. It began as a game but now it's a habit. Mutesi strongly disapproves—he is only six years old. Six! Why are they teaching him to behave like a soldier? Children should never be soldiers. Never. *Never.*

'Mummy lost her phone,' he says. 'She rang it but the battery was flat and now she has to go *straight away* because she has an important meeting.'

He has plenty to say about the lost phone, the bad words Mummy used and how he heroically found it in the bathroom. Mutesi keeps her listening face on for him, but she and Brigitte are both distracted by raised voices nearby. A young fellow—wild hair, wild eyes—is yelling at the café's owner. *Why didn't you tell me? I've come to get her! What the fuck have you done with her?* Robert is making *calm down* gestures, pressing downwards with his big hands as he talks. He seems to find the whole thing quite amusing. He may be a generation older than the shouting boy, but he's a head taller.

There's a powerful shove to Robert's shoulder, a final curse—*fucking evil*—and words that Mutesi doesn't catch over the music and a roaring coffee grinder. The whole thing is over as suddenly as it began. The young man bangs out through the street door, briefly colliding with a woman in a dark overcoat who's just coming in. The next moment he's pelting past the windows.

Café life pauses. There's a collective moment of nosiness. Then the milk frother starts up, and the smoothie blender. Someone laughs. Conversations resume. Robert's joking with a group of women in jogging clothes, tapping the side of his head. They're chortling. The woman who was almost knocked over is waiting at the counter, talking on her phone.

'That man used his outside voice,' says Emmanuel, pouting in disapproval. 'And bad words. Uh-uh. Naughty.'

Mutesi tugs gently on his ear. 'Maybe he didn't like his coffee.'

'Or he didn't take his pills this morning,' says Brigitte. 'I must go. Emmanuel, you'll read to Grandma, ask her to sign your reading diary?'

Emmanuel's hand is back in the air.

'I forgot my book. I think it's in my bed.'

'Not again!' Brigitte rifles through his bag. 'Miss Soames will fuss.'

'Look who's back,' says Mutesi, nodding at the door.

Brigitte is too vexed to look up from her search. 'It's been a crazy weekend. Isaac's flight to Montreal was delayed and—'

Her sentence ends in a shriek as Mutesi hurls herself at both mother and son, shielding them with her own body.

'Get down,' she says. 'On the floor. *Now.*'

FOUR

Abi

Her hand is on the door of the café when it swings towards her and someone comes thundering out.

'Sorry,' she mutters instinctively, stepping back as he barges past without so much as a glance in her direction. *Charming.* She has a fleeting impression of furious energy. Curly hair, heavy eyebrows. Grey cable-knit sweater and jeans. Not at all bad-looking, actually—*hot*, her vacuous sister Lottie would say—but seriously short on manners. He's obviously in a hurry. Well, fair enough. So is she.

Tuckbox smells of coffee and toast, and it's heaving this morning. The place aims for functionality alongside shabby comfort: a brushed cement floor, crimson walls, black-and-white photographs of sweeping landscapes, newspapers scattered around. Customers can choose between wooden tables, retro-style booths with red vinyl seats or worn leather armchairs grouped near the front window. Abi immediately notices a heavily pregnant woman making camp with a toddler and an elderly man. The young mother's in maternity jeans and fleece-lined boots, sporting a *Baby on Board* badge. *Go on, Ms Fertile, rub it in.* The little girl has white hair tied like a miniature fountain. Spindly legs in woollen tights stick straight out as she perches on her chair. She's pretending to spoon-feed a toy Roo, opening and closing her own mouth while scolding the baby kangaroo in a bossy imitation of a grown-up. Abi watches, enchanted despite her jealousy, aching with the absence of someone who has never existed. She forces herself to look away, only to spot Renata from number 96 and her posse of yummy jogging mates. Dear Lord, was there no escape?

The barista catches her eye and taps an espresso cup to show she's already on to it. Funny how matey you can become with someone you meet for only ninety seconds every day. It generates a kind of intimacy. Sofia is from Italy but she has a Romanian boyfriend. She's here first thing in the morning, often locks up at night. She'll do anything for her employer. *Customers can be such jerks, but Robert's a great boss*, she once said. *Treats us all like family.*

Right now, the man in question is delivering coffee to Renata and the yummies. He's in pretty good shape for an older guy: strong jawline, waves of dark hair with a frosting of silver, and he does this eye-crinkling thing when he smiles. He's dressed as always in an open-necked shirt. Renata is flirting openly with him, throwing her head back as she laughs. Despite being the mother of four-year-old twins she has the body of a teenager, which perhaps explains her choice of lycra for early-morning jogs on Tooting Common.

Abi's phone is ringing again. Might be the clinic.

No, not the clinic. Charlie.

'Charlie! What's up? I'm in Tuckbox, just about to grab my coffee. Bit short of time.'

'Of course you are. It's your default setting. Sorry, I can't stop thinking . . . Have you heard anything yet?'

He sounds so very hopeful, just as she was until she did that bloody test last night. He's on tenterhooks, and he's going to be broken-hearted. She wishes she could spend today with him.

'It's only seven-thirty,' she says. 'Give 'em a chance.'

'Let me know when you hear, won't you? Whatever the news?'

'You could call them yourself if you like.'

She's watching the coffee machine, mesmerised by dark liquid spilling into a cup. She doesn't have time right now for either his hope or his disappointment. She doesn't even have time for her own. She doesn't have time for agonising discussions about whether they should finally accept defeat. She hasn't time for being hurt again. All of that can wait. She glances at her watch. Four minutes to the train. It's enough. She'll be into the station, up the stairs and onto the platform with a good twenty seconds to spare. She will think about Kelly Bradshaw today.

'Um, did you do a . . . you know, a test?' Charlie's anxiety jabs at her across the ether. 'I saw the empty box in the bin earlier.'

Someone's screaming obscenities. Who the hell would be starting a riot in a café at this time of the morning? *Ah.* It's the curly-headed guy. He's back. She presses her palm over her free ear.

'Sorry, can't hear you—some idiot's yelling. I've got to grab my coffee and run.'

'We'll try again if it's negative, won't we? Abi?'

It's just sound. She's stopped listening. For the first time in days—in months—in years—she isn't even remotely thinking about either childlessness or work.

'Fuck,' she says. 'He's got a—'

The world explodes. A single report, a shock wave so shattering that her eardrums seem to burst. She's hurling herself to the ground. As both hands jerk to cover her ears, her phone spins from her grasp.

Pandemonium. The café's erupting like a fairground ride gone wrong: high-pitched screeches, someone screaming, *It's a bomb!* People are crawling under tables while others claw their way through a panicking bottleneck at the door. A little boy crouches on the floor beside a woman in a beret. The child's arms are curled over his head. A man in a suit actually trips over the poor kid—falls against a chair, scrambles up and legs it. Sofia has grabbed a couple of schoolgirls by their clothes and is dragging them towards the courtyard at the back, yelling for others to follow. *This way! Come on, come on!*

The second shot is overwhelming. For a full minute Abi can hear nothing except ocean waves. The air is opaque with gunpowder and fear.

She meets all kinds of second-hand violence in her work: endless lurid photographs of wounds, bloodstains and bodies in mortuaries. She's heard witnesses describing attacks, pathologists discussing fatal trauma—but it's all two steps removed. By the time it arrives in court there's a pattern to the violence. There's an order. It's neatly packaged.

The real thing isn't ordered at all. She knows this now. It's barbaric and ugly and confused and unimaginably loud. Her first instinct is to get out of Tuckbox, her second to tell Charlie what's happening. That's when she misses her phone. Every contact, photo, message and diary entry is stored in that little object. It's her handle on life. While sane people are running for their lives she's wasting precious seconds in turning back and bending to snatch it up from the floor.

She never sees who hurtles into her. Someone heavy, someone running full tilt. The impact knocks her off balance as she stoops, sending her sprawling, her forehead knocking against the radiator with a sickening thud. The pain is immediate. Her vision swims, her knees buckle. She's conscious, but for a moment or two her mind seems blank.

It's all over. Tuckbox seems to have been abandoned. The radio is playing a jolly Christmas song but there are no other human voices. By contrast with the *Mary Celeste* eeriness inside the café, a human herd is stampeding out on the street. Pounding feet. Shouts. *Leave this area now, get back, move!* Car horns, a roaring engine. A motorbike mounts the pavement as it U-turns. Painfully, dizzily, she uses the radiator to support herself as she stands up. *It's okay, it's okay.* The gunman will be long gone by now. She'll leave her contact details with the police, catch the next train, get to court, take a couple of ibuprofen and begin the Bradshaw trial.

As she turns to leave, she realises her mistake. The gunman is still here. He's about six feet away from her, pacing in manic circles with a shotgun in one clenched fist. Tuckbox looks like a battleground. Abandoned bags, coats and pushchairs lie scattered haphazardly between the tables. A mountain buggy has somehow ended up on its side. The pregnant mother, elderly man and toddler are all trying to hide under one small table. The schoolboy is clinging to the woman in the beret. Abi hears him whisper: *Mummy, is that man going to shoot us too?* His mother lays her mouth on his head. She's in tears. *Shush. No, but shush.*

But the really, really terrible thing is happening on the kitchen floor. The café's owner is dying, cradled in the arms of a man in a red-and-blue bobble cap. She thinks of a painting, a Renaissance pietà with its limp body and grieving bystanders, though instead of Jesus there's a middle-aged guy in jeans and a paisley shirt. Blood is coursing out of his neck, soaking his clothes, pooling on the shining concrete. So much blood. He seems to be staring at the ceiling through half-open eyes. It's deeply unnerving. *Dead on arrival at St George's Hospital*, the notes will say, but she suspects this man was more or less dead on arrival on the floor of Tuckbox Café.

Someone crouches over him, holding towels to his wounds while speaking into his ear. She's past middle age, a black woman in slacks and a cardigan. She catches Abi's eye.

'Would you please call for an ambulance?'

Her accent is strong, but her words are clear. Abi nods, immediately tapping 999 into her keypad. The woman raises her voice, calling to the people across the café.

'Everyone should leave now. Brigitte, please take Emmanuel away. Just go quickly. I will see you later.'

It's good advice. Best not to hang around. Abi is almost at the street door—her balance still unsteady, phone clamped to her ear—when she finds herself face to face with the gunman. He's standing right in her path, breathing like a wounded animal, chest and shoulders rising and falling fast. His gaze is fixed on her face as though he has something vital to tell her.

'I think I've killed Robert. I think I've killed . . . Jesus, have I killed Robert?'

'He'll be fine,' she lies.

She's racking her brains to come up with a strategy. She's met plenty of off-the-wall guys in her work, but none of them were carrying loaded shotguns. All she can come up with is an article she once read in a magazine in the fertility clinic: 'What to Do if You're Hiking in the Wilderness and Meet a Bear'. You keep absolutely still, apparently. Don't run. Don't shout. On no account must you panic. Speak calmly and reassuringly (what is reassuring to a *bear*, for God's sake?). Back away, keeping your eyes on the animal at all times.

'Look,' she says, 'this has nothing to do with me or any of these people. Just move away from the door and we'll all be on our way.'

The emergency operator's voice is loud, clear and penetrating.

Emergency. Which service do you require?

The crazy guy seems horrified by the voice. He's shouting incoherently, and he's a blur of action—breaking open the gun, shoving in cartridges from his pocket, slamming it shut again, all in a couple of seconds. In the same movement he's taken aim at Abi's phone. It's his sheer competence that appals her. She's pretty sure he could have reloaded with his eyes closed. A whimper of dismay ripples from the people behind her.

Emergency. Which service do you require?

Until this moment her own mortality has seemed the least of her problems. It's a mythological thing; a bit of a bugger, but it won't matter until she's too old to care. Now death has her in its sights, at close range, down a side-by-side pair of murderous barrels. Mortality is real. She loosens her fingers, letting the phone clatter to the floor.

'It's fine. It's okay,' she whispers, despising herself for the facile words. There's nothing remotely *okay* or *fine* about this situation. She's backing towards the counter, keeping her eyes on the bear.

The emergency operator isn't giving up.

Are you there, caller? Hello, caller?

A flash bursts from the barrel, another appalling blast of sound. Splinters of her beloved phone fly across the concrete. She dives behind the shelter of the front counter, close to where Robert is sprawled across bobble-cap man. The gunman is still yelling though she can't make out any words. Perhaps his voice can't ever be loud enough to express whatever hell is raging in his head.

In the chaos, a phone begins to ring from the overturned pushchair. As if on cue, another starts up on one of the tables. Both are calling out at once, in a shrill chorus. Perhaps customers who escaped are looking for one another; perhaps the news is already out, and people are calling their loved ones to check they're okay.

The gunman grabs both phones, drops them onto the floor and brings his boot down hard, crushing them.

'Any more?' he bellows. 'Over here. All of them, over here.'

Nobody's prepared to argue. Phones are obediently slid to him across the floor, and his solid boot stamps the life from every one of them: *smash, smash, smash.*

He's a total screaming maniac, thinks Abi. He could kill any one of us, any time. He probably will.

She inches further under cover until she feels something touch her calf. Her fumbling fingers find a shoe, then a leg—a dead man's leg. And the warm stickiness—she holds up her hand to her face, and instantly feels revulsion—is a dead man's blood. She recognises the butcher's shop smell. A glinting trickle is nosing its way across the floor towards a central drain. It looks like a living thing.

In this moment of nightmare, there's a new sound—faint at first, but rapidly swelling. It's intensely familiar, something every Londoner hears through the day and night, but right now it has an almost miraculous significance. Sirens howling, their tones intertwining, fading and reappearing. The cacophony seems to come from all directions at once. Sanity is on its way, pelting through the streets with blaring horns and flashing lights.

'Music to my ears,' mutters the man in the bobble cap.

The sirens electrify the gunman. His free hand goes to his head, clutching a handful of hair. He spins in a complete circle before rushing to the front windows where he pulls down all the blinds. He does the same to the street door, locking and bolting it before tugging the blinds over its four panes of glass. Working one-handed, still gripping his shotgun, he drags three heavy wooden tables in front of the door, tipping them over as makeshift barricades.

The wailing sirens reach their peak. Blue lights pulse through the blinds, rippling across his face.

The sheriff's here, thinks Abi. Thank God. Everything's going to be all right.

FIVE

Sam

Nothing is going to be all right. Nothing, ever again.

Lights are flashing through the curtains, making a blue river on his bedroom ceiling. Why are there lights in the middle of the night?

Someone's shrieking. It sounds like Mum, but she never shouts. The voices of strangers: *Up here, is he?* Heavy footsteps, *thud, thud*, on the stairs, past his bedroom door. An army has invaded his safe world. Now there are people in his parents' room. *Angus, can you hear me? Angus? Angus?*

He's lying like a puppet under the dinosaur duvet with his arms and legs stiff and straight and his eyes wide open and he mustn't blink, *I mustn't blink, mustn't blink*. It's hard for him to keep still, but if he doesn't move even once, everything might be all right. If something terrible happens it will be his fault for blinking.

•

Everything had been fine just a few hours ago. Summertime. Haymaking. The weather forecast said it was going to be raining cats and dogs later in the week, and the mower had broken down again. Dad was worried, working late into the night to fix it before the rain came. He'd tried phoning all the local contractors but they were up to their ears.

So there Sam and his dad were, in the tractor shed. Dad was wearing his blue overalls, a smudge of oil on his nose and stalks of hay in his hair. He was drinking coffee from a mug, though it had gone cold and husks were floating on the surface. Sam was in charge of the red metal toolbox. He knew what everything in that box was for. He was eight years old, and an apprentice farmer.

'You're falling asleep, Sammy,' said Dad, smiling as Sam handed him a spanner. 'Better hit the sack. You've got school tomorrow.'

'School. Yeuch.'

'I know. Yeuch.'

'I'll stay till we've got this fixed.'

'We've done it, son! We've saved the day.'

Sam wanted to stay there forever. He loved working with his dad more than anything in the world.

'Why do I have to go to school?'

'Bit young to be a dropout.'

'I'm going to be a farmer. I can learn everything I need from you and Mum.'

Dad thought about this. He liked to think before he spoke. He was careful with words.

'First,' he said, 'you can't be sure what you want to do with your life until you've tried a few things. Keep your options open. And, second, you need a good education to run this farm, or any farm. As the world changes—and it's changing pretty fast nowadays—you're going to need your education more and more.'

'No, I'm not,' Sam declared, folding his arms. 'I'll help you all day.'

'Aw, Sam, I wish you could. But, hey, good news! The summer holidays are coming. They go on forever. We'll have ages, son. Weeks and weeks.'

At the open doors of the barn, Sam paused to glance back. Dad was kneeling in the pool of light thrown by the powerful lamps they'd set up. Moths spun in the light. Bouncer and Snoops were sprawling on hessian sacks nearby. Bouncer was the old dog, Snoops not much more than a puppy. The glare made Dad's face look white and his nose bigger than it really was. He held up a ratchet, saluting.

'I'll just throw it all back together. Be in soon.'

'Okay.' Sam lingered for one last moment. 'Night, Dad.'

'Night, son.'

SIX

Eliza

She hears it first from the radio in the shower: an incident in progress near Balham station. Reports of gunshots and hostages, at least one witness talking about a suicide bomber. Both tube and railway stations are out of action. All streets within five hundred yards have been closed off with resultant traffic chaos. Local businesses are in lockdown; four schools have been closed. There's no statement yet from the police but a deluge of public speculation that this is yet another terrorist attack.

Not an off-duty day after all, then. She'll hear from the coordinator within minutes, and Richard's going to milk the situation for all it's worth. Before the news is over she's dressed and hauling her negotiation kit out of the cupboard: a blue sports bag stocked with an assortment of oddments. Painkillers, clothes, an empty water bottle, binoculars, torch, spare phone, charger, USB stick, peppermints, teabags, sachets of ready-mixed coffee.

Liam's still bashing away on the piano downstairs, mangling 'The Entertainer'. She imagines her son's unsmiling face, his head bent close to the keys. He's repeating the same phrase again and again and . . . she pauses, halfway through the act of zipping up her boots . . . *yep*. Again. Poor Liam. It's the school talent quest today. He's longing to show his classmates he's good at something. He just wants to have a friend or two—not much to ask, is it? But Liam isn't like other thirteen-year-olds. He doesn't seem to be on their wavelength, doesn't understand the rules of their social games. When they invite one another to their houses, he's never on the list. And the awful thing is, he cares.

The news ends with another mention of the incident in Balham. People in South London have started declaring themselves safe on Facebook. By the time Eliza reaches the kitchen her phone is pinging with notifications—*X has declared himself safe*, *Y has declared herself safe*—as though all their friends are frantic with worry.

Richard's still pretending he can't remember behaving like an arse on Saturday night. He spent yesterday clutching his head, knocking back painkillers and feigning amnesia. *Did I say that? No, I wouldn't have said that.* An apology would be nice. He still looks haggard this morning but he's acting all jolly, yelling encouragement through the hatch to Liam. Meanwhile, the baby lounges in his highchair, ferrying yoghurt from bowl to mouth but mostly missing the target. From time to time he carefully drops a dollop over the edge, watching as it lands on Yoda the cat.

'This thing at Balham station a job for you then?' asks Richard. 'Got the blue bag, I see.'

'I'm on the rota.'

'They're saying it could be a suicide bomber.'

'Might be a hoax.'

Richard's wiping yoghurt from Yoda's head. He's a draftsman, self-employed. Often not employed.

'Something always seems to happen when you're on the rota,' he says. 'It's uncanny.'

'Sorry.'

'Are you?' He's smiling, but he's not really smiling any more than she's really sorry.

Like all hostage and crisis negotiators in the Met, Eliza has a day job, in her case in the serious crime unit. She volunteers to be on call for negotiation during her off-duty time. It's become more of a problem since Jack's unexpected arrival. Everything's become more of a problem since then.

Richard's phone pings three times in quick succession.

'That'll be more drama queens declaring themselves safe.' He takes a look, snorts. 'Yup. See that? My own sister! She's getting comments—*Oh, hon, thank God you're okay.* Of course she's sodding okay! She's nowhere near Balham. Eight million people live in this city. Some of 'em are going to die today, it's a statistical inevitability. By her logic we should all declare ourselves safe every time we get into bed at night.'

'The Entertainer' comes to a thumping end. There's a blessed four-second silence before it starts again from the beginning. This time Jack joins in the concert, bashing his plastic cup against his table while bellowing *Da! Da! Da!*

'I'm too old for this,' mutters Richard. He's wearing a fleece inside out over his pyjamas. 'Why don't kids have volume controls? It's a design flaw.'

'I see now why my father went so deaf so young.' Eliza pours two mugs of tea.

'The milk's gone off.'

'Have to be black then. Last night when I was in the supermarket with Jack, the check-out woman congratulated me on having such a beautiful grandson. Grandson! Seriously?'

'Technically, we could easily be his grandparents. Forty-five.'

'Do I look like a granny?'

'No. Silly check-out lady, should've gone to Specsavers.'

The years have certainly been kind to Richard. Physically, anyway. He has the same straight eyebrows and tidy features that struck her the day they met, on a crowded train to Edinburgh. By York they'd swapped life stories. By Newcastle they'd swapped phone numbers. By the time the train pulled into Edinburgh

Waverley their lives had changed forever. It was romantic stuff, love at first sight, a shining tale to tell the grandchildren. But seventeen years on, chips and cracks mar the glossy paintwork.

A text arrives on Eliza's phone.

'That's my marching orders,' she says, sending a rapid reply.

When she tries to give Liam a goodbye hug, he slides away along the piano stool, still playing.

'Get off!' he growls. 'I've got to play the whole thing without a single mistake three times in a row.'

'Remember I said I was on the rota today?'

The music stops. He glares at the keys, his back hunched in mutinous disappointment.

'You won't be coming to the talent quest.' It's a statement, not a question.

'I will if I can.'

'Means you won't.'

'I'll do my best.'

'Huh.'

She squats down beside him. 'You'll blow their socks off! Tell me all about it this evening. Okay? Okay, Liam?'

He lifts his hands high, thumps them down. He doesn't play with panache or wit or any apparent pleasure. He plays with gritted-teeth determination. *Plink-plonk*.

Richard brings Jack to see her off at the front door. The baby makes a grab for her hair when she kisses him. As a teenager she spent her paper-round money on conditioner and straighteners, trying to turn a wire pot scrub into silky tresses. She's long since given up. She wears it in a blunt cut, shorter than her jawline. Jack has a fistful in his tiny fingers. There's grey among the mousy strands.

'Aw, look, he wants a souvenir of his granny,' says Richard.

'We are not amused.'

He knots the tartan scarf around her neck, not quite looking at her, his gaze sliding past her left ear.

'Who's on the negotiation team today?'

'Luck of the draw.'

'Paul Shackleton?' he persists.

'Possibly.'

Jack is squirming on his hip, stretching out his arms towards Eliza. She stoops to kiss her son again—his nose, his sticky hand—wishing she had time for a proper cuddle.

'Would Paul stay home to look after your children while you save the world?' asks Richard. 'Would he emasculate himself?'

'Not this again.'

'Bet he wouldn't.'

'He's got his own family to think about,' she says, sighing. 'He's of no relevance to mine. He's not a rival to you.'

'He's divorced.'

She blinks. 'Richard, why are we having this conversation?'

He drops the scarf, turns and walks back into the house, shutting the door behind him.

SEVEN

Neil

He only came in for a cuppa and the toilet. Somehow he's ended up on the concrete floor, cradling a wounded man in his arms. Blood is pumping out of a pulpy mess in the guy's neck, and his eyes are rolling. He's making an unearthly gurgling sound. If he has any consciousness left at all, Neil's might be the last human voice he ever hears. Quite a responsibility. He has no idea what to say.

'You're okay, mate.' The lie is instinctive. 'You're okay, you're okay. Just hang in there, mate, I'll stay with you, you're okay.'

He heard the barney on his way back from the toilets, and paused to see. Nothing like a good old slanging match to liven up a Monday morning. The curly-headed lad seemed irate—a bit nuts, really, not making much sense. Once he'd stormed out, the café's owner made a joke of the whole event. *Bring on the men in white coats*, he said, tapping his temple. He seemed to find it all very funny.

And that was a pretty serious miscalculation, as it turns out, because he only had about a minute left to live. The lad was back, and this time he wasn't empty-handed.

The first shot hurled the café guy backwards into a fridge. He hit the white door with a high screech, like a fox in the night. When the second shot came, Neil was already dodging through the gap between the cabinets, lunging towards the staggering figure with his arms outstretched. He did this instinctively—someone had to do something, and there wasn't time for weighing up the pros and cons. They both went down hard, Neil breaking the wounded man's fall.

And now here he is, sitting in a lake of blood, trying to comfort a dying human being. The gurgling sound horrifies him. He feels cold sweat on his own forehead, the clutch of nausea. This can't be real. It can't be.

To his relief, somebody kneels down beside him. He's not alone anymore. It's a woman, might be sixty, hard to tell. She takes a look at Robert and seems to know exactly what to do. She rifles through several of the kitchen drawers, snatches out a pile of tea towels and presses a fistful against the pulsating tear in Robert's neck. She hands some to Neil too, muttering, 'His chest, press hard.' Then she asks someone to call for an ambulance.

Seconds later the maniac has reloaded and fired for the third time, screaming blue murder. A youngish woman in a smart coat comes hurtling down behind the coffee machine.

'Fuck,' she mouths.

He bets she isn't used to grovelling around on the floor. She has pearls in her ears, dark hair brushed across her forehead and pulled into a no-nonsense ponytail. Her face is dominated by wide-set green eyes, and right now they're fixed on the nutter. While he's yelling and smashing everybody's phones, she's on her hands and knees, keeping low as she shuffles further behind the counter. Her hand touches the wounded man's leg and is daubed with his blood. Neil watches as she holds her palm up in front of her face. She looks sickened. Her nail polish perfectly matches the smears.

Not too long after that, he hears the first siren from outside. It's joined by another, and another, and another. Soon it sounds as though the entire Met is descending on Wilton Street, wailing and yelping. There'll be an ambulance too. Medics. People who can help this poor café guy.

Music to my ears, he thinks. Then he says it aloud, to cheer up the smart girl.

Too late, though. Too late for the café man. He senses life itself draining out of the body in his arms, pooling on the floor. It's a horrible sensation. The older woman is taking the wounded man's pulse when the gurgling sound stops. She speaks loudly into his ear: 'Robert, Robert, can you hear me?'

Robert. Good to know his name at least.

She looks into his face. 'Robert? Can you hear me?'

There's no flicker, no movement. She holds the back of her hand close to Robert's bloodied mouth, leaving it for thirty seconds or more before taking his pulse one more time. She touches his neck, stares into his face again. Finally she looks at Neil and shakes her head.

That's it then. Failed again. Weakness overwhelms Neil. His heartbeat is racing, his legs and chest crushed by Robert's weight. Sounds seem to be coming from far away. He's dimly aware of the nutter thumping about at the front of the café—dragging furniture, maybe. He shuts his eyes, lets his head drop back against the fridge.

A touch on his hand makes him start. The older woman is assessing him through glasses with tortoiseshell rims. She has a bobbed hairdo—thick and heavy, framing her face like curtains.

'Are you all right?' she asks quietly.

'Better than this poor sod.'

She lifts her head to look over the counter towards the gunman. 'He's busy barricading the doors. Good. That's distracted him for a few minutes. I'm going to move Robert off you right now.'

Robert's a big man. She sizes up the task before hooking her arms under the lifeless shoulders, pulling him away from Neil and beginning to haul him along the smooth floor. The smart girl pitches in to help; once she's got over her initial revulsion she's no wilting violet. Between the three of them they manhandle the dead man until he's lying flat on the floor at the very back of the kitchen, near a swinging door. The whole exercise feels surreal. This poor guy was cleaning cabinets just a few minutes ago, and now a broad trail of blood marks the pathway to his resting place. His eyes and mouth are wide open. He looks clownishly surprised, gaping up at the ceiling.

A loud crash sends the three of them ducking for cover. Sneaking a wary look through a glass cabinet, Neil can see that the gunman has tipped over another table and is dragging it towards the courtyard door at the far end of Tuckbox. He seems obsessed with barricading every entrance.

'He's afraid,' whispers the older woman.

The smart girl is shrugging out of her posh overcoat.

'He can have this,' she whispers, jerking her head towards Robert. 'Let's cover him up, for God's sake.'

'You sure?' asks Neil. 'Looks like a nice coat.'

'It was. I won't be wearing it again. It's all splattered with—' she grimaces '—God knows what.'

The older woman takes the coat and carefully spreads it over the dead man. As shrouds go, this one is luxurious: charcoal cashmere with a peacock-blue satin lining. Robert was six foot something. The coat covers only his head and about half of his body. His legs are sticking out: jeans, red-and-green-spotted socks and brown leather shoes. The effect would be comical if it weren't macabre.

'That's better,' she says. 'And now we face whatever is coming next. We face it together! Hello. My name is Mutesi.'

Neil is intrigued by her accent. It's from somewhere in Africa, he's sure, but there's something else as well. Maybe French? Every syllable is stressed. The effect is rhythmic. Hypnotic. Under any other circumstances he could listen to her voice all day.

'Neil,' he gasps. He's shivering now.

Crash. Another table hits the dust. Blood has splashed onto their hands and clothes and shoes; it's spread along the floor, sprayed up the walls and kitchen surfaces. One great smear of crimson is streaked across the white fridge.

'I'm Abigail,' murmurs the overcoat girl. 'Abi. What the hell just happened?'

Neil tries to wipe his hands on his jeans but it's hopeless, there's too much blood. It's crawling over him. It's sticking to him. He's gulping.

'Might be going to throw up.'

'Don't worry about the blood,' whispers Mutesi. 'It's just mess like any other.'

'It's everywhere.'

'It will wash off, I promise you.'

'I dunno if it will. Feels like it's part of me now.'

She takes a firm hold of his shoulder. 'That's the horror playing with your mind. But it is *not* part of you, it will wash off. And you have blood on you because of your kindness. I saw you run to Robert.'

'Didn't even know I could still run.'

'I saw. You're a hero, Neil.'

Gratitude swells in his throat, making his eyes water. It's been a long time since another human being has looked him in the eye, called him by name and voluntarily touched him. Most of the time he feels less visible than a traffic cone. Even when giving him money or food, most people drop it beside him without breaking their stride. There are acts of kindness: the curate who tried to get him into a shelter, the barista who sneaked him pies. People buy his *Big Issue* and sometimes stop to chat for a moment and pat Buddy. But for the most part Neil is Mr Cellophane.

The radio news comes on. Shots fired at a café in Balham, armed police deployed, a tense stand-off is ongoing. Local schools are closed, businesses and transport systems all being locked down.

Neil listens with a sense of unreality. They're talking about us, he thinks. We *are* the people on the news.

The gunman seems to have finished dragging furniture around and has taken up position behind the street door barricade. He's leaning down to peer out through a place where the blind doesn't quite cover the window, and jumping at shadows. When a helicopter passes low overhead, he shouts at it and fires through the door. The shot slices the blind and obliterates a pane of glass. Neil can hear Buddy just outside, whining and squealing in terror. Poor old boy! Neil should tell gun-nutter to bugger off, bust his way through the barricade and charge outside to comfort his best friend.

But, no, he doesn't do that. Instead he lies flat on his face behind the counter, trying his best to be invisible. And this, he thinks with self-loathing, is how tyrants rise to power. People like me do nothing. Cowards like me abandon our loyal old friends. Heads down, mouths shut. It feels like a long time before Buddy is quiet again.

'Was that your dog crying?' whispers Mutesi.

'Yes, he's—hey, how d'you know I've got a dog?' He lifts his head to squint at her. 'Hang on . . . did you put four quid into my cup this morning?'

'Mm. And if I hadn't, I bet you wouldn't be here. So don't you even think about being grateful.'

He feels the pressure of her fingers on his shoulder before she gets to her feet. She's a plump woman with a casual, rolling gait. There's a confidence about her. He watches in admiration as she turns off the ovens and gas hobs with their abandoned cooking. She strolls out from between the cabinets, flicks off the radio and crosses to where people are cowering on the floor.

'You need to move well back from the windows,' she tells them quietly. 'There may be shots from outside. You understand me? From *outside*.'

They seem too dazed to see what she's getting at. Only the

gunman understands. He takes her advice, rapidly retreating further from the street door.

'Why, Grandma?' asks the small boy. 'Is there someone outside who wants to shoot us?'

'No, not us! But accidents happen. Look, we'll sit in this booth. Sir, wouldn't you like a more comfortable seat?'

She helps the elderly man out from under the table and onto his feet. He's tall, stooped, his trousers pulled up high on his waist. He's wearing a tie and a tweed jacket. The small boy finds his walking stick and flat cap on the floor and brings them along too. Within a minute Mutesi has coaxed everyone into a crescent-shaped booth with vinyl seats. There are sachets of sugar, a bucket full of serviettes and a plastic tomato for ketchup. Mutesi ferries mugs and plates of abandoned food to another table. She looks serene, as though she's ready to order lunch.

One by one the sirens stop. The helicopter drones away into the distance.

And then there's nothing. No traffic. No footsteps. No voices. No rescue party. Nobody.

EIGHT

Eliza

Not a hoax, then. She's been given further details on her journey to the scene. Shots fired, at least one confirmed casualty.

By eight twenty-five Eliza is at the outer cordon, ignoring the stares of a crowd of onlookers as a uniformed constable holds up the tape for her. The wind is punishingly cold. Her face is stinging. This end of Wilton Street is mostly lined by Victorian terraces, though she can see a concrete block of flats and a school with a metal fence. Towards the High Road, homes give way to commercial premises, cafés and shops.

'Morning,' she says, ducking underneath the tape. 'Not a good day for standing at a cordon.'

'Glad you're here, ma'am. This incident isn't stable. We've just had another shot come out through the door. We're evacuating more properties.'

'Where is this café?'

'High Road end of Wilton, right-hand side.' He jerks his head towards the top of the street. 'A temporary command centre's being set up in that building on the corner. Barnett and Hughes. They offered their premises straight away.'

It's a double-fronted house, an estate agent's office festooned with photos of properties for sale. The cordoned-off street outside has become the car park for an assorted collection of vehicles—squad cars, an ambulance and a couple of vans. Paul is waiting for her at the door. She feels her spirits lift at the sight of her friend's broad-shouldered bulk and hopelessly misshapen nose. The man has no ego, or if he does he leaves it at home. He looks like a prize-fighter—broad, battered, surprisingly light on his feet—but he was a counsellor for a decade before he joined the police.

'Hello, you ugly bastard,' she calls genially.

'Likewise.' A shop bell tinkles as he opens the glass door. 'I'm meant to be painting Dad's garden shed today.'

'Macho.'

'Mm. The old man isn't happy with me. Says I promised.'

'Snap. I'm in the doghouse too.'

'They've stuck us in a room on the top floor.' Paul keeps talking as they hurry through an open-plan office. Every second is vital, especially during the first hour or two of a stand-off like this. People are moving furniture and equipment around, settling in for what could be a long haul. Eliza spots a stunned-looking group who might be witnesses. A woman in jogging gear is talking stridently as they're all shepherded towards a room at the back.

'The good news,' says Paul as he leads the way up a narrow staircase, 'is we've got fast broadband, landlines and a view of the place. Bad news is it's a bit damp up there.'

The negotiators' home for the duration turns out to be an attic room with a sloping ceiling. Once, perhaps, it was a maid's quarters. Cardboard boxes and filing cabinets barely leave space for an oval table, a freestanding whiteboard and four plastic swivel chairs. Someone has turned the radiator on but it hasn't yet taken the edge off the cold, nor dispelled a mustiness in the air. The familiar array of phones, headsets and other tools of the negotiation trade are being carried in and set up on the table.

Nice to see that. There have been crises in the past when she's had to improvise. No equipment or chain of command, just Eliza and a loudhailer.

'This is all very efficient,' she remarks, crossing to the sash window.

'Howard's the incident commander.'

That explains it. Superintendent Malcolm Howard is a magician when it comes to managing the practicalities of an incident like this one. He's on the verge of retirement, though Eliza can't imagine him playing bowls. Perhaps he'll just dissolve like an Alka-Seltzer when he takes his uniform off for the last time.

'That's Tuckbox,' says Paul, pointing across a jumble of tiled roofs. 'Other side of the street, down the end. With the blue-and-white striped awning.'

'Has there been any contact yet?'

'Not yet. The coordinator suggests you're primary negotiator on this one. I'm number two and Ashwin's number three. He's being briefed—ah! Talk of the devil. Morning, Ashwin.'

The third member of the team rolls in, puffing slightly after his climb up the stairs. Ashwin Anand is in his forties, a uniformed sergeant and the beleaguered father of five daughters. He looks stressed this morning, but then he generally does. His job as third negotiator involves sifting intelligence, building up a profile of their attacker and acting as the link with other teams.

'Salubrious quarters, I see.' He throws himself into a chair, dropping a sheaf of notes on the table. It takes him several seconds to get his breath back, but he's clearly keen not to waste any time.

'Right. First reports of shots fired came in at seven thirty-two this morning,' he says, putting on reading glasses as he hunches over the notes. 'Two initially, two more at intervals, one of 'em a few minutes ago—came through the glass door, possibly prompted by the helicopter passing. We know there's at least one casualty: Robert Lacey, who owns and runs Tuckbox. He's still on the premises. Witnesses believe he was hit at least once, probably twice, but we don't know the nature of his injuries. The witnesses were running.'

Paul has pulled up a chair to the table and is taking notes. 'Anything known about Lacey?'

'Not a lot. Fifty years old, lives at an address in Wandsworth Town. Nice guy by all accounts; none of the witnesses can think of any enemies. His wife died of cancer a couple of weeks ago, so he's not having much luck. He's the only confirmed casualty, except one poor sod who broke his ankle climbing out of the courtyard. Several witnesses are still deaf from the sheer volume of those shots in a confined space.'

'What's known about the perpetrator?' asks Eliza. 'Mad, bad or sad?'

'One witness thinks there were two of them. Nobody else saw that. The consensus is we're dealing with a lone male, aged anywhere between eighteen and forty, armed with one shotgun. Not sawn off.'

'Definitely no automatic weapons?'

Ashwin shakes his head. 'Just the shotgun. We've got a witness who saw it from close up, and she's a keen shot herself. Renata Forbes. She's very certain that she was looking at a twelve-bore side-by-side shotgun. In all the panic she left her two dogs outside.' There's a brief twitch at the corner of Ashwin's mouth. 'She wants us to negotiate their release before we do anything else.'

'Is she serious?' asks Paul. 'Higher priority than a wounded man?'

'*Much* higher. She's downstairs, kicking up a storm.'

Paul leans far back in his chair with both hands laid flat on his head. It's his thinking position.

'Have we ruled out a terror attack? Could this guy have brought in any explosives?'

'He's wearing jeans and a jersey, not carrying a bag. Unlikely he's hiding an explosive device. We can't see into the place because he's pulled down the blinds, and there's no listening device as yet, but this doesn't look like a political or religious thing. He and Lacey behaved as though they'd met before. They knew one another.'

The tension lifts a little. Eliza has never had to negotiate during a fatal terror attack, and she hopes she never will. Fanatics—whatever their beliefs—don't tend to follow the rules.

'It doesn't look like a robbery gone wrong either,' adds Ashwin. 'The attacker comes barging in, there's a barney—witnesses give different accounts, but it seems he's asking Lacey about someone. He's saying something like: "Why didn't you tell me?" and "I've come to get her." At some stage he may have asked: "What have you done with her?"—or it might be "What did you do to her?"'

Paul's already on his feet, writing along the top of the whiteboard:

I've come to get her.

Why didn't you tell me?

What have you done with her/what did you do to her?

'Who is "she"?' Eliza asks Ashwin.

'None of the witnesses have any clue who "she" is. It seems Robert Lacey isn't helpful to the perpetrator, who leaves briefly before reappearing with the shotgun. He discharges it twice, apparently wounding Lacey, though nobody was sticking around to check.'

Paul stands a couple of paces away from the whiteboard, chin in hand, looking at the words he's written.

'How many hostages?' he asks.

'Also unclear.' Ashwin turns a page of his notes. 'The barista thinks there were upwards of fifteen customers at the time the incident began, plus five café staff, including Lacey. We know at least twelve have come out. One waitress hasn't turned up, a woman called Rosie in her early twenties. There's also an Abigail Garcia, thirty years old. Barrister. We've heard from her partner. He was actually talking to her on the phone, heard what he thinks was a gunshot, lost contact, called emergency services.

She hasn't been seen since. He's a lab technician at St George's Hospital. He's downstairs now, offering to take Garcia's place in the café.'

'How noble!' says Eliza as she shrugs out of her coat. 'Does he mean it?'

'If he's not serious he's running a hell of a risk. He's making a lot of noise. Someone might take him up on his offer.'

Paul's whiteboard marker squeaks as he adds the names. He has very regular, copperplate handwriting.

Rosie (staff, 20s)

Abigail Garcia (lawyer, 30)

'The barista remembers a woman with a toddler,' continues Ashwin. 'A small girl. Mother's heavily pregnant, might not have been able to carry her child and run. Apparently it was a scrum in there. Also a schoolboy in uniform, aged about five, well-known to café staff because he's often in with his grandmother. Those four people haven't turned up. Finally, there's a third dog outside. Nobody's claimed it.'

The whiteboard list is growing.

Pregnant mother + toddler

Grandmother + schoolboy aged ? 5

Dog owner

'What does the boss want?' asks Eliza.

'He wants to know who's in Tuckbox Café right now, what state they're in. Lacey's condition. He wants to know what happened to the third shot—the first two were aimed at Lacey, the fourth came out through the door. Did the third injure anyone? He wants this guy's motivations and likely next moves. He wants your threat assessment. If this is going to blow up in our faces he wants to know about it. Any and all demands are to be passed on to him immediately, regardless of how unrealistic they are.'

Nothing unexpected there. Gather intelligence, assess the risk. Eliza's listening while she checks the phone system. Four shots fired and at least one casualty. Robert Lacey could be bleeding to death at this very moment, just down the street. Multiple hostages, including two children and a pregnant woman. She has a fair idea of the tactical team's contingency plans: overwhelming firepower, snipers, maybe chemical agents. They'll be getting into position right now. She needs to make contact as soon as possible.

'Do we have a phone number?'

Ashwin slides a photocopied A4 sheet in her direction. It's covered in handwritten notes, with a floor plan of the café.

'The number at the top is the café phone, used when people text in their orders. The barista reckons it's your best bet for making contact. It's got a very annoying ringtone apparently, and it's always kept on full volume so they can hear it above the coffee machine and things. Some old pop song, she says.'

'Okay.' Eliza reaches for a headset, sliding it over her ears. 'Let's give 'em a call.'

NINE

Neil

We're stuffed, he thinks, tugging his hat off his head. This is it. This is how it ends. He's a gambling man—that's an understatement—but he wouldn't put a fiver on his chances of surviving this day.

It's been an hour. He and Overcoat Girl—Abi—haven't dared to stir an inch from their refuge behind the counter. Not that it's much of a refuge, because they're a pair of sitting ducks. She's taken off her shoes and is trying to hide beneath the coffee machine, knees tucked up by her chin. The milk frother hisses gently every few minutes, letting off steam. The barista abandoned her post mid-latte.

They can hear the nutter roaming and muttering, sometimes sobbing. Maybe he's getting up the courage to top himself and take them all with him, even those two little kids. He might have other weapons hidden on him somewhere. There might be a suicide vest under that baggy grey jumper. He might be ISIS, he might be a common-or-garden psychopath, he might have just escaped from some secure institution and think he's Al Capone. The street outside Tuckbox will become a shrine, paved with flowers and teddy bears and messages from strangers who suddenly love their fellow man. The hostages will all be saints for a week, the dead children will be angels. Media pundits and politicians will talk about the Mental Health Act, demanding to know why a killer was at large in the community.

The combination of silence and terror has a weirdly mesmeric effect. Flies keep arriving and strutting purposefully around the misshapen lump under its cashmere shroud. Flies, in midwinter? Bloody opportunists. Neil leans across to brush them away. His foot slides on a patch of blood, painting another streak on the floor.

Abi's about to cough. She jams an elegant hand over her mouth, her body racked by shudders as her gaze meets Neil's. It's getting the better of her. Her cheeks are bulging, her eyes streaming. Any moment now she'll explode, and God knows what the nutter will do then.

Just as she begins to cough, a blast of noise erupts from Robert's body. Fright makes Neil spin around, his heart thudding. It's a human voice, and it's coming from somewhere near the dead man's crotch. For one truly bizarre moment, Robert seems to have been resurrected.

It's Elton John, belting out 'Rocket Man'.

Abi

Jesus Christ, 'Rocket Man'?

This is a nightmare. It has to be. A zombie nightmare with an Elton John soundtrack. A bubble of hysterical laughter is filling her throat, even as she coughs.

'What the fuck?' yells the gunman.

'I think it's his phone,' replies Neil, his voice cracking with the strain. 'The café guy. His phone. In his pocket.'

The music blares on. And on. Abi desperately hopes that whoever is on the other end of that line isn't calling to order three lattes and a skinny mochaccino. *Please, God, let them have a magic wand.*

Eliza

The café phone rings eight, nine, ten times.

She isn't alone—Ashwin has gone to speak to witnesses, but Paul is listening in through his own headset—and yet she feels profoundly isolated. She always does during this first call. She's trying to contact an armed man whose stress level will be right off the scale. It's *her* voice he will hear. It's *she* who must build rapport. It's she who will be haunted if people die. Two terrified children are depending on her for their lives.

In crisis negotiation there's a chance to reach into the tragedy and change its course. That's the buzz. That's why she will never give it up, despite the grief it adds to her family life. She has sat alongside people as they balance on the parapets of bridges and multi-storey car parks. She's waded up to her waist in the Thames, listening to a mother who planned to drown herself and her baby. She's talked through a window to a man holding his boss hostage with a nail gun. They're all still alive today, so far as she knows. But occasionally things go wrong. Horribly wrong.

For a dizzying moment it seems the call has been answered. There's a click—another click—a long moment of silence. Eliza feels a surge of adrenaline as she prepares her first words. She forces herself to breathe steadily, to pitch her voice in a low register. She's intensely alert. Every word counts. Every nuance counts. There's no room for mistakes.

Voicemail.

Lacey's voice is an affable bass. He sounds caring.

Hello! This is Robert at Tuckbox. Thanks for your call. You can text us your order, or if you want to leave a message, go ahead. I promise I'll call you back.

I doubt it, thinks Eliza grimly.

'Hi. My name's DI Eliza McClean. Eliza. I'm a negotiator with the police. I'm here to help. You can reach me on this number.'

Paul's calmly noting the time, the outcome of the call and their plan to try again in fifteen minutes. As secondary negotiator his role is to keep a log, to be a sounding board, even to take over the negotiation if necessary. The roles are interchangeable. Sometimes it's he who does the talking, she who supports.

Two children, a wounded man.

'I'll keep calling,' she promises Robert Lacey's voicemail. 'Let's work this out.'

TEN

Abi

Elton cuts off abruptly, in mid-yell. No magic wand. The silence is crushing. It sounds like abandonment.

A migraine is beginning to flash in the periphery of her vision; at least, she hopes it's a migraine, not concussion from bashing her head on that bloody radiator. There's no pain yet, just the familiar white stars, pulsating through unnerving patches of blindness. She's used to suffering migraines, especially since she started pumping herself full of hormones for IVF, but no matter how bad it gets she has never missed a single day of work. It's an obsession with her. She's got some hefty drugs which generally stop a migraine in its tracks. They're in her case—which she last saw somewhere near the street door—along with her robes, her laptop and a load of books and briefs, including *Bradshaw*.

She covers her eyes with her hands, but the flashing carries on behind her lids. Poor Kelly Bradshaw will be arriving at court soon, dressed in her tidiest clothes, sheet-white with terror and mourning for her baby—who may never walk or even eat unaided, and who she'll probably never see again. This is one of the worst days of Kelly Bradshaw's life. She's relying on Abi. She'll be looking for her.

When Abi uncovers her eyes, she sees that Neil has pulled his beanie off his head and is holding it between his hands. Matted hair, a grizzled beard, vertical lines down thin cheeks. His eyelids look raw with some sort of eczema. He doesn't smell great: stale sweat, grease of some kind. She has a suspicion he's homeless. His anorak and jeans definitely haven't been near a washing machine for many a long day, and now he has Robert's blood splattered all over him too. His walking boots have seen some action. The laces have broken and been knotted many times, the soles are peeling right off. She can see his feet inside them. He catches her eye and smiles, raising both his thumbs. It's not a convincing thumbs-up—she suspects he's at least as frightened as she is—but she's grateful to him for trying. She smiles back. His eyes are blue. Creased and bloodshot, but still blue.

The other hostages sit horrified in the booth as the gunman paces up and down. After a while the small boy tugs on his mother's jacket, murmuring, *I need the toilet.* Abi's heart melts. Poor little chap, with his wide eyes. He shouldn't be caught up in this. Neither should the tiny girl, who is kissing her Roo in a determined, motherly way, telling him not to be scared. Something has to be done! Abi loathes passivity—sitting here like a helpless pudding while children suffer. This is a kitchen, for God's sake. There must be a whole arsenal of weapons. Surely they can overpower one person if they all act together? Where are the chef's knives? She looks around. There—black handles arrayed in a steel block. Or maybe she could cosh the prick with a frying pan? Right! It's time to take action.

She levers herself to her feet, blinking at the flashing lights that have expanded to fill her vision.

He's close by—much closer than she expected. He looks and moves as though he's fit, twitching, taut with furious energy.

Several days' stubble, and reddish-brown hair in a curling tangle over his collar. There's some kind of injury on his forehead: a swelling bruise, a gash, dried blood in his eyebrow. He never lets go of that loaded gun. He could use it in a split second.

Suddenly he spins around to stare straight at her. His eyes are shining, but not in a good way. He stares with shocked intensity, as though he's ardently in love—or murderously angry. He takes a step closer. Abi hits the deck, and fast.

Her dad would laugh himself hoarse if he could see her now, cringing behind a counter. Her father has no time for humankind. According to him there's no such thing as loyalty or honour or even love.

'Love? What the hell does that mean?' he asked once, during an especially bitter rant over Christmas dinner. Red-faced. 'All these beautiful ideas are fantasy. When the chips are down, they melt away like a snowman in hell. People would murder their grandmothers to save themselves.'

Abi was a teenager at the time and had long ago decided that her father was an utter jerk and her mother a fool for sticking with him. She got up and walked out of the room. Nobody bothered to follow her.

She can't remember when she's sat so still, for so long, with nothing to do but wait. Her fingers itch for her phone. The clinic must have called by now. And she needs to ring her chambers, get her clerks to sort out the St Albans disaster. She longs to surf the news sites and find out what the police are doing. She could even tweet: *Trapped in Tuckbox! Help!* But her phone is in pieces, scattered across the concrete floor. No communication, no information. Blind, deaf and dumb.

Exactly fifteen minutes after the first call, Elton sings again. And again, fifteen minutes after that. And again, fifteen minutes after that. 'Rocket Man' is their only lifeline. Abi has begun checking the time, waiting for the next call. Counting on it.

Eliza

It's a knife-edge. She urgently needs to make contact, but call too often and she risks driving this man over the edge. The early moments of a siege are the most dangerous. Attackers panic. The lizard brain takes over: the primeval fight-or-flight response, smothering rational thought. They can't run, so they lash out. They do appalling things: things that their friends and family can't believe of them; things they can't believe of themselves when they look back later.

For a fifth time she dials, waits, holds her breath: *Come on, come on.* A scene of tragedy is lurking at the back of her mind, bodies strewn around a café. Two of them are very small.

Hello! This is Robert at Tuckbox. Thanks for your call.

'We've been trying for an hour,' she frets, standing up.

Paul checks his watch. 'He'll answer eventually.'

She hates this; she hates the waiting. Digging her binoculars out of her bag, she leans against the windowsill. Wilton Street is a ghost road. A grocery delivery truck stands with its back doors wide open, presumably just as it was when the driver legged it. Pallets and boxes lie scattered on the pavement. She can make out the door to the café, a couple of small tables with chairs, the jaunty TUCKBOX sign. There's a Christmas tree under the awning, twinkling with fairy lights, and tinsel looped around the windows.

Ah, and those poor dogs. A pair with tartan jackets lie close together, sheltering in the lee of an A-frame blackboard—perhaps with the day's menu scribbled on it. They seem a privileged duo, in their matching attire. They'll be the ones whose mistress is demanding their release. The grey, scruffy one is the largest of the three. He ignores his well-heeled companions. He's sitting up, never taking his eyes off the café's door, as though expecting someone to come out at any moment.

A movement further down the street has Eliza swinging the binoculars around. Five specialist firearms officers are making their way towards Tuckbox, holding shields, their faces hidden by helmets with visors. They move with surprising grace as they hug the fronts of buildings, staying well out of line-of-fire of the café. As she watches, the group ducks into the recessed doorway of a drycleaner's shop two doors down from Tuckbox.

The grey dog has seen them too. He's on his feet, tension in every line of his body, watching intently. His tail is slowly waving: hopeful, suspicious.

'Hey.' Eliza lowers the binoculars. 'If those dogs start barking there's going to be a problem.'

'Why would they do that?' asks Paul, without looking up from his notes.

'SCO19 are trying to find a nice spot for a picnic.'

The grey dog's tail has stopped moving. Eventually he sits again. Now he has two things to keep his eye on: the door of the café as well as the strange marauders nearby.

Those five officers won't be the only ones. She'd guess that others have been deployed around the back of the café, perhaps in the courtyard she can see marked on the plan. Marksmen will be looking for vantage points. They'll be prepared to wait for as long as it takes. Just in case.

Just in case I fail. No pressure then.

They might be about to storm the place. She'd be the last to know. As number three negotiator, Ashwin might be aware that the tactical team is ready to do something drastic but the chances are he wouldn't tell her. Keeping the principal negotiator in the dark avoids the risk of her accidentally giving the game away. The boundaries are clearly marked: *Negotiators negotiate*, runs the mantra; *commanders command.*

The Christmas tree lights are flashing. Tuckbox looks jolly and welcoming, a nice place to go for coffee and a mince pie, a good old-fashioned London café. Behind those blinds are ordinary folk who dropped by on their way to work or school this morning, maybe meeting old friends. Doing normal things, living normal lives. Until today.

ELEVEN

Rosie

It's like playing sardines, but you're hiding from death.

She's been in here for . . . how long? Feels like hours. She hasn't moved an inch in the hellishly cramped space. Even breathing feels loud and dangerous. She's not had an easy life, but she's never, ever been terrified like this before.

The sirens have stopped. Perhaps everyone has escaped except her. She could be alone with him and his gun. Her hiding place is dark, apart from a faint gleam from around the cupboard door. It smells of rotting wood, bleach—and there's something really disgusting coming from the pipes. Liquid from the U-bend of the sink is dripping gently onto her jeans. She's curled on her side among the cleaning products, knees bent, her neck held at a painful angle. Her right arm is shaking with the stress of holding the door closed; her left is pinned under her body, which is compressing her bruises. They're aching. Something hard—maybe a scrubbing brush?—keeps jabbing into the back of her head. She's desperate to yank at whatever it is, but that might set bottles and cans and God-knows-what cascading out of the cupboard. It might lead to disaster.

She spotted that madman pelting back into the café with his gun. It was the most terrifying sight she'd ever seen. Even before the first shot was fired she'd turned around and sprinted in here. She stood in the dim light, shaking and gasping at the sound of shots, and screams, and Sofia's loud yells—*Get out, this way! Get out!* But there is no way out from the back kitchen, not without passing right through the main area of the café. She was caught, a rat in a trap. Her only chance was to hide. The staff toilet is in here, through the alcove with the freezers, but it's the first place he'd look, and even with the door locked it would not be a sanctuary. One good kick would break the door down. So, in her panic, she pulled a couple of boxes and bottles out of the cupboard under the sink and crawled in. Once she'd jammed herself onto the lower shelf she pulled the door behind her, and held her breath, and waited. And waited.

She can't stop thinking about her daughter. Poor little girl, she didn't want to be left at nursery today. She never does. She worries all the time. She's afraid of being abandoned—and who can blame her, after all the upheaval and loss in her life? This morning she sobbed and clung and wouldn't let go. *I want to come with you, Mummy!*

'They won't let me bring you to work, angel. Hey, will you paint me a picture for when I come to get you?'

'When will you get me?'

'Four o'clock. And then you and me will go home and make spaghetti.'

'Promise you won't be late?'

'Promise. Four o'clock. See the little hand on the clock? See where the four is? Well, when that hand points to four, and that bigger hand points to twelve, I'll be there.'

I'm sorry, I'm sorry, I'm sorry.

TWELVE

Abi

A voice quavers from among the frightened people in the booth.

'Excuse me.'

It's the woman in the beret—though she's taken it off now, revealing a mass of short braids. A slender hand is half raised. Her other arm is wrapped around her son, hugging him close.

'He needs to visit the toilet,' she whispers. 'He can't hold on any longer.'

The gunman approaches, glaring with his over-bright eyes.

'This is Emmanuel, my grandson,' Mutesi remarks cordially. 'He's six years old and he likes to read. He's been in here for three hours now. That's a long time for a little boy, isn't it? His mum is Brigitte. She's a social worker, she's meant to be at a case conference this morning.' She smiles. 'And I'm Mutesi. I am a nurse in a rest home. I just came off my night shift.'

Bold move, thinks Abi. Bold and clever. Mutesi is humanising our huddled group. My turn.

She clears her throat, slowly standing up. 'My name's Abi. I'm . . .' She hesitates. Actually, who *is* she, in this context?

'I'm not meant to be here. I was on my way to St Albans. I'm meant to be in court.'

It's Neil's turn, but he says nothing. He shakes his head and sinks lower behind the counter. There's a long pause.

'Um . . .' The pregnant woman presses a hand to her mouth. She's staring at the table as she whispers, 'I'm Paige. Um, Paige Johnson. This is Lily.'

'You forgot Roo!' pipes Lily noisily, waving the toy in her mother's face.

'Shh, Lily,' murmurs Paige. 'Please.'

It's as though the gunman has only just noticed the little girl. He stares at her, and he's trying to smile—or maybe he's in pain. Or both.

'Um, and this is Arthur,' adds Paige, squeezing the elderly man's arm. 'Arthur Beaumont. He's our neighbour but he's like a granddad to me. He's meant to be at a clinic at the hospital. That's where we were going today.'

'Won't make it now,' mutters Arthur. His voice is hoarse. 'They'll take me off their list. They fuss like anything if you don't turn up.'

Mutesi smiles at him before turning back to the gunman.

'So that is us! And what is your name, sir? May we know it?'

He jerks his chin, motioning towards the bathroom. It's on the left at the back of the café, where the room is narrower.

Brigitte slides out of the booth, never letting go of her son's hand. They're a dignified pair. The boy rubs his eyes, dusts his knees. They creep to the toilet like two cats: in slow motion, careful to make no sudden moves.

'Where they going?' asks Lily at the top of her voice.

Paige throws a terrified glance at the gunman, pressing her finger to her lips.

Lily adopts a stage whisper. 'Where are they going, Mummy?'

'Shh. To the bathroom.'

'Why?'

'They need the toilet.'

'Why?'

'Hey, it's time for Roo's nap. He's tired.'

The stage whisper is abandoned. 'No, he's not! Roo's not tired!'

'Shush, Lily. Please. Shush. Rock Roo to sleep.'

Lily huffs in indignation and begins to croon loudly, shaking the toy up and down with the kind of violence that would have the social services involved if it were a real baby, like poor Carla Bradshaw. Paige looks close to tears, and for the first time Abi feels almost grateful that Charlie and she are childless. There's too much to lose. Imagine the paralysing terror. Imagine trying to keep your bored, tired toddler quiet, fearing she could be murdered for having a tantrum.

'We're meant to be at the clinic,' fusses Arthur. 'They'll have called my name by now.'

'It's okay, Arthur,' says Paige.

'Okay, Arta,' echoes Lily.

Abi can tell that the little girl is ready for a sleep. Her mouth has turned down. As time passes she stops crooning and slumps against her mother with her thumb in her mouth, rubbing Roo across her nose.

Emmanuel and Brigitte have been gone for a while. Could they have escaped, somehow? Abi rubs her temples, trying to picture the layout of the place. Perhaps the bathroom has a window, and maybe it opens into the courtyard. She likes that spot: a miniature haven with mellow bricks underfoot and high walls all around. There are wrought-iron tables, geraniums in pots and a wisteria drooping through a trellis. She and Charlie have spent many happy hours out there, in the summer. Saturday mornings in the leafy suntrap, after a lie-in. Coffee, breakfast and newspapers. Just the two of them. No guns. No dead bodies with spotty socks and lace-up shoes. They love one another's company, that's the thing. They're lucky, really.

It occurs to her that Charlie must have heard that first shot, before she dropped her phone. She knows him. He'll have dialled 999 straight away, and then he'll have left work, got into an Uber and headed straight down here. He's probably somewhere nearby right now. He can't help, of course, but it's a cheering thought.

Brigitte and Emmanuel reappear and make their anxious way back to the booth. Mutesi moves to let them in, mother and grandmother working together to shield their child as best they can. The little boy is sturdily poker-faced, his lips pressed hard together. Abi's nephew has an expression like that when he knows he's in big trouble and is trying not to cry. It's cute. Heartbreaking.

'Sir,' says Mutesi suddenly, turning to the gunman. 'Won't you let these people leave? Old men, pregnant women, children . . . your war isn't with them, is it? I will stay. I will be your hostage.'

He stops pacing and turns to look at her.

'Come on,' she wheedles. 'Life can't be so bad. Why throw it away? You live in this free country.'

He laughs at that. It's a short, incredulous *huh*, almost a sob.

'You have a lot of tomorrows,' urges Mutesi.

Again, that sob-laugh. 'I've no tomorrows.'

'Yes, yes.' Mutesi's voice is soothing. 'You're young, you have your life ahead of you. Your whole life. *Your whole life.*'

To Abi's astonishment, the nurse is easing herself to her feet as she speaks, confidently stretching out one arm towards him as though she'd just like to take a casual look at his gun. She's closer, closer . . . and then her fingers are around the barrel. She doesn't shift her gaze from his face.

'Won't you give this to me, son?' she asks quietly.

He reacts without warning, erupting in rage, shouting, '*I'm not your son! I'm not your fucking son!*' In one fluid movement he's raised the gun to his shoulder and is aiming straight at her forehead, the barrel inches from her glasses.

It's too much for Emmanuel, who lets out a piercing wail. Paige has shrieked too, an involuntary sound that she immediately suppresses with both hands. Lily copies her mother. Neil's on his feet and yelling, '*For God's sake, put that thing down! Put it down!*'

Abi finds herself bursting from behind the counter to grab a wooden chair, intending to use it as a weapon. She can't just sit there and watch that woman get shot! But even as she swings the chair up high, she checks herself. It's too dangerous. Smashing anything onto this guy's skull will only make him pull the trigger.

Amid all the fear, all the uproar, Mutesi's reaction is extraordinary. She stays absolutely still, her face alight with a broad smile.

'I am not afraid,' she says.

The group in the café form a horrified tableau. Abi stands frozen, holding a chair above her head. Emmanuel's screams have turned to sobs. He and his mother hug one another while tears course down both their cheeks. Paige presses Lily's face to her chest so that the little girl can't watch. Arthur is gripping the table, staring open-mouthed at the scene.

'I am not afraid,' repeats Mutesi. 'Even if you kill me, I will not be afraid.'

Ten seconds. Twenty. Sixty.

Mutesi

So here it is at last. Violence and death have caught up with her in the end.

She's been waiting for them. She was never supposed to be the survivor. No. She was destined to travel with her family on the next journey, but she somehow got left behind. All these years she's wondered why she was the one to live when they died in agony and terror. She's had a full life since then, she's seen her surviving child grow into a fine, successful man and become a father himself. She's the lucky one. But it has all been borrowed time, every precious second of it.

The killers were so close. So close. They trampled the bushes all around her hiding place, calling out cheerfully as though she and Isaac were pet dogs. She could smell their hatred, she shuddered at the swish and bite of their machetes through the leaves. Yet they didn't see her. Why didn't they see her?

'I am not afraid,' she says.

It's a lie. She is very, very afraid, but not for herself. Only for Emmanuel, who is watching. She can hear him crying. His life is all that matters. He and his father are all that remain of her family, and in him rests the purpose of her existence. For his sake she will smile in the face of this terrible thing. She doesn't want her grandson to be haunted as she has been, lighting candles in the darkness for the rest of his life. *I am not afraid* is her message to him, and to the man he will become.

She looks past the silly gun and into the face of the boy who holds it. Yes, he *is* afraid. He's haunted too. She has looked into the faces of men who take joy in slaughter, and he is certainly not one of them.

My fate is in the hands of God, she tells herself, not the hands of this frightened boy. There is a plan for me. Perhaps I'm about to join Mrs Dulcie Brown and Robert. Perhaps all my family are waiting excitedly to be reunited with me. Jesus, bring me home.

Silence. Fear. A smile. 'Rocket Man'.

Eliza

'The boss is looking at tactical options,' says Ashwin, already talking as he hurries into the attic room. 'They've had a dress rehearsal.'

It's the last news Eliza wants to hear.

'Slow him down,' she says.

'I'm doing my best but he's getting jittery. He says it's been three hours since this incident kicked off, we've been calling every fifteen minutes and we've still got no idea what's happening in there.'

'We have to be prepared to play a long game.'

The statistics are on her side. In a situation like this one there's often pressure on negotiators to get fast results, but containment and negotiation work. In ninety-five per cent of cases a hostage crisis will end with no loss of life. By contrast, rescue attempts can be catastrophic. Yet sometimes it takes nerves of steel to hold off.

Paul's been listening to this exchange.

'I still think our man is going to answer soon,' he says. 'These fifteen-minute calls must be driving him nuts, right? If the ringtone's loud in a crowded café, it'll be worse in a quiet one. But he hasn't turned off that phone. He's keeping the line of communication open. Why? Because he wants help.'

The three negotiators are anxiously discussing their options—not that they have many—when Ashwin's mobile rings. He answers, listens and runs to the window.

'Screams,' he announces urgently, peering towards the café. 'SCO19 just heard a male voice shouting and children screaming. Something's kicking off in there. They want to go in.'

'No—tell the boss to hold off another minute.' Without waiting for a reply, Eliza makes the call.

She listens as it rings, agonised, her heart racing. *Come on, come on.* She has seconds left in which to make contact. All hell is on the point of breaking loose.

Answer, answer, answer.

THIRTEEN

Neil

Elton bloody John, while a woman stares straight down the barrels of a shotgun. The bloody police, messing about with phones instead of sending the SAS or someone crashing in here. What the hell are they playing at?

But it works. It's like a miracle. The lad lowers the gun, wipes his eyes in the crook of his arm. His whole face is quivering. He looks as though he's woken up to find he's been sleepwalking and was just about to step off a cliff. Neil's met a lot of young blokes in trouble, both in classrooms and on the streets. He has a feeling this one could do with some help right now. He speed-crawls across to Robert's body, closing his nose to the smell of butchery, and follows the source of the music until his fingers close around cool metal. He hasn't held a phone in years, can hardly believe this smooth object *is* a phone. It's silver, wafer-thin, vibrating as it blares out the song. Space age. How can something so impossibly light make so much noise?

'Hey!' he cries, scrambling to his feet. 'I think this is for you.'

The gunman's curly head turns. Neil waves the phone at him. 'Aren't you sick of "Rocket Man"? I know I am.'

Once upon a time—long, long ago—Neil had a little flutter on religion. He was a chemistry student and struggling with anxiety when a girl invited him to her wacky church. For a month or so he was intrigued by the music and general friendliness, but once he started asking questions it became obvious there was no evidence to support the existence of a deity of any kind. Quite the opposite. Of this he's pretty certain; so certain that he hasn't said a prayer in three decades. He's never even prayed for a horse to win—not that he doesn't harbour his share of superstitions: crossed fingers, lucky numbers.

But this is an emergency. Belt and braces. Better safe than sorry.

Lord, I know I've been a waste of space, but there are two tiny little kids in here who definitely haven't. Help them now.

He stretches across the counter, holding the phone out towards the lad with the gun.

'They're not giving up. Do us all a favour. Answer the bloody thing.'

Amen.

Eliza

Buzz-buzz. Such a humdrum little noise, the ringing tone. *Buzz-buzz. Buzz-buzz.*

She's tensed over the cluttered table, jabbing at her notebook with her biro. *Answer. Answer. Answer.* Her colleagues are listening in through headsets. Ashwin's visibly sweating, his forehead slick. He sits hunched like a man in an ejector seat, bracing himself for the blast. He's whispering into his mobile phone, giving Inspector Howard a running commentary.

Paul is updating the log in his elegant handwriting: *Report of disturbance in Tuckbox. Screams/shouts. Call 9 made at 10.32.* He seems calm enough, but she's not fooled. He uses routine to keep himself from panic.

Answer, answer, answer.

The buzzing has stopped. She blinks rapidly, dreading the sound of Robert Lacey's message.

Silence.

Or is it silence?

She looks up, meets Paul's eye. All three negotiators instinctively lean forwards, straining their ears for the slightest sound. No, not silence. Someone is breathing. It's fast and shallow, only just audible, but definitely breathing. A human being is on the other end of this line.

'Hi,' says Eliza. She's careful with her tone: calm, but not patronising. Warm but not chirrupy. 'My name's Eliza. I'm a negotiator with the police. I'm here to help you.'

She lets the pause drift. Ten seconds, twenty seconds. *Come on, come on.* The breathing grows more laboured. Eliza covers her eyes with the palm of her hand.

'I'm still here,' she says.

At last there are words. A male voice, though not deep. Slightly slurred.

'You can't help.'

'I can start by hearing what's been happening to you.'

'What for?'

There's misery in this voice. Anger too, but mostly misery. The spoken word only represents about ten per cent of communication. Much of the rest is body language, useless down a phone. Eliza seizes on non-verbal cues that can be heard: breathing patterns, silences, changes in pitch and inflection.

It's like defusing a bomb: cut the wrong wire, use too much force, and it could all be over. *Boom.* It's no good trying to fix the whole thing right at the start. That's dangerous. The first priority is trust. She needs this man's trust above everything else, or he'll never let her over the doorstep and into his world.

'I want to understand what's brought you here today,' she says.

'You mean you want to talk me into coming out.'

'No. I want to help find a way out for you. We'll do it together.

First, I need to know whether everyone in there is safe, including you.'

'Safe?' He seems to muffle the phone, but after a moment he's back. 'Yeah, I think so.'

'Anyone need medical help? Including yourself?'

'Er . . . medical . . . no. No.'

'Can you tell me what's happened today?'

'He fucking . . .' There's another long pause; heavy, agonising gasps, a falsetto moan. 'He destroyed her.'

'Who?'

The voice is disintegrating. She hears garbled words—*I'm sorry, I'm sorry*—as the line goes dead.

She waits to be sure the call is over before sliding off her headset. Ashwin has already stepped outside, speaking quietly into his phone. He returns after half a minute or so, mopping his brow with a tissue.

'The boss says to carry on,' he says. 'For now.'

FOURTEEN

Sam

I'm sorry, I'm sorry, I'm sorry. I'm worthless. This brave lady is worth a hundred of me.

All she did was call him 'son'. That's all she did. Hardly a crime, was it? For a moment it seemed she was mocking him, mocking his father, and the rage came pounding back. Dad used to call him 'son'—with such pride and such a smile, as though Sam was the only son anyone had ever had. But how could she have known that?

Dad would be shocked and disgusted if he saw Sam threatening the lady. He'd be livid, even if he knew the safety catch was on and Sam would never have pulled the trigger. Sam's just broken the golden rule of gun safety, the one Dad taught him the very first time he put the old .410 into his hands and took him out to shoot tin cans. He used a capital-letter voice: *Sam, remember the golden rule: NEVER POINT A GUN AT ANYONE. Never, ever, even when it's not loaded. Not for a joke, not in a game, not by mistake when you're cleaning it. If you break this rule I will confiscate this gun forever. Understand?* Father and son used to recite the unbreakable commandment every single time they opened the gun safe: *What's the golden rule? NEVER POINT A GUN AT ANYONE.* It was drummed into Sam's consciousness.

The little guy—what's his name, Emmanuel?—well, he's beside himself. He's got his face buried in his granny's cardigan, and she's hugging him. Six years old, and he's just watched Sam point a gun at the head of someone he loves. He'll probably have screaming nightmares for the rest of his life. Sam knows exactly what that feels like. *Sorry, sorry, sorry.*

Oh, how he loved his own grandmother. She was a bit like this Mutesi in that she was never scared of anyone—though even she couldn't win against Robert. She lived in the middle cottage of a row of five. She called it her doll's house: just two rooms on the ground floor, a staircase so steep it was almost a ladder, two rooms upstairs. Apparently it was built in the time of the Elizabethans—who, Sam used to think, were some kind of tribe with blue war paint on their faces.

Granny used to collect him in the afternoons after primary school and take him home for tea. It was always the same: Amir the grey Persian cat would be snoozing on the grey Persian rug by the fire. Radio 4 would be on, droning voices. The cottage smelled of incense sticks, and the sofa was covered in cushions Granny brought back from her holidays in India. Sam's feet stuck out straight when he sat on it because he was a little runt at seven or eight years old. Granny had a map of the world in a frame on the wall, and a carved coffee table from her travels. They used to pull it up close to the sofa. Earl Grey for her, orange squash for Sam, and scones and jam if he was lucky.

She didn't behave much like his friends' grandmothers. She was lean like Dad, with hair the colour of storm clouds. She wore it in a plait that hung all the way to her waist. She used to ride Sundance Kid, her old piebald horse, until Sundance hurt his back and had to retire. After that he lived the life of Riley, just mooching around in his field by the spinney while people brought him apples and other goodies. The spinney was a small wood—though it seemed like a giant forest to Sam when he was little—and one of Dad's favourite places on the farm. It was part of a network of ancient woodland, he said: oak and ash and hazel and field maple, home to a host of species.

One afternoon, Granny showed Sam a photograph in a silver frame.

'Found this down the back of my desk. D'you recognise any of this horrible mob?' she asked, as she poured her tea.

'Yep,' he mumbled, shoving a massive piece of scone into his mouth. 'Mum and Dad getting married.'

There was a wedding photo on the dresser back home, just his parents cutting a cake. This picture of Granny's showed a big group. Mum stood out a mile in her white dress, her hair a bird's nest of curls, flowers everywhere. Dad looked even thinner back then, with high cheekbones and his sandy hair really short. Both of them were laughing. Mum's dimples were very dimply.

'There's Aunt Monique. Yeuch!' He made a face at Mum's gruesome sister. 'And there's you.'

'Mm, yours truly. And Grandpa John.' Granny was looking at a man with a beard and epic eyebrows, like a chimneysweep's brushes. 'The old man got quite emotional that day.'

Sam couldn't remember meeting either of his grandfathers. His mother's father died quite young after having lots of small strokes, and then bigger ones, and ending up sitting in a chair in an old people's home, even though he wasn't that old. Sam didn't know what a stroke was, but he knew his mother was scared of them. Then there was Grandpa John, with the beard. Like Sam, he was born in Tyndale farmhouse. He farmed the land, and so did Sam's dad, and so would Sam one day. He had no doubt at all about that.

Granny was still talking, naming all the aunts and uncles and cousins in the photo. Boring. It was old history, like the Elizabethans.

'You're wearing a *ginormous* hat,' he said, interrupting her.

'I was trying to be conventional. Your dad told me I wasn't to make an exhibition of myself on his wedding day. Then he said my hat was outrageous and constituted making an exhibition of myself. Ha! There's no pleasing some people.'

'You look much younger in the photo.'

She put on her thoughtful face, chewing one side of her mouth.

'Well, it's all relative. I was . . . let's see . . . I would have been about two hundred back then.'

He giggled, spitting crumbs. Then he spotted someone standing among the bridesmaids.

'Is that Robert?'

'Mm.'

'Why's *Robert* there?' He felt as though the man had jumped onto the photograph like a flea.

One of Granny's eyebrows went up. 'Lacey was best man.'

'No, he wasn't! *Dad* was the best man.'

'No—well, yes. Angus is of course the best man in the world, but being best man at a wedding is a job. He's the groom's side-kick on the day, making sure he's all scrubbed up and doesn't leg it out of the back door of the church while the bride's shimmying in the front. And if the groom doesn't show up, the best man is supposed to marry the bride instead.'

Sam made a gagging noise, and Granny joined in.

'Nasty thought, isn't it? Never understood why your father's so fond of the man. They met at university.' She was slotting the picture back among the others on her mantelpiece. 'Handsome brute, I'll give him that. He's a bit like a toothpaste advert—all teeth and smiles. By Jove, he can turn on the charm. The bridesmaids were scrapping over him.'

Sam didn't like Robert. He didn't want him in his parents' wedding photo. He had no idea why bridesmaids would scrap over him.

'*I'm* dad's best friend.'

'You certainly are! But you weren't born back then. You weren't even a twinkle in your father's eye.'

It was years before he worked out that she'd said something a bit naughty. He was still fretting about Robert being Dad's best man.

'I hear Lacey's turned up in this neighbourhood,' mused Granny, as she sipped her tea. 'Like a bad penny.'

'His wife was mean to him.'

'Connie? Is that what he's saying? Hm.' He saw her mouth tighten. There were little creases all around it.

'They got divorced.'

'There's a surprise.'

Sam was enjoying her disapproval. 'He's cooking in Jackson's Lodge. Mum looks after the garden. She says Jackson's is really posh and she'd like to have dinner there on her birthday.'

'I hope she gets her wish.'

'Robert's been showing her how to decorate cakes.'

'*Has* he now?' Those lines again, and the empty voice adults used when they had something they wanted to say but knew they mustn't.

'He says I'm spoiled.'

Her teacup smacked down onto its saucer with a sharp rattle.

'You're not spoiled, Sammy! You're loved. Loved, loved, loved. There's a world of difference.'

He imitated Robert's deep voice. 'D'you *ever* stop talking, little squirt?'

Robert used to say it with a grin that showed those white teeth, head tilted to one side as though he was being playful and jolly. He'd tickle Sam under the arms while he asked whether he *ever* stopped talking. You laugh when you're being tickled. You can't help it—you have to laugh, just like you have to sneeze when you breathe in dust from the grain dryer. It doesn't mean you're happy. Sam was never happy when Robert tickled him; he wanted the man to leave him alone. He felt angry about him being the best man before Sam was even a twinkle in Dad's eye. He felt hot and fidgety just thinking about it.

'He says I've got ADHD because I never keep still.'

'He should keep his opinions to himself. Don't let anyone stick labels on you, Sammy. Hey, grubby little urchin—stop wiping jam on your school trousers. Harriet will have my guts for garters.'

She was always saying Harriet would have her guts for garters. Sam didn't think his mum would do that. She used to tell her friends that she had the best mother-in-law in the world.

'Robert did the writing on my birthday cake,' he said. 'Mum says he's got steady hands.'

'Steady hands, eh?'

Amir stood up and stretched himself like a croquet hoop, his tail all fluffed out along his back. He had a squashed face as though he'd just run into a wall. Sam slid down from the sofa to lie on the rug by the fire, curling himself around Amir.

'Steady hands,' repeated Granny. 'Wow. Well, I'm surprised Robert Lacey's got time to be decorating cakes with his steady hands, being such an important chef and all. Now, where's your homework? Your mum says I have to be the enforcer.'

He had a maths sheet to finish, and a reading book, but he had no intention of doing either of them. Homework was torture. Last year, his parents had tackled his class teacher about how he struggled to read and write. He was in the room at the time, 'reading quietly' in a corner—which meant holding up a book and flapping his ears.

Mrs Poulson said he was educationally challenged. It didn't go down well.

'You mean slow?' asked Dad.

'I never use that word.'

'You've just implied it, and you're wrong. Sam grasps new concepts faster than most adults. He's always questioning what he sees in the world around him. He's an excellent shot—that takes concentration. He can spot what's going on with a broken bit of machinery just by looking at it. He's competent with stock. If I'm in a jam with something on the farm I know I can call on him for help. There's nothing wrong with his cognitive abilities.'

'Could he be dyslexic?' asked Mum.

Mrs Poulson wasn't having a bar of it. She didn't like Sam, and the feeling was mutual.

'Dyslexia is sometimes used an excuse for laziness and poor time management. Sam would have an easier life if he would only sit *still*. He needs to stop losing things, take more care with his written work and get his head out of the clouds.'

So his parents researched dyslexia, using the library and the old dial-up internet that took hours. They contacted the Dyslexia Institute. Thanks to their determination Sam now had a special teacher once a week and extra time in exams. His parents were his champions.

'I haven't got any homework,' he told Granny. 'I did it all at break time.'

'Oh yeah? Was I born yesterday?'

He closed his eyes and pretended to snore. Granny was laughing as she carried the tray away. After a while he heard the clink of glass and knew she was pouring herself a brandy from her decanter. It was warm by the fire, and it had been a long day at school. He didn't see the point of school. Amir's purring was peaceful, especially when he rubbed his squashed nose against Sam's cheek. He was as soft as a cloud. Sam could see the point of Amir.

If being happy and feeling loved meant you were spoiled, maybe he *was* spoiled. But not for much longer.

Eliza

One of the facilitators during the gruelling weeks of negotiation training was an ex-FBI negotiator called Ethan. He pretended to be a bookish type, with his round-rimmed glasses and wispy beard, but in a past life he'd been a fighter pilot. His trademark obsession was his insistence that negotiation and flying had a lot in common.

'You have to be completely attuned to ten things at once,' he told them. 'Monitor data in three dimensions, control movement across three different axes. At the same time, you're listening for the engine note, watching for subtle changes, constantly checking instruments, coaxing twitchy, unforgiving controls that could flip out any moment. It's pitch-black, you're flying down a canyon at the speed of sound. One mistake and you're embedded in the cliffs for eternity.' He scratched his nose, looking around the group. 'You don't get a parachute.'

The remark wasn't very funny, but it earned a murmur of laughter.

'Word of advice,' added Ethan. 'Never look down. Whatever you do, don't *ever* look down.'

He had a point. She nips into the kitchen, makes a mug of coffee. Then she leans her elbows on the crazed paintwork of the windowsill, squinting towards Tuckbox. An image of those frightened children keeps barging into her mind. *Don't look down.*

'Got something for you,' says Ashwin, returning from a briefing meeting. 'CCTV footage from two points shows our guy heading down Wilton Street towards Tuckbox at seven twenty-five.' He lays two photos on the table, side by side. One is a grainy close-up of a face. 'Fits descriptions of the attacker. Looks like an injury to his forehead, see?'

Paul holds the close-up to the light. 'Yes, I see it.'

'Here he is again, sprinting back in the direction he's come from, two minutes later. And look at this—' Ashwin lays down his last photo '—there's our lad, on his way back towards the café for a second time. You can see the shotgun in his right hand. They're running his image through facial recognition software. Nothing yet.'

'Any idea where he fetched this gun from?'

'Glad you asked. They've found a Land Rover down a side street, blocking the entrance to a furniture removal business. Ancient thing, apparently, but in good nick. Someone's loved it. Driver's door wide open. There's a child's pedal car on the back seat. Shotgun cartridges all over the floor, and a canvas gun case on the front seat.'

Eliza clicks the end of her biro, ready to make a note. 'And the vehicle is registered to . . .?'

'Samuel John Ballard. Born 1994, so the age fits. He's got an address in Sussex: Tyndale Farm, Holdsworth. Local police are on their way out there. Samuel John Ballard could be sitting at home, minding his own business, totally unaware everything's kicking off. He's got no criminal record. Our attacker might have swiped his vehicle.'

'Holdsworth? I drove through there a couple of years back,' says Paul. 'Stopped for a pub lunch with my ex. Sleepy little place, picture-postcard.'

Eliza picks up each of the photos in turn, trying to get a feeling for her man. There's frantic urgency in the blurred figure, curls flying around his head. He seems so young. He'd look angelic if it weren't for the shotgun in his right hand.

'Who are you?' she asks aloud. 'And what do you want?'

Rosie

Nothing but damp and darkness, screaming muscles and the chanting of her thoughts. *I didn't even want to come to work! I didn't want to be here.*

The chill has penetrated right to her bones. Her bruised arms throb, her twisted spine feels as though it's going to snap. And the icing on the cake? She's coming down with a cold. It began as tightness in her throat last night but now it's taken hold, raging through her sinuses and making it painful to swallow. She longs to stand up straight, to stretch her arms and rub her aching neck.

She longs to be able to sneeze without terror. She keeps imagining a hot bath with Radox and a cup of Lemsip, or maybe red wine.

He's still here, and it sounds as though he's got some people trapped with him. Fuck, what's he planning? She'd heard more screams and yells a little while ago. She risks letting the cupboard door swing open an inch and holds her face to the crack, peeking out. Only one light is on in the storeroom: a single bulb, not bright. Borrowed light gleams from the customers' bathroom, through a high window. She can just make out the shapes of shelves and equipment, the industrial-sized fridge and freezers, the coat rack. The staff's abandoned coats and jackets look like a line of people, all hanging from the hooks.

Her phone has been close by all this time, so tantalisingly available—just there, in the pocket of her denim jacket, which is hanging on those coat hooks. If she could only get hold of her phone she could let the police know she's here. She could leave some kind of message for her daughter, in case they never see each other again. She might be able to text other people too, people she didn't think she cared about. Especially her dad.

But the moment she comes out from her hiding place she'll be risking her life. She keeps screwing herself up to make a break for it—I'll go! I'll run across there, grab the phone, be back in twenty seconds—then she remembers the terrible sound of gunfire and the weird animal shriek that followed it, and she shrinks back again.

Robert's been shot. She's pretty sure of that. It might even be him she heard making that awful screeching sound. He can't be dead, though. He *can't* be. He has such energy, such effortless control of everything and everyone. Robert Lacey always comes out on top! He'll have found some way to survive. He can talk his way out of any kind of trouble.

Her boss had been sitting on the edge of her bed at six o'clock this morning, with a towel around his waist and his hair wet, smacking her bottom as she lay face down—playfully, but not quite painlessly.

'Ouch!' she protested.

'Come on, that didn't hurt.'

'It did.'

He rubbed the place where he'd slapped her. 'Well, it shouldn't have. You're getting too skinny, Rosie! Nothing of you. I might as well be sleeping with a boy.'

She pulled the duvet over herself, and he laughed as he stood up. She heard him moving around the room. He told her he'd see her at work at seven-fifteen, and she'd better not be late again. Or else.

'Or else what?' she asked, turning over to look up at him. He was pulling on his jeans.

He leaned down, smiling; put his hands each side of her head on the pillow. She could smell his cologne as he kissed her.

'That's for me to know and you to find out.'

It was the very last thing he said to her.

Just a few hours ago. He's got so much life in him. He can't possibly be dead.

FIFTEEN

Neil

Water steams and gushes from the taps. He's filled the basin and stripped down to his vest, squeezing frothing mounds of soap from the dispenser before using a towel as a flannel to scrub his face and arms and neck. *That man's blood. That dead man's blood.* Rusty streaks spiral into the vortex of the plughole. But no matter how hard he scrubs—how much soap he uses and how hot the water—he can't get clean. He'll never get clean. He's just brought up everything he's eaten in the past day, which isn't much. It's a relief to hide here in the bathroom, to have a break from watching that crazy lad charging around in circles. It's a relief to take five minutes away from feeling like a snivelling coward.

He has to give the police full marks for persistence. Hats off. The negotiator keeps on calling, time after time, even though her only reward so far has been incoherent mumbling and yells. Neil has taken to watching the clock, waiting for 'Rocket Man'. It makes him feel less alone. He's pretty sure the crazy lad has been watching the clock too, perhaps for the same reason.

The bathroom consists of two cubicles built into a square room with a tiled floor and wood-panelled walls. A vase with sprigs of holly fills one end of the vanity; at the other there's a basket of hand towels and one of those bottles of scented oil with bamboo stuck in it. He's never quite seen the point of those. An enormous mirror dominates the basin. He's careful to avert his eyes from that. The last time he glanced in a mirror it gave him a hell of a shock. The guy he saw was a shambles. Finished. Washed-up.

Oh, how he wishes he could talk to Heather. He wishes it every day, but never more than now. He was a despicable husband and he'll regret it to his dying breath—which might be today; he has to face that. He imagines her in this room beside him, leaning against the baby-changing table with her arms folded. Heavy brown hair, hazel eyes. He tries to conjure her voice, lilting, teasing. *What kind of a scrape have you got yourself into this time, Neil?* You can take the girl out of Liverpool, she used to say, but you can't take Liverpool out of the girl.

She ran the office at the first school where he taught. That's where he first clapped eyes on her, on his first day as a qualified teacher. He had asked for directions and she promptly left her desk and walked alongside him, chatting all the way. By the time they arrived at the staffroom she somehow knew most of Neil's life story. He'd worked for a company making medical equipment before deciding on a career change.

'Why teaching?' she asked.

'I had a fantastic chemistry teacher. Mrs Weddell. She inspired me—she's the reason I'm a chemist. I thought I should pass it on.'

'Hmm. Nervous?'

'A bit.'

That was the understatement of the year. His stomach had been squirming for days. Last night he'd only just resisted the urge to buy a packet of cigarettes, though he'd long since given up. She didn't promise it would all be fine; she was too honest for that. Later, she admitted she'd felt sorry for him. *A lamb to the slaughter.*

'You know where I am,' she told him. 'Drop by at lunchtime. I'll be keeping these crossed. And my toes.'

He can see it now. She's standing with both hands held up, fingers twisted around one another. She has freckles all over her face, and her eyebrows arch high when she smiles. He's wondering whether there's a boyfriend in the picture.

The memory brings tears to his eyes. He seems to cry all the time nowadays, daft old sod. If he dies here today, she might never know. She doesn't even know what city he's in.

He's pulling his clothes back over his head when he notices a narrow window above the basin. It's a horizontal oblong, perhaps two feet by three. Leaving the tap running to cover the noise, he carries a wooden chair across and climbs onto the vanity with an agility he didn't know he still had. Balancing with one foot each side of the basin, he peers through.

It's no good. Even if he could open and squeeze through the window—unlikely, he's no gymnast—he'll have got nowhere. He's looking into a windowless space, about the size of a large garage. There's a double sink, kitchen equipment, an alcove with some freezers and beyond those a door with STAFF on it—probably a toilet. There's no daylight, no sign of any windows. By craning his neck he can see another door to the left, but it must lead back into the café. In fact, now he thinks about it, Robert will be lying right behind that.

He's about to clamber down when he spots movement. He can't believe his eyes. A door beneath the sink is inching open. There are fingers curled around the edge. It's creepy, the sight of a disembodied hand in that gloomy room. A person rolls out—onto her knees at first, before getting to her feet. A young woman: slender, very short hair with a floppy fringe, tight jeans. She straightens slowly, clutching her back. If she's been hiding under that sink all morning she must be knotted like a pretzel. She's looking all around her, hyper-alert like Neil's foxes as they slink out from under the hedge. She stretches her neck to one side and the other, rubbing it.

He's seen this girl before. She works here. She's wearing the staff uniform, a black T-shirt with TUCKBOX across her bust. There's a tattoo; some kind of plant curling up her left arm. Yep, it's her all right.

When she spots Neil's face at the window, she jumps. Poor lass. She literally jumps, covering her mouth with the palms of both hands. He waves his arms, trying to let her know he's harmless, and she stands like a horrified statue, hands still jammed over her mouth.

Someone's knocking on the bathroom door behind him—*Neil, Neil?* He hurriedly climbs down and puts the chair back, bundling his shirt, sweater and anorak into his arms.

The knock's becoming more urgent.

'Neil! Sorry, you've got to come out. Now.'

He opens the door to see Abi standing there. She's looking strained.

'He's paranoid,' she whispers. 'He's decided you're up to something.'

When he returns to the café, the other hostages are clustered in a tight knot of frightened humanity in the booth. Neil can see why. The lad's out of his tree again—screaming about how snipers are hiding behind every door and every window and they're going to blow his head off the first chance they get.

Fair enough. They probably are. Let's hope they take a pot shot soon.

'You've been letting them in!' he yells, advancing on Neil.

Neil takes a step back, holding up his hands. 'See for yourself, there's no way anyone could get in here.'

The lad doesn't believe him. He creeps to the bathroom door, rushes inside and spins in circles. When he notices the window, he stops dead, staring up at it.

'Just a storeroom next door,' says Neil quickly. 'There's no way through there. Nobody can come in or out.'

The lad lays one hand flat on the edge of the vanity, holding his gun in the other. He's young and fit, he doesn't need a chair to hop up beside the basin. Any second now, he's going to look through that window. Any second now, he's going to see a terrified girl.

That's when the dogs begin to bark.

Rosie

The place has been quiet for a while. Now's the time.

She rolls out of the cupboard and onto her feet, ears pricked, watching the swing door for any kind of movement. If he walks in here now, she won't have time to hide. She will be the fish in the barrel. She may be about to die in the attempt to get her phone. Oh, but it feels fantastic to be out of that hell-hole! It's a luxury just to be vertical, to stretch the tortured muscles and joints in her back and shoulders, to rub her sore neck. She allows herself several precious seconds to make the most of her temporary freedom.

That's when she happens to glance up at the internal window. Her heart gives one massive thud, as though a mallet has smashed against the inside of her chest. It leaves her breathless. There's someone watching her. All she can make out is a sinister silhouette and blurred features—the outline of shaggy hair, perhaps a beard.

He begins waving, gesticulating. After a few moments he abruptly drops away from the window.

She doesn't move. She's never been paralysed by fright before—never imagined what it would be like. Before she's gathered her wits, angry shouts are erupting from the café. That galvanises her. Forgetting about the phone she scrambles back under the sink, pulls the door behind her and curls up again.

She's fighting to control her breathing. *Shh.* She lies absolutely still, straining her ears for footsteps or the creak of the door.

Instead she hears another, unexpected sound. It's faint, perhaps coming from the street outside. But somewhere, not far away, dogs are barking.

Eliza

'Bloody hell,' she mutters to Paul, as they watch from the attic room. 'That's a high-risk strategy.'

A pair of firearms officers are trying to get closer to the café, creeping out from the drycleaner's doorway. As they approach Tuckbox they come face to face with the biggest of the dogs. He's sitting up on his haunches, following their every move. They freeze for a good half-minute before trying to edge past him.

'Might be okay,' whispers Paul. 'They're moving slowly.'

But this is clearly an excellent guard dog and he takes his duties seriously. Eliza doesn't hear his first bark, but the other dogs certainly do. Within seconds they're all in full cry, yapping and baying like a pack of wolves. The little white one is actually springing up and down, all four paws leaving the ground. The officers beat a hasty retreat, but the damage is done. The hullaballoo could wake the dead.

'This isn't good,' gasps Eliza, rushing back to the phone. 'This isn't good, this isn't good, this could be a flashpoint. He'll be going nuts in there! I'm going to call him, try to calm him down.'

The gunman answers straight away, and she was right. The barking has hurled him back into panic. His first words are high-pitched shrieks, almost unintelligible.

'Call them off!'

'There's nobody, it's just the dogs.'

'They're coming to kill me. Call them off. Call them off! I mean it, I'm warning you!'

His terror resonates in her headset, fracturing his voice into jagged splinters. She's heard screaming meltdowns like this before. The lizard brain has taken over again. He's cornered. He's dangerous.

'I can hear that you're scared,' she says, but he's still shouting.

'Call them off! I know they're outside, the dogs are barking.'

'I'm a negotiator, I don't make those decisions, but what I can tell you—' she pauses, waits for a break in his yells '—listen,

listen—listen! What I *can* tell you is that as long as the people in there with you are safe, I'll keep talking to you. I will keep listening. There'll be no need for any other police action. Okay?'

'They're right outside that door! I'm dead.'

'No—hey, listen to me for one second! I know the dogs barked, but nobody is coming in.' She hopes it's true. 'Nobody wants this to go wrong. Not me, not you, nobody. We all want the same thing. We *all* want to find a way out of this for you.'

He's quieter, but he's still terrified. It sounds as though he's shivering.

'You're keeping me talking while they sneak up. I can hear them next door too. Through the wall. I can hear them everywhere.'

Paul shoves a post-it note in front of her: *Paranoid. Ground him in reality? Focus on what he can see?*

'Can you tell me what's happening inside Tuckbox right now?' she asks. 'What exactly is the situation in the café?'

During the silence that follows, she mentally zips her lips. Silences make her edgy. In social situations—lunch with Richard's parents, work bashes, the neighbours' bloody awful Christmas party on Saturday night—she makes it her duty to fill the awkward pauses. She's the one who thinks of the funny story to tell, who spurts desperate inanities about the weather. Ethan pulled her up on it during one of the simulations in her training. *Stop fearing the silence, McClean, for Pete's sake. It's one of the most valuable tools in the box. Keep your trap shut. Zip your lips. Give 'em time to think.*

She keeps her trap shut now, counting the passing seconds. *Twenty, twenty-one, twenty-two, twenty—*

'Robert's dead,' he says.

She exhales carefully, glancing at Paul.

'Thank you for telling me that. It's much better that I know.'

'I killed Robert. Can't believe it.'

'Are there any children in Tuckbox?'

'Um, yeah. Two.' She detects a note of shame. Perhaps there's leverage there.

'And it's still the case that nobody needs medical help?' she asks. 'Including you?'

'No.'

'That's good. That counts for a lot, the fact that everyone else is okay. I know things can happen fast and situations sometimes get out of hand. But since this began you've kept things under control, and everyone else is safe. You've done well.'

'Don't patronise me.'

'I'm not—'

She winces as the headphones magnify his shout.

'Are you seriously going to pretend this has all been a bit of a misunderstanding? I killed an unarmed man in his own café. That's murder, isn't it? Murder. I can't come back from this. I won't be walking out of here.'

'Why won't you be walking out of there?'

'I'm never going to prison.'

Ashwin slides into the room, placing a note in front of her before donning his own headset.

Samuel Ballard. Sam. Dob 10/5/94. Robert Lacey is his stepfather.

Samuel. Sam. She doesn't change her tone, doesn't hint at what she now knows. It's far better if the information comes from him. She's getting a feeling for him now, for his speech patterns. He seesaws from rage to fear to horror, but he's no fool. She's been in danger of underestimating him. Her response needs to be tailored to him. It's no good being Tigger if he is Eeyore.

'I'm getting the feeling Robert and you have a history?' she prompts.

'You can say that again.'

'Tell me. It sounds as though a lot's gone on.'

'Why would you care?'

'Because it's my job. Right now, today, my whole focus is on you, on what's brought you here today. I really do want to understand what's happened to you. I want to listen.'

Ethan was right: telephone negotiation is like flying blind. You have to develop a sixth sense. The floodgates are opening. She can hear Sam's breathing becoming louder, more choppy and uneven, until he cries out. 'People didn't see it!'

'See what?'

'He plays the fucking saint to a tee. Nobody would listen to me, nobody would help me, they couldn't see what he was doing to us. Nobody, nobody . . .' His voice disintegrates into a long, despairing moan—*ohh!*—like a heartbroken child. It's a desolate sound. It tugs at her. When Liam was four, he somehow got lost at a funfair. After a frantic search she found him standing alone in the vast crowd—a tiny figure, completely ignored by passers-by as he wailed to himself. She still feels guilty. Sam sounds exactly as Liam did then.

'What was he doing to you?' she asks.

'I don't want to talk about Robert.'

Paul's scribbling: *YES HE DOES!!*

'Okay, we won't talk about Robert,' she concedes, nodding her agreement with Paul. 'But maybe you could tell me your name? It feels wrong, calling you "you". I'm Eliza, as you know.'

There's a crack in the plastered wall of the attic room. It begins near the ceiling, zigzags down the magnolia paintwork and disappears behind a filing cabinet. Her gaze follows its hairpin bends as she counts. *Keep your trap shut, McClean. Thirty-one, thirty-two* . . . She's chewing her lower lip, willing him to answer. *Come on, come on.* If he is prepared to trust her with his name, she'll have one foot over the threshold.

'Sam,' he mutters at last. 'Sam Ballard.'

Yes. She gives a silent shimmy of celebration.

'Is there anything you need, Sam? Anything practical we can deliver to you? How about food and hot drinks?'

A grunt of laughter. 'Are you serious? We're in a fucking café.'

'True.' She allows herself to echo his laugh, matching his change of mood. He's shifted gear again. It's tricky to keep up.

'There *are* some things I want,' he says. 'I bet they're asking you, "What are his demands?" Are they? Are they asking that?'

'Of course.'

'Well, here I come with some demands.'

'Let's hear them.'

'Right. Right. Erm . . .' He swallows. He sounds nervous. Playing the role of demanding hostage-taker doesn't seem to come naturally to him. 'Yeah. I didn't expect to be here, so I haven't got a plan worked out, but . . . okay. I want to talk to Nicola. Face to face. Not on the phone. Face to face, in here. And she's got to bring Julia with her, okay? I must see my daughter. I *must* see my daughter. That's my demand. That's not negotiable.'

Ashwin has sprung into action: he's typing into his tablet, skimming through notes.

'Just so I understand,' says Eliza, playing for time now, 'you'd like to talk to someone called Nicola?'

'And Julia.'

Ashwin is shaking his head, mouthing *no way* as he highlights something on his tablet and slides it across to Eliza. It's some notes from the officers who visited Ballard's address and spoke to the owner of the Holdsworth village shop.

Long-term relationship with Nicola ?? family name. Broke up earlier this year. One child Julia 2 or 3 y/o. Court case? Not sure of outcome.

'Okay,' says Eliza, rapidly scanning the message. 'I've heard your request. But you know, Sam, that's quite a big ask. All I can promise to do is to pass it on and see where we get.'

'It's not negotiable.'

'Let's start with finding Nicola. What's her family name? D'you have any contact details?'

To her surprise, this easy question seems to be like a red rag to a bull.

'Come on! Think I'm stupid? I bet she's standing right beside you, laughing her head off.'

'She isn't. We haven't had any contact from a person called Nicola.'

'She was in Tuckbox when I came in. She saw me, I saw her. There's no way on this earth she won't be talking to the police at this moment, telling them what a raving psycho I am.'

Eliza is scanning the list of witnesses, double-checking that Nicola wasn't among those who escaped from the café this morning. *Nope.*

'She's not here. We didn't know she existed until just now when you—'

'Of course she's fucking there.'

'I promise you she's not. Do you have an address for her? A phone number?'

'You know full well I don't! What's the point of talking, if you're just going to lie?'

'Sam, I'm not—'

'Jesus Christ, what's the point? Fuck off.'

'Sam?'

He's gone. With a groan, she lets her forehead bang onto the table.

SIXTEEN

Mutesi

So, his name is Sam. They know this now.

He never stops moving: a caged bear, striding three paces, swinging around, three paces back. From time to time he takes a pill out of a foil packet and crushes it in his teeth. She imagines it must be some kind of stimulant.

'Grandma,' whispers Emmanuel, 'why's that man eating pills?'

She strokes his head, hushing him.

'Don't worry. They make him feel better. It will be all right.'

Mutesi has long been a fan of Elton John. She used to listen to him on the radio years ago in Rwanda, but she never expected his music to take on a life-or-death significance. 'Rocket Man' is the hostages' link to sanity. They eavesdrop on Sam's phone calls in watchful silence. His world is theirs now; his fate is linked with theirs. Once or twice Mutesi catches the voice of the negotiator, a woman who speaks as though she has all the time in the world, absorbing all the emotion Sam hurls at her—yes, even when he tells her to fuck off.

'They're stalling,' he rages, hurling the phone across the room. 'Fucking lying to me.'

Neil gets up, limping across the room to retrieve the phone. 'Why would they do that?'

'Nicola's pulling their strings.'

'How d'you know that?'

'She has to be with them!' Sam turns in a circle, banging his head with his fist. 'Christ, we were together long enough, she knows me. Why doesn't she just say, "Okay, I'll talk to Sam. I'll go down there and talk to him." Why? *Why?*'

'Why isn't your ex-girlfriend volunteering to drop in here for a bit of a chat? Hmm.' Neil lets his gaze rest on the shotgun in Sam's hand. His lips twitch. 'It's a mystery.'

•

At about midday Sam makes a hurried visit to the toilet, taking Neil with him as a hostage. He's barely out of sight before Abigail is springing to action.

'Quick,' she hisses, sliding on her stockinged feet towards the makeshift barricade. 'We all have to lift these. We can't drag them, it'll make too much noise.'

Mutesi and the two other women hurry to help, each taking a side of the nearest table. The children watch wide-eyed from the back corner of the booth. Lily is chewing Roo's ear. Emmanuel puts his arm around his even smaller companion.

'Don't worry, Lily,' he whispers affectionately, hugging her. 'They're going to open the door and let us out.'

The table is one of the biggest ones, solid and unwieldy. They manage to lift and shift it several feet before one leg scrapes the concrete floor with a horrifying shriek, triggering a yell from Sam in the toilet. The next moment the rebels have thrown themselves back into the booth while Sam charges in with Neil behind him. He strides to the barricade, bellowing something obscene as he shoves the table back into place.

It's all too frightening for Lily. Mutesi sees the toddler's upper lip wobble, and the next moment she's demonstrating just how loudly she can scream.

'I want to go from here, Mummy,' she wails. 'Go home!'

Paige cradles her daughter on her lap, rocking from side to side. 'Please let us go,' she begs Sam. 'She's just a baby. She's still in nappies. Please, please let us go.'

Sam looks at Lily with his unnerving, intense gaze, twisting a handful of his own hair. He's stopped shouting. Three paces one way, swing around, three paces back.

Lily is inconsolable for a long time, but little by little her screams become sobs, and then gulps, and then hiccups. Her face takes on a small, blank look. Mutesi's daughter Giselle used to have that same expression, when she was overtired and needed a nap. They are two tiny girls from almost opposite worlds, decades apart, and yet so much the same. Lily sits with her thumb in her mouth, leaning against her mother's pregnant stomach, occasionally heaving a sobbing sigh. Mutesi smiles and winks at her. Lily solemnly winks back—though she has to hold one eye open while she shuts the other.

'She okay?' Sam asks suddenly.

Paige pulls her daughter closer, glaring up at him. 'What do you think?'

'They'd never bother talking to me if I didn't have you lot with me.'

Abigail swivels on the vinyl seat, eyeing him. The failed escape attempt seems to have infuriated her. Her lips are pursed, her jaw clenched.

'So keeping us here is all about getting yourself a platform, is it? I've got a client accused of GBH and child cruelty—her own baby, just imagine that for a moment—and her trial was meant to be today, she's been dreading it, and I've let her down because you need bargaining chips! Is that fair? *You* want a voice? Well, I'm *her* voice. That young mother. There must be better ways of getting what you want than using innocent kids as pawns.'

'Jesus Christ!' Sam slaps his wounded forehead so hard that Mutesi winces. That has to hurt. 'It's me that's the pawn. I've been begging for help since I was eight years old. Nobody wanted to know, nobody's ever wanted to know. You're Mrs Privilege! You're a lawyer. I bet people have always done what you tell them to.'

'I wish,' says Abigail.

'You say jump, they say how high.'

'Ha! I say jump, they say fuck off.'

Mutesi is sure there's a creasing at the sides of Sam's mouth, a lightening in his eyes—a brief glint of a smile—before he turns it into a scowl. It's the first sign. Fleeting, quickly suppressed, but hopeful. There *is* a human being in there.

'Sam?' she says.

The pacing falters. He's listening. Now is her chance.

'Sam, I am wondering. You say you've been begging for help since you were eight years old. Is that really true?'

He bends his head, rubbing his face on his upper arm as he paces. He has a gun in his hand, but Mutesi can see the lost eight-year-old.

'Whatever happened to you?' she asks. 'Tell me.'

Three paces, swing around, three paces, swing around.

SEVENTEEN

Sam

He can't. He can't tell it. He lives it every day but he can't tell anyone. The scents of the summer night, the hay, the blue river of lights.

He left his dad in the tractor shed and trotted across the yard to the house, thinking all was well in his world. Apart from stupid school, his life was lovely. Just lovely. Tyndale Farm was a part of him. He was born there. He spent half his life perched beside Dad in the tractor, looking back at the ploughed rows. Sunshine and rain. Clouds billowing on the horizon, white seagulls wheeling on the wind like a cloud of snowflakes. If he lifted his earmuffs he could hear Dad humming songs, *hummm*, vibrating along with the tractor's big motor. *Pom, pom, pom.* That was the sound of safety and contentment and home. When Dad was humming, all was well in the world.

As soon as Sam could talk, they talked. Father and son rambled on for hours and days and weeks and years about everything and anything. Might there be life in outer space, and if so what would an alien look like? Did King Arthur and his knights really exist? How does an aeroplane fly? What's in a seed? Sam learned ten times more from his dad than he ever did in a classroom.

His parents lived as though they were singing a duet. When he thinks of his mother back then, she's always laughing herself into hiccups. He feels her warmth beside him on the sofa. To this day he can't hear that cheery *Thomas the Tank Engine* tune without a sad echo of happiness.

He's never forgotten his joy that haymaking night; end-of-term joy that made him jump up the kitchen steps with his feet pressed together—*hip, hip, hop, I'm a kangaroo.* The mower was mended! Dad was happy! Four more days till the summer holidays! It was a warm evening and the kitchen door was wide open. Mum was sitting at the table doing the farm accounts, wearing her patched jeans and singing along to the radio. He doesn't remember changing into his pyjamas or brushing his teeth or nosediving into bed, though he must have done all those things, same as he always did, every bedtime.

He doesn't remember falling asleep. He will never forget waking up.

The tawny owls were hooting. He knew them well, that pair. They lived in the spinney in Sundance's field; he'd often seen and heard them swooping through the dusk with a whirr of wings. Their descendants live there still.

But it wasn't the owls that woke him. It was a human voice. Blueness was flashing through his curtains, making underwater patterns on his ceiling. He watched the watery dance, and wondered. Maybe they were the lights of the tractor? Perhaps Dad had got up early to get everything done before the weather changed. Sam's bedroom window was open. He could smell the night-scented stock Mum had planted in the front garden. Honeysuckle too, and mown hay. A ram bleated down in the orchard beside the house. It was a sleepy sound.

Back in those days, Sam used to do puppet shows in a miniature theatre his dad had made out of some wooden crates.

They weren't good puppet shows but his parents were a very enthusiastic audience. People gave him all kinds of puppets, and he'd built up a collection. The only puppet he didn't like was a weird one his mother's sister Monique brought back from a holiday. It was a two-faced doll. One face was a jolly man, with a kind smile and cheeks that stuck out like bright red apples. He looked a nice old guy, maybe Santa Claus without the beard. But when you turned him around you saw his other face—and that gave Sam a fright, the first time. He was a devil with bright red eyes and wicked shark's teeth, his mouth wide open in a snarling kind of grin as though he were going to eat you. He was evil. Mum said Monique had no children of her own, so perhaps she didn't realise it could give a wee person nightmares. It seemed rude to throw it away—and Monique would be bound to notice, and would kick up a fuss—so they sat it on the mantelpiece in Sam's bedroom with all the others, smiling face looking outwards.

And now that puppet looked so, so happy as it turned blue in the flashing lights. Santa Claus was sitting on the mantelpiece, laughing at Sam as footsteps thumped past his bedroom door, as someone who sounded like his mother spoke in a voice that was nearly screaming, as Sam tried not even to blink. He kept hoping to see Dad's cheerful face looking around the door. Dad would explain why there were strangers in their house at night, and why Mum was nearly screaming. Maybe she'd met a burglar.

After a while the footsteps passed his room again, heading down the stairs. They weren't running anymore.

When someone finally looked around his door, it wasn't Dad. It was Mum. Electric light flooded in from the landing behind her. She was wearing a nightie with a cardigan over the top of it.

'Sweetie,' she whispered. 'Are you awake? You need to get up.' She came into the room and picked his clothes off the floor, the ones he'd dropped there when he went to bed. 'Just chuck this sweater on over your pyjamas. Dad's not well.'

He didn't understand. He rolled off the bed, pulling on his

sweater as they hurried down the stairs. He shoved his toes into his shoes at the kitchen door but before he could tie the laces Mum had taken his hand and was running with him towards the car.

'Where's Dad?' he asked.

'In the ambulance.'

'Why's he in an ambulance?'

She started the engine before he'd got his seatbelt on. As she swung out of the yard and into the lane, they saw the flashing lights up ahead.

'Why's he in an ambulance?' he asked again, but she still didn't reply and he stopped asking because he was afraid of the answer. She drove like the clappers down the narrow lanes. He watched their headlights on the hedgerows, and rabbits scurrying out of the way, and the blue lights ahead of them, and he had this awful sinking feeling in his stomach. Then they were running into the hospital through sliding glass doors. Mum had got a long way ahead of him. He was trying to keep up, scared she'd leave him behind.

The rest of the night was like a whirlpool of weird, horrible things. A hot room with a sofa, magazines, toys and a water cooler that made a glugging sound. A smell that reminded him of the vet's surgery. Mum hugging him much too tightly. Granny bursting in with her storm-cloud hair all in a mess, rushing up to his mum with her arms held out. Sam had never seen Granny's hair loose before. There were people who dressed like the doctors he'd seen on television. People saying they were sorry. Sam didn't know why they were sorry, but it made his stomach hurt when they said it. People giving Mum leaflets and numbers to phone. People saying that Dad had been arrested.

'By the police?' he asked.

'No, sweetie,' said Mum. 'Not that kind of arrest.'

All the strange hospital sounds melted into one another. He lay on the sofa with his head on Mum's lap. She was stroking his hair.

'I'm not sure whether I want to see him,' she whispered to Granny. 'Do you?'

'Yes.' Granny's voice had a shake in it. 'Yes. I'd like a little time with him. There are things I want to say. Things I should have said every day of his life.'

'Are we going to see Dad now?' Sam hopped off the sofa, feeling perkier. 'Where is he?'

'Sweetie.' Mum pulled him close. He felt wetness on her face.

'Why are you crying?' he asked.

She was trying to speak. She made her mouth into the right shape to say the word *Dad,* but no sound came out. This frightened him so much that he started needing the toilet. He had to hop from foot to foot.

'Sammy, Sammy, your dad has died,' said Granny. 'I'm sorry.'

'But he has to get the hay in.'

Granny knelt on the floor beside him, hugging Mum and him together, repeating over and over that she was sorry.

They were wrong! Dad would come alive again, like Baloo in *The Jungle Book*. He'd smile and chat and everything would be all right. Dad hadn't had time to get ill and die. He was fixing the mower. He was happy. He'd said, *Night, son*.

'But when did he die?'

'In the night,' said Granny. 'His heart stopped while he was asleep. Sometimes that happens even to young people like him.'

'They can start it up again, can't they?'

His mother made a sound like a laugh, but it wasn't a laugh.

'Don't worry, Mum,' he whispered, wiping her wet cheeks with his hand. He desperately wanted to cheer her up. 'They can start it again. They'll have a gadget. Like a battery charger thing.'

Granny pressed her fingers over her eyes. Dark blue veins on the backs of her hands. They were the two women he loved best in the world, the two who made things safe. It was terrible to see them crying.

'I want to find him,' he said. 'Where is he? Where is my dad?'

Mum stood up. 'You're right, Sam. Come on, let's go and say goodbye.'

Granny looked shocked. 'Really—Sammy too? D'you think that's a good idea?'

'I don't know.' Mum sighed. 'I'm off the map here, Patricia. A few hours ago Angus was getting into bed, banging on about how he'd fixed that bloody mower. I hardly even spoke to him! I just said, "Oh good, clever boy," rolled over and went back to sleep. How could I not have at least given him a kiss? I'll regret that for as long as I live.'

'You didn't know what was coming.'

They found a nurse nearby. She showed them along the corridor.

'We've got him all ready for you,' she said, as though Dad was a wedding cake she'd iced, and she was quite proud of the effect.

She ushered them into a white room, only about two doors down from where they'd been waiting. Sam was surprised to discover Dad had been here all the time. The room had a metal basin and plastic chairs. It smelled so strongly of the vet's that Sam was almost sick as soon as they walked in. He never forgot that smell. It stuck to him forever. Years later he learned that the smell was a combination of death and disinfectant. The nurse pulled back a white plastic curtain, revealing a waxwork dummy. She said they were to take as long as they liked. Then she left.

Dad was there. Dad wasn't there.

The dummy's presence filled the room. It was lying flat on its back on a kind of giant ironing board, with a sheet covering its body up to its shoulders, and its face was the colour of Blu-Tack. It had Dad's hair, Dad's long feet sticking out the other end. No clothes. Its eyes were closed but its mouth was a little bit open. Dad was handsome and always smiling, but this dummy was ugly and bony and it looked as though it had never smiled. Sam really didn't want this version of Dad to wake up. It would be a horrible zombie if it did.

Mum was crying softly. Granny whispered, 'Angus, my son,' leaned over the dummy and kissed its forehead. Her long hair fell forwards across its chest. Sam watched her lips meet the smooth Blu-Tack, and he smelled that awful smell, and he had to get out of the room.

'It's not him,' he squealed, dragging Mum towards the door by both her hands. 'Let's go, let's go, it's not him!'

She let him tow her into the corridor. Perhaps she was glad to escape too, because his dad was made of Blu-Tack and reeked of something that wasn't human. A weight was crushing Sam's chest, as though he was trapped in the vice in the toolshed. It stopped him breathing. He let go of Mum's hand and pelted down the corridor, past all the trolleys, into the waiting area with people sitting in rows—but he still couldn't breathe, so he burst through the sliding doors and out into the car park.

Tomorrow had arrived without them noticing. The sky was pale blue with a bright yellow horizon. Blossom glowed on a chestnut tree. Cars were being parked, people were waiting at a bus stop. Dad could not be dead in the daytime. It was all wrong, wrong, wrong—the sun should go out and the sky turn black, and there should be thunder and lightning. Sam pelted around the grass verge, shrieking at the top of his voice until he tripped and fell hard. He'd wet himself when he was running and his pyjama bottoms were soaking. It felt clingy and warm at the tops of his legs. Normally he'd have been mortified but now he didn't care. He lay face down on his front, sobbing and sobbing.

He heard his mother panting as she trotted up. *He worshipped Angus, I'm not sure how he's going to get through this.*

A deep voice answered her. *Poor wee chap.*

Someone was on the grass beside him. A heavy hand was rubbing his shoulder.

'Robert's here for us, Sam,' said Mum. 'He's going to drive us home.'

Robert! He crawled away and sat with his back to them and his hands over his ears.

'Go away,' he mumbled. 'We don't want you here.'

He heard Mum apologising. Robert was telling her not to be silly, the little guy was in shock, it was a bloody awful thing to happen to a kid. He said he'd drive them home in their car and take a taxi back to collect his later.

'How're you feeling, Harriet?' he asked, as he turned onto the road.

'It hasn't even begun to sink in. I'm dreaming, I'll wake up and it's all . . .' She looked across at him. 'Thank you for coming. You must be shaken too.'

'It's a dark day.' He seemed to choke up for a while. 'God. A dark, dark day, especially for this little man. Harriet, remember I am here for you. Whatever you need. A shoulder to cry on, anything at all. Just ask. I mean it. I am at your service.'

He came into the house. He made Mum tea with lots of sugar and Sam hot chocolate with marshmallows floating on the top. *You're so kind, Robert.* He put breakfast in front of them and insisted they ate. He changed the sheets in Sam's parents' room. She watched him, with Dad's pillow held tight to her chest. It still had the dip in it where his head had been.

'Thank you, Robert. I was dreading this job.'

He took the pillow out of her hand, punching it hard with his big fist until the Dad's-head-shaped dip was gone. Sam didn't want him to do that.

'Are you sure you wouldn't rather sleep in the spare room?' he asked.

'No, I'll stay in here.' She touched Dad's side of the bed with her fingertips. 'He feels closer.'

Robert took the next few days off work. He never stopped doing things for Mum—all kinds of things. He mended a broken pipe under the sink, and did the shopping, and made phone calls to the bank and to suppliers and contractors and the lawyer, and drove Mum to sort out the death certificate. He answered her mobile phone whenever it rang, which was all day long. He talked to the undertaker and the vicar. He met people who came to the door, thanked them for their flowers and cards and messages, but he wouldn't let them in. He said Harriet wasn't in a state of mind to see anyone.

He cooked in their kitchen, or brought meals he'd made at home. His cooking was much, much posher than they were used to. It looked and tasted like restaurant food. On the third day, Sam upended himself in the freezer and found some cottage pie his father had made, and Mum heated it in the oven. So they got to eat a Dad cottage pie one last time. They both cried as they ate it. Sam sneaked away the leftovers and hid them under his bed until they were covered in a cloud of fluffy mould—orange, blue and white. He tried eating what was under the mould, because Dad had made it, but it tasted so rotten that he had to spit it out.

Robert even tried to stop Granny visiting, but she wasn't putting up with his bossiness.

'My son,' she said, pushing past him at the kitchen door. 'My grandson. My daughter-in-law. I think we should all grieve together, don't you?'

Robert bowed his head and murmured, *Of course, Patricia, so sorry.* Granny had brought hundreds of photos in a suitcase. She and Mum went through them, choosing which ones should be printed on the order of service. Granny had strong views about the readings and the coffin—it *had* to be wicker—and the music, and the wake afterwards. She had opinions about everything.

After she'd gone, Mum and Robert took glasses of wine and sat in the garden. Sam was riding his bike around and around the fishpond. They thought he wasn't listening because he was busy. People often assumed that about him. *Sam's a* busy *child, isn't he?* they'd say. That was code. It meant he was annoying and fidgety and he was driving them nuts. But what they didn't know was that he was alert while he was doing those other things. He listened, he understood and he remembered. His dad used to call him a maestro multi-tasker.

'She's just expressing her own grief,' Mum was saying.

'Mm, poor Patricia. Burying her only son—it doesn't bear thinking about.' Robert rubbed his jaw with the palm of his hand. He'd grown a bit of stubble. 'But she's steamrolling. She's not thinking about you.'

Mum had tilted her head back and was gazing at the summer sky as though she were searching for something.

'My mind's playing tricks. You know? I keep thinking he's just out on the farm. I hear his footsteps in the yard, and walking through the back door. His clothes are still in a pile on the chair where he left them that night. They smell of him, so I can pretend he's just nipped out for an hour. His toothbrush on the basin, his socks with bits of hay stuck in them, all those scruffy to-do lists in his handwriting.' She gave a sad little laugh—*ha!* 'Even those awful oily overalls. They're the last bit of him. I keep trying to talk to him . . . I keep remembering the moment I woke up and reached out to him and he was cold.' Her voice went high. She covered her face with one hand. 'Sorry.'

Sam knew what she meant. That morning he'd felt something warm nudge his fingers and hoped his dad had come to see him. But, no, it was just Snoops. He'd cried.

Robert leaned across from his deckchair, running his knuckle down Mum's arm.

'I'll keep Patricia at bay for you, shall I?'

'That seems wrong. Her heart is broken too.'

'She's got such a powerful personality, that's the trouble. No boundaries.'

'Are you talking about Granny?' Sam asked as he whizzed past on his bike.

Robert snatched away his hand.

'Big ears,' he said.

Sam kept riding around the fishpond but in his head he was yelling at Robert. He remembered Granny saying the man was all teeth and smiles. He considered telling him so, but thought better of it.

Robert was Mum's best friend through those sad times. Her very, *very* best friend. She was so tired that she couldn't think straight, so Robert helped with all the complicated arrangements about money and the will, and the farming business. He contacted the life insurance people. He arranged for a neighbouring farmer, Mr Appleton, to take over the management of Tyndale. To start with it was an emergency measure, but Mr Appleton leased the farm and ran it alongside his own land for years after that. He took Dad's guns and kept them in his own safe, because nobody had a licence in their house anymore.

Mum worried that she should be managing her own affairs, but Robert wouldn't hear of it.

'I'm doing it for Angus,' he insisted. 'I loved the guy. He would have done the same for me in a heartbeat.'

He was *so* kind to them, and Mum was *so* grateful. She didn't know *how* she'd have coped without him—as Sam heard her telling people again and again at the funeral.

'He's been my rock,' she said.

'Is that what you call it?' muttered Granny. 'Huh! Steady hands.'

'Robert Lacey's a lovely, lovely man.' This was Marjorie from the Holdsworth village shop. 'When he comes in for his paper, I always end up feeling good about myself.'

Oma turned up for the funeral. Sam's other grandmother reminded him of Miss Trunchbull in *Matilda*, except she had a Dutch accent. She said whatever nasty things came into her head. She told Mum that being a gardener isn't a career; she bragged that Monique was a skinny accountant: *at least one of my daughters had brains, and a waist as well.* Sam didn't think Mum was lucky with her parents. She used to say she didn't know happiness until Angus came along.

But, boy, did Robert turn on the charm for Oma! He had her eating out of his hand. Literally. He offered her the triple chocolate mousse he'd made at Jackson's Lodge. After the first spoonful she was purring like a cat. Soon she was inviting him up to London for the theatre and talking about how she had a lovely spare bedroom.

Even Aunt Monique was under his spell. She took the train from Manchester and stayed the night of the funeral. She'd met Robert years before but they'd both been divorced since then. She and he went for a long walk around the fields, and Sam spied on them from up in the poplar tree as they returned through the farmyard. He heard Robert telling her the sad story of how his dad—a carpet layer—had run off with a rich client, and his mother brought up her two sons single-handed. Monique was making lots of poor-you noises.

Later, she cornered Mum and started blathering on and on about Robert.

'He's simply there for you, Harriet!'

'I know.'

'No strings attached. Nothing is too much trouble. What's the catch?'

Mum looked confused. 'Catch?'

'Is he gay?'

'Don't think so. He was married to Connie for years. I'm not really in a mood to notice these things.'

'Mm, well, I am. He certainly doesn't make my gaydar bleep.' Aunt Monique pretended to fan herself. 'Far from it! That smile, those brown eyes. The man could be a film star.'

'What's gaydar?' asked Sam, but he got no answer. Monique was still raving on.

'Sensitive, intelligent. Good teeth.'

'You make him sound like a horse,' protested Mum.

'And—on top of all that—the man can cook!'

'True.'

'Can I have him?'

Mum shrugged and turned away, but Sam saw her smile.

It wasn't just the women who liked Robert. Men also seemed to think he was a great bloke. He organised five of Dad's friends—plus himself, of course—to carry the coffin out of the church. He played host at the wake, made sure everything ran smoothly, behaved as though it was his own brother who'd died. Sam overheard heard him telling people that Harriet's boy was a 'troubled' kid.

Sam hated him. He hated his stupid handsome face and his deep voice. He hated the way he was so nice to everybody. He hated everything about him.

He wasn't the only one. Tammy was Mum's old school friend; she was also Sam's godmother—which meant she gave him Christmas presents. She used to visit Tyndale at weekends and often sat on the steps outside the kitchen door, smoking. She had orange hair and a loud voice, wore big billowing dresses and called herself 'cuddly' or 'curvy'. Sam's mum was pretty much the same size and shape, except she wore jeans and called herself 'fat'. In the good old days Tammy and Mum used to stay up and chat half the night, laughing their socks off down in the kitchen.

'Don't you think Robert Lacey's a bit creepy?' Tammy asked soon after the funeral, when she, Mum and Sam were out walking the dogs. 'Feels like he's trying to get his feet under the table.'

Mum sighed. 'Oh, Tam! Not you too.'

'I've met his ex-wife. It was a ghastly marriage.'

'He's just being loyal to Angus.'

'Yeah, but why is he always here?' Tammy slid a cigarette out of a packet and stuck it in her mouth. She took a moment to light it. Sam watched the smoke curling. 'Hanging around.'

'As are you.'

Tammy made a face and muttered something about hoping she wasn't getting in the way. They didn't see her much after that, which was a shame. Sam missed hearing Mum and her laughing their socks off.

Once the funeral was over and Aunt Monique had gone, Sam took the two-faced Santa Claus snarling-devil puppet off his mantelpiece, put a sock over its head and shoved it into the back of his cupboard. And he named it Robert. Because it *was* Robert.

EIGHTEEN

Rosie

It's just over there. Just there. So close.

She has to move. She can't stand it any longer. Three-two-one-go! She's on her knees, on her feet, scurrying across to the coat hooks and grabbing her phone from her jacket—got it—then fifteen seconds to pee in the staff toilets before forcing herself back into her lair. Only when she's inside, with the cupboard door pulled nearly shut, does it occur to her that she could have put the jacket on.

For a time she is exultant. The phone gives her light. It gives her hope. Somehow it keeps her company even before she's spoken to anyone. She has no idea how to text the police, and dialling 999 is too risky. She daren't even whisper—she might be more audible in the café than they are to her. She finds *DAD* in her contacts and sends a text, begging her useless father to let the police know she's trapped in Tuckbox Café.

Hiding under sink back kitchen. Robert shot I think HELP

This will be the first time she and her dad have been in contact since . . . when? June? They don't get on. She despises him, and he claims to disapprove of her life choices. Frigging hypocrite!

Please, Dad, answer. She imagines him in a grubby T-shirt, rolling a cigarette in his thin fingers, shaking from a night of weed or whisky or whatever it is he's doing these days. He's only forty-five. Younger than Robert. Different species to Robert.

Five minutes pass, and he hasn't answered. Perhaps he's lost his phone. Perhaps he's turned it off, or forgotten to charge it. That would be typical. Perhaps he's gone off on some kind of meditation retreat. She'll have to try somebody else. She brings up her contacts and begins to text her half-sister.

The screen is suddenly flashing in the darkness. So much light, using precious battery life. Someone's trying to ring her. *DAD.* She cuts off the call, texting furiously with both thumbs.

I can't talk!! Please tell police I'm here

The phone vibrates as he replies.

OK will do worried sick

It's an old phone, doesn't hold a charge for long. The battery's already down to thirty per cent. She can't afford to waste it.

She sends one more message. It might be her last, for all she knows.

Love you dad xxxx

It's true. True-ish. She sometimes, almost, kind of loves him. On a good day. Or a really bad day, like this one.

And then she waits. She waits. She waits.

Eliza

The fragile rapport she's so painstakingly built has been shattered. Four calls in a row have ended badly.

'This is your final chance,' he warns, his voice flat. 'Don't call again unless it's to tell me Nicola and Julia are on their way over here.'

'We haven't found them yet.'

'You're the police, aren't you? You've got access to every database there is!'

'Listen, Sam—'

'No, *you* listen. Nobody is leaving this café until I've seen my family.'

'I understand you're frustrated and—'

'You don't understand shit!'

A post-it note from Paul. *Talk about Julia?*

'You're right, I don't,' says Eliza quickly. 'Sorry. I don't understand, but I really do want to. Tell me about Julia. How old is she?'

'Don't bother calling again until you've got them.'

'Sam, can we just—Sam?'

It's no good. He's gone. Eliza rips off her headset.

'Damn! Where the hell *is* this Nicola person? How come we haven't got her here yet? Is she deliberately avoiding us? He says she was in the café, so why didn't she fetch up here, with the other witnesses?'

Paul is logging the call—what was demanded, what time it ended.

'D'you think Sam might be getting tired?' he asks. 'I thought I heard a bit of exhaustion in his voice.'

'He must be. He can't rest at all, can he? But he's not so tired that he'll be giving up—it's just enough to make him dangerous.'

Eliza has often tried to imagine what it would be like to be the person at the other end of that phone: to be so alone, a public enemy, unable to let your guard down for a single second. The idea first caught her imagination when she was twelve and watched a real-life prison drama unfolding on the local news. A middle-aged man had somehow got onto the highest roof of Edinburgh Prison. He'd always protested his innocence but the courts wouldn't hear his appeal. *Hear me, hear me*, he kept shouting. He'd been balanced on a ledge for hours. *Will somebody please hear me!*

'He must be getting really tired,' Eliza had said. 'Poor man.'

Her brother Aaron pretended to play the violin. He was incapable of putting himself into anyone else's shoes. He's in insurance now, with four kids and two ex-wives. Eliza dislikes him intensely.

'How my heart does bleed for the poor murderer or paedophile or whatever he is,' he'd simpered, imitating her. 'Boohoo.'

'He says he didn't do it.'

'He would, wouldn't he? If he can't do the time, he shouldn't have done the crime.'

Instead of going to bed that night, Eliza wheeled her desk chair into the middle of the room, clambered up and stood on the seat. After fifteen minutes she was cold and bored. After half an hour she was cold and bored and longing to be in bed. After an hour she was almost in tears from sheer exhaustion. The chair kept wobbling. It was after midnight when she finally gave in, tumbling from chair to bed and snuggling under her duvet. That lonely man was probably still standing on the prison roof, surrounded by arc lights and people like Aaron.

By morning the crisis was over. He'd given himself up. She hoped they were letting him sleep.

'*I've come to get her*,' muses Paul, squinting at his own handwriting along the top of the board. '*What have you done with her? What did you do to her?* D'you think we can assume "she" is Nicola?'

Eliza stands up, walking around the table to join him.

'I'm not sure we can. Not if he's already seen Nicola in the café. It doesn't really fit.'

'Julia, then? His daughter?'

'Maybe.' She gazes up at the board. '*What did you do to her?* I'm beginning to wonder whether something terrible has happened to that child.'

Paul's job is to be a dispassionate adviser, to keep his emotional distance. He's not the one pouring his soul into building trust and rapport with Sam.

'Even if—*when*—they find Nicola,' he says, 'his demands aren't going to be met. You do know that? You'll never get the boss to agree to a gamble on that scale. Taking a kid into a murder scene, delivering her up to an armed killer? Heck, no! Can you imagine what the media would have to say?'

'What if two other children were released in return?'

Paul is shaking his head.

'This Nicola is obviously a love affair that's turned to custard. Why d'you reckon he wants to talk to her? Same reason he wanted to talk to Robert?'

'Possibly.'

'Right.' Paul draws his finger across his jugular. 'And we all know how *that* ended. This guy's got nothing left to lose. He might be looking for an audience for his suicide. Or, worse, he might be planning on taking his family with him.'

He's right. Of course he's right. She hates the fact that he's right.

'Nicola might agree to act as an intermediary on the phone,' she suggests.

'She might, if we find her. But that's also a risk, isn't it? Speaking to his ex might turn out to be the final tick on his bucket list.'

Right again. They've both been involved in crises where a phone call has been used to say goodbye. Eliza turns away from the whiteboard. She's getting cabin fever. She needs to be out of the room for a few minutes, maybe make a cup of coffee.

'Nicola can't have disappeared into thin air,' she says. 'I'm sure she's the key.'

Hurried footsteps rattle on the stairs. The next moment Ashwin's standing in the doorway. He looks stunned.

'Nicola,' he says.

'Tell me you've found her,' begs Eliza.

'Um, yes and no. She's in Tuckbox.'

His colleagues frown at him, doubting.

'She's never left that bloody café,' he insists, gesturing wildly out of the window. 'She's the missing waitress. She's Rosie. Turns out her surname's Rosedale. Rosie. Geddit?'

Eliza blinks. This simply does not compute.

'No. That's not right. Sorry, Ashwin, your intelligence has to be wrong. She definitely isn't in Tuckbox. I've just spoken to Sam, and he's—'

'She's about fifteen feet away from Sam Ballard. Hiding in a cupboard. Texting goodbye messages to her family.'

NINETEEN

Mutesi

The negotiator hasn't called for a while now. Perhaps the police are scouring the country for this woman Nicola.

The hostages have drawn together in the booth, six adults keeping Emmanuel and Lily as far from that gun as possible. Abigail and Neil sit side by side, a meeting of the immaculate and the shambolic. Lily has fallen asleep at last, sprawled on her mother's lap. Emmanuel is somehow managing to make himself very small. Mutesi sees his wide eyes peeking out, following Sam as he paces.

Mutesi and terror are old acquaintances. She knows that it has peaks and troughs. She and Emmanuel's father, Isaac, once spent five weeks hiding among a cloud of flies. Isaac was a very small boy then, just as Emmanuel is now. Every moment was laden with the threat of death. Each morning, when strips of sunrise glittered through the gaps between the boards, she knelt on the dirt floor to bargain with the Lord. At each sunset she thanked him. Yet Isaac and she weren't in a state of panic for every second of those weeks. They read, they played quiet games and wrote in the dust with sticks, they whispered stories.

Sometimes they even laughed—silently, agonisingly, until tears ran down their faces.

She sees the same resilience in these people. After hours of fear their collective lives are beginning to take on new rhythms. As Sam paces, paces, paces, the hostages exchange words of comfort and whispered snippets of themselves. Sam doesn't seem to hear them, or care if he does. They're beginning to establish a community. Neil has turned out to be a mine of information on the private lives of foxes; Paige's husband is a tube driver, their unborn baby is a boy and they're going to call him Harry; Abigail was suffering from a migraine but it's better now that she's managed to get very strong pills from her bag-on-wheels. Her court robes are in there too. She brought them out to show Emmanuel, who forgot his fear for a moment as he tried on the wig.

'I very nearly died here, long ago,' says Arthur.

Everyone looks at the elderly man. He's been quiet until now. When he does speak aloud it's with great care, as though he has to retrieve every word from his memory.

'Here?' asks Mutesi. 'You almost died *here*?'

'Balham tube station. In 1940.'

'Not now, Arthur,' says Paige, laying a hand on his arm. 'Don't tell them this story. It's too sad.'

'Was it the bomb?' asks Abigail.

'That's right!' Arthur beams at Abigail. 'You've got it! The bomb.'

'There's a plaque on the wall at the tube station. What happened?'

'Well . . .' Arthur swallows, taking time to gather his thoughts. 'The platforms were air-raid shelters, you see? During the war. People used to sleep down there during the raids, the place was always packed to the gunnels. My family too. On the fourteenth of October a bomb landed a pretty direct hit. Tunnels collapsed.' He swallows again. He seems quite breathless suddenly. 'Sixty or seventy people dead. Pitch-black, tunnels flooded. Gas too. Horrendous thing. There were children. A girl in my class at school was killed down there. But . . . you see—' he peers at Abigail with beetling brows '—that was the one night my family didn't go to the shelter.'

'Oh! You were lucky.'

'The *one* night. It was random chance, you see? Like being in here today. This was a random chance too. Paige kindly said she'd drive me to the clinic this morning. I said okay, thanks, but let me buy you scones and tea in Tuckbox first. I'm always awake very early and so is young Lily. She's an early bird.'

'She doesn't sleep,' says Paige. 'Always up by five. I don't know how we're going to manage when the new baby arrives.'

'It's going to be hell,' mutters Abigail.

Paige grimaces, moving Lily's head into a new position on her lap.

'You okay?' asks Abigail. 'Please tell me you're not going into labour. That's above my pay grade.'

'*Ow.* No. Heartburn. The baby's shoving everything out of place and Lily's not helping, she's heavier than she looks.'

'I've got these for heartburn.' Abigail fishes in the pocket of her jacket then produces a packet of antacids. 'Here you go!'

'Thanks, but I'd better not take anything. I try to avoid chemicals.'

Tenderly, Paige presses her stomach with both hands, as though she really can touch her unborn child. Abigail mutters, 'Suit yourself.' For a fleeting moment Mutesi senses rage in her—a stiff shrug, a deepening of the vertical lines around her mouth as she drops the pills back into her pocket. She's too thin, that girl. Her eyes are shadowed. There's something wrong, for sure.

The group falls silent, and with silence comes a new cloud of fear. The caged bear keeps on pacing. Three paces, swing around, three paces, swing around.

'Emmanuel,' whispers Mutesi, 'what have you got in your school bag? Is there something to do?'

Her grandson grins, straightens and grabs his bag. He and Brigitte rootle in it. *There*. Coloured pencils and an exercise book. Everyone joins in, talking whispered nonsense about Emmanuel's tidy handwriting and his brilliant artwork. The scribbles on those pages are exactly what you'd expect of a six-year-old, but the silly conversation lightens the mood a little, makes their captivity seem less terrifying. Sam still doesn't seem to be listening to them. He's in a world of his own.

'This picture is of Alphonse,' announces Emmanuel, pointing to an orange and black blob.

'Who's Alphonse, then?' asks Neil.

'My cat! My big ginger cat! Did you see this picture I did of Alphonse, Mum?'

Brigitte doesn't answer. Poor girl, she can't. She's biting on her lips, facial muscles working furiously to stop any sound from escaping. Tears are coursing down her cheeks. Any second now, Emmanuel is going to look around and catch his mother crying.

It's Neil who comes to the rescue. Neil, who caught Robert as he fell, who persuaded Sam to answer the phone; Neil, who looks as though he hasn't any other clothes but the rags he's wearing.

'Hey, young man, would you draw a picture for me?' he suggests, with a sympathetic glance at Brigitte. 'I see you've got some very smart pencils.'

Emmanuel is pleased, his mouth pursed with pride as he reaches for his pencil case.

'What of?'

'Whatever you like. Surprise me.'

'Okay.'

Bless you, Neil. Soon Emmanuel's head is tilted to one side, tongue between his perfect little teeth, fingers gripping the coloured pencils. He's drawing a stick figure with a red top, green trousers and a comically broad smile. 'It's Daddy,' he mutters anxiously, and Mutesi's heart throbs. Isaac has flown to Montreal to present a paper on genetics. He'll be waking up in his hotel room about now, blissfully unaware that his wife and son and mother are in such terrible trouble. Or perhaps he's already been woken by a knock at the door to find police standing there. Surely they'll help him to get a flight straight home?

Emmanuel looks so very like his father when he was a little boy. Until now her grandson has lived in a different world—and yet here they are again, hiding from death. He scrunches up his small cheek when Mutesi leans down to kiss it. Suddenly he drops his pencil and turns to hug her, clinging fiercely with all the strength of his arms.

'Don't be scared,' he says. 'It will be all right.'

She presses her brave grandson to her chest, loving him with all her soul and wishing she could somehow make him invisible. They're wrapped around one another.

'Daddy's going to be flying a kite in the picture,' he whispers into her ear.

'Oh good! What colour?'

'Um. Green and purple and yellow.'

After a little while he goes back to work, drawing what might—with a *lot* of imagination—be a kite. He's murmuring to Mutesi as he colours it in.

'Are you hungry, Grandma?'

'A bit. Are you?'

He shakes his head, but she sees him glance hopefully towards the cabinets.

'I think it must be lunchtime,' Mutesi announces to the world. 'My stomach tells me so.'

She stands up, ignoring Sam. He doesn't try to stop her—he still doesn't even seem to notice—as she raids the kitchen, returning with a haul of ready-made sandwiches, sausage rolls and mince pies piled up on a large oval plate. She's a firm believer in the healing power of normality. The ordinary little things: the sharing of stories, of food, of smiles, of small comforts. These are the key to survival. These are what kept her from losing the will to live after her country went mad. Brigitte has recovered herself a little now, and is finding more distractions in the school bag.

'Will you join us?' Mutesi asks Sam.

He has stopped in his tracks, staring feverishly at a blank stretch of wall. If Mutesi remembers correctly, there's a news-agent's shop on the other side.

'Hear that clunk?' he asks.

'I didn't hear anything.'

He strides across to place his ear against the paintwork.

'That clunk, sounded like something metal against the wall. It's them. They use thermal cameras through the walls. They'll be in there, trying to find a way to shoot me.'

Neil looks intrigued.

'Really? Thermal cameras? How does that work?'

Sam's ear is to the wall, his back turned to the hostages. He seems completely engrossed in investigating this new danger. This could be their only chance. Mutesi has a heavy plate in her hands. She might be able to smack him very hard over the head. Then, while he's stunned, they could all overpower him and snatch away the gun. She moves closer, gripping the plate, willing herself to raise it high and bring it smashing down. She imagines the food falling as she raises it, the violence of the impact with a human skull—*crack!*—and is horrified.

Abigail has had the same thought. Picking up a glass water jug, she silently skims around the table towards Sam. She meets Mutesi's eye, glances at the plate and nods. She's swinging the jug by its handle—it's above her head—she's going to do it! Neil too is on his feet, tensed and ready to pile in. Paige is easing the sleeping Lily to one side, preparing to move fast. It's all come so suddenly, this moment of rebellion.

Lily chooses this precise moment to wake up and protest with an ear-splitting wail. She makes a lot of noise for one so small. Everyone jumps. Abigail and Mutesi drop their arms just as Sam turns around to look.

While Abigail hurries away to fill the empty jug with water, Mutesi lowers herself into the booth, breathlessly nagging everyone to eat. She tries to sound innocent but her heart is palpitating painfully—*bom-bom-bom-bom*. She's not a soldier. She can't break someone's skull, especially not with Emmanuel's bright eyes watching her. From now on she will do what she does best: stay calm, and try to keep Sam calm too.

They're all taking part in the pantomime—pretending that food is the only thing on their minds. Neil is just about take a bite out of a meat pie when he hesitates, glancing unhappily towards the back of the kitchen where Robert's body lies.

'It seems a bit disrespectful. You know, tucking into his food while he's over there.'

'This was his café,' retorts Mutesi. She's still puffing with the stress of nearly attacking Sam, nearly being caught. 'D'you think he'd want everything to go to waste?'

'There's no arguing with my mother-in-law,' says Brigitte quietly. 'She persuades people with dementia to eat even when they're throwing their dinner at the walls. Take my advice.'

Neil shrugs and begins to make short work of the pie. One by one the others join in, all except for Arthur Beaumont, who says he's not hungry. He looks ashen-faced, poor man. He should be asleep in his armchair at home.

It's as Mutesi expected: the very act of sharing food brings some calm, even in this strange captivity, with a dead man on the floor and his killer prowling around.

'I just wish I could get something out there to Buddy,' says Neil, as he starts on his third sausage roll. Now that he's begun to eat, his hunger seems insatiable.

'How did you come by him?' asks Mutesi.

'Found him in a squat in Vauxhall. He was with this young couple. They rescued him from a nasty piece of work who used to bash him.'

Abigail sticks out her lower lip. 'Aw, poor Buddy! He's had a hard life, hasn't he? Didn't the young people want him anymore?'

'They couldn't take care of a dog—couldn't even take care of themselves. They'd run away from home and come to London expecting gold-paved streets. The lad was the kind who'd have pratted about in the back of my class when I was a teacher. He'd have failed every exam, but when it came to the practicalities he was a genius. He managed to wire the squat so we had power. God knows how he did it.'

'Stealing, really,' says Paige. She sounds disapproving.

'Yeah.' Neil shrugs. 'You ever lived through a winter without heating, not even a kettle, broken glass in the windows? We were freezing and it was nice to have a few home comforts for a change. I paid my taxes for years, and power bills. I didn't feel too much of a criminal this once. Anyway, we all got evicted. The kids were offered a room in a bed and breakfast, and a place on a back-to-work scheme. It was a lifeline for them but they couldn't take Buddy, so I said I'd have him.' Neil's eyes have reddened. 'Best thing I've done in years. Buddy *is* my buddy. He's company, he's warmth, he's security. He'll be wondering why I walked in here this morning and never came out again. I told him I wouldn't be long.'

Out of the corner of her eye, Mutesi sees that Sam has paused in his terrible pacing. He's watching. He's listening. *At last.*

Neil picks up an empty sugar packet. He examines it carefully, turning it around in his hands.

'It's my birthday today,' he says.

None of the adults seem to know how to react. The usual social rules don't apply; after all, this may also be the day he dies. Emmanuel is the one who behaves properly.

'Happy birthday!' he cries brightly, holding his hand in the air.

'Thank you, young man.'

'I'll draw you a birthday card. After lunch.'

Abigail gestures around the café. 'This isn't a very conventional party, is it? But happy birthday anyway.'

'It's all relative,' says Neil. 'I've had worse. I've had better. Not so very long ago, I went on holiday to Mauritius with my wife to celebrate our joint birthdays. I haven't always been on the streets.'

'You don't seem the type to be—' Abigail squirms a little. '—you know.'

'A rough sleeper? There are plenty like me, for plenty of different reasons.' Neil's playing with the paper sugar sachet, folding it up as small as it will go. His fingers are red and raw, with painful-looking cracks around the nails. That would be the cold. Mutesi makes a mental note to seek out a first-aid kit when she gets a chance.

'I've worked in academia. In industry, in teaching. Had a wonderful wife and two fantastic kids. I chucked it all away, Abi.' He sighs, shaking his head. 'I danced with the devil.'

'Which devil?'

His head is bent over the sachet, tangled hair tucked behind his ears, concentrating on that little paper envelope as though his life depends upon it.

'You don't really want to hear this, do you?'

'Why not? We're a captive audience.' Abigail casts a covert glance at Sam. 'In every sense of the word.'

'True.'

'Hardly the moment for small talk, is it? Come on, Neil. Spill.'

TWENTY

Neil

Perhaps there's a limit to how much terror a person can experience: an upper level, above which it trickles away down the overflow. He woke up this morning cold, hungry and—more pervasive than all his other sources of misery—lonely. Now he's none of these things. He's connected to other human beings, sharing an experience with them. The people with him now aren't scurrying commuters grabbing a *Big Issue*, keen to get home to their central heating. He hasn't shared a day like this for a very, very long time.

'I've been a complete and utter knob,' he says.

Abi chuckles bitterly. 'Doesn't disqualify you from high office. There's quite a few knobs running countries right now, and they're not living on the streets. You had a career, a family. What went wrong?'

He likes her. She's impatient, maybe a bit arrogant, but she's honest. She doesn't mince her words. He can imagine her cross-examining some stammering witness in court. She's probably not much older than his Belinda, but he suspects the two wouldn't get along at all.

What went wrong? If he traces the river of his self-destruction back through the years, where will he find its source?

'I was a teacher for twenty-five years,' he begins. 'Married almost as long. Two children, Belinda and Jesse. It wasn't till near the end that the stress got on top of me. I'm not making excuses.' He considers this statement. 'Yes, I am. Making excuses, yet again. Stress began the downward slide. Day after day, year after year. Parents, management. Paper trails, Ofsted inspections. I taught in a challenging school in Bristol. "Challenging" is doublespeak. What it means is bedlam. Kids bringing knives and drugs in.'

Abi has turned sideways in the booth, so that she's facing him. 'Knives. Too many of those around nowadays.'

'They said they were for self-protection, when I rumbled their cache. *I need it to protect myself, Mr Cunningham.* We had a lot of hungry kids so I tried to set up a breakfast club.' Neil scratches his chin under his beard, reliving the disappointment. 'I tried pretty hard but it never got off the ground. No funding, no interest from management. My dad died; he was a good friend and suddenly he was gone. Every day it seemed harder to get out of bed in the morning. I couldn't achieve anything. I felt I was failing. I *was* failing.'

Mutesi shakes her head. 'Teachers shouldn't feel like that.'

'I don't think mine ever did,' says Abi. 'Half of them flew on broomsticks, the other half had 'em shoved up their arses. Sorry, Neil.' She turns back to him with a wide smile. 'I'm sure you're the exception that proves the rule.'

'I've got a feeling you went to a different kind of school.'

'Possibly.'

He unfolds the sugar packet, smoothing it flat with the pads of his fingers. He's getting to the part of the story that makes him want to cry.

'One day I was off sick. I called it flu but really I just couldn't face leaving the house. I was on my laptop, looking for a new job. We had a massive mortgage. Anyway . . . this advert popped up on my screen. An ad for online gambling, you know? They're always there. Bright colours. Flashing. A disco on my screen. I didn't even know how to play the stupid game but I thought, *Why not? Might be fun*. So I put on a fiver and I won. Hooray! That win gave me a bit of a high. I put the whole lot back on, won again—*Blimey, I can do this, I'm good at it, I can win*—ridiculous 'cos there was absolutely no skill involved. I was like a kid in a sweetshop. For once in my life I was a winner! By the time Heather came home I'd made us thirty quid. I didn't tell her because in my heart I was ashamed. But I was in a better mood; I'd had a few hours off from the stress. A little holiday.'

'Maybe they let you win at first?' Brigitte suggests. 'To get you hooked.'

'They do exactly that. And it works. It switched on a circuit in my mind that I hadn't known existed—the gambler part of me. I imagine it as flashing disco lights in my brain.'

Neil discards his sugar wrapper. Now he's telling the story, he feels a compulsive need to confess. He wants these strangers to know what he is. Even the lad is listening. The killer. He's just a boy really. Hair that hasn't seen a comb for a while, stubble, the weary droop of a sixth-former who's had a heavy weekend on the tiles and chemistry first thing Monday morning. True fact: as you get older, doctors, coppers and murderous hostage takers just seem younger and younger.

'I had another flutter the same night,' he says. 'And the next. It was a nice distraction. I was putting back too much whisky in the evenings but I didn't smoke, didn't do anything really except work. I didn't think of it as getting addicted, I told myself it was just a game, but I was gambling every evening after Heather had gone to bed. Other husbands watch porn every chance they get. Not me. Never watched a single minute of porn.'

'Charlie claims he hasn't either,' says Abi. 'Might be more fun if he did.'

'Whoa!' protests Neil, holding up a hand. '*Way* too much information. Young women have changed since my day. Anyway, I might have been better watching porn because, before I knew it, I was possessed. I gambled in every way known to man. Casinos, bookies, slot machines. I kept expecting the Big Win, that marvellous, wonderful day when Heather and I could give up our jobs, pay off our mortgage and give the kids better schools and holidays and . . . Jesus, I was a knob.'

He's feeling it now: the sickening ache in his stomach. The shame. The lies. The lies.

'When our mortgage payment wasn't going to go through, I borrowed from my mother to fill the gap. I told her a pack of lies. I got more credit cards behind Heather's back. Before I knew it I'd maxed out three cards, couldn't afford the interest. Christmas was coming, we had to buy presents and food and the bank was doing its nut. I went to all kinds of lengths to catch the post before Heather saw the threatening letters. I ended up getting a stomach ulcer.'

Arthur winces. 'Nasty. I've had one of those.'

'Well—you'd know then, Arthur. I was more or less catatonic by this time. I wasn't sleeping, kept flying off the handle. Got myself a written warning for swearing at a pupil.'

'Heather must have noticed something was wrong?'

'Oh God, oh God.' He presses his palm to his eyes. 'She asked and asked. I denied there was a problem. Denied it to myself. I thought: *I'm a scientist, I can beat those bloody algorithms.* I sat down and worked out a system to win everything back. The week before Christmas I borrowed from a loan shark and put all the money on one horse. I had a good feeling about that horse. I still hoped I could save us.'

'Oh dear,' murmurs Abi. 'I think we can all see where this is going.'

'You've guessed it. Lost the lot.'

'Heather found out in the end?'

'Heather's no slouch. She suspected I was having an affair so she searched my drawers, found the credit card bills and letters from the bank and the loan shark and the receipt from the pawnbroker who had my wedding ring and my collection of vinyls and even Jesse's silver cups that he got for skating. She went through my internet browser history and that told her all she needed to know.'

He remembers the day with horrible clarity. Parking in the drive, walking into an eerily quiet house, the Christmas tree drooping in the corner with its lights turned off. Tinsel. Presents in a pile; presents that they couldn't afford. Heather, sitting on the sofa in the dark. He confessed before she accused—blurted out the whole story. He felt relieved.

'She left me for a month,' he says. 'Took the children and went to her parents. They were all a lot more forgiving than I deserved. In the February she gave me a second chance. Her parents bailed us out financially. I signed up to Gambler's Anonymous and started seeing an addiction counsellor. I promised, promised, promised. I stayed off the websites and out of the casinos and bookies—swore I'd never touch them again. We had a chance of getting back on our feet thanks to Heather taking a second job as a fees clerk. We staggered through to summer when her parents paid for us to have a week in Wales. That was nice. Until one day . . . one day . . .' He stops, trying to swallow the aching tightness in his throat. 'I let my guard down. Someone gave me a hot tip for a steeplechase. I was such a stupid . . . I listened to this little voice in my head whispering, *Go on! You're not a gambler anymore. This is just a bit of fun.* I put on a tenner.'

'And won?' asks Brigitte.

'Bloody won.' Tears are dripping from Neil's nose. Abi passes him a serviette and he presses his face into it.

'Possessed again, worse than ever. Lying, stealing. Heather was keeping really tight control of the finances now but I found ways . . . I fiddled my expenses for a school Duke of Edinburgh trip. I meant to pay it back. I was lucky not to be prosecuted, but I had to agree to resign immediately. The deputy head personally escorted me to collect my things and marched me off the premises. Heather gave me a week to leave the house but I left the next day. I ruined her. We went bankrupt. *Bankrupt.* It's not a concept people really understand unless it's happened to them. The shame. Heather couldn't hold up her head, we owed so many people money. Belinda and Jesse got bullied at school. I ended up on the streets. Served me right.'

'Why the streets?' asks Paige. 'You must have family or friends.'

'It took a while. My mum was in a nursing home. She's died since. My sisters weren't speaking to me after they found out I'd spent all her savings. Most of our friends were avoiding me. To be fair, I'd borrowed from most of 'em. I didn't have a car, a job or an address. I had literally no money—I left my last pound coin on the kitchen table as I walked out. All I had was what I could carry. In the end I left Bristol, hitched to London where a guy I knew from my student days let me sleep on the sofa. I looked for jobs . . . no joy, except I weeded people's gardens for the odd hour or two. I overstayed my welcome. The people I was dossing with said they were sorry, but they had visitors coming. I said, *Righto, cheerio, I've got somewhere else lined up*. I didn't. I'd run out of mates.'

'What did you do?'

'Phoned home. Used up all my credit.'

That was the last time he'd heard Heather's voice. He had told her he'd landed an interview for a job in pharmaceuticals, that it was a dead cert, and he'd gone back to Gambler's Anonymous.

'Give me one more chance,' he'd begged. 'Please.'

'Oh, Neil.' A ragged sigh. 'Don't. Just don't.'

The love had flatlined; the love that had bounced them so carelessly and hopefully into marriage and kids. It was dead. She'd finally had enough and nobody on this earth would blame her. She had wrung out every drop of faith, accepted his excuses and apologies and lies, given him chance after chance.

'There's been too much damage,' she'd told him. 'I have to think about the children now.'

'I promise—I've hit rock bottom.'

She'd said that she'd heard it all before and she couldn't believe a single word that came out of his lying mouth. She was right, of course. The new job was pure fiction, he hadn't been anywhere near Gambler's Anonymous, and he was a very long way from rock bottom, though he didn't know it yet.

'That was the first night I spent on the street. I've never been so scared in my life.' Neil glances at the gun in Sam's hand. 'Until today. London's like another city at night. I didn't sleep a wink; I was much too cold and scared. By the next morning I had an idea of what it means to be hungry. It took me another day to be desperate enough to start begging. You never feel the same about yourself once you've had to beg to survive, once you've been through rubbish bins. You feel subhuman. You stop mattering to anyone. I was sitting under a bridge and the rain was dripping through. I had a plastic cup in front of me. I *was* the beggar you walk past. "Spare change? Spare change?"'

He's never forgotten it: a figure in a mackintosh, barely breaking step with the marching tide of commuters. A male voice, brisk and businesslike—*there you go*—and then the saviour was gone, but there was money in the cup.

'One pound seventy,' he says. 'One pound seventy. I was so grateful, and so tired—*so* tired—I started blubbing.'

'What's happened to your family?'

'I didn't stay in touch. Don't want them to see me in rags. I hear Heather's got someone else now and I really, really hope she's happy. Belinda moved in with her childhood sweetheart. I've got a grandson somewhere, never met him . . . Jesse went into the navy. He gave me a black eye last time I saw him. Fair enough.' He hesitates. 'I've got a confession to make to you, Mutesi. You gave me four quid this morning. Thanks. I was planning to lay it on a dead cert at Haydock.'

Mutesi smiles, wagging a forefinger. 'You need to cut that out.'

He stops, exhausted by the sound of his own voice. He hasn't talked this much in years. There are plenty of things he hasn't told them. The indignities; the nagging internal voice telling him he'd be better off dead. The violence. People piss on you when you're asleep. They empty their McDonald's over your head, or give you a swift kick as a reminder of what a loser you are. It never ceases to amaze him just how viscerally some people hate rough sleepers. He knows a girl—nineteen, Irish, clever—who was outside the National Portrait Gallery when her sleeping bag was set alight with her in it. Sometimes the danger comes from your own: a month ago a young guy, off his head on artificial cannabis, mistook Neil for an anaconda and tried to throttle him. Might have been curtains for Neil if Buddy hadn't come to the rescue.

While he's been telling his story, the little girl—Lily, is that her name? Yes, Lily—has been chattering and babbling to her soft toy, bouncing it up and down old Arthur's arm. She's a real sweetie, only just learning to talk. She has a turned-up nose.

'Arta,' she says. 'Roo's jumping on you. Look, Arta!'

When Mutesi glances around at the child, her indulgent smile fades.

'Arthur? Are you feeling all right?'

There is urgency in the nurse's voice. Following her gaze, Neil sees the reason for it. Arthur is sitting bolt upright, gripping the edge of the table with both hands, staring rigidly at the opposite wall as though his life depends on not closing his eyes.

'Not great,' he wheezes. A sheen of sweat glistens on his face.

'Any pain?'

'Here.' His fingers flick across his chest. 'Hoping I don't keel over, make a real fool of myself.'

'He's got a heart condition,' says Paige. She's loosening his tie and undoing his top button. 'That's why we were going to the clinic at the hospital today. He has some pills but they won't be on him—have you got your pills with you, Arthur? Arthur? Can you hear me?'

Lily joins in. 'Arta? Arta?'

Arthur has begun gasping for breath. Mutesi leans across the table, running her fingers around his thin wrist. Whatever his pulse is doing, she doesn't seem happy about it.

'Not good?' asks Neil.

She meets his eye with a rapid shake of her head. 'If someone presented like this at my work, I'd be calling an ambulance and telling them to hurry up.'

'What can I do?'

'We have to get him out.' She straightens, her chin jutting. 'Sam? Sam! I need you to listen to me. This man may be having a heart attack.'

The lad is watching nervously, shifting his weight from one foot to the other.

'Come and see for yourself,' urges Mutesi. 'Stress and exhaustion: these are triggers. Arthur has suffered both today.'

'You're just trying to trick me into opening the door.'

With a cry of exasperation, Abi slides out of the booth. The next moment she's facing Sam down, her eyes snapping with anger. There's not a hint of fear in her. Neil admires her for that.

'Seriously? *Seriously?* Fuck, Sam, get over yourself! Have you looked at him? D'you want another dead man on your conscience?'

'I'm all right,' gulps Arthur, but he isn't. A grey pallor is spreading across his face, tinges of blue around the lips.

Sam moves closer, his brow furrowed. 'He says he's all right.'

'He's almost ninety, you moron,' snarls Abi. 'He's been through wartime! His generation doesn't complain even when they're at death's door. Let him go right now, for Christ's sake—let the kids go too. I'll help you get them out, I'll put all the tables back after they've gone. I promise I'll help you. Just get him out of here and off to hospital—or you will have been a double murderer today.'

Sam's next step brings him up short. He's clearly horrified at the sight of Arthur's face.

'Fuck,' he mutters. 'Fuck, this is . . . he's . . . why can't they just let me see Nicola and Julia?'

'I don't know,' says Mutesi. 'I'm angry with them too. I wish they'd give you what you want.'

'It's on them if he dies. It's on them.'

Mutesi's hands are on her hips. Light from the window glints on her glasses. 'You don't believe that.'

Sam looks towards the barricaded door—at Abi, who is already beginning to drag a table to one side—and swings back to peer at Arthur. He's rubbing his nose, his chin, muttering to himself.

'What are you going to do?' asks Mutesi.

TWENTY-ONE

Eliza

She's been holed up in this oppressive little box all her life. It's her universe.

The negotiators are forcing down plastic sandwiches from a local bakery. Ashwin's looking slightly less stressed than he was earlier, perhaps because he's made some progress.

'I can add to our profile of Ballard,' he says, dunking a biscuit in his mug. 'I've just talked to someone who used to be a neighbour, a retired farmer called Appleton. I didn't give him any information about what's happened. He's known the Ballard family forever. Knew Sam's father, took over the farm after he died. He reckons Sam Ballard is . . .' He turns a page in his notebook. '*A fine lad, conscientious, first-rate farmer.* Says Sam dotes on his little daughter, takes her absolutely everywhere with him—or did, until she was hauled off to live elsewhere. Appleton didn't have much to do with Robert Lacey. He doesn't like Nicola Rosedale one little bit. He thinks she's a gold-digger. *Out for whatever she could get. Everything had to go her way.*'

'Sounds like a loyal friend of the Ballard family,' says Paul.

'Yes—and maybe he's got rose-tinted specs on when it comes

to Sam. He was the referee for his gun licence years ago. He swore to me he'll eat his hat if Sam Ballard has ever—*ever*—discharged a shotgun unsafely.'

Eliza pulls the ring on a can of diet Coke. 'Oops. Time to look up hat recipes.'

'I also tracked down Sam's only aunt, Monique Bond.'

'Father's sister?'

'Mother's. She's an accountant, lives in Manchester. Big fan of Lacey's, reckons he's a saint walking this earth. She's not so fond of Sam. According to her he was nightmare as a child—*spoiled . . . deluded . . . unhinged . . . evil on legs*—ruined the Laceys' wedding by deliberately messing up a poem he was meant to read and moping about like a wet Wednesday. He had it in his head that Lacey killed his father. Her theory is that he's got some kind of Oedipus complex. She hinted darkly about incestuous obsession.'

'Heart-warming stuff,' says Eliza. 'Good old Aunty Monique.'

'She says he has ADHD, diagnosed thanks to Lacey. If true, that might account for some poor impulse control? She told me this weird story about a puppy.' Ashwin pauses to take a bite of sandwich. 'D'you think this is meant to be food? I've eaten cardboard boxes with more flavour.'

Paul has got to his feet and is updating the whiteboard.

''Fraid the best café in this neighbourhood is closed today,' he says, without turning around. 'Unforeseen circumstances. What's the puppy story?'

'So . . . Lacey bought the kid a very cute, very expensive puppy as a peace offering. Sam took one look and threw a world-beating tantrum. Screamed, trashed the house, almost killed the poor animal. Lacey had to give it back to the breeder. He was very shaken and phoned Monique Bond to cry on her shoulder. She assured him she wouldn't blame him if he left her sister.'

'Nice,' says Eliza. She's taken a strong dislike to Aunt Monique. 'Nothing like a bit of disloyalty to hold a family together.'

'She also says . . . erm . . .' Ashwin's scanning his notebook. 'Lacey put up with what she calls Harriet's "neuroses"—a whole host of insecurities and an eating disorder which began after their marriage and continued right up until Harriet's death last week.'

'Did she have a single good thing to say about her only sister?'

'I don't think they were very close. Monique didn't make the journey down to the funeral. She had a long-awaited knee reconstruction booked and decided not to cancel it. Without any prompting she asked me whether Sam has killed Robert.'

Eliza narrowly avoids spitting out a mouthful of Coke. '*What?*'

'I didn't tell her what's happened today, but she came out with . . . hang on, I made a verbatim note, 'cos this was startling. *Has Sam attacked Robert? He's wanted to kill that man since he was eight years old.*'

Paul has turned away from the whiteboard. He's frowning, his burly arms crossed.

'So the aunt—Monique Bond—really believes this was Sam's childhood ambition? To murder his stepfather?'

'That's what she said. If she's right, Lacey's death is starting to look planned. Ballard brought a shotgun all the way from Sussex. This was an execution, not a catastrophic breakdown. Nicola could well be next on the list.'

The sandwiches really aren't worth the effort. Eliza abandons hers and stands up.

'Where exactly is Nicola hiding? Do we know?'

'We do. I've taken over text contact with her.' Ashwin pulls out the floor plan and the three of them lean over it. 'She's under this sink, here. It's a back kitchen, used mainly for storage and as a staff cloakroom. She's terrified—not surprising, given there's an armed man wandering around looking for her. It's cold and cramped in her cupboard and she keeps sneezing. There's only a swinging fire door between her and the café. One loud sneeze and the whole thing blows up in our faces.'

'And where's Julia right now?'

'Day care. Arrangements are being made for her after that. There's a court battle ongoing.'

'I suppose there's no way to smuggle Nicola out through the back?'

'Nope. I double-checked with the barista. Hang on . . .' A text has arrived on Ashwin's mobile. 'The boss wants our input on the next press statement. Any thoughts on that? How d'you want to play it?'

The three spend several minutes discussing their approach. The media may very well be broadcasting straight into the café, so the press statement is a useful tool—perhaps a way of getting a message to Sam as well as to the hostages.

'Talk about how there are children trapped in there,' suggests Eliza. 'How young they are, how their families are terrified. I think Sam's feeling guilty about them. After all he's a father himself, he's been kept from his own daughter. There must be relatives of hostages downstairs?'

'A guy just phoned to say he thinks his wife and two-year-old daughter were going to Tuckbox this morning with an elderly friend. Paige Johnson, seven months pregnant, and Lily. The descriptions fit. He's a tube driver, got the news at work when they were told not to stop at Balham. He's on his way here now.'

'Could you get a quote from him for the press release? Sam's daughter Julia is a very similar age to Lily. There has to be some leverage there.'

Once Ashwin has headed downstairs, Eliza stands at the window for perhaps the hundredth time today. There it all is: the café, the colour-spangled Christmas tree, the three anxious dogs and—just visible—an SCO19 team, armed to the teeth, who must be running out of enthusiasm by now.

'Why?' she asks Paul. 'Sam Ballard's never been in trouble before. His neighbour clearly respects him. Why would he suddenly run off the rails so spectacularly?'

'He's just lost his mother. A grieving mind is wounded, it

can malfunction—sometimes a grieving mind will play tricks on people.'

'Yeah, but murder and hostage-taking?' She's rolling her shoulders, trying to release an ache in her neck—until her gaze sharpens.

'Hey, Paul, take a look,' she murmurs urgently, reaching for her binoculars. 'I think something's happening. Could be an escape attempt.'

She hears his chair tip over backwards, hitting the carpeted floor. Seconds later he's joined her at the window. They both lean close to the glass.

The street door of Tuckbox has opened. It swings outwards just a foot or two, enough for a person to slide through. All three dogs are alert and facing that way. The smallest one begins to bark.

Other pairs of eyes are watching. Eliza trains her binoculars on one of the firearms officers, who is observing developments from around the edge of his hiding place. He motions to others behind him, and they immediately fall into position.

Yes. A diminutive figure is emerging through the narrow opening of the door. A woman. She moves onto the street, holding both hands high up in the air. She's wearing a puffer jacket, a beret on her head. She stands for perhaps ten seconds with her arms up, turning from one side to another. It looks as though she's shouting something.

Others follow her out: a second woman, very pregnant, with a small child balanced on her hip. The woman's arm is wrapped around a stooped man in a pale coat. He's leaning on both her and on a walking stick, wisps of white hair blowing in the wind. Judging by the woman's posture, Eliza suspects she's carrying much of his weight.

And now there's a boy with an old-fashioned satchel. He emerges last but hurries to hold on to the first woman's puffer jacket with both his hands. He's wearing an anorak with fur around the hood. As Eliza watches, he throws some objects towards the dogs—*one, two, three.* They immediately stop barking and begin to eat. The door of Tuckbox closes again.

'Has that child just fed the dogs?' Eliza asks, handing Paul the binoculars.

He takes a look. 'Mm. Pies, I'd say.'

'I don't believe it.'

The nearest firearms officer is beckoning to the hostages from around his sheltering doorway, but it seems that the elderly man is unable to walk, even with the support of the two women. Progress is desperately slow until a couple of officers sprint out to meet them.

Eliza is still transfixed by the scene when the negotiators' phone rings.

'Incoming,' she gasps, hurling herself across the desk.

Her caller is using the café phone. It's not Sam, though. This is a female voice, low-pitched and unhurried. She has a marked accent but there's no difficulty in understanding her.

'Hello? Hello? Yes . . . This is Mutesi Nkunda. You need to send an ambulance right away. As close as you can get it, please.'

'Okay. Have you—'

'Please, just listen. I can't answer any questions. The man who has just left is in need of urgent medical attention. Tell them he's eighty-seven years old with a history of heart disease. He has pain in his chest and breathing difficulties. His pulse is extremely fast and weak, he cannot walk unaided. His name is Arthur Beaumont.'

'Right,' says Eliza. 'We've got an ambulance on standby. It should be with him within a minute.'

'Thank you. That's all I can say.'

Eliza speaks fast, words tumbling out of her. This is too good an opportunity to waste.

'Mutesi—wait—are you still there? Please thank Sam from me. That's important. Thank Sam from me.'

Mutesi seems almost to be singing. 'Yes—yes! I will tell him.'

And she's gone.

The siege is entering its seventh hour. The remaining hostages must be exhausted as well as terrified. Yet Eliza is left with the strange conviction that the woman she's just spoken to was smiling.

Mutesi

'Yes—yes! I will tell him,' she agrees cheerfully, just before Sam takes the phone out of her hand.

'You look happy,' he says.

'I *am* happy. You have done a very good thing. She asked me to thank you.'

Sam wasted no time, once he'd made up his mind to release the five. He was like a different man. He and Abigail rapidly moved the tables before ushering Brigitte out, followed by the others. Brigitte insisted on going first, in case there was any accidental gunfire.

'Pronto,' Sam kept urging, 'pronto, pronto, before the snipers work out this door is open.'

It was he who had the wonderful idea of feeding the abandoned dogs. He ran to the cabinet, grabbed three pies and gave them to Emmanuel.

'Chuck these to the dogs,' he suggested, putting them into the little boy's hands. 'They might be hungry.'

Emmanuel hung back. 'What about you, Grandma?'

'I will stay a bit longer,' said Mutesi, giving him a gentle push towards freedom. 'But I'll follow you soon.'

And now the ambulance is coming for Arthur, and Abigail is helping Sam to drag the tables back into place in front of the door—just as she promised she would. Neil's in the storeroom, looking for a defibrillator. Of course there won't be one, and anyway Arthur has gone now, but Neil still hasn't come back. Maybe he's found a secret door and has run away! *Ha! Good for him!* Mutesi wants to dance—she could take this curly-headed young murderer by the hand and make him jive with her. She could kiss him on his beaten-up forehead—why? Because Emmanuel is safe, Emmanuel is safe! What does it matter if she is a hostage? What does anything matter?

'They had an ambulance ready,' she says. 'If you go to the window I am sure you'll see it.'

Sam looks at her with amazement, as though she's got two heads. 'You think I'm going to press my nose against that window? Some bloody crack shot will blow it right off.'

Mutesi laughs aloud. 'I expect they're equally afraid of the crack shot in here.'

'I'll look out of the window, Sam,' says Abigail, pulling down one of the slats in the blind. 'You can stand behind me if you want, so you'll be safe. Hey, Mutesi's right. There's the ambulance—they've parked out of range behind that porch, but you can just see the back corner, and the lights flashing.'

Sam takes cover close behind her. The pair of them are craning their necks in their efforts to watch.

'I think they've shut the back doors,' says Abi. 'Yes—hear the siren? They're off.'

'Will that old bloke be all right?' asks Sam.

Mutesi is dancing as she moves into the kitchen.

'Yes, I think he will,' she assures him. 'With medical help, and with the grace of God.'

'Hope so.'

'Tea?' suggests Mutesi, rubbing her hands together. 'Come on, Sam, drink tea with us. What else is there to do?'

'You're crazy.'

'Probably.'

He looks suspicious. 'How do I know you're not going to slip me a mickey finn?'

'Slip what?' It takes her a moment. English is her third language and sometimes the idiom still baffles her, though she's lived in London for well over twenty years. Then she remembers.

'Oh! A mickey finn. I know. You mean a sleeping pill or something?'

'You work in a nursing home. I bet you're always dropping tranquillisers in the old folks' tea.'

'Well, no. I do not like to drug my friends. Not with tranquillisers in their tea at least. Maybe Risperidone in their yoghurt. Sam, I don't carry medicines home. I would be sacked if I did. Look—' laughing, she holds her arms out to each side '—you see? No pockets at all! You're welcome to search my bag and my jacket and even look down my socks.'

In order to reach the shelf of white teapots, she has to lean across Robert's body. It doesn't bother her. She's seen plenty of those in her time. Plenty of blood, too. Plenty of murder.

And anyway, Emmanuel is safe.

TWENTY-TWO

Sam

As soon as he looked into the old guy's face, he knew he was in serious trouble. He recognised the Blu-Tack.

If someone had been awake when his father's heart faltered and stalled, especially someone experienced like Mutesi, maybe he would have lived. But life and death are totally arbitrary. Every day is a roll of a dice. Sam learned that when he was almost as small as Emmanuel. One moment Dad was fixing the mower, happily planning all the fun they'd have in the school holidays. *Night, son.* By three o'clock the next morning, for no reason at all except some misfire of the electrics in his heart, he was dead. Two weeks later he wasn't just dead, he was non-existent. He'd been burned to nothing but ashes in a furnace. They'd put him in a green plastic tub with a screw-top lid. Mum, Granny and Sam were setting him free.

Mum waited for a windy day because she wanted Dad to be able to fly. Bouncer and Snoops came too. Those poor dogs had worshipped Dad and they were lost without him. They seemed to understand that the three humans were doing something very solemn. Even Sundance joined in the procession, walking along with his nose butting on Granny's shoulder. Mum chose a place by the spinney in Sundance's field, because Dad had loved this spot so much. For a while they all stood and waited for a good strong gust of wind. When it came, Mum held up the green tub and turned it upside down.

Sam wasn't sure what he was expecting, but he was surprised when a stream of very fine dust came pouring out of the mouth of the tub and billowed around in a cloud. He tried to catch some of it in his hand, but Granny shook her head.

'Don't, Sam,' she said. 'Don't keep him. Let him go.'

So he stood and watched as the wind caught the ashes. They flew and tumbled, swooping across the field like a swarm of bees before merging into the summer blue. He imagined it was Dad's spirit. He wanted to fly with him.

'Bye, Angus,' said Granny.

'Bye, Dad,' said Sam.

Mum didn't say goodbye. She stood with the plastic tub in her hand and sobbed—quietly at first, then louder and louder until her sobs sounded like yells of pain. Sam put both his arms around her waist and his cheek against her tummy and hugged her as hard as he could, trying to comfort her, but she didn't seem able to stop. She got down on her knees and washed the green tub in Sundance's trough, to make sure Dad was all gone. She was still sobbing while she did that.

'Come on,' murmured Granny, putting her arm around Mum and taking Sam's hand. 'Home. Tea.'

•

For a while, they kept the plastic tub on a shelf in the larder.

'I can hardly put Angus's urn in the recycling, can I?' asked Mum. 'I'm not sure what to do.'

Robert offered to take care of it, and she was so grateful. *Oh, Robert, would you?* He smiled, carried it away and shut it in the boot of his car. Sam was ready to bet he dumped it in the nearest rubbish bin on his way home.

Not long after they scattered the ashes, Mum said she was ashamed of making such a scene in Sundance's field. *It wasn't fair on you, Sam.* She announced that it wouldn't happen again, and she succeeded in her mission. Sometimes Sam heard her crying in her bedroom at night, but by the next morning she'd be cheerful again.

So his father was alive and well one day, and two weeks later he was a cloud of dust. Sam tried to keep him alive. He stared at shadows and imagined they were Dad's. One night he looked out of his bedroom window and almost—*almost*—saw Dad in the orchard, stooping to pick up apples to give to Sundance. He was wearing his floppy canvas sunhat—Mum said the hat was ridiculous, but she liked it really—and his baggy overalls with their smell of straw and engine oil and soap and sometimes cowpats.

And there were the dreams, so real that Sam woke up thinking everything was all right, Dad was sleeping next door. Then the sadness came crashing in again. That was like him dying every day.

In one dream, Dad and Sam were visiting Sundance Kid up by the spinney. They'd brought apples from the orchard. Bouncer and Snoops came too, lolloping through the dry summer meadow with their tongues hanging out.

'How's Mum?' Dad asked.

'She only cries at night.'

'Doesn't she remember me during the day?'

'Yes, but she's being strong for me.'

'Give her my love.'

Sam leaned his chin against a warm fence post, closed his eyes and let the sun shine on his face. He loved Sundance's horsey smell and the chomping sound as he munched apples with his big teeth. He was happy to be here, with Dad. It didn't matter about him being dead.

'Robert turned me into dust,' said Dad.

'The doctors think it was the cardi thingy.'

'It was Robert.'

'How did he do that?'

'It was Robert.'

When Sam opened his eyes, Sundance was still munching and drooling juice. But Dad had gone. A cloud of grey dust was swirling away, like a swarm of bees.

TWENTY-THREE

Rosie

Someone called Ashwin is texting her. He says he's a negotiator. *Hi Nicola. I'm Ashwin, I'm here to stay in contact with you and make sure you're okay.* She takes comfort from imagining this person. She knows nothing except their name, but pictures a fatherly, solid guy in uniform, unflappable and caring.

But he isn't in Tuckbox. He's safe in some office, far out of the range of Sam's shotgun. He can't really help her at all.

Ash get me out of here pls for gods sake

We're doing all we can Nicola. Are you still safe?

NO!!! He cld find me any second he will kill me

Our advice is to stay where you are.

Can't you gas him or shoot him?

Please stay hidden. We're watching your situation, you are surrounded by police. Try to stay calm.

She's shivering now, suppressing sneeze after sneeze. Hay fever, colds, they all set her off. It's hard to sneeze quietly.

How did this happen to her? How did she come to be hiding

in a tiny little cupboard under a sink, scared half to death? Her dad was right; she shouldn't have got mixed up with any of these people.

She'd only just come into work when it happened. She was at least ten minutes late—again. Well, Robert could deal with it. There had to be some privileges when you were shagging the boss. Julia's nursery only opened at seven; it's impossible to get her ready and dropped off and then run around here before seven-fifteen. She'd hurried in without glancing at the clock, heading past Robert who was cleaning cabinets. He looked up, raised one eyebrow and smiled. They had to be very discreet. There was plenty of loyalty to Harriet among the Tuckbox staff. People wouldn't understand.

She hung up her denim jacket in the back kitchen and immediately got to work, running a toasted sandwich out to a customer. When Sam first came pelting into Tuckbox, she ducked behind a table before nipping into the customer toilet, hoping he hadn't spotted her. Best to stay well out of it. She hadn't seen him in months. She felt guilty about him—worried about him—but now was definitely not the time. Not when he was angry and shouting, not when she was at work, and certainly not when Robert was in the room.

Once the coast seemed to be clear she made a beeline for the main kitchen, hoping to have a word with Robert and find out what had just gone on between him and Sam. But Robert was too busy flirting with some female customers to speak to her, and the next moment Sam was charging back. She spotted him through the window, carrying that bloody gun of his. Lucky she happened to glance out there, and lucky he was so fixated on Robert. It all gave her a few extra seconds—just enough time to escape.

When her phone dies she'll be alone again. No more Ashwin, no more Dad. The battery's already dropped to twenty per cent. She turns off the wi-fi and location and dims the screen, desperately trying to conserve the power. Another sneeze is gaining traction somewhere at the back of her throat. It begins as a tickle, steadily building. She buries her face in the crook of her arm, trying to muffle the sound—three wrenching, half-suppressed explosions, one after the other.

So loud! Too loud.

Someone's coming into the back kitchen. She recognises the squealing protest of the fire door, the heavy metallic clunk as it settles back on its hinges. Terror surges through her brain, numbing her body. Her pulse is pounding.

He heard me. He's looking for me. I'm dead.

She holds her breath.

Footsteps on the concrete floor, heading straight for the sink.

She stares into the blackness.

Neil

Ah, that lass in the cupboard. Ever since he spotted her through the bathroom window, Neil's been hoping for some way to make contact. His chance came while Sam was busy shifting the street-door barricade. Muttering about looking for a defibrillator for Arthur—a weak excuse, but people were too distracted to notice—Neil stepped past Robert and slipped into the back kitchen.

He leans down to the cupboard door.

'It's okay,' he whispers. 'I'm on your side.'

She's an oval of white in the gloom, with shadowed hollows where her eyes should be. Pale fingers are curled around a phone. She seems winded; he can hear her struggling to inhale.

'Oh my God, oh my God . . .' She manages a gasping breath. 'I thought you were him.'

'Sorry.'

'I thought I was dead.'

'Sorry, sorry.'

He lowers himself onto one knee, and then sits on the floor beside her.

'Robert?' she asks. 'Was he shot? Is he dead?'

Neil has already decided to lie. She's stuck in this room by herself; she doesn't need to know that her boss's corpse is just through the door.

'I think he'll be okay,' he says.

She's crying quietly. Her eyes are closed, she's covering her mouth with her wrist.

'It's me Sam's after. I'm his ex.'

'Nicola?'

'Please go away, before he comes looking for you.'

Neil thinks for a second. 'He's a lot calmer now. It might be okay for you to come out.'

He intended to reassure her, but his words have the opposite effect. It's like watching a clam retreat. She shrinks into the darkness, grabbing at the door to pull it after her, begging him to leave her alone. Fear can do that. Neil has often spent nights curled up under bushes and behind dustbins.

'Is there anything you need?' he asks.

'Just don't let him know I'm here. Don't let him know.'

He promises not to betray her presence to Sam, and heads back into the café. To his astonishment he's met by the sight of Abi and Sam standing close together, both of them looking out through the blinds. Sam's sheltering behind Abi, peering past her shoulder. They're similar heights, similar builds. They could be siblings.

And good old Mutesi! She's making tea again, pouring boiling water from the hissing tap into a round white pot. Of course she is; this is what she does—but Neil reckons she's streetwise, that Mutesi. There's a lot more to her than meets the eye. She's a master at the art of bringing people down from orbit. While waiting for her tea to brew she sways from side to side, singing in a mellow contralto. It's a pretty melody, obviously a church thing: *Jesus, sweet Jesus, bring me home.*

Well, fair enough. Live and let live. Neil's prepared to overlook this display of superstition. The woman's glorious optimism—if not her faith in an imaginary friend—is irresistible. He limps behind the counter to lend a hand.

'You're a box of kittens,' he says, as he fetches milk from one of the fridges.

'Kittens! I like that.' She has a dazzling smile. 'We must make the most of these calm moments, don't you think?'

She rummages in a cabinet, emerging with a slice of carrot cake with butter icing and sugar carrots. She sticks a fork into it as she carries it across to a table.

'Sit down, Sam,' she orders briskly. 'How about this chair?'

Doing the Right Thing about Arthur seems to have put Sam into a better headspace. He obeys—awkwardly, and with his shotgun in one hand—but it's an improvement on one-two-three-swing, one-two-three-swing.

'I know for a fact that you haven't eaten one single thing today,' scolds Mutesi, sliding the plate in front of him. 'Your blood sugar will be low. Having low blood sugar makes people cranky. Eat this. No, don't argue. There is no mickey finn of any kind.'

Sam scowls and says he's fine, for God's sake; but he takes a forkful of cake—and another—and stops talking. The gun is resting on the floor, barrel facing the ceiling, gripped in his left hand.

Mutesi watches him with folded arms and a fond smile, as though this young criminal were a favourite grandchild.

'Thank you for letting Arthur go,' she says.

He shrugs.

'And the others too.'

He speaks around his cake. 'The kids were scared.'

'Yes.' She makes a loud, disapproving *tock* somewhere at the back of her mouth. 'Of course they were scared—and so were their mothers! Very scared. You're a father, aren't you? How would you feel?'

He looks up at her, muttering something that might almost be *sorry*.

Abi seems to have caught Mutesi's upbeat mood.

'Hey,' she cries, heading for the front counter, where the retro radio jostles for space among jars of biscuits and coffee loyalty cards. 'How about we have a listen to the news? I bet we'll all be celebrities by now.'

Neil would hardly recognise Abi as the immaculate suit who power-walked in here this morning. She's pulled out her hair tie and is wearing it on her wrist. Dark hair is hooked messily behind each ear. Without those elegant court shoes her gait seems flat-footed, even clumsy. The white shirt might as well be a dishrag: it's come untucked from her skirt, crumpled and blood-spattered. She's rolled up the sleeves.

She switches on the radio without waiting for an answer from Sam, and immediately the café is flooded with Mariah Carey singing 'All I Want for Christmas Is You'. It's been everywhere recently. Neil's heard it floating out of shops and pubs, even from the boom boxes kids bring along when they're skateboarding under the arches.

'Eh!' cries Mutesi. She dances back to the teapot, swinging her hips, snapping her fingers.

Abi blocks her ears with a silent scream. 'You have *got* to be kidding me. What does a girl have to do to escape from this effing song?'

'There's no escape from some things,' says Neil.

If turning the radio on was Abi's cunning plan to make things seem more normal, it's worked. Neil feels better for being bombarded by Christmas music, by frivolous things, by human voices. Even the advertising slogans have a certain reassuring inanity. The presenter begins a phone-in competition, playing excerpts from three songs, starting with 'Nights in White Satin'—which takes Neil straight back to his wedding day, because Heather chose it for their first dance. Callers have to guess the connection between the three songs. The prize is a weekend on Dartmoor for two, courtesy of the Devonshire Tourist Board. People keep phoning with suggestions.

You can hear their nervousness at being live on air, making wild guesses while the presenter scoffs mercilessly.

Mutesi delivers tea all round. She takes a sip from her own mug before stretching herself along the vinyl seat of the booth, complaining that she was on a night shift and has heavy eyes.

'Bizarre, isn't it?' says Abi. 'We're in here, Robert's down there on the floor in a pool of . . . but London carries on exactly the same as normal. Listen to those smug twats with their jolly phone-in and their ads for plumbers.'

'And that is only right and proper.' Mutesi stifles a yawn. 'Why should our problem spoil everyone else's day?'

The half-hourly news leads with politics. The third item is a bulletin about shots fired at a café in Balham.

'Here we go.' Abi turns up the volume. 'Our five minutes of fame.'

Hostages . . . ambulance seen leaving with lights and sirens . . . specialist firearms officers . . . no end to the stand-off in sight.

There's a brief interview with a police spokesperson, studiedly calm as he follows his script in a monotone: *Not being treated as a terrorist incident. Our priority is to ensure the safety of members of the public and all those involved. I can tell you that a few minutes ago two young children were released unharmed, along with three adults. One male has been transported to St George's Hospital as a result of a medical condition. The release of five hostages is obviously very good news, and we hope to bring this incident to a peaceful resolution as soon as possible.*

'What about casualties?' asks a journalist. 'Can you confirm reports of at least one fatality?'

No, he can't confirm that. *The incident is ongoing. We're not prepared to release any further information at this stage.*

The reporter seems extremely enthusiastic about having a siege to cover. He's done a bit of digging, it seems, and has found an anguished family member to interview.

'I've been speaking to Charles Bowman whose partner, criminal barrister Abigail Garcia, is believed to be in Tuckbox. He's been waiting here for news since early this morning. Charles, have you been told anything at all by police?'

Abi has whirled around and is glaring at the radio, her eyebrows drawn together. Charlie's speech is clipped. He speaks rapidly and almost without inflection.

'Not a lot,' he says. 'They're playing it close to their chests. I'm hearing all kinds of rumours. I'm pretty sure someone's been wounded.'

'I think you heard the first shot?'

'I did. I was talking to Abi on the phone at about seven-thirty. I heard shouting and a loud bang, and lost contact with Abi, so I contacted the police and came straight down here.'

'You must be very worried,' says the journalist, oozing faux sympathy.

'That's putting it mildly.'

'And do you feel the police are doing—'

Charlie interrupts him. 'There's something I want to say,' he declares curtly. 'This is a message to the hostage-taker. I don't know who you are and I don't care. If you're listening, I have a request. Let me swap places with Abi. She's a great deal more valuable than I am, for all kinds of reasons. The world without her would be impoverished. I'll take her place.'

'Bowman! Put a sock in it,' mutters Abi, as the news report comes to an end.

She's blushing. Neil's surprised by her vehemence.

'Why?' he asks.

'It's too public. Bloody hell, I never would have picked Charlie for a media babe.'

'Would you let him take your place?'

'Of course not.'

'Because you don't want to put him in danger?'

'Because you can't weigh the value of human lives like that.

It's endearing—I'm touched and I'm sure he means it, but . . . I owe him now, because he's offered to risk his life for me. He's done it in the hearing of about a million people. Anyway, why should he swap with me? Because I'm a woman? Does he think I'm some kind of princess in a tower?'

'That's not how it comes over to me.' Neil scratches his head. 'Sounds to me as though he loves you.'

'He probably does—and he's just proved it by offering to make the ultimate sacrifice. How can I ever repay that?'

'I get it.' Sam's nodding as he polishes off the last crumbs of cake. 'I get what you mean, Abi. Nothing comes for free.'

Blimey, thinks Neil. Some people are hard to please. Greater love hath no man than that he puts a sock in it and lets his friends take their chances.

A traffic and travel update follows the news, heralded by a merry little jingle. The incident near Balham station has been causing all kinds of headaches for beleaguered commuters. Neil listens with bemusement. Shoot a man, take a load of people hostage, and you still come after Brexit in the news; mess up the Northern Line at rush hour and you make an enemy of the entire city.

Sam happens to be sipping tea when 'Rocket Man' starts up again. Neil watches as the young man carefully puts down his white mug before pulling the silver phone from the pocket of his jeans. He could be just an ordinary lad, enjoying a cuppa in a café—at least he might, if it weren't for that shotgun.

'Hello?' he says.

Eliza

'Hello?'

There's far less energy in his voice. Less panic, less fury. Time is doing its work at last. Time, the crisis negotiator's friend. His adrenaline levels are falling; perhaps sheer exhaustion is setting in too.

The negotiation cell is no longer working in the dark. Paige Johnson's been taken to the hospital for a medical check-up, but Brigitte Uwase has described the scene in the café in meticulous detail. Thanks to her, police now know that three hostages remain: Mutesi Nkunda, Abigail Garcia and an ex-teacher from Bristol called Neil, of no fixed abode. Brigitte was astonished to learn of Nicola's presence in the back kitchen.

'Hi, Sam!' Eliza pitches her tone somewhere between enthusiasm and concern. 'How are you doing in there?'

'You got Julia yet?'

She's ready for this. The negotiators have decided on a tactic—though *tactic* seems a grand term for what amounts to stringing the man along while trying to distract him with good news.

'I know you want to talk about your family,' she says. 'But let me tell you about Arthur Beaumont. He's at St George's Hospital. He's stable now, sitting up and talking. They're saying he can go home tomorrow.'

'Hang on,' he mutters, and she hears him relay this information to the others. *Arthur's okay.*

'The doctors think he might have died if you hadn't got him out so fast,' she tells him. 'It's lucky he wasn't at home by himself, which he would've been by lunchtime today. So in a way, what's happened in Tuckbox may actually have saved his life.'

'Huh.'

'I want to thank you, Sam.'

'Yeah, yeah. Mutesi said it was stress and exhaustion that set him off. So what I actually did was almost kill him.'

'You made a good decision in the end.'

'Cut it out, will you.' He doesn't sound annoyed; she senses that he's pleased. 'I know what you're doing. It's like getting the Sunday school prize for "most improved student". All it means is you were really, really shit to start with and the teacher still hates your guts but you did quite well in the Bible knowledge test so they reckon they ought to give you something.'

Eliza finds herself smiling. After all, it's true. That's exactly what she's doing.

'Is that what happened to you?' she asks.

'Yep. Got some dinosaur stickers.'

'Nice! In my case it was swimming club when I was twelve. They gave me a certificate: *Eliza McClean, most improved swimmer*. Most improved! I thought it was downright insulting.'

'Could you even swim?'

'Took me twenty minutes to paddle the length of the pool. Everyone else was dressed by the time I got out.'

'Pathetic.'

'Oh—and could you tell Mutesi her son Isaac is on his way from Montreal?' suggests Eliza, hoping to build on this lighter moment.

'Okay. Montreal.'

'The Canadian police have been great.'

'Okay. Right.' He sounds vague, suddenly. His mind is beginning to lead him down some other, more dangerous path. She needs to bring him back.

'It'll be dark soon,' she says. 'Have you got central heating? This room I'm in is freezing.'

'Yeah, we're okay.'

'I can arrange to have blankets dropped off. Let me know what you need.'

'I dunno. I dunno . . . it's not . . . fuck, did I really kill Robert?'

'Stop,' she says firmly. 'Park that thought for now.'

'I killed someone today. How the hell do I park that?'

He's going off the air again, spiralling into agitation. She's getting used to these abrupt changes of mood. Brigitte Uwase saw them at first hand, and her observations are summarised on the white board:

Loose cannon. Mood swings—impulsive/reflective
Capable of compassion. Not a natural killer?
V nervous of attack from street/sniper

Never lets go of gun, seems experienced in handling it
Taking pills regularly—speed?

'I hated Robert Lacey,' he's saying. 'And I had bloody good reason to hate him, and he hated me, but I can't believe I killed him. He's got parents. Have you found them?'

'They haven't been informed yet.'

'How are they supposed to get over this? And a brother, I think he's in Hong Kong.'

'That's right.'

'He'll be hearing the news any time now. Some twat shot his brother.' There's a long pause. 'I'm getting a bit tired now, Eliza. I'm so fucking tired. I'm taking Ritalin to keep myself awake but Jesus, I'm . . .'

The sentence drifts into nothing. Paul is already running a Google search on the effects of misusing Ritalin.

'You'd like to sleep?' asks Eliza.

'To rest. D'you think people really rest in peace when they die?'

'I don't know. I often wonder. What do you think?'

'I just hope the hurting will stop. I think it will, because there won't be any brain activity to feel it. I'm looking forward to that.'

'Tell me about the hurting.'

'It fucking hurts.'

Eliza has begun to doodle on her notepad, drawing heavy, straight lines. Bars, bars. Anxious bars. She adds others at right angles to make a blue-ink lattice of bars. A cage. She knows what question must come next, but she always has to steel herself to utter the words.

'Sam,' she asks, 'are you thinking about killing yourself?'

It sounds as though he's dropped the phone, or maybe he's just shifting it from one hand to another. After a moment, he's back.

'Of course I am. I think about it all the time. I've been thinking about it for years. I dream about it, like other people dream of . . . I dunno, winning the lottery. Every time I get my head above water something comes and knocks me down again. In the end you just get too tired. You've had enough. You want out.'

'Are you thinking about killing yourself right now?'

'I've got a shotgun in my hand.'

'Is that your plan? To shoot yourself?'

It was Ethan, the ex-pilot, who taught the recruits to ask these questions. *Suicide's the elephant in the room. You won't tip a suicidal person over the edge by talking about it. If you think it's on the cards, for Pete's sake don't fanny about—ask them straight out. If they say yes, ask them for details. Ask them when. Ask them how. Ask them:* What's your plan? *Focus on the damned elephant. Turn a spotlight on that big grey bastard, so it has nowhere to hide.*

Then he'd strolled among the group, looking into the eyes of each trainee, insisting that each of them ask him the question out loud.

Are you thinking about killing yourself, Ethan?

Not good enough. You sound shit-scared. Let's hear it again.

Are you thinking about killing yourself, Ethan?

Better. Yes, I am.

Have you made a plan?

Yes.

Would you tell me about your plan? When? How?

They were disturbing questions to ask, even to a smiling Californian in a brightly lit room at Hendon Police College. One of the recruits—Andy—took three attempts before intoning the words with such wooden insincerity that he had the rest of the group giggling. It was only later that they learned his sister had hanged herself at the age of thirteen. He dropped out of the course.

'Sam,' Eliza says now, 'you and I will sort this out. We can find a solution if we work together.'

'We can't.'

'We can, if we—'

'Eliza, please don't give me any more bullshit. Please don't tell me it's all going to be okay. It's not going to be okay. Robert can't be resurrected. If I walk out of here I'll be in a cell tonight. I'll be spending the rest of my life behind bars.'

'Not necessarily.'

'I wish I'd never come near Tuckbox. I wish I'd got back in the Landy and driven away. But I didn't. Killing another human being is a humbling experience.'

'Humbling?' Eliza writes it on her notepad—*humbling*—and immediately begins to scrawl more straight lines around the letters. Her jotter's becoming cluttered with dark-blue bars. 'Why humbling?'

'Because it makes your own life less than worthless. It makes you wish you'd never been born. If I'd never been born, Robert would still be swanning about the place. His mother would still have both her sons.'

'We've made enquiries,' she admits. 'I know Robert was your stepfather.'

''Course you do.'

'Can you tell me why you argued with him today? Can we start with that?'

'What's the fucking point?'

'So I can understand why you *didn't* get back into your Land Rover and drive away.'

She listens to his breathing, and draws bars. The nib of her biro rips right through the paper.

'I don't know where to start,' he says.

TWENTY-FOUR

Sam

She sounds nice. She really does. She has what Granny would have called a *pleasant* voice. Scottish, he thinks. Yes, definitely Scottish.

He knows she's not really on his side. She's just doing her job. She's a professional Nice Person with her Pleasant Voice, and in the background there's an army of professional Nasty People ready to shoot him less pleasantly if they get the chance. Good cops, bad cops. But she's making a fine job of pretending to care whether he lives or dies. It's better than nothing.

There's a weird kind of peace in Tuckbox now. Mutesi is lying flat on her back in the booth with one arm behind her head. Neil has pushed an armchair over to a radiator and is looking happy as a clam, doodling on a serviette with Emmanuel's coloured pencils. Those two seem to have decided just to listen and let the negotiator do her job. Not Abi, though. She hasn't let down her guard for a moment. She's found a booklet of instructions for the espresso machine and is pretending to flick through them, but he's noticed her surreptitiously eyeing his gun. She's thinking up plans to take it off him, and she'll act fast if he makes a mistake. *Can't blame her for that. I'd do the same in her shoes.*

'I don't know where to start,' he tells Eliza.

'You could just start at the beginning.'

'A very good place to start?'

She laughs. Pleasant laugh.

It's a quote from *The Sound of Music.* Sam once gave Granny the video for Christmas, and she used to chortle about how devilishly handsome Captain von Trapp was. She reckoned under all that singing-naval-officer charm he was a man like any other and probably snored his socks off.

The beginning.

Dad was the beginning. He dredges his memory for snippets of Dad, up to and including the night his heart stopped. He tells Eliza about the blue lights and the Santa Claus devil and that monstrous Blu-Tack; how he sees his father's dead face often, especially in the middle of the night, and how the death-and-disinfectant fills his nostrils and smothers his breath, and he wakes up yelling at the top of his voice. That's something he's never told anyone—except Nicola, of course, though it turned out she was the last person he should have trusted.

Eliza is patient with his rambling on. She mutters the odd remark—*did he?* or *oh no!*—but she doesn't interrupt. Not once. That's a first. Nobody has ever let him tell the whole story without butting in.

'D'you really want to hear about this?' he asks, taking a look at the clock. He's been talking non-stop for over half an hour.

'I really do.'

'I'm kind of imagining Nicola and a load of coppers sitting around with you, taking the piss out of every word I say.'

'It doesn't work like that, Sam. This conversation is between you and me. Negotiators stay separate from everyone else. I'm in a small room set aside for negotiation, and right now the only other person in here is my colleague. His name is Paul. Believe me, Paul is the last person in the world to laugh at you.'

'Okay. Okay. I believe you, dunno why.'

'So,' she says. 'Go on.'

When he comes to the part about running out of the hospital and falling down in the car park, he hears something real in her voice. She's upset; she's not pretending. It's as though she is there in the hospital grounds, watching eight-year-old Sam wetting myself.

'Sam,' she whispers. 'Sam, Sam. That must have been the worst day of your life.'

'It was like having a bloody great trapdoor open up under my feet. I've never felt safe again. And Robert was right there—the caped crusader—ready to swoop down and turn our tragedy into his triumph.'

'You sound bitter.'

'I *am* bitter. Robert Lacey stole my mother and then he destroyed her. It was all a game to him.'

'A game.' Eliza's silent for a moment, perhaps making a note. 'Tell me what he did.'

'It's really hard to explain. He was clever. He didn't bash us with sticks or starve us or lock us in cupboards. The way he abused people, he left no marks. It was slow, it took years. That's why nobody ever listened to me.'

'Well, I am. I'm listening right now.'

There's so much to tell: all those years of Robert World. To this day, Sam can't pinpoint exactly when the man got his hooks into Mum. Looking back, he spots subtleties that passed him by when he was a child. The look on Granny's face, the tiny lines around her mouth. *Steady hands, eh?*

'I'm not suggesting Mum and he had an affair back then, when Dad was alive,' he says. 'I mean . . . she wouldn't. She adored my dad. She would never have done that.'

'It sounds as though you're doubting,' says Eliza.

'I'm not. I'm sure she was faithful to Dad. And Robert would have hated that. He always had to be the centre of attention. He had to be loved and admired and above all he *had* to win every battle. There was one thing my dad had that he didn't.'

'Your mum?'

'Got it in one.'

•

By the time the funeral was over, and all the very-very-sad-for-one-day people had stopped hugging one another and scurried back to their own lives, Robert was a fixture. He claimed to have a soft spot for Sam, and was always turning up with presents or treats.

'I knew he wasn't real, though,' he tells Eliza.

'How did you know he wasn't real?'

'You should have seen the expression on his face when Mum wasn't looking. He wished I'd do him a favour and drop dead too.'

Mum was dreading their first Christmas without Dad. Tammy came to stay at Tyndale but there weren't any gales of laughter. Robert invited everyone for lunch at his house, including Granny. He cooked a traditional Christmas dinner and Sam had to admit the food was spectacular, especially the brandy butter. He had seconds of everything and felt sick. An awful lot of wine was drunk. Robert proposed a toast—*To Angus!*—and the four adults clinked glasses. It was one of those times when people make loads of noise but you don't hear a single genuine, happy laugh all day. Granny and Tammy kept looking at one another with sly little smirks. In the car on the way home, Mum told them both off.

'He went to *so* much trouble,' she scolded. 'He wanted to help us through our first Christmas without Angus. No ulterior motive.'

'Yeah, right,' snorted Tammy. She was slurring her words a bit. 'And I'm the Madonna.'

'Why do you two have to be so cynical?'

'I talked to Connie again. She finally dumped him after she caught him shagging a waitress in the walk-in fridge. She hasn't got a good word to say about Robert Lacey. She ended up on antidepressants, anti-anxiety meds, in psychotherapy. He gaslighted her for the entire five years, made her think she was going mad.'

'He's told me all about that. Connie's a compulsive liar! You can't believe a word she says.'

'Pots and kettles,' said Tammy.

•

One freezing winter evening, Granny turned up unexpectedly. She and Sam went to make sure Sundance was all bedded down in his stable. It was already dark and the air tasted of ice, but the stable smelled of warm horse and sweet hay. It was a happy time.

'I wish Dad was here,' said Sam, as they were tugging off their wellies at the kitchen door.

She put her arm around him. 'We've still got each other, Sammy.'

She only dropped in for a cup of tea, but of course Mum asked her to stay for supper. Granny sat in one of the two little yellow armchairs while Mum pottered about. Sam lay on the rug by the Rayburn, doing boring homework and looking forward to mutton casserole. He could smell it in the oven, and his mouth was literally watering. It was tricky to write while lying on his stomach but since his teacher never gave him good marks anyway, he didn't bother to move. *Careless mistakes, Sam. Please copy this out again. Sam, spelling! Sam, this is too untidy. Sam, you must take more care with your handwriting. Sam, Sam, Sam, blah, blah, blah.* Silly cow.

The adults were talking about a decision Mum had to make. She'd been offered a full-time job as head gardener for a stately home just outside the village. It was open to the public. She'd have three people working under her.

'We could certainly do with the money, but I'm not sure it's the right time,' she told Granny, as they laid the table together.

'Gosh, what a fabulous opportunity!'

'It is.'

'The Hamley House garden is glorious,' said Granny. 'Prestigious too, always winning awards. What a feather in your cap! If it's Sam you're worried about, don't be. I'll happily collect him from school.'

'Robert thinks I should turn it down.'

Granny was rummaging in the cutlery drawer. He can still see it now, that storm-cloud plait hanging down her back, and the way she stopped clattering the knives and forks.

'Robert,' she said. Just the one word. *Robert.* She made it sound empty.

'Mm, he's dead against it. Thinks I shouldn't take on such a big challenge.'

'You could do that job standing on your head.'

'He's worried I'll get too stressed.'

'And why, pray, does Robert Lacey's view have any bearing on this decision?'

'Oh, Patricia.' Mum slammed the Rayburn door with her foot. She was holding the casserole dish in her oven-mitted hands, and the smell of it wafted around the kitchen. 'He's kind to Sam. He's kind to me. He's a genuine friend.'

Granny wasn't having a bar of it.

'He's a pervasive weed. Convolvulus. It looks quite pretty but it takes over the whole garden once it has its nasty roots down. You can't get rid of the stuff. Chokes all the other plants.'

'That's bloody rude.'

Mum didn't often swear. Sam sat up, silently cheering. *Go, Granny!*

'Someone has to tell the truth,' retorted Granny. 'Lacey's winding himself around you. He's throwing out his tendrils.'

Mum's cheeks were flushed as she dumped the casserole onto the table.

'He's simply a friend.'

'Ah yes. A friend.' Granny was chuckling. 'But what sort of a *friend* is he, I wonder?'

'One I can rely on. Are you suggesting we're . . .?'

Sam was all agog, waiting for her to finish the sentence. *What? We're what?*

'I don't know,' said Granny calmly. 'Are you? Will you?'

'How dare you!'

'That's not an answer.'

At this point Mum spotted Sam listening with his mouth open, and her expression went blank. It was as though she'd closed a door in her face.

'I'm not discussing my personal life with you, Patricia,' she said. 'And Sam doesn't need to hear your sordid insinuations. Robert is a loyal friend. End of story.'

Granny said *hmm*, chucking a pile of cutlery across the table. Usually Sam's mother and grandmother chattered over a meal—like two budgerigars, his dad used to say—but this evening they were more like two angry cats. Sam was wolfing down his third helping when Granny started up the argument again.

'You own Tyndale Farm now,' she said. 'Angus left it all to you. Not in trust for Sam. Just you.'

Mum lifted one shoulder. 'So?'

'It's been in the Ballard family for four generations, if you count Sam. Angus hoped Sam would take over from him one day.'

'I know that.'

'I'm worried.'

'Patricia, this really is none of your business. You were bought out long ago. I've got the mortgage payments to prove it.'

Granny looked really upset. She put her knife and fork down on her plate before reaching out her hand to touch Mum's sleeve.

'Please, just be careful. That's all I'm asking.'

'Careful of what?'

'Convolvulus.'

'For heaven's sake!' Mum snatched her arm away. 'You seem to think I'm a brainless bimbo who can't make decisions for myself.'

'I think the exact opposite. I admire you, Harriet. I know you're heartbroken to lose Angus, but you're not the sort to be defined by widowhood and you're more than capable of managing the Hamley House garden. I just don't understand why that smiling assassin, Robert Lacey, is deliberately trying to undermine your confidence. I think it's sinister.'

'Perhaps you'd like to be running Tyndale Farm yourself? You never wanted to leave in the first place.'

'Good Lord.' Granny laughed aloud. 'There's a new one. Is this the gospel according to Mr Toothpaste?'

Mum opened her mouth but shut it again without replying, and Sam knew why. That was exactly what Robert said about Granny. *Good old Patricia, she never really gave up this place, did she?*

He listened to every word the two women said, and understood much more than they might have liked. It used to amaze him, the way adults could have what sounded like two different conversations at once—the farm and Hamley House—and yet really it was all about another thing altogether. Robert.

•

The following evening the man himself turned up, carrying two bottles of red wine and a cloud of what Sam now knows was ridiculously expensive aftershave. He strode into the kitchen on his long legs, sat and listened and tutted while Mum complained about Patricia being so *patronising* and *controlling*. At one stage he covered her hand with his. She had gardener's hands: freckled, often a bit muddy. Short fingernails. Robert's hands were large and hairy and . . . *yeuch*. How could she stand it? By the end of the first bottle she'd decided not to take the job at Hamley House. Halfway through the second, she agreed to see less of both Granny and Tammy.

'They're motivated by love,' she said, sounding uncertain.

Robert moved a little closer to her along the sofa.

'Oh yes—of course they are! But they've each got their own agenda. Tammy struggles with jealousy. She can't get over the way your life turned out, while she's bitter and single and childless. She's pretty loud, isn't she?'

'Um . . . I'd call her bubbly.'

'*Has* to be the centre of attention. It's all about her. She sees you as the foil to her flamboyance.'

Mum was fiddling with her wedding ring. 'Maybe.'

'And Patricia just cannot—*will* not—let go.'

'You could be right.'

'Of course I'm right. I'm always right.' He stretched his arm along the back of the sofa so that his fingers touched the back of her neck. '*You* are what matters now.'

Sam was on his way to bed when Robert remembered that he had to drive home, and he'd be well over the alcohol limit. Mum said that was no problem. They made up the bed in the spare room at the top of the stairs.

'Can't he get a taxi?' asked Sam, as he watched the pair of them wrestling with a duvet cover and plumping up pillows. They were giggly. Two bottles of wine.

'Much more fun if he stays, though,' said Mum. 'He can make some of his special pancakes for breakfast!'

'Lacey's gourmet stack,' said Robert, and then they giggled even more. They fell about laughing.

Hours after Sam had gone to bed, two sets of footsteps passed his door. Creaks. Whispering. Quite a while later he heard Robert cry out as though he'd been tickled. The sound made Sam feel horrible.

When everything had gone quiet, he slid out of bed, fetched the Robert devil out of his cupboard, took the sock off its head and began to bash its two faces against the wall. Ten times. Twenty times. *Bash, bash, bash*, as hard as he possibly could.

But the devil doll didn't care at all. Neither of its faces would stop laughing.

•

He's talking and he's talking and he's bloody talking like a maniac, and someone is finally listening. He's telling Eliza his whole life story—not every detail, but a hell of a lot of it—and the more he talks, the more he remembers. He dredges for memories, sitting there with a gun in his hand and a phone clamped to his ear. He needs her to understand. He needs her to see how Robert slithered into the space where his father had been and poisoned Sam's world.

It's as though the past is pushing itself out of a chrysalis, opening its wings to reveal all those patterns and colours that make a childhood: Dad's boots crunching in the frost in the early mornings; his parents chuckling in the front of the car while he dozes on the back seat. A flying clay exploding into fragments, Dad shouting, *Good shot, son!* The snuggliness of lying between Snoops and Bouncer, the peaceful clanging sound of the Rayburn door. The blue-grey of a dead father's face. Robert's smile.

Granny tried her best, but in the end she couldn't help. The more they saw of Robert, the less they saw of her. He was coming around all the time, cooking meals and 'staying in the spare bedroom'. Huh! Did they really think he couldn't hear their voices through the wall? He didn't want to know what they might be doing in there. He tried not to think about it.

'He treated Mum like a princess at first,' he tells Eliza. 'Always saying she was talented and beautiful and unique. And the presents—bloody hell, you should have seen the presents! A bunch of roses every week. Poetry books. A mohair throw for her bed. He bought me things too. Stuff I really, really wanted, like a camera for my ninth birthday.'

'That's quite a gift for a child who's not your own.'

'Mm, and this was a digital one, back in the day when they weren't in every phone. Poshest thing I've ever owned. He knew full well I was going through a photography-mad phase and I'd sell my soul for one of those. And I *did* sell my soul, because I had to make him a card to say thank you. Mum insisted I draw a picture and write at least *three* sentences, in *legible* handwriting. Almost killed me. It was like being invaded by presents. I know how those poor sods the Trojans felt when the wooden horse turned out to be full of crack troops.'

That bloody camera. He still feels like throwing up when he remembers the stupid card he made, a goofy picture of a horse with the caption *SUNDANCE KID*. The horse looked as though it was on some serious drugs, but the writing inside was the most humiliating thing. Trying to write legibly was torture for Sam. Writing to thank Robert was triple torture.

Dere Robut,
Thank you for the camra. Its digtal which is grat. I will take a lot of fotos.
Yours faythfly,
Samuel John Ballard

Robert laughed out loud at Sam's stoned horse and stupid baby handwriting and bad spelling and general uselessness. Mum said, *Sorry, he's terribly dyslexic, top end of the scale, and he also has dysgraphia so his handwriting doesn't reflect his intellect at all.* Robert ruffled Sam's hair and claimed to admire his boundless energy.

'You've got the patience of a saint, Harriet,' he told her. 'You give this fellow every ounce of yourself, don't you?'

What a wanker. What a mealy-mouthed, evil snake.

One night, Sam saw something that made him want to gouge his eyes out. He'd gone to bed—which took a while because he always strung out the rituals of teeth, pyjamas, reading, hugs—and after the lights were out he rolled around and fretted and his mind seemed to race. This happened most nights. He started thinking about an experiment he wanted to do with his camera, using the flash. He decided to nip downstairs and grab it. Mum wouldn't mind, he was often up and down like a yo-yo. He'd left her watching telly by herself. She might make him some hot chocolate.

He slid down the bannisters, trotted into the sitting room and skidded to a halt with a scream in his head. Mum wasn't alone anymore. Robert must have parked in the lane and crept into their house. Mum was sitting in her usual armchair with one leg stretched out, toes pointed like a queen. Her skirt was all up around her waist. Robert was kneeling on the floor, kissing the arch of her foot with the whole of his mouth. She was laughing—low, slow laughter, not her usual giggle—hair all over her face in a happy tangle of curls. Robert's pink stripy shirt was unbuttoned. Sam glimpsed the dark shadow of hair on his chest. He was making pretend growling noises as though he was eating her foot. Sam was gobsmacked. He couldn't imagine what on earth they were playing at. He honestly thought they'd gone nuts.

'Oh, Sam, darling!' gasped Mum, when she caught sight of him. Her cheeks flushed crimson as she shot out of the chair. 'What are you doing up? It's after midnight!'

There was his camera, on the mantelpiece. He darted in, grabbed it and scurried out again without a word, hating Robert's deep laughter that seemed to chase him as he fled back upstairs and pulled the duvet over his head. He wished—*wished*—Robert would drop dead. You can't unsee a scene like that. It's still seared into his memory: Robert's horrid mouth all over Mum's tanned foot, and the weird way she was laughing. The musky-lavender-rum smell of Robert's cologne was still lingering in the house the next morning—in fact he keeps getting whiffs of it now, years later, in Tuckbox. It's on this phone he's using, making him feel sick. It's a snazzy phone, silver-shiny. Of course it is. Robert would have the best and flashiest. All bought on stolen money.

Not long after the freaky foot incident, Robert came to live at Tyndale and all those lies about the spare bedroom went out of the window. He was quite openly sleeping in Dad's bed, with his head on Dad's pillow. His clothes were in Dad's chest of drawers, his toothbrush was plonked into Dad's mug. The house was full of Robert: his voice, his smell, his things, his rules. A thousand digital cameras wouldn't ever in a million years make that okay.

Robert moving in was the worst thing that had ever happened to Sam, apart from Dad dying. One day Mum and he were still a team: the two of them against the world. The next day Robert was making him eat mushrooms—he hated mushrooms—and enforcing bedtimes and chores. He reckoned Sam had run rings around his long-suffering mother for too long.

'It's *our* house,' Sam protested to Mum when she was driving him to soccer. 'Yours and mine. Not his! I don't want him here.'

'I know you don't like change, Sammy.'

'I don't mind change. I just don't like Robert.'

She wouldn't look at him. She kept on staring through the windscreen.

'That's because you're still grieving for Dad. I am too. But Robert wants to make us happy. We make *him* happy. Poor man, he's not had an easy life. His wife was cruel to him.'

Tammy hit the roof when she heard he'd moved in. She drove straight down to the farm, bailed Mum up in the kitchen and told her she was making a catastrophic fucking mistake. Sam was under the table at the time, playing with the amazing Lego set Robert had given him. Pieces were scattered all across the floor.

'Harriet, wake up and smell the fucking coffee!' raged Tammy. 'Can't you *see* what he is?'

'Actually I can. He's a good man who's been quietly carrying a candle for me for years.'

Tammy pretended to stick her fingers down her throat. 'Oh, puh-*lease*. Do me a favour. That sleazeball?'

'It happens to be true, Tam.'

'Loving you from afar! Bring me the sick bucket.'

It took Mum a while to answer. She was finding mugs in the dishwasher and filling the kettle.

'That's right, loving me from afar. His marriage was a nightmare.'

'Yeah, it was—for Connie! She's only just getting her mojo back.'

'Connie's not a victim. She's a manipulative, nasty woman.' Mum was putting coffee powder into mugs. 'Robert and I have both been given a second chance at happiness. I don't think Angus would want us to throw it away. I think he'd be giving us his blessing.'

'The man's a narcissist, Harriet! A sociopath. I can see straight through him.'

'With your X-ray eyes.'

'How d'you know it isn't Sam he's really after? I wouldn't be surprised if he turns out to have kiddie porn on his computer.'

'Oh dear God. Seriously?' Mum slammed the coffee jar down on the bench. 'Listen to yourself. Just listen to yourself.'

Tammy was picking up her car keys. Her voice had gone flat and quiet. 'I just hope you know what you're doing.'

'I do, thank you.'

'Good. Great. Marvellous.'

But Tammy obviously didn't think it was marvellous at all. She didn't stay for her cup of coffee. She clenched her jaw and said she was leaving and don't worry, she wouldn't be back in a hurry. She crouched down to plant a kiss on top of Sam's head, muttering *poor little bastard*, and then she slammed out of the house.

Sam crawled out from under the table. He ran to the door to watch her car headlights as she drove away. He felt lonely.

•

As soon as Robert had officially moved in, Granny stopped visiting Tyndale. Amir the cat was run over by a lorry, and that seemed to break her heart all over again. It broke Sam's too. Amir had been his friend. They wrapped him in a sheet and buried him in Granny's back garden. They both cried as they filled in the hole. When Granny collected Sam after school—which was less and less often in those days—she looked sadder than he'd ever seen her. She'd lost her sparkle. She seemed to float around like a ghost in her empty doll's house.

'Why don't you come and visit us anymore?' he asked her.

'Well, you know. I don't want to get in the way.'

'Is it because of Robert?'

'Winds of change,' she muttered hoarsely, sipping her brandy. 'Winds of change, Sammy. They're blowing. And by golly they're cold.'

•

She married him. Of course she did. He was eleven years old and their bloody pageboy, all dressed up and on display for a ceremony he was dreading. Mum kept asking him if he was happy. He kept saying no, he wasn't—to which she'd smile sadly, promising he'd understand when he was older.

She'd suggested a quiet wedding, but Robert wouldn't hear of it. *Harriet, you deserve a party!* It was years before Sam worked out that his father's life insurance paid for his widow's lavish wedding. Granny booked a holiday to India so that she could avoid the whole thing. Tammy wasn't even invited. It was mostly Robert's friends who showed up.

Sam had to do a reading in the registry office: a soppy poem about love. He rehearsed it about a million times but when his big moment came he messed up all the most deep-and-meaningful words, missed out whole lines and gabbled so fast it didn't make any sense at all. This was nothing to do with dyslexia. No. He couldn't read it because he wanted to tear out the page and spit and shout the filthiest words he knew. He could feel a hundred pairs of eyes fixed on him as he stumbled through it. He could feel Mum's embarrassment.

Robert winked at him as he trotted back to his seat with his cheeks on fire. Sam was scowling to stop himself from crying. Robert's grin never slipped at all.

The reception was in the ballroom at Jackson's Lodge, filled with round tables with white cloths. There was a dance floor and a band playing jazz. Mum was wearing a floaty blue dress that matched her eyes, her hair pinned up in a bun on the back of her head and spangled with blue flowers, lots of little curls falling around her face. She looked like a summer's day. Robert wore a silk waistcoat in the same blue as her dress. He gave a speech in his deep voice, choking up when he mentioned *Angus, the finest friend a man could ever have.* He finished by turning to Mum. *I've made a few false starts, but today I married the love of my life.* He took her face between his two hands, smiled into her eyes, and kissed her. Everyone in the room went *awww!* as though they were watching a cute cat video. Sam didn't. He was thinking about Dad's shotgun, which was in Mr Appleton's safe. He imagined shooting Robert with both barrels. He imagined his enemy falling face first into his own wedding cake.

Most of the guests drank a lot and either ignored Sam or asked stupid questions—*And what do you think of your new stepdad?*—to which Sam knew he was *not* allowed to reply: *I think he killed my actual dad, I hate his guts and I'm imagining how fun it would be to shoot him.* For most of the evening he wandered around by himself, taking photos with his precious camera and feeling like a total goon in his pageboy outfit. People kept slapping Robert on the back and telling Mum what a great bloke she'd landed, but Sam felt as though there was something else going on at that wedding. Something fake. Something mean. He stopped to listen to a loud group, yelling to one another across their table—they'd overdone the bubbly and were wrecked. *Is the merry widow knocked up? Five years older than him, what a cougar! I reckon our Rob's after the money.*

They were in hysterics when Robert strutted up with his arms held out wide like a conquering hero. They changed their tune—*Hey, hey! Here's the man of the moment!*—and there was jolly banter about what a bloody lucky guy he was. If Robert heard what they'd been saying seconds earlier, he didn't let on. His grin still didn't slip at all.

At ten o'clock Aunt Monique drove Sam home. The *newly-weds*, as she kept calling them, were going to sleep in the bridal suite at Jackson's Lodge. This thought made Monique smirk.

The farmhouse was empty and cold when they walked in. Aunt Monique was empty and cold too. She'd never liked Sam. The feeling was mutual.

'Well!' she sighed, as she took off her pointy-toed shoes. 'I must say, I think you and my sister have fallen on your feet. I'm not quite sure how she did it. You couldn't ask for a better stepfather.'

It was too much.

'He killed my dad,' Sam blurted.

Her eyes flew wide open. She raised her hand as though about to slap him, and he ducked.

'Now look, you vindictive little monster,' she hissed, 'if I ever . . . *ever* . . . hear you say that again, you'll regret it. Okay? Comprendo? It's against the law to tell lies like that. You'll go to prison!'

'No, I won't.'

'Oh yes, you will.' She was nodding and nodding. She looked a little bit crazy. 'You will! Prison! Your mummy won't be coming there with you. And you don't want to know what happens to good-looking boys like you in prison.'

'What happens?' asked Sam.

She told him in graphic detail. She was a good storyteller. His eyes grew wide with horror as he listened. According to Aunt Monique, being in prison would involve people's bodies, including Sam's, being used in ways he'd never begun to imagine. She said bullies would torture him and he'd be screaming for help, and they'd tear his bottom, and nobody would stop them. They would do it every single day. She said he wouldn't survive a week in there.

He knows now she was making it all up, just trying to frighten him. For a start, kids don't go to adult prisons, do they? But he's never forgotten the sick fear he felt while she was describing it. He was crying by the end.

'Robert Lacey had nothing to do with your father's death,' she said.

'How do you know?'

'Didn't Harriet tell you? No? Well, she should have done—then you'd know not to go accusing people. They cut Angus open and took out all his organs. His brain and everything. It's called an autopsy.'

This was an even worse idea than the one about prison.

'They didn't cut my dad open,' he insisted.

Her smile was small and mean. 'The man's heart was a ticking time bomb. He was never going to make old bones. Robert Lacey is a saint to take you on, and don't you forget it. A saint. Nobody else would be saddled with you.'

'Why not?'

'Because *you*, Sam Ballard, are a big problem.'

Alone in his bedroom, he dug the Santa Claus devil out of the cupboard and fetched a pair of nail scissors from the first-aid kit in the bathroom. He sat on his bed and stabbed the puppet in both its chests. He dug in the pointed blades of the scissors and tore the fabric until yellow lumps of foam stuffing spilled out. *It's called an autopsy.*

But neither of its grins ever slipped at all.

•

He has to stop talking. He can't go on.

The Ritalin's not working so well anymore. His mind is jangling and full of screams and his forehead's throbbing where he bashed it and his mouth feels weirdly dry despite all the tea Mutesi's been pouring down him and he's longing to curl up in one of the booths and fall asleep and he . . . what were they talking about? Sleep. Deep, deep sleep so that he can stop struggling and forget everything that's ever happened. Forever.

'Forever,' he mumbles.

'I'm still here,' says Eliza. 'You okay, Sam?'

She's trying to keep him from sliding away, but she can't. Julia will grow up with no dad. She's much better off that way. She's his little smiling friend, who skips beside him wherever he goes. He loves her so much. It will be awful when she gets to school and other kids tease her and say her dad was a murderer. Kids can be mean. But at least she won't have a father in prison, and at least Robert won't be there to ruin her life. He's achieved something, hasn't he?

'You there? Sam?'

'Let me see Julia. Please let me see Julia. Just once.'

Her next words are drowned out by the jangling. When he can hear her again, she's trying to convince him that it's impossible to bring Julia.

'My boss isn't allowing her to go into Tuckbox. There's Robert dead in there, and . . . let's be honest, it's a crime scene. No place for a child, is it?'

He only wants to say goodbye. This morning, when he ran back to the truck, he still had choices. He could have hopped in and driven away. He could have emigrated to Australia or something. He could have chosen to live, but he didn't. He came charging back in here and shot Robert, and in that moment he made his choice.

It's almost dark outside. Today is almost over. He's running out of lifetime.

'Hey,' says Eliza. 'What's that beeping noise? Is your phone's battery going flat? Sam?'

TWENTY-FIVE

Rosie

The whole of her left side is numb now. She feels as though she's rotting away along with the wet wood of the cupboard. She's still holding the door shut, and her curled fingers feel brittle. She imagines trying to straighten them, imagines them cracking.

She checks the time on her phone. Nearly four.

When will you get me?

Four o'clock. See the little hand on the clock?

Julia will have put her own coat on by now. She's clever like that. She'll be all ready, sitting on the chair near the door, swinging her legs, singing to herself. She might be holding a picture she's painted today, or scones they've made in the nursery kitchen.

She'll be waiting and waiting. Soon she'll be getting worried. She's always had a fear of being forgotten but these past few months have been much worse. She was taken away from her dad—it was his fault, really, but how could a three-year-old understand that? She saw him shouting and attacking her mum. She left the only home she'd ever known and then she lost her granny. Too much sadness for a very small person.

This day may leave Julia without parents or grandparents, and there's nobody else she knows. She might end up in a children's home, or with foster parents! That would break her heart.

I'm sorry, I'm sorry.

The battery is down to fifteen per cent. Just enough. Soon it will die. She squints into the dark, wondering how to pack a lifetime of love into one short message.

Abi

She's a prisoner, trapped with three total strangers, drinking builder's brew tea out of a white mug. She's watching the setting sun touch the face of a murderer.

Kelly Bradshaw will have been given bail and sent home by now. Charlie might have phoned the clinic. Poor Charlie. It's negative. She knows it is, because at two o'clock this morning she did a home pregnancy test. Stupid thing to do. They say not to—it's too early, can give a false negative, better to wait for the more reliable clinic result—but she was *so* hopeful. She felt different. She imagined waking Charlie up then and there, with a kiss and the magical news. She imagined the look on his face and she just couldn't wait! She was so sure, so excited when she opened the box.

But no. Instead she lay in a sleepless mess of disappointment, wondering whether they could go through it all over again. Perhaps they should start telling the world the truth. *We can't have kids. It's not happening.*

She invited Rory and Renata around for a drink when they first moved into number 96. It seemed the neighbourly thing to do. Mistake. *Big* mistake. They left their dogs at home but turned up with identical miniature demons called William and Albert. Bill and Bert. It took Renata three minutes to ask The Question.

'So you're dinkies?'

Abi froze. 'Sorry?'

'You know: dinky. Dual income, no kids yet.' Renata's gaze was darting around the obviously-child-free courtyard. No plastic slide, no sandpit or paddling pool, no baby gym.

Charlie was opening a bottle of wine at the time, screwing in the corkscrew, mouth pursed in concentration. She wanted to hug him.

'That's us,' he said quietly. 'Yup. Dinkies.'

'Our lifestyle's not really compatible with a family,' added Abi.

It was their go-to lie. It avoided the pity, the questions—*What's the problem? You? Him? You don't know? How can you not know?* That particular evening she'd been pumping herself full of hormones for their second round of IVF. She felt as though she was dragging a heavy weight around. Every joint ached.

'Oh, it's *never* the right time!' Renata stooped to drop nauseating little kisses onto Bill's head—*mwah, mwah*. 'You've no idea what you're missing.'

Of course bloody Rory piled in. He's in advertising, spends more time with his Tesla than he does with his family, but—like everyone else in the world—he's an expert on the joys of parenting.

'You just have to get on with it,' he urged, with a jab of his right fist. 'Jump right in.'

'I don't have a maternal bone in my body,' said Abi.

''Course you do.'

Charlie knew this game. 'We won't be cluttering up the planet with resource-guzzling little clones of ourselves.'

It was easier, this: to be rebels who'd cheerfully plumped for child-free living rather than a desperate duo who traipsed to and from the fertility clinic, suffering indignity and pain and cost, trying to achieve what other people did so easily.

Abi shakes herself, dragging her thoughts back from private sadness. Sam's still talking. This negotiator has the patience of ten saints. Sam seems to be returning to his most agitating memories again and again, leaping backwards and forwards in time, yet the even-toned murmur on the other end of the line never seems to hurry him. Abi would have snapped by now.

'I don't think he loved Mum at all,' he's saying. 'I think he got off on control.'

Yep. The man was a bastard. Now can we cut to the chase? You have precisely one minute to answer the following questions—One: Why'd you kill him? In a nutshell, please! Two: What exactly are you hoping to achieve? Three: When do we get out of here?

If armed responders are lined up along Wilton Street they're in for a long, cold wait. The winter sun is almost gone, its last rays seeping between the blinds. Zebra stripes glow on Sam's deathly pale face and strike copper sparks in his hair. He looks young, as though he's been transformed back into the bewildered boy whose story he's telling. Even his voice seems to have become more infantile, his vocabulary simpler, his pitch higher. He's never still. Some part of him is always moving: a foot tapping, a knee jerking, fingers twiddling his ear. Fidget, fidget. Abi can relate to that. She's a fidgeter herself. She loathes inactivity. Beach holidays are pure hell.

We're all a part of his story now, she thinks. Mutesi, Neil and me. Even the ever-so-patient person on the other end of that line is being swept up in it. Our lives collided with Sam's today. We were rolling merrily along in different directions until he smashed into us and knocked us all off course. Now we're travelling together for a while.

She's glad the others got away. Those little children, and Brigitte, and lovely old Arthur who narrowly avoided the Balham station bomb, only to be caught up in Sam Ballard's private war. She's glad to see the back of Paige too, but not for such charitable reasons. Abi feels more attuned to Sam than she does to that woman, with her baby bump and pushchair and polka-dotted changing bag and maternity jeans and scruffy fleece-lined boots, and that ostentatiously messy hair with dark roots showing, just like Lottie's—*Sod it, Abi, I haven't got time for the hairdresser, I'm a mother, not a model!*

Mutesi is still stretched out in a booth. She looks supremely comfortable, though from time to time she stirs. Abi suspects that her languor is an act, that she's alert and listening intently. Neil is microwaving himself a fish pie in a glass dish. He keeps frowning towards the front window. Probably worrying about his dog. The wind's getting up now, and rain is forecast for tonight.

A twinge of cramp throbs in Abi's right knee. She grabs her ankle and pulls her leg high up in front of the chair. She's beginning to feel . . . no, surely it's not possible. Her life is in immediate danger, she's making headline news, there's a bloodied corpse developing rigor mortis under her favourite coat. She can't possibly be *bored*.

The films have it all wrong. She and Charlie have watched *Die Hard* almost every Boxing Day since they met. It's their happy tradition. Bruce Willis, turkey sandwiches, the bottle of bubbly Great-Aunt Phyllis gives them every year. There's not a dull moment in the *Die Hard* siege: it's a white-knuckle roller-coaster ride with one crisis after another. Completely unrealistic, she now knows. The challenge in Tuckbox isn't just terror, it's passivity. It's helplessness. It's being forced to wait for others to act.

When Abi was about six, Great-Aunt Phyllis gave her an illustrated version of the story of Rapunzel. At first Abi loved the book and pored over its sumptuous pictures: Rapunzel, a beautiful prisoner in her tower, with her blue eyes and golden river of hair. Eventually Abi outgrew fairytales and put away childish things.

She was sixteen and cynical when she next flicked through her old favourite. Well! What an irritating story. Rapunzel, she now saw, was a total drip. All that golden hair, useful only as a kind of coiffured ladder for witches and men. Teenager Abi despised the moronic girl and her annoying prince. She covered the pages in felt-tip pen graffiti: twirly moustaches on Rapunzel, with speech bubbles to make her say things like *I'm a boring virgin*. She turned the prince into a fairy with wings and ballet shoes. The only character she left intact was the witch. The old bat might be wicked but at least she got things *done*; she didn't wait around for some man to rescue her. Abi determined that she never would either. The witch was the only character she respected. She'd far rather be a witch than a princess.

Famous last words. Here she is, making friends with her captor, meekly waiting to be rescued by a load of macho guys in combat gear.

Something nudges her upper arm. Neil's elbow. He's scoffing fish pie and resolutely keeping his gaze fixed on Sam, but his hand has slid along the table towards her. She looks down to see a serviette with a single line of handwriting in green pencil.

Nicola's hiding in a cupboard in the back kitchen

Nicola. Nicola. Who the hell is Nicola?

Hang on—*Nicola!* The woman Sam's been raving about—the woman who seems to be the cause of this whole disaster. How the hell can Sam's ex be in the back kitchen? How? *Ah*. The penny drops into place. Nicola, who saw Sam and legged it. She never actually got out of the café. It's farcical—it's almost hilarious. Abi has no sympathy at all for a princess who left Robert to stop a bullet on her behalf. Maybe she should have stayed to fight her own battles. Serves her right if she's stuck in a cupboard.

Smoothing the serviette, she slides a biro from her handbag and scribbles rapidly.

She's got to come out and talk to him.

When Neil shakes his head, she writes: *Less volatile now, be ok*

'Are you prepared to bet her life on that?' Neil whispers out of the corner of his mouth. 'She's not.'

So we deal with her ex for her?

Neil grabs the serviette, crumples it up and shoves it into his pocket. Abi has a good mind to march back there, find this mythical female and haul her out to face the music. Nicola's the one person who might be able to bring all this to an end.

She's distracted by a change in Sam's voice. Something is going wrong with his phone call. He's on his feet, glancing anxiously around the café.

'That noise? Yeah, you're right,' he says. 'It's the battery. What do I do?'

'Hell,' groans Abi. 'No, no, no! This can't happen. That bloody phone's going flat. Hang on, Sam! I'll see if I've brought my charger. Okay?'

She dives for her handbag and begins rifling through it.

Has to be in here, has to be in here . . .

She's sure she dropped her portable power bank into the side pocket before leaving the house this morning. It's bright blue, about the size of a lipstick, cost less than a tenner—but right now it's the most precious commodity in her world.

Don't tell me today's the one day I left it at home.

She has a mental image of the little blue tube, plugged into the laptop on her side of the bed. She tips the bag upside down onto the table, frantically shaking it until she's emptied every pocket. Sam has turned away and is talking to the negotiator again.

'You're like Mary Poppins,' whispers Neil with awe. 'Sure you're not packing an Uzi in there?'

'I wish.'

He glances over his shoulder towards Sam. 'Would you use it, if you had?'

'Shoot him in the leg. Wouldn't you?' She gives the bag a final shake. 'I'm normally packing a power bank. Okay—c'mon, let's look in the kitchen. There has to be a charger somewhere. They use that phone for people to text in their orders. I texted one myself this morning. Never did get that sodding espresso.'

The pair of them scurry behind the counter, searching in nooks and crannies. Sam is still talking to the negotiator while looking along the front service counter. Mutesi swings her legs off her bench and joins in the hunt. All hands on deck. The last thing they need now is for Sam to be cut off from that soothing voice.

'No, I haven't got another phone,' Sam's insisting. 'Mine will be at home, it was the last thing on my mind when I left. I was in a bit of a state . . . What? Nobody here's got one, I don't think. They did have, but I, um, shot 'em. Or stamped on them. I wish I hadn't now.'

He's listening again, shaking his head emphatically as he glances towards the door.

'No. No! Don't send anyone . . . I don't want that . . . Hang on, are you still there?' His voice is rising in both volume and pitch. 'You there, Eliza? You there? Eliza?'

Eliza

Bugger, bugger, bugger. Just when she was getting somewhere.

She drops her headset in disgust. 'I don't believe it. How come he didn't notice the battery was getting low?'

'He's just shot his stepfather,' suggests Paul, who is calmly updating the log. 'He maybe isn't concentrating on those teeny details.'

'We've got a problem if he can't get that phone charged. I haven't been able to sort out a safe way to deliver another one to him.'

'He'll manage. Lacey will have had a system. But hey—you've made enormous progress! Sam's talking, he's trusting you. You're in through the front door and heading upstairs.'

'And I could lose it all again because of a flat battery.'

She feels like running down to the café and knocking on the door. She knows Sam now. She's filtered out her own preoccupations, the world around her, everything except Sam's voice. She's noticed every nuance, followed the wild zigzags of his emotions. She's walked in his shoes. Rapport goes both ways. *Monitor data in three dimensions, control movement across three different axes.* It's exhilarating to be flying down a canyon in the dark. Sometimes it feels more real, more valid than anything else in her life. Sometimes she almost forgets her own family.

Richard knows this. She's never admitted it to him, but he knows. He reckons the only way for him to get her full attention would be to hijack a bus. This was his punchline on Saturday night, at the neighbours' Christmas bash. He'd put away half a bottle of Scotch in short order. Never a good sign with him.

'Has to be worth it, doesn't it?' he asked the assembled company. 'Hijack a bus and threaten to blow everyone up. Just so my wife—Detective Inspector McClean, Eliza, my clever, highly trained wife—will come rushing along, lights and sirens—*nee-naw nee-naw*—to spend hours and hours hanging on my every word. She'll use all those natty little tricks like *reflecting* and *paraphrasing* and *minimal encouragers* and she'll be ever so empathetic. She's a terrific listener, you know. She's a people-whisperer . . . yep, a people-whisperer.' He'd raised his glass towards Eliza. 'Just so long as you're not married to her. When you're married to her, she finds you pretty boring.'

Awkward tittering. Someone face-palmed. Their host muttered *ouch.*

'Shut up, my darling,' hissed Eliza, smiling sweetly. But he didn't shut up.

'She and her bestie, Paul, spend hours and hours huddled together, saving lives, while I change nappies and do the school run. Then they go to their local and . . . you know.' He knocked back another mouthful of whisky. 'They *debrief*.'

He'd crossed a line. Muttering apologies through gritted teeth, Eliza manhandled her swaying husband out of the party and back to their own home four doors down. The babysitter tactfully made herself scarce. Eliza was ready for a major showdown—the kind of furious, gloves-off confrontation that can end a marriage—but she never got the chance. Richard collapsed on the sofa and was comatose when she came downstairs with Jack the next morning. The poor man had never looked less attractive: chilled, shivering, his complexion a faint pea-green. He swore he couldn't remember a thing. *I did what? I said what? No! Are you sure?*

She let it go. She was afraid of where a fight might lead, because she knew he had a point. She may not be guilty as charged, but she's not entirely innocent either. The intensity and high stakes of crisis negotiation is like a drug. It can be difficult to come down once it's all over, so she and her colleagues sometimes stop for a swift drink or two—or three—in a quiet corner of the Black Lion. Sometimes it's just Paul and Eliza. And why not? They have shared experience. They talk, they listen, they support. It's never been more than that. Not physically, anyway. Not really.

She stands and stretches, massaging the small of her back. The plastic swivel chairs are exquisitely uncomfortable. She cracks her knuckles.

'You'll get arthritis,' scolds Paul, without looking up.

'His mother was pretty quick to move on, wasn't she?'

'Not for us to judge.'

Eliza's taking up position at the window. 'She had an eight-year-old son to think about. She might have waited ten minutes before installing the new model.'

'Maybe she thought it was best for Sam to have a father figure.'

A sudden gust of wind sets the glass shuddering. After a final burst of brilliance the winter sun has slid below the rooftops, leaving an inky smudge of cloud in its place. Lights have been set up at the cordons, and bars of yellow gleam from between the blinds in Tuckbox's windows. The rest of Wilton Street is in darkness. No streetlights at all. It will be a tactical decision, to use the falling of night to the advantage of the besiegers. All kinds of things can be put into place in the shadows.

Rain begins fitfully, spitting out of the dark, and within minutes the heavens have opened. Uniformed officers down at the outer cordon are pulling on waterproofs and retreating to shop doorways. The crowd of curious onlookers and media has magically thinned. The dogs are cowering under the awning.

'I think we're sinking,' she says, without taking her eyes off the distant café lights. 'Richard and I. I'm not sure we can keep afloat much longer.'

'I'm sorry.'

'Sometimes I wonder whether Liam's problems stem from us. All the tension, the silences, the eye-rolling. All the jealousy. All the boredom. We're both guilty.'

She can't see Paul's expression, but she senses his stillness.

'Don't give up yet,' he says.

Ashwin chooses this moment to stride in, waving a cardboard file above his head.

'From Nicola Rosedale's solicitor. Not good.' He slaps the file onto the table. 'These are copies of court documents. Our boy's got a recent history of violence towards her. He's made threats to kill both her and Robert Lacey. I've highlighted the relevant bits.'

Eliza and Paul flick through the pile of paper. Sam clearly doesn't have legal aid and has made his application for contact without a solicitor's input. His statement is brief, with the occasional spelling mistake. It describes a very ordinary tragedy: two young people met, fell madly in love—well, he did—and once he'd taken over his family farm she moved in with him. They had a daughter, conceived accidentally but loved fiercely, and for a couple of years they were content. *We were so happy*, writes Sam. *Things were so good. Not long after Julia was born we became engaged.*

Then came the Ice Age. Late one night Sam woke up to find that the woman he loved was in the act of leaving him and taking his child. To add insult to injury, she was running off to stay with Robert Lacey. His final paragraph is bewildered:

> *Julia has never been away from me before, hardly even for a night. She's never lived anywhere but in this house. I can't sleep for worrying about her. I've begged Nicola to bring her to visit but she refuses. She says Julia's frightened of me but I don't believe this. I want to know she's ok. I just want to be her dad.*

Nicola's statement is longer, more detailed, more coherent. She's got herself a solicitor and it shows. Her ducks are in a row. Disaster is laid out in order: heartbreak, rage and abandonment regimented into numbered paragraphs. Her take on their history is almost diametrically opposed to Sam's.

4. Things have never been good between us. By the time I became pregnant I knew that Sam was unstable. He has ADHD though he denies this. He's always late, he acts impulsively and lives chaotically. He cannot control his anger, especially when under any kind of pressure. I tried to break off our relationship when I found I was pregnant but he pressured me to move in with him so I reluctantly agreed. I did this for the sake of our unborn child.

'She can't bring herself to admit they were happy once,' Eliza mutters, turning the paper over as she reads on. 'Why not? They must have been. Unless the neighbour is right and she's a gold-digger?'

5. Our life together was fraught with conflict from day one. It was a living nightmare. I had to be constantly on my guard with what I said or how I behaved as Sam would fly off the handle. Julia and I lived in fear, walking on eggshells at all times. He has never shown any real interest in Julia. I believe he resented our very close mother–daughter relationship.

6. In May of this year, Sam was given notice that Tyndale Farm is to be sold. It belongs to Robert and Harriet Lacey but is heavily encumbered with mortgages and they need capital for a new business venture in London. The notice period they gave Sam was generous. He is not a competent farmer and was unable to earn enough to pay a commercial rent, so it was inevitable that the Laceys would have to sell.

7. Once Sam knew that he was losing the farm, he became untethered. He was extremely angry and depressed. He ranted about Robert Lacey, even accusing me of sleeping with him. I was disgusted and hurt by this suggestion. I became more and more afraid for Julia's safety as well as my own.

8. On 15th July I telephoned Robert to wish him a happy birthday. Sam flew into a rage, shouting and throwing things around the house. Julia was terrified. I decided I must leave immediately. The Laceys had offered shelter if I ever needed it. Because I feared Sam's reaction I had no choice but to leave secretly in the middle of the night. I had our bags by the car and Julia in her car seat when Sam woke up and confronted me. He screamed in my face that he would kill both me and Robert. I was petrified. I ran to my car and tried to lock the door, but he chased after me and wrenched it open. He gripped me around the shoulders close to my throat and shook me while attempting to pull me out of the seat. I believed he was going to throttle me. I truly feared for my life. I still have bruises on my collarbone as a result. I drove off in order to free myself. As I did so he was still banging on the windows. Julia was inconsolable. Since this event she's had constant nightmares and will only sleep in my bed.

9. I have had to rely heavily on the help of the Laceys, who have supported me financially and been wonderful grandparents to Julia. I stayed with them until Robert found me alternative accommodation in a flat belonging to a friend of his. Robert has given me work with flexible hours in his business, a café called Tuckbox.

10. Julia is terrified of her father and constantly seeks reassurance that he won't be coming to our home. She has nightmares about him attacking me and banging on the car windows. It cannot be in her best interests to force her to have contact with someone she fears. I do not believe that the Respondent has any genuine interest in seeing her. He has never been much involved in her life. I believe he is only making this application in order to harass me.

11. I am living at an address in South London. I ask the court's permission not to disclose it as I fear the Respondent's reaction. He may try to snatch Julia. If he discovers my address, I shall apply for a personal protection order against him.

Eliza reads to the last page, shaking her head.

'It's been months. How come he still hasn't seen his child?'

'According to the solicitor, Harriet Lacey was diagnosed with cancer soon after the application was made. That slowed things down.'

'Gawd, she makes him sound like Heathcliff! This lowering, gothic presence, all moods and violence. But if you look at the timeline he's actually been quite patient.'

'Not quite the word that springs to mind,' says Ashwin. 'There's a dead man in Tuckbox.'

'He's tried to work through the legal process. Until now.'

Paul is leaning perilously far back in his chair, tipping it onto two legs, hands on his head.

'I think it changes our threat assessment, and we have to let the boss know. Look, Eliza, even if he's nursing a legitimate grievance—moot point—Ballard's got to be treated as an extremely high risk to Nicola, hasn't he? He's threatened to kill both her and Lacey. One down, one to go.'

'I'm not convinced,' says Eliza. 'This threat—this *alleged* threat—was in an unusual situation. She was taking his child away!'

Ashwin's been bringing something up on his phone. He hands it to Eliza without explanation. She reads it, and sighs.

Battery v low. Julia cld go live with my dad?? She doesn't know him, not great but family at least and best I can think of. Pls pls tell her I LOVE YOU FOREVER AND BACK JULIA. So sorry XXXXX

'The woman who wrote those words is within feet of Ballard,' says Ashwin. 'She's alone, in the dark, with a fading mobile phone. Trusting you to save her life.'

TWENTY-SIX

Mutesi

She indulges in a moment of self-congratulation when she finds that blessed charger. It was obscured by plates of half-prepared breakfasts, plugged into a socket on a steel work surface immediately above Robert's body. The others have instinctively been avoiding the grim lump on the floor, and missed it. With a shout of triumph she yanks it out of the wall.

'Brilliant!' cries Abigail. 'Gimme that phone, Sam. I'll plug it in by the radio.'

Sam obeys meekly. He seems dog-tired. The cut on his forehead has broken open, and a thin trail of blood is heading for his right eye. The phone's battery is pancake-flat, so they're going to be off the air for a while. Might as well make use of the time.

'Has anyone seen the first-aid kit?' asks Mutesi. 'There must be one. I'm going to fix up that mess above your eye, Sam.'

He touches his forehead. 'You're not.'

'Oh, I think I am.'

'What's the point?'

Good question, she muses wryly as she searches along the shelves. What's the point of cleaning the minor wound of a man who has absolutely no will to live, has just blasted his stepfather into kingdom come, and who seems to be planning on following him very soon?

'Deckchairs on the *Titanic*,' mutters Abigail.

'The point,' says Mutesi, 'is that I am a nurse and you have an injury that needs treatment. Neil, we will put something on your cracked fingers too. Ah! There it is, on the corner shelf. Can you reach it for me, Neil?'

The fight has gone out of Sam. His shoulders slump. His face is twitching. For a moment he seems tempted to drop his forehead down to the table, though he checks himself.

'Go on then,' he says. 'But it's pointless.'

The kit is well stocked. Mutesi sorts through the box to find saline wipes, butterfly stitches and plastic gloves. She gives Neil a pot of petroleum jelly with instructions to rub plenty of it into his sore fingers. Finally she takes a chair next to Sam.

'Now,' she tells him, looking into his face. 'Listen to me. Are you listening? I am not going to try to overpower you or take that gun away. That is my promise to you. I swear it in Jesus' name, and for me that is an unbreakable vow. All right? Do you believe me?'

Sam meets her eye for a moment before managing a sullen nod.

'Good. I'll take that as a yes.' She's pulling on the gloves. 'But in return I need you to keep still. Will you put that gun down? No? Well make sure your hand is *well* away from that horrible trigger. Your job is to make sure this thing doesn't go off accidentally. All right? So . . . ready? I'm going to touch your head right now. Okay, here we go.'

She cleans the wound with slow, gentle movements, careful not to cause any sudden stab of pain. The injury looks nastier than it really is: livid bruising and swelling around a star-shaped laceration. There's no permanent damage. Blood has clotted among the hairs of his eyebrow. She hears wind outside, and a smattering of rain. The temperature is dropping fast.

'How did you do this?' she asks as she snaps open a phial of sterile solution.

'Banged my head against a brick wall.'

'What, literally?' asks Abigail. She's standing on one foot, grasping the other behind her in a stretch.

'Yep. Literally. About five times.'

Abigail winces, her mouth forming a silent *ooh* of empathy. 'That had to hurt.'

'It hurt like buggery. That was the point.'

'You banged your . . . five . . . I mean, why on earth would you *do* that?'

He blinks up at the lawyer, lifting a hand to the wound.

'Keep still,' scolds Mutesi. 'You're like a jumping spider. I can't do this properly with you leaping about the place.'

'Sorry.'

Mutesi smiles to herself. He threatened to shoot her just a few hours ago. Now he's apologising like a small child, just for fidgeting.

She takes her time in cleaning around the wound. Physical contact and care are tools of her trade; perhaps the most powerful tools, when used at the right moment.

'Where did you train to be a nurse?' asks Abigail.

'In Rwanda, at the government nursing school. Then I worked in a small hospital, in a town beside a lake.'

'Rwanda's beautiful, isn't it?'

'Very beautiful. A paradise.'

'My cousin travelled through there,' says Abigail. 'She went to see the mountain gorillas.'

'Ah, yes! The gorillas. Your cousin will have been in the Virunga Mountains.' Mutesi takes another wipe out of its sachet and continues to clean. There's no harm in talking while she works, in fact it may help to distract Sam. 'The land of a thousand hills. Sometimes a morning mist settles in the valleys, but then the sun warms everything. Plants and trees grow even as you watch them. You see colour everywhere. Colour and light. It's not dark and grey like London can be.'

'You sound a bit homesick.'

Sometimes she curls up on the sofa in her bedsit and allows herself to remember things that make her weep. Family, more family. Old friends and neighbours. Her boys setting off to school, Giselle's little feet. Sunlight on the path to the church.

Sam's eyes are bloodshot, drooping at the corners. He can't keep still. She suspects he truly isn't capable of it. He twitches, sniffs, rubs his nose.

'Do I seem scary?' he asks.

'Scary?' Mutesi looks him up and down. 'You don't. But your gun, that's a *very* scary thing. I wish you would just lay it on the floor.'

'I don't want to scare Julia if I see her.'

'Your daughter?'

'Mm.'

'Tell me about her.'

'Wish I had my phone. I'd show you a photo.'

'How old is she?'

'Two.' He winces as Mutesi closes the wound. 'Ouch! No . . . three now. I missed her birthday.'

Three years old. Giselle was three. The past lives in your memory. It doesn't leave you. It never leaves you.

'Three going on thirty,' says Sam. 'Julia's the boss of me.'

Mutesi chuckles. 'I bet she is.'

'I haven't seen her for five months. That's a long time in a kid's life, isn't it?'

'That *is* a long time.'

'Even an hour would be too long. We used to be together all day, every day. I've been taking her to work on the farm with me ever since she was a baby.'

'That's very special,' murmurs Mutesi. She's concentrating hard on her task, trying not to leave any space in her mind for a child's screams. The sound will drive her mad if she doesn't keep chasing it out. 'Very special.'

'How many children d'you have, Mutesi?' asks Abigail. 'Apart from Emmanuel's dad?'

It's one of those questions people ask. Idly, politely. A conversation starter. They don't know what they're asking.

'Four boys and a girl,' Mutesi replies without hesitation, as she always does. It's not a lie. It's not the truth. She begins to hum, hoping the next question will not follow. *And what are they all doing now?*

Sam raises his eyes to look at her. 'D'you think Julia will still remember me?'

It's the simplicity of the question that moves her. *Poor boy.* Her heart swells for him.

'You're her daddy! She will always remember you.'

'She'll have to do without me.'

'No, no,' Mutesi murmurs as she takes out another butterfly strip. 'She will always need her daddy. It doesn't matter what mistakes you've made. She will always need you. Don't leave her alone. Don't do that. Don't do that.'

'There's no coming back from what I did this morning.'

She ponders on his words as she presses the last strip into place. It's clear to her that Sam intends to make an end of himself. Today, probably. He's run out of hope, just as she herself did once. Without hope the darkness is monstrous.

'You can come back,' she says. 'I've known men who killed, and yet themselves still live. Some of them have found forgiveness.'

'Who?'

'Just some men.'

They hunt her through her dreams, drunk with hatred. Some of them live in that same place to this day, even in the graveyard of her family. She sometimes wonders whether she's in their dreams, as they are in hers. She wonders how they can sleep at all.

'All done,' she announces brightly, shutting the first-aid box and stripping off the gloves. 'In a month's time there will be nothing but a little scar. Julia's daddy is as good as new.'

What Julia's daddy needs most of all is sleep. She sees it in every line of his body, in the heaviness of his head on his neck, in the effort it takes him to speak. He presses out another pill and crunches it between his teeth.

'How long can you carry on doing that?' asks Abigail.

'I don't actually know.'

'What is it?'

'Ritalin. Keeps you awake if you take enough of it.'

'Useful stuff!'

For a moment there's the flicker of a mischievous smile on Sam's lips, a glimpse of what he must once have been. Long lashes, fine features. A handsome boy, if he wasn't so broken. And charming too.

'Want some?' he asks, but he's joking. The pills are already back in his pocket.

They work quickly. Within minutes he's more alert. More nervy too. His mood has swung from despair to a brittle, jarring animation. He's on his feet again, and pacing. It's not good at all.

'Best not take any more of those pills,' suggests Mutesi. 'They're not soothing for your brain.'

'I have to. No sleep since Friday. If I drop off now I'll wake up in handcuffs.'

'What if we promise that won't happen?'

'Promise all you like, I won't believe you. Nope. Sorry, but I have to see this through.'

'See *what* through?' demands Abigail.

'The end.'

'Agh!' Abigail looks as though she could strangle him. 'The end, the end! What does that even mean? What *is* the end? Where is all this going, Sam?'

'I'll know when I get there.'

Mutesi is trying to catch Abigail's eye, willing her to stop pushing. Every instinct tells her that it's counterproductive to force this unstable young man into a corner. But tact is not Abigail's strong point.

'We've been prisoners all day,' she persists. 'We've been threatened, covered in blood, watched a guy get shot. Aren't we entitled to know what the finishing line looks like? Why do you want to talk to Nicola? What exactly would you say to her?'

'I don't know.'

'We might be able to help. You never know.'

At these words Neil, who has been entertaining himself with Emmanuel's pencils, leaves the booth and hurries across to join them. He looks concerned.

'You can't help, Abi. He can't talk to Nicola, 'cos she's not here.'

It's odd, the way he says that. There's something pointed about it, and a meaningful look passes between him and Abigail. Mutesi is baffled. What is going on? Then the shutters come down over Abigail's face, and she turns back to Sam.

'I'm good at problem-solving,' she tells him. 'But I need to know what problem it is I have to solve. I need to understand the causes, the ramifications and a range of possible solutions. Then we work out how to fix it. So come on: tell me exactly what you're trying to achieve, for God's sake, and let's all get out of here.'

'I don't know.'

Abigail folds her arms. 'Could do better.'

'I want for none of it to have happened,' he says helplessly. 'I want to go back in time.'

A series of gusts rattle the awning. The metal frame clatters, the plastic flaps. Freezing air is rolling in through the broken pane in the door. From somewhere out on the street comes the sound of gurgling and spattering, perhaps a broken gutter. A dog begins to whimper.

'That's Buddy,' says Neil. 'It's raining pretty hard now, from the sounds of it. The dogs will be getting wet.'

'Shit.' Sam seems stricken. He stares towards the window. 'The dogs! I forgot about the dogs.'

'What about if I get them inside here—or I could let them off their leads at least?'

'I forgot about the dogs,' Sam says again.

'That's okay, we can put it right.' Neil takes a step towards the door. 'I'll let the other two off, shall I? Bring Buddy back in here with me.'

He takes another step. Another. Then three more, until he reaches the barricade. Mutesi holds her breath as she watches. Perhaps he's planning to run off as soon as he's safely outside. She wouldn't blame him, in fact she'd cheer him on, but she and Abigail will be left to deal with the consequences. Or maybe he'll open the door, step out there and invite the police to burst in. Yes, that seems very likely.

Neil heaves each table aside, making enough space so that he can slip past them to the door. He crouches to slide the bottom bolt, reaches to undo the top. Finally he turns the key. Then he twists around to look back at Sam.

'I think I'll just let those other two dogs go,' he says quietly, meeting Sam's eye. 'The police will pick them up in no time. But Buddy won't leave me in a month of Sundays. He'll sit right there on the pavement where I left him, no matter what happens. So I have to bring him in. D'you follow me?'

Sam nods. It's a small acknowledgement, but it's enough. Neil turns the handle and pushes the door, and it swings open.

There's no light out there. Normally this area in the early evening, just before Christmas, would be bright and bustling with traffic, commuters and shoppers. It's strange to see total darkness through that door. The sound of gushing water is louder now.

Neil glances at Mutesi and at Abigail, one after the other. He raises his eyebrows. He steps outside. The door swings shut behind him.

TWENTY-SEVEN

Sam

He forgot the dogs, and it's pissing down out there. How could he have forgotten the dogs? What kind of a monster is he?

All his life, he's had dogs trotting at his heels. Most farmers around him don't use them—they don't have enough stock—but his father and grandfather both did, mainly because they liked them. Bouncer was born the same year as Sam and they grew up together. Eventually he started having trouble with arthritis in his knees, so Dad brought Snoops home: a glossy, black-and-white puppy in a basket. He was a collie too, but leaner and faster and much busier. Dad said Snoops was a clever chap, trouble on four legs, and he and Sam were one of a kind. Bouncer wasn't very bouncy; he was always ready for a nap. All he wanted to do was snooze by the Rayburn or out on the front step where the sun warmed the black parts of his coat. Snoops used to explore in the sheds, barking at rats. He liked to roll in the dust in the yard making yapping, snapping noises. Sometimes Sam would roll around beside him and the pair of them would end up covered in dust. Snoops and Sam were both just young lads when Dad died.

Robert showed his true colours when it came to the dogs.

'Those two greedy so-and-sos are redundant now the farm's leased out,' he said one day, not long after he and Mum were married.

Mum was feeding them at the time. Sam was kneeling down on the floor with his arms around their warm necks, one each side. They used to come into the laundry for their dinner. Sam or Mum would pour the food into their brown clay bowls, and they'd scoff the lot in ten seconds.

'Not really redundant, are they?' puffed Mum. She was lugging the bag of dog biscuits back into the wooden cupboard. 'They're family, not employees.'

'But a working dog needs to work.'

'Nah. Not these ones, Robert. They're pets as much as anything. Bouncer was already semi-retired and Snoops is such an airhead, he runs away from sheep. But Angus loved them to bits, and they loved him.'

Robert was quiet for a while, watching Bouncer lapping water very noisily and messily. Then he put his arm around Mum's waist, dropping his mouth onto her neck so that his words were muffled.

'Sometimes,' he said, 'I feel I can't compete with Angus.'

She hugged him with both her arms, kissing his cheek, whispering in his ear. He'd got exactly what he wanted.

Sam forgot about the conversation almost straight away. Robert didn't. Oh no. And the thing about Robert was that once he decided he wanted something—or *didn't* want something—he would never give up until he'd achieved his aim. It was a point of honour with him. What he wanted most in the world was to erase every memory of Dad, everything to do with Dad, anything Dad had owned or loved or touched. That included the dogs, the farm, Granny, Sundance Kid. That included Sam. Perhaps it even included Mum.

He bided his time until the weather turned and the leaves came spinning down from the poplar tree by the stable. The days grew wetter and colder, the dust in the yard turned to squelchy mud. Bouncer and Snoops would pad into the house with grubby feet and dripping coats, leaving two trails of paw prints. They lay by the Rayburn with steam rising from their coats. The kitchen smelled of wet dog.

'Why don't you let me do that? You're far too beautiful,' said Robert, when he saw Mum mopping up muddy prints from the kitchen floor. He took hold of the mop and gently tried to prise it from her hands. Sam was sitting at the table, trying to fix a broken drill of Dad's that he'd found in the shed.

'Back off, buster,' protested Mum, holding on to the mop. They had a friendly little tug-of-war, both of them chuckling. 'My dogs, my problem.'

Robert accepted defeat and got out the red coffee pot and some delicious pecan pie he'd brought home from work. He was always producing sticky goodies that he'd made in the big steel kitchen at Jackson's Lodge. Sam used to tuck in, even while he fantasised about rubbing Robert's face in the stuff.

'Those dogs aren't yours really, are they?' he said to Mum. 'They were Angus's obsession. Look, this is just a suggestion, but how about if I find a new home for them—both together, in a working environment where they'll have exercise and stimulation. Then we could get a puppy instead! Something small and child-friendly, that doesn't need much exercise and can live indoors.'

Mum dumped the mop into the bucket and pushed straggles of hair away from her face.

'I don't think . . . no, Sam loves our two guys.'

Sam stared hard at the broken drill. He was good at pretending he was in another world. From under his eyelids he watched as Robert sidled closer and put his hand on her bottom.

'A puppy, though,' he wheedled. 'We'd *all* love a puppy, wouldn't we? Hmm? For Christmas? Georgia breeds Border Terriers—she's got some ready to go quite soon. How about it?'

Georgia was the manager of Jackson's and an exotic figure in Sam's world. She was a widow like Mum, but very unlike her in every other possible way. She made Sam think of a woman from a World War II film: always dressed up to the nines with a nipped-in waist and swirling skirts. She wore her hair in corn-coloured plaits curled around her head. Her throaty laugh did strange things to Sam.

'Ooh, tempting,' whispered Mum. 'Georgia's are nice dogs, I must admit. But we can't part with Snoops and Bouncer.'

Sam was mesmerised, watching Robert's big hand slide up and down his mum's behind. She was wearing one of her faded old pairs of jeans. They'd got a bit tighter recently. She used to say that Robert's cooking would be the ruin of her.

'I know you,' he murmured in his deep voice. 'I know you better than you do yourself. You'd adore one of those little Border Terriers.'

'We could have a puppy *as well as* Bouncer and Snoops,' Sam piped up.

Robert tweaked his ear as he walked past. 'Big ears. Three dogs! How much mopping d'you expect your mum to do?'

He made their coffee while she put the mop away. Sam lay down on the rug between Bouncer and Snoops.

'Don't worry,' he told them. 'I love you. I'll never swap you for a puppy.'

•

On the last day of the winter term, Sam was invited to his friend Jake's house after school. They were forming a band together—Jake on drums and Sam on the guitar and both of them doing what they thought was singing. Jake's parents must have been very tolerant people.

Mum collected him after dinner. She and Sam spent the drive home warbling along to the car stereo while he played air guitar. She'd spent the day in London visiting Oma, a duty she always dreaded, so she was relieved it was over. By the time they turned in at their gate it was dark and pouring with rain. Mum parked close to the porch steps and the pair jumped out and splashed through the puddles, giggling as they charged into the house. Robert was in the kitchen, leaning against the sink, wearing one of his trendy fleece tops and a smug smile. Their laughter stopped as soon as they saw him. Sam hardly ever laughed with Robert around.

'Hello, you two!' he said, looking extremely pleased with himself. 'I've got someone for you to meet. A very nice girl.'

'Oh dear, a visitor?' Mum started trying to straighten her hair. 'Who? Where?'

Sam heard a tap-tapping of little feet as a biscuit-coloured puppy came pottering across the floor towards them, making miniature barking-crooning sounds, clumsy paws sliding on the tiles. She was only about the size of a bag of peas.

'So cute!' cried Mum. 'Whose is she?'

Sam squatted down to pat the tiny dog. She rolled onto her back and let him tickle her tummy.

'Ladies and gentlemen,' crowed Robert, 'I give you Maggie! The newest member of the family.'

'What family?' asked Sam.

'Our family.'

Maggie's fur was wiry, her body sturdy. She bent her head to lick Sam's fingers. He could hear Mum asking Robert something in a whisper, but he wasn't really listening. He was too engaged in playing with the puppy. What eleven-year-old boy wouldn't be?

Gradually he began to notice that the adults were arguing. Robert's rumbling voice was easier to hear.

'Look at him,' he said. 'He loves Maggie. I did it for him.'

'Yes, but—' Mum leaned closer and whispered again. She sounded upset. Sam heard the words '—just can't do it. You'll have to get them back.'

Robert spun around to face her. His fingers were gripping her elbows.

'I don't believe this. You *did* agree. You absolutely did.'

'I didn't.'

'Jesus Christ, how can you not remember, Harriet?' He shook her by the arms, as though he was trying to wake her up. 'Seriously, do you not remember?'

'When did I say that?'

'In here. When you were mopping up the mess those collies made. You were all for it. You agreed Snoops needed more exercise and stimulation and it wasn't good for him not to be working. You said you liked Georgia's dogs.'

'I remember saying I liked Georgia's dogs, but—'

'—and then you asked me to organise this.'

'I didn't!'

'What are you talking about? Of *course* you did.'

'I don't—I—this is awful. Did I really?' She didn't sound sure. She sounded scared. 'You must have got the wrong end of the stick.'

Sam was listening with his ears out on stalks. Maggie unrolled herself off her back and clawed her way onto his lap.

'You're really worrying me,' Robert was telling Mum. 'You've got gaping holes in your memory. You forget whole conversations.'

'I don't. I don't!' She stared up into his face. 'Do I?'

Poor Mum. She feared losing her memory because her father lost his. It started with small things and gradually got worse. He turned into a broken old man when he wasn't even old. She used to say he rotted away.

'You're secretly relieved they've gone,' said Robert. 'You know you are. Admit it.'

Sam had an awful, awful thought. Snoops and Bouncer weren't loafing on the hearthrug. He put Maggie off his lap and ran outside into the darkness, pulling on his wellies in the porch. He ran all over the yard in the rain, calling for his friends. They weren't in their favourite rainy-day spot—the hessian sacks in the tractor shed. They weren't in the barns. Their kennel doors were hanging open. No dogs.

He started to cry, stumbling back into the kitchen without taking off his wellies, tracking mud and wet leaves across the floor. He was panting with so much running and shouting and crying.

'Where are they?' he demanded.

Mum looked at Robert as though it was his job to answer. He smiled down at Sam. *Big* smile.

'Mate, they're working dogs.'

'No, they're not. Bouncer is retired and Snoops is scared of sheep.'

'Well, I have a supplier at Jackson's who's farming sheep and beef organically. He came and collected them first thing this morning. They were born and bred to work. They'll be much happier.'

'Bring them back!' yelled Sam. He kicked off his left boot and it flew across the kitchen, scattering mud. Maggie grabbed it and started chewing.

'It's okay, Sam,' said Mum.

'It's not okay! Bring them back, bring my dogs back!' He was shrieking at the top of his voice. It left him hoarse. When he kicked off the second boot, it spun fast and low and hit a cupboard door, right next to where Robert was standing. It only just missed his leg.

'Hey, hey! Steady!' Robert was still smiling. Santa devil. He looked at Mum. 'Are we going to let him act like this?'

Sam lost it. He grabbed a kitchen chair and—*crash*—hurled it at the ground. Then another one. He heard Mum pleading with him to stop, but there was nothing in his head except the need to smash things. He spotted a paper packet of flour on the table, along with sugar and cocoa—Robert's bloody cooking, they always had to be so bloody grateful—so he grabbed it in both hands and hurled it onto the floor. The bag burst, flour billowed out across the tiles. Then the sugar—*wham*—then the dark brown cocoa—*bam*—and all the time he was screaming as though someone had stabbed him. He had Robert's very posh electronic kitchen scales above his head and was ready to smash those too when Robert grabbed him, took the scales away and grasped both his arms really hard. It hurt. Robert was muttering in his ear, *Oh no, you don't, you little bastard*.

The mess was shocking, even to Sam. Flour and sugar and cocoa and mud. Mum was crying. Sam was crying. Maggie squatted down and peed in the cocoa powder, a yellow stream spreading through all the other chaos.

'Pleased with yourself?' asked Robert.

Mum ran into the laundry. He heard the whoosh of taps, the clunk of the tin bucket they used for mopping.

Robert bent down to Sam's level, looking him in the eye.

'Why do you do this kind of thing, Sam? Why? You're making your poor mum sad.'

'I'm not! I'm not, you are!'

'Listen. Can't you hear her? She's crying her eyes out. You did that.'

'She's sad because you sold Snoops and Bouncer.'

'I tried to do a nice thing. It's *your* reaction that's made everything go wrong. *You* are the problem. You could have been pleased with such a sweet puppy, you could have just behaved like a normal child and played with Maggie, you could have made your mum happy. But you chose to be a selfish little twat.'

'I didn't.' But Sam wasn't so sure now.

'You're ruining her life. You're making her ill. Is that what you want?'

No, he didn't want to make Mum ill. If she was ill she might die. All he wanted was his dad back, his dogs back, everything back—just the way they used to be. What he got was Robert's craggy face six inches away. What he got was Mum, who always tried to be so cheerful, crying as she blundered about in the laundry. He felt as though she hated him. He felt as worthless as he ever had in the whole eleven years of his life.

Robert took Maggie back to Georgia that same night. They never had a dog again. The house seemed lifeless and lonely without any animals, and it was all Sam's fault.

After that day things went from bad to worse. Sam was the problem. Sam was always the problem.

•

The homeless guy. The scientist, teacher, gambler. He said he was going outside to look after the dogs, but as the seconds pass the truth dawns on Sam. Half the Met will be right outside that door, armed with assault rifles, or submachine guns, or whatever. That's why they've turned out the streetlights. Neil has opened the door for them; he's made it easy. Right now, he'll be telling them exactly where Sam is standing. He's fallen for it hook, line and sinker.

This is it, then. He faces the door, raises the gun to his shoulder. It's over. He's living the last seconds of his life. The safety catch is on and his finger is nowhere near the trigger—hasn't been since this morning—but they can't know that. Whoever is first through that door will be a brave person, someone's father or mother or son or daughter. When they see him ready and aiming at head height, they'll shoot him dead. They'll have to. They'll have no choice. Saves him finding the courage to do it himself.

He can hear Mutesi and Abi beating a hasty retreat down the back of the café, like people do when you're lighting fireworks. From the sound of their footsteps he'd guess they're heading into the toilet. They're not stupid. They know what's coming and they don't want to be caught by a stray bullet. Good. He's glad they've had the sense to get clear.

He can hear Neil chatting away to the dogs, out in the darkness and rain. Chatting, chatting. It's part of the ruse. They'll have told him to keep talking while they get into position. Still, Sam likes the kindness in his voice.

'Go on, you two,' he says. 'Get out of here . . . no, *that* way, you daft animal. You too, little fluffball, go on. Bye bye. C'mon Buddy, let's get you inside. You're all wet, you poor old boy! That was a long cup of tea, wasn't it? I'm sorry. I'm sorry, mate.'

Sam hopes they finish him off fast with a volley of shots, like Butch Cassidy and the Sundance Kid. That brilliant final freeze frame shows them in the split second before they die. They're still whole and young and alive, fighting their way out of trouble, immortalised in a bright moment of hope. They won't ever grow old or face the long dark days of failure. They'll never be prisoners. Sam wouldn't mind an end like theirs.

The street door is opening inwards now. Sam clamps his teeth together, forcing the stock into his shoulder to keep the barrel under control. He's waiting for the shouts and smashing of glass, the fusillade of bullets. He's committing suicide at last.

But there is no onslaught. Just Neil's quiet voice.

'It's me, Sam. Okay? Yeah? It's Neil. For God's sake, don't shoot me, will you? I'm coming back in now.'

Slowly, slowly, his bearded face inches around the door until he's looking straight into Sam's sights.

'Mate,' he says, almost without moving his lips. 'That makes me pretty nervous.'

As soon as Sam has lowered his gun, Neil slides back inside, leading a dog by the collar. 'C'mon, Buddy, it's okay, you're allowed.'

It's that grey dog Sam glimpsed this morning. Enormous paws. Perhaps he's got some Irish wolfhound in him. He's holding his tail low and sticking very close to Neil's legs, nearly wrapping himself around them. Both man and dog are dripping wet.

Sam breathes again, though his pulse is roaring in his ears. He can't quite believe he's still alive. Neil has shut the door again. He's trying to lock it too, but his fingers are trembling and he fumbles at the bolts, so Abi comes running to do it for him. Then she helps him to push the tables back into place. Everything is done in silence.

The dog gives himself a shake—droplets flying—looking up into Neil's face. Bouncer and Snoops used to gaze adoringly up at Dad like that. Time is playing tricks on Sam today. He's in a kaleidoscope, jumbling past and present, tumbling memories into crazed new patterns.

'Thanks, Abi.' Neil drops his hand onto her shoulder. '*Whew.* Lordy, lordy, that was a mission. Everyone, meet Buddy.'

These words are greeted by cries of welcome from the two women. Mutesi brings a towel from the bathroom, and Abi throws herself on one knee to dry the dog's wet fur. 'Hi, Buddy, aren't you gorgeous? Were you cold out there, hey, were you?'

It's all a bit over the top, a bit unreal. Abi doesn't strike him as the gushing type. Probably never behaved like this before in her life. He reckons it's relief, because she and Mutesi were braced for World War III to break out. There's a shimmer of hysterical celebration in the air, and he's being carried on it. He can't believe Neil walked out of here, got his dog, came back alone and barricaded the door again. He didn't have to come back. Why did he do that?

Mutesi has filled a plate for Buddy: sausages and ham sandwiches. Food—and tea, of course—is that woman's go-to, fix-it remedy for every problem. Sam's ready to bet the old folks in her care are never hungry for a single minute. He bets she force-feeds grieving relatives sugary tea and biscuits when their dad or mum dies. He bets they love her for it. He wishes she'd been with him when he heard his own mum had died.

'Is he allowed these things?' she asks Neil.

'Mutesi, my friend—' Neil gives a gentle little tug to Buddy's ear '—this fella eats out of dustbins. He'll worship you like a goddess if you give him a feast like that.'

He's right. The dog wolfs up his meal in double-quick time and licks the empty plate, shoving it around with his nose.

'Are they out there?' asks Sam.

Neil blinks innocently. He really is a terrible liar.

the phone from Abi, typing a short reply as best he can with his shaking fingers.

All ok here will call soon

Mutesi brings him the promised mug of tea. Then she sinks into a leather armchair nearby, pulling her cardigan close around her, complaining that the room is getting colder.

'What did you mean?' Sam asks her. 'About the men who killed?'

She cradles her own mug close to her chest. 'Oh, just some men.'

'Who though?'

'Leave it, mate,' warns Neil.

'I only—'

'No, really,' says Neil. 'Let it go. I don't think you've got any idea what you're asking.'

There's an edge to his voice, a bossiness that doesn't match the way he keeps getting tearful. Sam can see the school teacher in him now. What's he fussing about? Mutesi is just a cuddly grandmother, for God's sake. She's wearing a cardigan, she sings gospel hymns and fusses over people's little cuts and bruises. She makes endless pots of tea. How disturbing can her memories be?

Neil lays his hand on a radiator.

'You're right, Mutesi! This is cooling down. The café would normally be closed by now, and the central heating will be on a timer. I'll have a look in the back kitchen, shall I? See if I can find the override. I should be out there in the rain selling *Big Issues* at this time of day, freezing my bollocks off.'

As Neil mentions the back room, he glances at Abi. Fleetingly, Sam wonders whether he could be trying to communicate something—but, no, that's impossible. Abi and Neil have never met before today, so they can't have any dark secrets. Sam has been into the back kitchen; he helped install some equipment when Mum and Robert first bought Tuckbox. He's certain there's no outside door or window.

'Go on then, Neil,' he says. 'Crank the temperature right up, let's make a sauna in here. Robert's estate can pay the electricity bill.'

'Um, who?'

'A load of guys with rifles.'

'Oh, right,' says Neil, rubbing his nose. 'Nah, I didn anything like that. They're down the street. Police cars things. Pretty sure I could smell burgers too; they're m a night of it. They've got lights set up. Those other two headed for them.'

What a whopper. Sam's guess is that Neil was able to sig somebody much, much closer, maybe even have a quick con tion. Makes it all the more amazing that he came back.

'Thanks,' he says, and then he finds he's swaying, b some kind of a reaction is setting in. He grabs a chai down hard. The room's spinning. He can't stop his teeth chattering.

'Now you know how it feels!' That's Abi's voice, a doesn't sound at all sympathetic. 'Thinking you're about t bullet in the face. Not nice, is it?'

'Tea,' says Mutesi. She's already pottering off to make

Buddy ambles over, and Sam reaches down to rub hi It feels comforting. He's missed having a dog. He sits for time, just touching Buddy's damp fur.

'This should have charged up a bit by now,' says Abi, up the café phone. She presses buttons and soon the listening to a flourish of electronic music as it fires up, f by the single *ping* of a text.

'Message from Eliza,' says Abi. 'Those two dogs Di Bella are safe and well, already reunited with their ghastly I can picture the scene. Renata will dine out on this for r She keeps reading. 'And Eliza wants to know how you'r Sam. I think she's hinting that she'd like you to call them

He doesn't want to start talking to Eliza again. Later but not quite yet. He feels overwhelmed by what's just hap facing what he thought was certain death, and finding still alive. He needs a bit of time to get his head together.

There are crow's feet around Neil's eyes, and they deepen when he smiles. He heads off with Buddy padding alongside him. That old dog is not going to let his master out of his sight again. They shouldn't be sleeping rough, thinks Sam. It's wrong.

Once they've gone, Mutesi stretches out her legs and starts humming under her breath. He likes being near her. Some people make him jittery, others are just naturally calming. Mutesi's one of those. He can feel his heartbeat slow down just because she's sitting there, blowing on her tea and humming to herself. She's . . . what's the word? Sturdy. He doesn't mean physically. She's certainly not wasting away, but it's not what he means. She's sturdy to her core.

'Sam,' she says. 'Your mother. Did she pass away not long ago?'

'She did.'

She murmurs *eee*, and does her tongue-clicking thing. To Sam, this seems to mean more than just sympathy; it's expressing disapproval of what a complete bastard life can be.

'Sorry.' She sighs with her whole body. 'Sorry, sorry.'

'Thanks.'

Mum seemed fine when he saw her last. Well, not fine. She was heartbroken because her husband and her son were almost coming to blows. Sam didn't know about the cancer then; he didn't know there was an evil alien growing inside her. Robert showed him the door, told him never to come back. *Ever.* So two evil aliens took his mother away.

'I didn't say goodbye,' he tells Mutesi.

'That is bad.'

Over by the counter, Abi's working out how to drive the coffee machine, turning knobs and frowning at dials. Neil and Buddy are back. The heavy fire door groans shut behind them, but it hasn't closed properly this time. Sam suspects the hinge is stuffed. Not his problem.

'Success!' Neil does a little jig and high-fives an imaginary person. 'Prepare for a sauna.'

'And an espresso.' Abi shoves a cup under the machine, flicks a switch, and—hey presto—there's a stream of something that looks and smells like coffee. Her green eyes light up.

'*Mwah!*' She's kissing her fingers like an Italian chef. 'I am a genius! Want some, Neil? Anyone?'

'No thanks,' says Neil. 'I'm about to taste my first ginger beer in years.'

Buddy's claws click on the concrete floor as he walks. Mutesi leans from her chair to stroke the dog's ears, crooning quietly to him while Abi brings her coffee and sits on the edge of the booth, facing outwards. She's not much older than he is. She's scary and impatient—and funny, and ballsy, and somehow angry. He thinks perhaps she and he could have been friends, if only he hadn't met her today, of all days. He feels as though he's known her for years.

He likes all three of these people. In fact, he's wondering whether he's got some kind of Stockholm syndrome but in reverse. It's *him* aligning with *them*, not the other way around. He certainly didn't foresee any of this when he drove away from Tyndale in the darkness this morning. He never dreamed he'd be having a mad tea party in an empty café with three complete strangers and a dog called Buddy.

He knows this time of peace can't last. It's an illusion. Killing someone is irrevocable. These people aren't his mates, they're his hostages. He keeps forgetting that. His head could be in some sniper's crosshairs right at this moment.

Well, so be it. I hope they get a clean shot.

'Um, Sam, this bloke Robert.' Neil has fetched himself a bottle of ginger beer out of a fridge, and is prising off the cap. 'He married your mum. Am I right?'

'Yep, he married her.'

'And then what?'

'It's complicated.'

Abi claps her hands together, startling everybody.

'Oh, come on, Ballard! We're none of us going anywhere, are we? And you've royally fucked up our day. All three of us had somewhere better to be. Except Neil, come to think of it. He would've just sloped off to the bookies and lost his shirt again.' She smiles at Neil. 'Anyway . . . I think you owe us an explanation.'

'I'm with Abi,' says Neil. 'That man over there on the floor? He died in my arms. The least you can do is tell me why.'

TWENTY-EIGHT

Eliza

Poor Ashwin is clumping up the stairs yet again. He's flagging. It's been a long day and Eliza knows he will have taken flak from all sides. It is he who's been trying to reassure the terrified Nicola Rosedale. He's been a conduit to the incident commander and tactical teams; he's had contact with witnesses and family members, absorbing their anger and fear and demands for action. He doesn't have the luxury of being cocooned in the negotiation room.

'Sick of those stairs?' asks Eliza.

'No need to go to the gym today, anyway. Okay, listen up.' He throws himself into a chair. 'The male who released the dogs? That was the rough sleeper Brigitte Uwase told us about. He tucked a note under the collar of the greyhound before encouraging it to head for the SFOs. The dog's owners have just found it.'

'That *is* resourceful.' Paul gives a low whistle of admiration. 'Using a dog to carry a message. Never come across that before.'

'And there's a bit of good news,' says Ashwin. 'He says they've got the café phone charging. Shouldn't be long now before we can re-establish contact.'

There's general relief in the negotiation room. Some minutes ago they sent a carefully worded text: *Hi Sam, the two dogs are fine and reunited with their owner. How are you doing in there? Have you got your phone charging?* But until now there's been no reply from Sam. Eliza and Paul have been brainstorming ways to get another phone into the café. No options looked at all easy.

Ashwin has a photocopy of Neil's note: several rows of neat handwriting, in what looks like green crayon.

Phone now charging. You're making progress. Sam calmer, has let Mutesi treat minor wound to his head. BUT still volatile, hyper alert, taking Ritalin.

NB! DO NOT storm the barricades at this stage. Let us talk to him.

NB! Nicola is in a cupboard in the back kitchen. Nervous but physically ok.

My ex-wife Heather Cunningham (now something else?) lives Bristol. If I don't come out of this, please inform her.

Neil Cunningham

'I hope the boss takes the man's advice,' says Eliza. 'No storming of any barricades.'

There's a thoughtful silence before Eliza's phone vibrates.

'Text from Sam,' she says, glancing at it. '*All ok here will call soon.*'

Ashwin laughs aloud. 'That's what I call a "sod off" text.'

'Really? Why?'

Ashwin's unwrapping a Twix bar.

'Because that's exactly what it means! My eldest daughter could have written that, especially at one o'clock in the morning when I'm nagging her about being late home from a party. It means: *Don't call me, I'll call you. Maybe. When I feel like it. Or maybe not. Sod off, Dad, you fussy, tubby old fool.*'

'What d'you do in that situation?' asks Eliza with genuine curiosity. 'I've got all this ahead of me.'

'I go and collect her anyway. I drive over there and knock on the door of wherever the party is and ask for Anita Anand, which makes me the most embarrassing wombat of a dad in the universe. I get a big telling-off all the way home.'

'Strong personality?'

'Oh yes. Anita rules our household.'

The three negotiators discuss their plan. Eliza's tempted to call Sam straight away, despite his sod-off text.

'We were really getting somewhere before his phone died,' she says. 'I don't want to lose momentum.'

Paul's reading their notes on the whiteboard. He seems completely relaxed.

'I'd suggest we hold off for another half hour,' he says. 'Give Sam some space, let him feel he's got some kind of control. I think he's blown a gasket today because of an overwhelming sense of disempowerment. Right? In his mind, Lacey has won every battle.'

'Until today,' says Eliza. 'Today, I'd say Robert Lacey has definitely come off worse.'

TWENTY-NINE

Sam

It took years for Robert to break down his mother and rebuild her in his own image, but he seemed to enjoy the journey. He liked to be God.

Selling poor Bouncer and Snoops into slavery seemed to be a decisive victory for him. He got away with it and sowed the seed in Mum's mind that her brain might be going the same way as her father's. From then on he began to do pretty much whatever he wanted. He was still keeping up his Santa Claus act, but the devil began to show its pointed teeth. And for every incident Sam saw, every nasty comment he heard, there must have been a hundred that he didn't.

The practical changes came first. The whole house was re-decorated, the furniture exchanged for newer, fancier stuff. It wasn't Sam and Harriet's house anymore; it was Robert's. Pictures and ornaments ended up collecting cobwebs in the old milking shed, replaced by arty photos taken by Robert's trendy friends. Photographs of Dad or Granny were swapped for ones with Robert in them. He was photogenic, all right: white teeth, broad shoulders, that crinkly-eyed smile Aunt Monique used to drool over. He installed a snazzy chef's kitchen. Out with the old, in with the new. Out went the shabby cabinets with their peeling blue paint and drawers that stuck; out went the comfy yellow armchairs and the rag rug Sam had played on since he was a baby. In came stainless steel: a vast fridge, two sinks with a weird kind of tap like the proboscis of a giant insect. Black marble slabs covered all the surfaces, just like a morgue. The wall into the pantry was knocked down, making it all open-plan. Granny nearly fainted when she dropped by. She kept whispering *hideous, utterly hideous* under her breath.

Mum protested too, because the renovations involved an increase on the mortgage. She lost the argument. Of course she did. Remortgaging Tyndale Farm was part of Robert's dastardly plan. He was playing a long game.

The kitchen got plenty of use. Robert was always throwing spur-of-the-moment dinner parties and asking people around for drinks. *His* friends, of course. Not hers. Mum was his precious, perfect princess—until suddenly she wasn't.

'Are we piling on the pounds a bit?' he remarked one day, when she was wearing her favourite short-sleeved top. He jabbed her arm with his forefinger: *poke, poke, poke.* Sam saw the red marks on her skin.

'Ouch!' she yelped, rubbing her arm.

'I hardly touched you.' He laughed at her. 'Good grief, my love, you can be quite the drama queen, can't you?'

'You don't know your own strength.'

'For God's sake.' His laughter morphed into a scowl. It suddenly seemed colder in the room. 'Don't make this into something it isn't.'

She tried to suck her tummy in.

'D'you really think I've put on weight?'

He was still scowling. 'Best if I don't say any more. I'm in enough trouble.'

Mum looked perfect to Sam, but later he saw her standing on the bathroom scales, squinting down at the dial. She jumped off again with a muffled squeal as though there was a scorpion between her feet. She never wore that short-sleeved top again.

That was the start of her dieting, of Robert 'helping' her—controlling what she ate and even what she drank. There were no more sticky goodies from Jackson's. From then on he did all the shopping and every month he'd scan the credit card bill. *What's this? What's that?* He set goals for her weight loss. He gave her a gym membership for her birthday and exercised alongside her. He bought her fitness gear—not too figure-hugging, though, *because you're lovely, darling, but let's face it, you're no gym bunny.*

Sam saw her refusing apple pie on one of the rare occasions when she and Sam visited Granny. It was a shame, because Granny had made the pie especially.

'Robert's right,' Mum told her. 'I've let myself go. I need to try harder.'

'Why?'

'It's not fair on him.'

Granny's left eyebrow shot way up. 'On *him*?'

'He has to look at me.'

'He's bloody lucky to be able to look at you.'

But Mum wouldn't budge, so Granny cut Sam a simply enormous piece of pie and poured on about a pint of custard, heavy yellow folds concertinaing onto his plate. She looked thin herself; her cheeks didn't have that lovely granny-ish bloom anymore.

It was several years before Sam began to suspect that Robert had been messing with the bathroom scales to trick Mum into thinking she was heavier than she really was. He once caught his stepfather sitting on the edge of the bath with the scales on his knees, fiddling with the dial. Robert smiled when he saw Sam watching. He said he was fixing them. He probably *was* fixing them, but not in a good way.

It wasn't long before he started controlling what Sam ate too. Things disappeared from the cupboard. Random things. No more cheese strings. No more crisps or pasta or sausage rolls—Sam loved sausage rolls, they made him happy. No more popcorn, for God's sake.

'Why can't I have cheese strings?' he complained. 'I always have them in my lunchbox on a Friday.'

'They're processed rubbish,' said Robert. 'Make you hyperactive. You're like a flea in a box.'

Mum was cleaning the oven, kneeling on the floor and wearing yellow rubber gloves.

'Couldn't he have a cheese string once a week?' she asked. 'They're not so bad, are they?'

The words weren't out of her mouth before he was rounding on her.

'Really, Harriet? *Really?*'

'I just think we need to be a bit flexible. They've always been Sam's Friday treat—his little reward for getting through the week. He loves his cheese strings.'

Robert looked as though he couldn't believe her treachery. 'We agreed about this!'

'When?'

'Are you serious?'

She was kneeling at Robert's feet. Sam didn't like that; he wanted her to get up off the floor and tell him to pack his bags and sod off out of their house.

'Do you realise how often you undermine me?' he demanded furiously. 'It's incredibly destructive.'

'I didn't mean to undermine you. I'm just wondering—'

'Oh, come on.'

'No, really, I promise. I—'

'You do it constantly!' Suddenly he was shouting. 'You do it all the time! All the bloody time!'

Mum covered her face with her yellow-gloved hands, rocking backwards and forwards.

'Robert, please,' she whispered.

He took a breath, held it in for a long time, let it out. When he spoke again, his voice was super-calm. Super-angry-calm. That was worse than the yelling.

'Now you're making me out to be an ogre. Seems pretty unfair when all I'm trying to do is help your son. I just can't win, can I?'

'I'm sorry. You're right. I'm so sorry.'

It was like a magic password. As soon as she'd apologised, he pulled her to her feet and kissed her really hard on the mouth. It didn't seem like a happy kiss to Sam. He couldn't believe she'd just said sorry when he was the one in the wrong.

'It's all for you,' he muttered in her ear. 'Everything, everything. My whole life. It's all for you.'

'They're just cheese strings,' whined Sam. 'They're not some kind of deadly poison.'

'Sammy, shush. Robert knows about nutrition.' Mum's voice was firm, but her face wasn't. She looked as though she was about to be sick.

She never bought cheese strings again. There were no more Friday treats. No more treats at all, in fact, unless Robert provided them.

It was around this time that Robert introduced the homework rule: Sam had to do sixty minutes of homework in his bedroom every night. He wasn't allowed to skip it, ever. Robert said he needed structure and routine, and would thank him one day. He was wrong about that. Sam never did thank him.

Those miserable years are jumbled in Sam's mind. He was about twelve when Robert killed Sundance. Mum and Sam went away for a weekend with the school soccer team and came home to an empty stable. According to Robert, Sundance had been in agony with colic. The vet thought he was suffering, that it was bound to keep recurring, he was very old and it would be kindest to euthanise him. The death sentence had been carried out straight away. Sundance had already been shipped off to a furnace somewhere. All done and dusted—literally. Sam's remaining childhood friend had been his calm, apple-munching self when Mum and he had left on Friday; now he'd been turned to dust. Like Dad. Just dust.

Granny, Mum and Sam stood at the stable door and cried their eyes out.

'Robert killed him,' said Sam.

Of course Mum protested. 'It was the colic. He's as upset as we are.'

'Robert killed Sundance,' Sam repeated stubbornly, and he added a silent promise to himself. *One day I'm going to kill Robert.*

After Sundance died, Sam threw in the towel. Nothing seemed to matter anymore. Darkness filled his heart and his head. He stopped playing soccer because he couldn't be bothered. He didn't want to be in the band with Jake. He gave up any pretence of trying at school. As the months passed and he became a teenager, he went from bad to worse: throwing things around in class, getting into fights, never doing his homework (despite Robert's stupid rule) and—most maddening for the teachers—staring out of the window for hours at a time. Mum hated going to parent–teacher meetings because it was one bitter complaint after another. She said she might as well wear a T-shirt with SAM BALLARD'S MOTHER on the front and YES, I KNOW, I'M REALLY, REALLY SORRY on the back.

One awful day, Sam accidentally broke Jake's brand-new Gameboy. It was par for the course, he was always breaking things, and he was mortified. Jake seemed to think it was the last straw. He shouted that he was sick of Sam and he'd never lend him anything ever again. Then he stomped off to the soccer pitch to play British Bulldog.

Jake was Sam's only close friend. Other people hung out with him because they thought he was a rebel and they had a ghoulish kind of interest in what hare-brained mistake he was going to make next. Many of his classmates looked like men by now and were already chasing girls; Sam was a scrawny runt for his age and—secretly—still enjoyed playing with Lego. Jake knew all this, yet he was prepared to be Sam's friend. Until now.

It was all too much. Sam was worn out by the darkness inside him. He was worn out by the loneliness. He felt as though darkness and loneliness had hollowed him out. For the first time in his life—but not the last—he seriously thought it would be lovely to be dead. Death sounded like a wonderful, peaceful holiday destination. He wanted to go on that holiday.

He trudged down to the boys' changing room in the basement, thinking he might hang himself from one of the coat hooks. The room smelled of sweaty socks and testosterone. He spent ages trying to make a noose out of his tie. He was picturing all the details of his funeral: Jake would be sorry about yelling, and Mum would be sorry she'd married Robert. Robert would deliver a moving eulogy with one hand resting lovingly on Sam's coffin. He'd cry, but there would be a grin on his other face. He would have won.

Sam abandoned his noose and began pulling every coat off every peg. He threw people's soccer boots down the toilets and slammed hockey sticks into the wall, making bits of white plaster and green paint fly around. He emptied lunchboxes and stamped on pots of yoghurt, which splattered under his feet. He turned on the taps in the basins and put in the plugs. Finally, he found a red marker pen in someone's smashed pencil case and wrote *FUCK LIFE* all over the walls.

He began to regret his five minutes of madness even before it was over. He wasn't nearly as much of a rebel as he pretended to be. He wanted the teachers to like him—he wanted everyone to like him, and was constantly perplexed that they seemed to find him annoying. He was horrified when he saw how much mess he'd made. He slunk out of the room, felt sick and cold-sweaty all through maths, especially when he remembered about leaving the taps on. He imagined a teacher's feet splashing through a lake on the floor.

His nightmare came true when a runner arrived with a note. The maths teacher read it and delivered the dreadful summons without even glancing in his direction.

'Sam Ballard! Head's office. Now.'

His knees nearly gave way as he left the room. There was a buzzing in his head, the sound of fear. The headmistress was a terrifying dictator called Miss Stephanie Hodgson, one of the youngest secondary school heads in the country—not that anyone thought of her as young. She was ageless, like dragons and gods, with a superhuman ability to teleport. She was always immaculately turned out: a helmet of black hair, little glasses with green rims. She made Sam feel like a lump of Play-Doh.

So there was Miss Hodgson behind her desk, melting Sam with her death stare. His dean was there too, though he hardly said a word. They sat Sam down in a chair. His feet didn't even reach the ground.

'Someone has done a lot of damage in the boys' changing room,' Miss Hodgson began. 'Anything you want to tell us about that?'

He fidgeted and stared at the floor. He was curling up, a leaf in a bonfire just before it catches flame.

'Really, Sam? Nothing at all?'

When he still didn't confess, she sighed and showed him the CCTV footage. He wished he could spontaneously combust. The quality wasn't great: the camera must have been high up, and only recorded a few frames a second, but he couldn't deny that the skinny vandal chucking stuff around and leaping up and down on lunchboxes was him. He was blubbing before it had played right through. His nose was running. He kept trying to wipe it on his sleeve.

'You've committed a serious criminal offence,' said Miss Hodgson, handing him a tissue from a box on her desk. 'I hope you understand that, Sam. I may have to call the police.'

No, no, no, no, no! Police meant prison, and he'd never forgotten what Aunt Monique had told him about prison. He would have given his right hand to go back in time, pretend he was too ill for school and stay safe under his Superman duvet.

They'd already phoned Mum and asked her to come in. She did—still in her work clothes, mud under her fingernails, shock in her voice. Her frizzy hair was a marked contrast to Miss Hodgson's sleek bob. She brought Robert with her and the first thing he did was stride across to lay a fatherly hand on Sam's shoulder. Sam muttered *geroff* and squirmed out of his grasp.

'It's not been easy,' said Robert, giving Miss Hodgson one of his rueful smiles. White teeth. 'As you can see.'

They showed Mum and Robert the CCTV footage. Sam wouldn't look at it again. He spotted a Rubik's Cube on Miss Hodgson's desk—she'd probably confiscated it from some poor sod—and had an all-consuming urge to fiddle with it. Mum's mouth fell open as she watched her criminal son rampaging around the coat pegs. She kept chewing her knuckles and gasping, 'Sam, Sam—dear Lord, Sam, why?'

He couldn't say he'd done it because Jake was pissed off with him. That would have sounded lame. So he mumbled, 'Dunno.' Miss Hodgson said *dunno* wasn't good enough. Sam added, 'Because I hate school'—which didn't seem to go down very well either.

Robert seized his chance. At the time, Sam thought he was just being bossy and a know-all, but in the years since he's had a lot of time to think about Robert's way of operating. He had an agenda. He was a master of the art of control.

'Look, Stephanie,' he said. 'I think of this young man as my son. We're very close. But perhaps I can be that bit more objective than a mother can ever be—especially this particular mother?'

He reached across to Mum and took her hand. His fist imprisoned hers. 'Harriet's not made of iron, emotionally. I think she'll acknowledge that. Hm, Harriet?' He smiled at her, affectionate and anxious. It was the perfect imitation of a caring man. 'Since Angus died she's tried to compensate for the loss of his father by giving Sam every bit of herself. She's ignored his challenging behaviour. In fact . . . well, in fact she's rewarded it. Frankly . . .' He made a ducking movement, a soldier dodging a missile. 'Better get my tin hat on! Sorry, Harriet, but maybe it's time to be honest—frankly, she enables him.'

'So all of this is my fault?' asked Mum.

'Darling, it's not a question of blame.'

'I don't enable him.'

Robert was gazing earnestly at Miss Hodgson now, as though he and she were the only adults in the room.

'I haven't wanted to say this, but I think I must. I'm sure Sam has ADHD. Denying the problem isn't doing him any favours.'

The talk went on and on, but Sam stopped listening. He was doing the Rubik's Cube in his head. Eventually Miss Hodgson glanced at her watch and said she'd be meeting with the disciplinary committee, but for now Sam was suspended. She said she'd consult with the dean and his teachers about making a referral for assessment. She seemed to want to get the family out of her office. She stood up, shook hands, saw them to the door.

Three minutes later Sam was in the back of the car and in disgrace. Robert insisted on driving, as always. *You're not in any fit state, Harriet, you're a cat on a hot tin roof.* At first they sat in silence. Sam kept tugging on his seatbelt because it dug into his chest. He wished he had wings so he could fly out of the car window and never come back.

'What's up with *you*?' Robert was looking at Mum. His voice was deeper than the engine note. 'You're stewing on something.'

'I don't know, I just . . .'

'Spit it out.'

She pushed her hair back from her face. 'I wish you hadn't said that about me. That I'm weak, I reward bad behaviour. That I enable him. It was embarrassing.'

'Jesus Christ, not this again.'

'And the ADHD thing. We've talked about that! You know

I don't want him labelled or medicated. He's functioning, isn't he?'

Robert laughed sarcastically. 'You call his performance in that locker room functioning?'

'Okay, but that discussion was one for you to have *with* me, not with Stephanie Hodgson *about* me. I felt about five inches tall.'

She hadn't finished speaking before he was erupting like a volcano.

'What are you talking about? What are you . . .? Jesus Christ! I can't say anything at all, can I? I have to watch every word. You take everything the wrong way.'

'That's just not fair.'

'You're creating a monster out of that child!' he snarled. 'He plays you like a bloody violin. Listen to me, Harriet—are you listening? It is *not normal*. People are always telling me so, people who care about you.'

'Who said that?'

Robert was gritting his teeth as he hunched over the wheel. There wasn't a trace of the calm, caring husband who'd sucked up to Miss Hodgson twenty minutes earlier.

'Who said that about me?' asked Mum again.

He muttered, 'Fuck this,' changed down a gear, revved the engine and pulled out to overtake a long line of cars. The poor engine was screaming its head off.

'Please pull back in,' Mum said. And then, a few seconds later, 'You can't see round that corner.' And then, 'Get back in, get back in, please get back in!'

They were hurtling towards the corner when a van appeared right in front of them. Mum screamed, 'Oh my God!' as Robert slammed on the brakes and swerved to the left. Someone honked—*baaam!*—Robert stuck up his middle finger, the van flashed its lights, Sam's seatbelt jerked against his chest and he bellowed, 'Ow!'

Robert kept driving. There was one of those terrible silences when you can hear people wanting to scream at one another and you feel crushed by all the anger. It lasted until Robert raised both his hands and smashed them back down onto the wheel.

'And here we go, yet again. Jesus fucking Christ, I can't take much more!'

'You might have killed us,' said Mum. 'You almost did.'

'I could see perfectly well. I could see *perfectly well*! Okay? It was a safe manoeuvre until you started squawking like a fucking banshee. You're nuts, Harriet, you're fucking nuts! I can't go on like this; it's like walking across a minefield every single minute of every day.'

Sam had never heard anyone shout so loud. They were turning into a lane near the farm now, the one with the high hedges. Driving along here always reminded him of the night they followed the ambulance with Dad in it.

'Who says I'm not normal?' asked Mum for the third time.

'Never mind. Forget it, for God's sake.'

'I do mind.'

'Please, *please*, give me a break. No more drama. You're tearing us apart.'

'But who says it?'

Robert looked at Sam in the driver's mirror. Their eyes met for several seconds, and Sam was sure he saw Robert smile at him. Then he came out with it: the nastiest, most poisonous lie of all time.

'Okay, if you must know, it was Angus who said that about you.'

'*Angus?*'

'Among others.'

'Angus would never have said that.'

'I'm afraid he did. He used to phone me and pour out his troubles. He was worried sick about the way you encourage Sam's behaviour. Letting him get up all hours of the night, letting him run riot, taking his side no matter what he—'

'That's a lie,' cried Sam from the back seat. 'Dad never said any of that to you.'

Robert swung around the corner into the yard, bouncing over potholes. He pulled on the handbrake even before the car had properly stopped. Sam's seatbelt jerked again.

'I'm sorry,' he said, 'but it's true. I hoped never to have to tell you this. Angus wasn't sure how much longer he could stick around.'

•

Mum waited until Robert had gone back to work before locking herself in the bathroom and phoning Granny. Sam heard, *Hello, Patricia?* He loitered close to the bathroom door but couldn't catch much of the conversation: just the murmur of talking, listening, talking again. The gist of it seemed to be that Mum was telling Granny he'd trashed the changing room and been suspended from school. His ears burned with shame.

But then he heard Robert's name, and that word again—*enable.* He felt more hopeful. He knew Granny would take his side.

Mum's voice grew suddenly louder: *This isn't about Robert!* And a few seconds later: *I should have known you'd turn this into a Robert-hating fest.* Finally, a curt: *Okay. Bye.*

There was a long, long silence before Sam heard a high-pitched moan, as though poor Mum had an awful stomach ache. He expected her to unlock the door, and was poised to dart off into his room, but she didn't. The basin taps were turned on, and off.

Then she was speaking again. Sam was determined to hear this time, so he jammed his ear hard up against the door. Her voice was lifeless.

Hello, it's me. Hi. Look, um, I'm just so sorry. I think I must be losing my mind.

She was talking to *him*. She'd rolled over. She was giving him everything he wanted. Total capitulation.

I know. I'm so sorry. I can't express how sorry. Yes, I promise. Yes, I do promise.

Sam wasn't savvy about the ways of the world, but the sound

of his mother grovelling to that man was one of the most terrifying things he had ever heard. It made a shiver go up his spine, quite literally. The devil puppet had hold of all their strings, and was making them dance.

•

'He's still pulling my strings,' Sam says now. 'He's dead on that floor, but I'm still dancing.'

'Your grandmother couldn't help?' asks Mutesi.

'She tried her best. He stopped her coming over, but she used to sneak in at break times to see me at school, just to make sure I was all right. When I was about fourteen, she went on some kind of yoga retreat in India. She was only meant to be away three months but she died there. The letter we got said it was a very aggressive virus. A broken heart, I think.'

Mutesi seems to listen to Sam with all her own heart, as though she's in her kitchen with a troubled grandson yabbering on. He can't decide whether she's forgiven him for aiming a shotgun at her this morning, or whether she's just clever at pretending. Meanwhile Abi kneels straight-backed like Buddha, perched on the vinyl seat. There's something hypnotic about her green cat's eyes. Sometimes a vertical furrow appears between them.

Neil has lowered himself awkwardly down onto the floor near to Abi with his left hand resting on Buddy's head. He says he's used to sitting on the ground, but Sam is pretty sure his knee is aching, or maybe his hip, or maybe both. Neil has one of those faces that betray everything he's thinking or feeling. He'd be rubbish at poker—no wonder he's such a loser when it comes to gambling. Some parts of Sam's story have his mouth twitching, some almost make him cry. He's a softie. No wonder he just about had a breakdown when he was teaching. The kids at Sam's school would have made mincemeat out of him.

The bit about Sam vandalising the changing room has him chuckling.

'Did you flood the place?' he asks.

'No, 'cos the water went down the overflow. I was lucky.'

'Didn't you know they had CCTV?'

'I forgot.'

'Oops.'

'Yeah. Oops. I ended up being assessed by a shrink. Robert insisted on coming along, of course, got in his side of the story. The next thing I know I'm taking Ritalin.'

Neil seems interested. He must have come across plenty of toe-rags in his classroom.

'Oh yes? Did Ritalin help you?'

'Put it this way: the stuff didn't transform my life like it does for some people. I could concentrate better maybe, but it gave me stomach aches, made me feel like an engine over-revving. I stopped taking it regularly as soon as I got out from under Robert's thumb.'

'But you're taking it today?'

'I use it every now and again, when I really need my wits about me.' Sam pulls the packet from his pocket. Only a couple of pills left. 'Like now.'

'So what happened after you were suspended from school?' asks Abi.

'After that . . . years and years of *him*.' Sam turns to look towards Robert. His stepdad's presence is all-pervasive. 'He got away with murder.'

Abi's frowning. It deepens the crease on her forehead. 'Just to be clear: are you suggesting he *literally* got away with murder? D'you believe Robert killed your father before marrying your mother?'

'Hamlet,' murmurs Neil. He leans down to pull something out of Buddy's fur.

He turned me into dust, insisted Dad in Sam's dreams. They were just dreams, of course, but they were so very vivid. They still haunt him. As for Mum, Robert certainly did destroy her. He turned her into grey dust before Sam's very eyes.

'Depends what you mean by murder,' he says.

'Come on!' Abi smacks her hand onto the table. 'I mean deliberate and unlawful killing.'

She wants concrete answers and she wants them right now. She's a bit like Miss Hodgson. It's not that easy, though. How can he describe such a slow, creeping kind of destruction? How can he make them understand? Years of drip-drip-drip, thousands of poison-tipped darts. Things said *to* Mum, things said *about* her, jokes which made all their friends laugh at her. Humiliating little digs, while he stroked her neck and smiled into her eyes like a snake, gently hissing, *Shhh, my love, you're making a fool of yourself.* Love and gifts one day, contempt and boredom the next. Sometimes he'd make a casual reference to her age: she was five years older and he never let her forget it. Or it might be a flick of his gaze up and down the outfit she'd carefully chosen. *Oh dear, my darling, what's happened there?* And most common of all: *It was a joke, Harriet! What's happened to your sense of humour?*

It worked. As the years passed, Mum stopped being Mum. She wasn't curvy and fun with crazy curls, she didn't loaf around in her gardening jeans. She didn't sing in the shower or thunder around the house, and if she laughed it could only be at one of Robert's jokes. She turned into a tiptoeing wisp of a woman with short hair and expensive clothes that she wore uncertainly, as though she'd stolen them from someone else's wardrobe. She even spoke carefully, testing the effect on Robert of each word. If he didn't seem happy she would immediately shut up. He suffocated her life force, drained away all her colour until there was just this obedient, anxious, Mum-shaped shadow left. By the time the cancer came there was nothing left for her to cling to.

As she diminished, Sam began to grow up. He finally got a growth spurt. His voice dropped almost overnight, which was a hell of a shock. He gave away all his puppets except Robert-devil-Santa, which he burned in the Rayburn. At the age of fourteen he was expelled from the church youth group after Donna Davies and he were caught half-dressed in a barn at the annual picnic. He changed mentally too. The darkness and loneliness never quite left him, but he gave up on trying to save Mum. He could see that was hopeless. Instead, he began to obsess about how soon he could leave home.

After turning fifteen he joined the local clay bird club, retrieved Dad's twelve-bore from Mr Appleton's safe, and applied for his own shotgun licence. He knew he was a good shot. He was just seven when Dad let him have a go with his own old .410. First time out, Sam hit all the tin cans they'd lined up along the fence. Dad whistled in amazement.

'You've got the knack, son! Your grandpa would be proud.'

Each week they moved a few paces further away from the cans. One morning Sam graduated to clays—smooth flying saucers that shattered in mid-air if you got it right. That was wonderful, but Sam's favourite bit of the day was cleaning their guns afterwards, sitting side by side at the table in the laundry. Father and son talked as they took them apart, then oiled and cleaned and reassembled them. Sam used to make the job last as long as possible. He revelled in the mingled smells of gun oil, Dad's instant coffee, the clean starchiness of clothes hanging on the airer.

'Was Grandpa a nice man?' he asked.

'Very.' Dad was rubbing walnut oil into the stock of his twelve-bore. The wood seemed to come alive under his fingers. Sam loved the intricate metalwork, the oval plate engraved with Grandpa's initials: *JHB*. 'He and I used to sit at this same table to clean these same guns. We used this cleaning rod, these brushes, the same type of oil. If he was here now he'd be telling all manner of tall tales.'

Sam took great pride in his cleaning. When he'd finished, Dad would hold the .410 up to the window, squint down the barrel and say, 'Look at that—beautiful job. Not a speck.' He'd slide both guns into their canvas cases and lock them in the metal gun safe. Then he would hide the key, even from Sam.

So when Sam reclaimed the twelve-bore from Mr Appleton, it felt like being reunited with an old friend. He sensed his father's and grandfather's touch on the smooth metal and wood; rested his own fingers in the grooves worn by theirs. Both those men had cleaned it at the same table, kept it in the same case and the same safe. As he carried out those rituals he felt a connection with them.

One morning he woke up to hear a flaming row going on downstairs. Mum and Robert. It sounded as though she was standing up for herself for once, and *that* Sam had to hear. He was well into his teens now, taller and lankier, so it was trickier to be invisible. He rolled out of bed and sneaked as far as the top stair. Robert was employing his usual tactic: attack as a form of defence.

'I can't believe you'd invade my privacy! Reading my texts? Scrolling through my—Jesus Christ, you must have used my password! How could you, Harriet? I don't know what's going on with you.'

She sounded timid but desperate, like a mouse trying to stand up to a cat.

'But who are they from?'

'How the bloody hell should I know? I get texts from customers, from staff, from suppliers, from all kinds of random people. That phone is a tool of my trade.'

'What about this one? *Thanks for last night. You are a magician*. And there's a winky face. What does that mean?'

Robert swore again. There was a pause, maybe while he looked at the screen. When he spoke again, he sounded much calmer.

'Okay.' He even chuckled. 'Okay, okay. Yup. I can see how that could be taken the wrong way, if you're a bit paranoid. I'd guess this message came from an octogenarian called Joan.'

'Joan who?'

'Brightwell, I think. Might be Bothwell. Something ending in *well*. She's talking about a fudge sundae I made for her eightieth birthday party at Jackson's. We had sparklers, the whole restaurant singing "Happy Birthday" when I carried it out. Joan was delighted—said it was the work of a magician. She's a real character. A bit flirtatious.'

'An eighty-year-old woman sent you a personal text?'

'Why not? Eighty is the new sixty. You can phone and ask her if you don't want to trust me. Go on. Be my guest.'

'No need for that.' Mum's voice had less conviction now. 'Well . . . but there's this other person, you've just got her in your contacts as "G". There are lots from her. *See you this evening honey kiss kiss kiss . . . How about a rematch, three question marks, kiss kiss kiss*. And you've replied to that: *I'm on my way*—with two exclamation marks. Here's another one from her: *Let's do coffee after lunch*—winky face—kisses. So . . . who is G?'

'This isn't sane.'

'If you could just put my mind at rest?'

'Hand over that phone again. Let's see . . . Ah!' Robert sounded amused. Not a hint of a guilty conscience. 'I thought so. Georgia. She talks to everyone like that, calls the whole world "darling" and "honey". She scatters all written communication with kisses. It's an affectation.'

'Georgia is predatory.'

'Oh, come *on*, now you're being ridiculous. You know Georgia! She's larger than life, flirts with absolutely everyone, regardless of age or gender—but none of it means a thing. Customers love it. She's also my boss so I can't tell her to cool it. You're not going to get all jealous again, are you?'

Sam had pricked up his ears on hearing Georgia's name. He had an adolescent crush on the manager, with her hourglass figure and blonde-bombshell hair.

Mum had one last try. '*Coffee*—winky face? Winky face! What's she winking about?'

Robert's voice took on a dangerous edge. 'You tell me. You've obviously got some kind of sick idea.'

'Well . . .'

'You think it's a euphemism for sex. Is that what's on your mind? You think I'd risk my marriage and my career and self-respect for . . . Jesus Christ, Harriet! Georgia is on a detox diet. She drinks a disgusting herbal thing made of dandelion roots, which she calls "coffee". It's a running joke. The other staff and I have coffee, Georgia pretends to.'

'Oh.'

The wind had gone from Mum's sails. Robert had an answer to everything. He always did. Always. He was Mr Teflon.

'Satisfied?' he asked. 'It's so hurtful, Harriet. It's so destructive. Your jealousy's putting our marriage at risk. I'm really struggling. I think you need some kind of therapy.'

There were footsteps and murmurs. Sam knew Mum would be saying sorry. It was her catchphrase. She lived in a state of permanent apology. *Sorry, sorry, fucking sorry.* He left them to it and wandered off to get dressed, thinking about Georgia's throaty voice and low-cut blouses. She made a point of standing very close to Robert, and Sam had seen the creepy way he smiled at her. *Winky face.* There was no way Mum should be apologising.

•

As soon as she got back from work that day, Mum rolled up her sleeves and cleaned the whole house.

'Help me, Sam,' she said. 'I want to make everything perfect.'

He did help, though she did most of the work. She laid the table, cut flowers from the garden and arranged them in a vase. She changed the sheets on her and Robert's bed—Sam refused to wonder why she'd be doing that. She washed her hair and straightened it with the gadget Robert had bought her because he thought her curls were 'a bit over the top'. She put on an outfit she knew Robert liked: a red dress and strappy sandals. She even wore make-up, which was rare for her. Sam looked in through their bedroom door and saw her concentrating very hard as she brushed mascara onto her eyelashes.

She also made a Thai beef salad. He ate his in front of *Top Gear*, but she wanted to wait for Robert.

'He's not got an evening shift today,' she told Sam, opening a bottle of wine. 'So he should be back any minute.'

She sat at the kitchen table while she waited. Everything in the house was perfect except for her. She looked fake, with her magenta lipstick and straightened hair. She looked like someone else's mother.

Hours passed. She was still waiting. She tried calling Robert's phone but he didn't answer. For no good reason, she filled a bucket and mopped the kitchen floor. She mopped in every corner, moving things around to be sure to cover every inch of the kitchen and laundry. Then she sat down again and fidgeted. Every few minutes she checked her phone.

'Ring him again,' suggested Sam.

She reached for the phone, grimaced, put it down, picked it up. 'I don't want to annoy him.'

'Just ring him. You're worried.'

'I could, but . . . no. I'll wait a bit longer.'

At about nine o'clock she did try to call him again. He didn't answer, but a minute later a text arrived.

'Oh dear, he'll be very late.' She was tugging at strands of her hair. 'Held up at work after all. There's a party. The other chef's off sick.'

When Sam turned in, she was still drooping over the kitchen table with an untouched bottle of wine. Her hair had turned back to frizz, her dress was crumpled, her lipstick a smudgy disaster. Maybe she sat at the table all night, all dolled up. Waiting. Like a faithful hound.

Robert finally appeared the next morning. Sam was eating Weetabix and scowled at his stepfather when he whirled in—whistling, patting Mum on the bottom.

'Where were you?' she asked.

'Didn't you get my text?'

'I did, but—'

'I said I'd be late.'

'Late, yes, but you didn't come home at all.'

His smile was stuck on his face. Painted on, like the devil puppet's grin.

'Never mind,' he said, with a horrible kind of false calm. 'I'm home now.'

'What happened?'

'We were booked out all night, two big parties, and half the staff were off sick. Some kind of flu going around. We didn't get cleaned up till nearly two o'clock. I had a brandy with the team—they'd worked their arses off and we all wanted to unwind. It was too late to call you and I didn't want to take the risk of driving home. So I stopped in one of the bedrooms at Jackson's.'

'Was Georgia there?'

'She was around.'

'Did she have a drink too?'

'Jesus Christ.' He rubbed his face with both hands. 'Not this again.'

'But if you'd just talk to me, tell me what's going on . . .'

'I *am* talking. I'm talking right now. It's you who isn't listening. Look, Harriet, for the last time: I am not having an affair with my boss, or anyone else. I work late. I work in hospitality. I work with all kinds of people, it's the nature of my job. This is all in your mind. Are you really going to let your delusions drive us apart?'

Wearily, he shook his head and headed upstairs to the shower. She trotted after him, tried to grovel, but he gave her the cold shoulder treatment for the rest of the day.

•

'You'd think it was Mum who was shagging around,' Sam tells the people in the café. 'She took the blame, every time.'

Abi's arms are folded. 'So d'you reckon Robert was having a fling with this Georgia woman?'

'He was. I know that for a fact.'

'Hmm. For a fact? Or is it more a kind of a wishy-washy metaphorical thing, like him being a murderer?'

'Oh yes, it was a fact,' says Sam, nodding furiously. 'When I took over the farm, I got the full story from people who worked with them. Everyone knew. Robert and Georgia were always nipping off for a siesta in whichever of the bedrooms was free. And Georgia wasn't the only one, not by a long chalk. There was a Jillian before her, and someone else after. Robert's a pathological liar. Lies drip off his tongue. I don't think he'd know the truth if it slapped him in the face.'

Abi raises one eyebrow. 'Or shot him in the chest?'

Sam wishes with all his heart that he'd never come anywhere near Tuckbox this morning. There's been many a time when he's fantasised about killing Robert. Well, now he's done it—and he doesn't feel liberated; he feels like a despicable coward. But when he remembers Georgia and all those other women, when he thinks about the hurt and humiliation inflicted on his mum, he feels like marching behind that counter and shooting the conniving bastard all over again.

Mutesi has taken off her glasses and is rubbing her eyes with her fingertips.

'Lies,' she murmurs. 'Lies, lies. They have too much power.'

She says it with such sadness. Sam wonders what she means, what she's seen. But the thought slides away again. All he can think about is Robert.

It wasn't long before the man unveiled a new plan, the next stage in his hostile takeover of Sam's future. It was the beginning of the end.

THIRTY

Sam

Robert was in full cry, striding up and down the kitchen.

'Jackson's Lodge is on the market!' he announced, and before Mum could get a word in he was telling her his plan. He was going to buy Jackson's and invest a whole load of money in making it a top-end boutique hotel, spa and restaurant.

Mum was doing the washing-up at the sink, Sam was drying. Her hands were turning lobster-red in the hot water. They say that if a frog is in a pot and you heat it up slowly, the poor thing won't notice it's being cooked until it's too late. Mum was that frog—except it seemed as though she was letting herself be burned. Perhaps she didn't think she deserved any better.

'The turnover's going up year on year,' enthused Robert. 'That's why the value of the business is so high. Georgia and I will transform the place into something very, very special. It's *such* an exciting opportunity.'

'It all sounds very expensive,' Mum said quietly, keeping her eyes fixed on the bubbles. 'We haven't got that kind of cash sloshing around.'

'We can raise it. I've already made enquiries at the bank.'

'So much debt though, Robert.'

He shrugged. 'Got to diversify to survive.'

'So you'd be able to borrow what you need against the restaurant business?'

'No. The bank's pathetically risk-averse. They think Jackson's premises will be overcapitalised. The loan would have to be secured on this place. That's no problem, is it?'

'This place?' Sam echoed. 'Whaddya mean, *this* place?'

'Tyndale Farm.'

'No way.' Sam wanted to punch him. He very nearly *did* punch him. His hands were balled up into fists. He was about fifteen but still nowhere near Robert's height or weight. 'No fucking way, Robert.'

'Shh, Sam.' Mum dumped a saucepan upside down on the draining board. White starch was streaked down one side.

'I'm bloody good at running a kitchen,' Robert was boasting, 'and Georgia's got tremendous flair! I've done the maths. Jackson's is a goldmine. We'll easily service the payments.'

'I wouldn't want to risk Tyndale,' fretted Mum. 'This farm is Sam's future.'

Robert went and stood close behind her, both arms around her waist, nuzzling her hair with his mouth. She froze. Baby rabbits froze like that when a dog was nosing around and they couldn't get to their burrow. They hunkered down in the grass and stayed completely still. You just saw their ears. Sam and his dad used to rescue them.

'Don't you trust me, my love?'

'Of course I trust you.'

He made a playful growling sound. 'Really?'

'Really.'

'You really are a very wonderful woman, you know that?'

Sam had to get out of there. He threw down the tea towel, stormed off to his bedroom and turned his stereo up to full volume—must have made the whole house shake—but for once

Robert didn't come thumping on his door. Of course he didn't. He had no need to. He'd won. Sam had lost.

At the time, Sam had no idea of just how much he'd lost. Over the next few weeks Mum signed everything Robert put in front of her. The farm was transferred into their joint names and used as collateral for Robert's new venture. Mum's lawyer had acted for her and Dad forever. He wasn't at all happy about the changes and insisted on seeing Mum by herself. Sam has sometimes wondered whether she hesitated before she picked up that pen to sign Tyndale away from him. Surely she did, at least for a moment?

But Robert was the puppeteer. He had hold of her strings, and he was making her dance and jump and clap her hands to his tune. In no time at all he was the owner of Jackson's Lodge as well as Tyndale Farm.

•

'They put in a heated swimming pool,' Sam tells the people in the café. 'And an orangery. A fricking orangery! They closed for months while the builders were turning the place into a palace.'

Abi's still in her kneeling Buddha pose, stretching her arms behind her back.

'Wow,' she says. 'I'm not sure I even know what an orangery is.'

'Georgia and Robert used the whole thing as an excuse for all their late nights together. They were blatant, but Mum never asked questions anymore.'

'So . . . did they make a big success of the place?'

'Nope. Just about went bankrupt. Georgia flounced off in a huff when Robert started on one of the chambermaids.'

'Bloody hell! Casanova got about a bit, didn't he? I didn't know him, obviously, but he seemed like a nice enough guy to me. Very pleasant to all his customers. Sofia the barista reckoned he was a great boss.'

'That's the thing. He could be great. He could even be a truly stellar stepfather, which messed me up because sometimes

I wondered whether I could have got him all wrong. One birthday—maybe my sixteenth?—he laid on a party for me, did all the catering, drove people around the countryside. Nothing was too much trouble. I spent all evening waiting for him to be a dick. I was looking forward to everyone seeing what I had to put up with—but he really let me down! He turned a blind eye to my mates smuggling in cans of beer. He chatted about films and Xbox games. He even handed out chummy advice about how to pick up girls.'

Abi curls her lip. 'Ew. That's really very creepy.'

'They didn't think so. Most of them stayed over, and when we crawled out of bed he rustled up a fantastic cooked breakfast he called "Lacey's famous hangover buster". He behaved like every teenager's favourite uncle. I kept trying to tell them he was a massive wanker but they couldn't see it at all. *Sam, you're off your head, you don't know how lucky you are.*'

It was Harvey who said that. Harvey, the school soccer star. What he thought really mattered to Sam.

'And I remember this other time, when Mum was visiting Oma for the night, he and I walked down to the pub in Holdsworth. Had pizza, played pool. He told me about his childhood, how his dad had walked out on the family and that's why he'd always wanted to be like a father to me. I started to think maybe I *was* off my head.'

'That's the point, though, isn't it?' says Abi. 'That was his M.O.—to keep you disorientated. Day was night. Up was down.'

'That's right! Thank you! Day was night, up was down. Mum and I were lost in Robert World. In Robert World, your dogs got sold and your horse disappeared and your friends were either exiled—like Tammy and Granny—or charmed, which was even worse. He was a shapeshifter. Everyone saw a completely different Robert.'

'Like the dress,' says Abi.

'Exactly like the dress.'

Neil's still sitting on the floor and has to crane his neck as he twists around to look up at Abi.

'Come again?' He sounds bemused. 'The *what*?'

'The dress,' she says.

'Nope. Still doesn't compute.'

Abi sighs. 'Where exactly have you been living, Neil? Pluto? It's a photo of a dress on the internet. Two people will look at the same photo of the dress and see completely different colours: either white and gold, or blue and black. Apparently it's all to do with neuroscience. For the record, it's white and gold.'

'Bollocks!' cries Sam. 'That dress is blue and black.'

Abi's roaring with laughter. She seems slightly stoned.

'Okay, okay!' She's putting up her hands in surrender. 'You're the man with the gun. I'd better pretend to go along with your fucked-up worldview. Blue and black it is.'

Neil's muttering that they're all crazy, that soon they'll be praying to the Flying Spaghetti Monster five times a day. It's funny. For a few moments Sam is laughing along with Abi. For a few moments he has almost forgotten the terrible thing he's done today.

And then they all stop laughing, and listen.

There's a new sound. It's coming from the back kitchen, and it's all too familiar. It twists an exposed nerve in Sam's mind.

He hates that noise. He *hates* that noise.

Abi

It's not 'Rocket Man'. This one has a brash vintage ringtone, the sort you'd expect to hear in the drawing room of an Agatha Christie play—which might be why the sound carries so clearly from the room at the back. Charlie can do a masterful imitation of this kind of ringtone. It's his party piece. Brings the house down.

'That's Robert's phone!' shouts Sam. He's already heading towards the back kitchen. 'I'd know it anywhere.'

Neil's trying to get up off the floor, but he's too slow. He looks anxiously around at Abi, mouths, 'Nicola.'

'I'll go and get it,' says Abi, leaping to her feet.

She overtakes Sam, skims behind the back counter, past Robert's body and through the heavy fire door.

Ringing fills the air, brassy in the gloom. She finds a panel of light switches and flicks on a couple more, while the door groans almost shut behind her. The ringing is coming from a row of hooks with jackets and bags. She rifles among them, throwing scarves and hats and gloves around. One of the coats is a waxed jacket with a corduroy collar. She shoves her hand into one pocket—no, those are car keys—then into the other pocket. *Bingo*. A white iPhone, much like her own. It's going nuts in her hand, flashing and vibrating.

She takes a look at the screen, and her heart sinks. The caller is *Mum*.

Robert Lacey has a mother. Of course he does. Why wouldn't he? A woman, a real person—who adores her son presumably; most mothers do—is trying to make contact with him right now, right at this moment. *Mum*. She will have seen Tuckbox Café on the news. She'll be so worried.

The noise stops. The screen darkens. Abi stands for a time, weighing the phone in her hand. There's a pattern lock on the screen. Pity. There are a hundred things she could do with a phone right now. She tries a few of the obvious patterns: an 'L' shape, a square, diagonal lines. No good. On the next try, she's locked out.

Something—a quiet sound, almost inaudible—makes her swing around to peer into the room.

'Nicola?' she whispers.

Sure enough, there's someone under the sink. She's making agitated movements with both hands, shooing Abi back towards the café door, mouthing, 'Go away, go away.'

Abi crouches down beside the cupboard. She can only just see the pale face.

'Look, you must be bloody uncomfortable in there. Don't you want this to end? He won't give himself up until you've come out and talked to him.'

'No! No way!'

Abi's not impressed. She'd dearly like to call Sam into the room. That might be the quickest way to cut through all this. If Nicola plays her cards right—and surely she knows how to do that?—their tiff could end in kissing and making up before Sam is carted off in handcuffs.

Then again, it might not end so well. It didn't end at all well for Robert.

'You'll have to speak to him sooner or later,' she hisses.

'No.'

'He's the father of your child.'

'I've nothing to say to him.'

'Nothing to say? Even though this whole thing seems to be because of you?' Abi shakes her head as she straightens. 'Well, you'd better start thinking of something.'

THIRTY-ONE

Sam

Abi looks poleaxed when she returns from the storeroom. She hands Sam Robert's phone without a word. When he sees who was trying to get in touch with the dead man, guilt takes a hefty swing at Sam and punches him in the stomach.

What's Mrs Lacey's name? *Sheila.* He met her a handful of times: a neat, energetic woman with sad eyes. She'll be about eighty by now. She brought up two boys by herself. She doted on Robert. Sam will have broken her heart today.

Someone's turned off the radio. Good. He doesn't want to hear another news bulletin about the hostage situation in South London. Poor Sheila. He imagines the old lady sitting by the phone, waiting for news.

'This Nicola,' says Abi suddenly.

'What about Nicola?'

She's tapping her fingernails, making weird shapes with her mouth. She's jittery—or is she fuming about something? She reminds Sam of himself.

'What about Nicola?' he asks again.

'Dunno. Just strikes me that Robert's dead and we're all stuck in here, in fear of our lives, because of a mythological figure. The face that launched the incident in Tuckbox Café. Must be a hell of a gal to cause all this fuss. I'm just wondering who the heck she is.'

•

He didn't know that summer evening was going to change everything. Twenty-one years old, in his shirtsleeves, riding his old Honda along the narrow lanes to the Wheatsheaf. He'd been haymaking on the farm where he worked, and they'd had a perfect week for it.

He left home at seventeen, when Robert bought Tuckbox. He had to. Tyndale farmhouse was rented out and there was no way Sam was going to move to a small flat in London with Robert and Mum. Over the next few years he jumped through all the hoops Robert held up for him: worked on a variety of farms around the country, managed one of them single-handed, scraped through a course at agricultural college. He never had trouble finding work. The darkness was always there, always lurking somewhere inside him, but he kept himself going with the promise that one day he would get back to Tyndale. When Tim Appleton announced that he was retiring and would be giving up the land, Robert couldn't find an excuse to put him off any longer. In a few months' time Sam would take over the lease. He was coming home.

He felt as though he was overflowing as he turned in at the Wheatsheaf. Midsummer evenings in Sussex always stirred him up. The happy scents of hay and clover, the lilac haze of dusk, the wrongness of blue lights through his curtains, the darkness swallowing him. It all seemed to be happening again, right now. Sometimes it only took the smell of newly mown hay to send his heart thundering into overdrive.

His clay bird club mates were already drinking in the beer garden. He could hear the noisy sods as soon as he took off his helmet. He stepped into the pub through the front door—stone flags, dark wood—and stopped at the bar to get himself a pint. And there she was.

He didn't believe in love at first sight; didn't believe in love at all, really. Dad had loved Sam and Mum, but not enough to stay alive. Robert was a monster who twisted love to make a net in which to entangle people. Sam looked at the new barmaid with her blonde boy-cut and her tight jeans and his first thought was that she was sexy. He had no interest beyond that. There had been a series of girlfriends since Donna Davies at the youth group picnic: one at agricultural college, another who did the accounts for a farm where he worked in Norfolk. He kept moving on. So did they.

He watched the barmaid stretching to get something off a shelf, chatting over her shoulder to a couple of middle-aged suits. A cropped T-shirt revealed a lot of flat stomach and a glittering green gem in her naval. She wasn't from around here, she told the suits. They said something cheeky about her being better-looking than Alistair, the grumpy landlord, and she hurled banter back at them while she took their money. She was nearly as tall as Sam and twice as confident. A tattoo of a vine wound all the way from her wrist to her shoulder. She caught him staring at it, and smiled. There was something about her smile, a gleam in the slate-grey eyes, as though she was thinking about some private joke.

While she was pouring his pint she asked if this was his local.

'No. Sort of. Yes.'

'No, sort of, *and* yes?'

'I'm here to meet some guys. The clay bird club.'

She raised her eyebrows, pointing with her chin towards the beer garden. 'That bunch of clowns?'

He nodded, feeling like a clown himself. She set the beer down in front of him.

'But you live round here?'

He rested his helmet on the top of the bar. Within a couple of minutes he was telling her all about how he'd soon be taking over his family farm. She walked around the tables, gathering glasses, asking where exactly was Tyndale, and why weren't his parents there now? That led to him explaining about Dad.

'Hey!' She came closer, resting her fingertips on his arm. 'That's something we've got in common. I lost my mum when I was nine.'

Maybe that was what first drew them together: the shared experience of learning at a young age that parents weren't immortal, and death was really real. Bereaved kids think differently to others.

The Wheatsheaf was pretty quiet that evening. Most customers were in the beer garden, buying drinks from grumpy Alistair through a servery window. Whenever she had a free moment the barmaid gravitated back to Sam. He learned that her name was Nicola. They talked about the year she'd just spent as an au pair in France, her ambition to train as an early-years teacher. He heard about her feckless kid of a father, whom she despised. When he asked what had brought her to the middle of nowhere, she laid a hand on her chest. Long fingers.

'Running from a broken heart. And this job, and a cheap place to live above the pub while I get on my feet. Alistair was in the army with my uncle. He's driving me spare.'

Sam felt as though he'd been reunited with a childhood friend. A couple of clay bird mates came in from the garden to use the toilets and spotted him, but once they'd worked out he was chatting up the new barmaid they winked and left him to it.

Sam and Nicola were still talking when Alistair called time, ringing the brass bell and bellowing like a bull: *Time, ladies and gentlemen, please!* It was the jolliest he'd been all evening, miserable sod. The man was a natural spoilsport.

Sam picked up his helmet. 'Well,' he said.

That gleam in her eyes. 'Well.'

'I'd better be off.'

'You know where to find me.'

'You're not going anywhere?'

'I'll be right here.' She made a *blah* face, sticking out her tongue. 'In my garret room. Come and rescue me, Sam Ballard.'

•

He was back two nights later, and then again, and again. The Wheatsheaf had become an irresistible magnet, and the summer obliged by providing one balmy evening after another. One night, as the pub closed, Nicola said she'd love to go for a blast on the back of Sam's bike and see where he grew up. So he lent her his helmet and blast they did, pelting through the fragrant darkness with her arms around his waist. The hedgerows gleamed white with elderflower and old man's beard.

It was midnight when Sam stopped at the top of the hill on the border of Tyndale Farm. They perched side by side on the five-barred gate leading into Sundance's field, sharing a bag of pork scratchings from the pub, while a full moon rose above sleeping woodland on the other side of the valley. The tawny owls were hunting. One swept close overhead with a whirr of wings, startling Nicola.

Sam could see the place where Dad's ashes had been scattered. A mare and her foal lay dozing by the very same trough where Mum washed the urn. He kept shtum about that. Bit of a passion killer, and he didn't want to spoil his chances by doing or saying anything stupid. The blackness inside him had lightened just enough for him to hope for the coming of day.

Instead, he pointed out Tyndale's boundaries to Nicola, naming the fields: Beacon Meadow, Weston's Laine, Poverty Bottom and the others—sheltered pastures bounded by hedges and copses, rolling swathes of maize and wheat and yellow oilseed rape. He knew every inch, every gate, every trough; the composition of the soil, what would best grow where, which corners were badly drained or awkwardly shaped or steep. They were as familiar to him as his own family.

The farmhouse lay just a couple of hundred yards off, tucked among the trees. A light shone from his old bedroom. A dog barked. Time rolled back: Dad was in the shed, Bouncer and Snoops were mooching about, Mum was doing the farm accounts at the kitchen table. Sundance dreamed in his stable, Granny in her doll's house. All was still well.

As they talked in murmurs, Nicola and he kept edging closer and closer together on the gate. Awkward but promising.

'And you're really going to come back and run this farm?' she asked.

'I am! In the New Year.'

'Don't you feel a bit suffocated by all that family history?'

'Nope. I feel suffocated without it. This is my home.'

She looked across the valley, towards the spire of Holdsworth church. 'Must be nice. Knowing where you're going.'

'Don't you?'

'I left my heart in Paris,' she said, sighing. 'He's an older man. *Much* older. Could be my dad. That isn't the problem, though. The problem is that he's married.'

'Oh.'

'But he's in love with me. I was au pair for their children. In the end I had to leave. He had to put the children first, which meant saving his marriage.'

Sam was shocked by this revelation. He wasn't sure how to react.

'Unhappily married,' she added, sounding defensive, so he muttered something about how that was fair enough and it wasn't for him to judge. Privately he thought the man sounded like a real prick. Slept with the pretty nanny, sacked her when it suited him. He sounded a lot like Robert.

After a while the dozing horses rolled to their feet and came over to say hello. Sam hopped off the gate to greet them. The foal kept nuzzling against his mother, tottering on spindly legs.

'So what's this spot called?' asked Nicola.

'Sundance's field,' replied Sam, stooping to pull up handfuls of lush grass from through the gate. 'On the farm map it's labelled "Frontacre", but nobody calls it that anymore. Sundance Kid was a horse who lived here for years.'

The mare snorted as she ate the grass. He felt the warmth of her breath on his palm. It was like his dream, when Dad became a cloud.

'My stepfather had Sundance shot,' he said.

'No! Why?'

'He claimed he had colic and was in agony and there was no choice, but he was lying. Of course the vet would have offered options. Robert went for the final solution.'

'He didn't like Sundance?'

'He didn't like my grandmother. Sundance was her horse.'

The moonlight made Nicola's hair seem luminous as she swung down from the gate. She put her arms around Sam's neck.

'Poor Sundance,' she said.

He took her hand and led her along the hedge, away from the trough and the spinney and the memories. She didn't ask why. They stopped in a sheltered corner of the field, where the gloom was splashed with glowing patches of buttercups. For a time he forgot everything else.

As he dropped her back at the Wheatsheaf, a world-beating dawn chorus was bursting from every copse and hedgerow—bursting from somewhere in his chest too. He felt light. He felt free. Something broken inside him had clicked into its rightful place, back there among the buttercups.

•

'She mended me,' he tells the listeners in the café. 'I was happy! *We* were happy. We went on holiday to Casablanca. Our friends started calling us Samola. You know, like Brangelina.'

'Please God, no,' mutters Abi.

'Yeah, yeah, sickening, but I was kind of chuffed. That was

our first and last proper holiday. At New Year the great day came, the moment I'd been waiting for all my life—literally all my life. I took over the lease at Tyndale. I hit the ground running because I knew Robert would dance a bloody jig if I bombed. Tim Appleton was a big help with the business side of things. I knew a fair bit about land management and could fix just about any bit of machinery that broke down, but there was a hell of a lot still to learn. I'd be out all day and up half the night, trying to get on top of the paperwork: accounts, bills, massive bureaucracy every time stock was moved on or off the place, hundred-page applications for subsidies. I was working sixteen-hour days when Nicola found out she was three months pregnant.'

'Oh dear.' Neil grimaces. 'Bit of a shock, I bet.'

'You can say that again. She wasn't going to tell me—she'd even booked herself in for an abortion—but one night she came out with it; said I had a right to know. We panicked and talked and panicked and talked, and finally decided to give it a go together. She moved into Tyndale. We got a collie puppy called Toby. I wanted my child to have a friend, like I had Bouncer and Snoops. I went along with Nicola for the scan. I saw that funny little shadow on the screen, and it was like being hit by a baseball bat, and I just . . .'

He can't finish the sentence. He can't. He'll start blubbing. This whole story is leading to Julia. The last time he kissed his little girl, she'd had her bath and was all tucked up and giggling under her dinosaur duvet in his old bedroom. Blue pyjamas and rosy cheeks. He sat on her bed while she snuggled up to him, just as close as she could possibly get. They read her favourite story, *The Tiger Who Came to Tea*. She was sucking her thumb. She was warm and soft and smelled of baby shampoo.

'I'd do anything for Julia,' he says. 'I've never known love like it.'

Mutesi smiles at him. 'There *is* no love like it.'

The nurse seems older than she did earlier. Her eyelids are drooping, her cheeks seem to sag. She came off a night shift this morning, he remembers, so she's been awake for . . . well, not as long as he has, but a very long time. Seeing him so upset about Julia seems to have knocked her. He wonders why. He wonders who she is, really.

Neil's still sitting on the floor with one outstretched leg across the other, head tilted back, staring at the ceiling. Abi has thrown herself into another armchair, turning it around so that it's facing Sam. They're all exhausted. Sam doesn't think any one of them is seriously frightened anymore. Not really. They've got the measure of him. They're stressed, they'd like to get out of here, for sure—at least the women would, he's not so sure about Neil. After all, he and Buddy haven't got anywhere else to go.

Silence is a funny thing. It can be throbbing with silent screams. It can be awkward as all hell. It can be companionable, like this one. Perhaps he's beginning to hallucinate. He's been doing that a lot lately. He's in some kind of weird prayer meeting with his three oldest friends in the world: Mutesi, Neil and Abi. He's pretty sure there's no afterlife; he doesn't believe in a spirit world. He really doesn't think there *are* more things in heaven and earth, Horatio. And yet at this moment he has an overwhelming feeling that his parents are very close by. They're waiting for him. He can hear Dad humming over the rumble of the tractor: *pom, pom, pom*. He can feel his mother's sadness. Perhaps it's time to pluck up the courage and join them? He's done enough damage here. He's *really* trashed the changing room this time.

Of course the downside could be that bloody Robert's somehow talked his way in. Sam will be seriously pissed if he gets to the pearly gates and spots that toothpaste smile ahead of him in the queue. He's picturing getting off a train at a celestial version of Victoria Station to see Mum and Dad standing side by side on the other side of the pearly barrier. Mum's wearing her patched jeans, Dad his overalls and canvas hat. Robert's waving as he waits for his ticket to get checked. *Yoohoo!* Meanwhile Sam is struggling along at the back of the queue, desperate to get his story in before that conniving bastard tells his parents that Sam murdered him.

'But there's nothing on the other side,' he says aloud.

'Sam?' Mutesi is leaning closer to him. 'Are you all right?'

Gradually her kind face swims back into focus. She's looking at the cut on his forehead. He knows he seems wild, bug-eyed, as though he's just woken up and doesn't know where the fuck he is. He used to do the same thing when his teachers told him off for staring out of the window. *Stop daydreaming, Sam!*

'Sam, Sam.' Mutesi sounds much gentler than any of his teachers. 'Isn't it time to give up?'

'No.'

'You're not really going to shoot Abigail, or Neil, or me. You are not. I know you are not.'

She's right, of course. He doesn't know how much longer he can go on.

Eliza

The wind has picked up suddenly, and now it's rattling the Victorian window frame. A crisp packet blows against the glass, peering in for a moment before whipping away into the darkness and rain. Every passing minute feels like a lost opportunity.

Eliza and Paul have followed up with two more texts to the café. The replies came from Abigail Garcia.

He says not yet. I think u should wait. Abi Garcia

Calm and talking to us. Abi

At seven, Eliza nips into the top-floor kitchen to call Richard.

''Fraid this isn't showing any signs of coming to an end. I won't be home anytime soon,' she says. 'Everyone okay?'

Richard sounds resigned. 'Jack's in his PJs, off to bed in a minute. Liam's had a bad day.'

Eliza feels her chest tighten. When she lies sleepless at three in the morning, it's generally because she hasn't had enough time during daylight hours to worry about her elder son.

'What happened?'

'The talent quest was a disaster.'

'Oh no! But he worked so hard, he could play it so well.'

'He went wrong. His fingers were shaking. He had three false starts until he gave up and walked away. He reckons the whole school was laughing at him. They were slow-clapping.'

She imagines Liam's shaking fingers on the keys, his rising panic. It makes her heart ache—literally, it aches.

'What the hell were the teachers doing?' she demands furiously. 'They must have been asleep at the wheel! Why was that kind of behaviour allowed?'

Richard doesn't answer. She knows exactly what he's thinking: *Where were you?* Perhaps, if she'd been there as she promised, Liam wouldn't have lost his nerve. Perhaps if she'd been there nobody would have dared to laugh or jeer or slow-clap.

'How is he?' she asks.

'Pretty upset. He's spent the evening asking when you'll be back.'

'Sorry.'

A sniff. 'Yeah.'

'There are hostages.'

'I know. We've been watching on the news.'

'It's not a good moment to be handing this on to another negotiator.'

'I'm sure it's not.'

She's trying to think of some way to cheer Liam. 'Tell him I'll take him ice-skating on Saturday.'

'I think it'll take more than ice-skating.'

She hears his muffled voice, relaying her peace offering with an undertone of sarcasm—*says she'll take you ice-skating at the weekend*—and a grunt from Liam.

'Tell him it will all come out in the wash,' she says. 'It won't have been as bad as he thinks.'

'Some of the little bastards were filming. They've shown him the video. It's far worse than he thought. He's saying he can't go back to school. Ever.'

'They haven't posted this video online, have they?'

'Christ, I hadn't even considered that!' Richard sounds appalled. 'D'you think they might? They'd bloody well better not! Anyway, he's having ice cream and we're going to watch *Dr Who*. We'll see you later.'

He's ended the call before she's had a chance to say goodbye.

She fills a glass of water, feeling weighed down by the image of her awkward son, trying so hard to do something right for once. Giggles, then gales of laughter, a heartless crowd slow-clapping him off the stage. Ooh, she'd like to have ten minutes with some of those kids. Her own cheeks burn with his mortification.

'Trouble at t'mill?' asks Paul, as she returns to their room. Her colleague seems as alert as he did first thing this morning, perhaps because he's on his zillionth cup of coffee.

'Liam. The usual kind of thing. I wish I could split in half and be in two places at once. Two people at once. Maybe three.'

'That would be a useful skill.'

'It would.'

He's gazing keenly at her. 'You all right?'

'Always. Just a godawful mother.'

'D'you want to think about handing over to me or Ashwin?'

'Over my dead body.'

'Okay. Good.' He looks relieved. 'But let's revisit that in a couple of hours. We'll have to pass this on to another team if it's going to run all night.' He hands her his tablet. 'Take a look at Ballard's Facebook page. See Julia? She's a sweetie.'

The first picture is a close-up of a very small baby snuggled in an adult's arms. Her mouth, nose and one tiny clenched fist are visible above a white blanket. A yellow cap covers the top third of her face. She seems to be fast asleep except that she's yawning widely. The yawn wrinkles her nose. According to Facebook, one hundred and twenty people have liked or loved the image.

In the next picture she looks about Jack's age, or maybe a little older—still a baby, really—dressed in dungarees and blue wellies. She's sitting in the grass with her legs stuck straight out in front of her, cuddling a very young, very woolly lamb. Wispy curls cling to the nape of her neck. Sunlight glows on her face and shines through the lamb's ears. She's squinting up at whoever's taking the photo, grinning from ear to ear. She hasn't yet got all her teeth.

'Pretty cute,' says Eliza.

'Hang on, there's a more recent one.' Paul takes the tablet back and flicks through the photos. 'Here we go. July this year, around the time Nicola left.'

This time the little girl is definitely that—a little girl, not a baby. She's squatting down with her feet flat on the ground, in that way very small children can, frowning in concentration as she lays a bright red brick on top of a tower of them. She's wearing a denim pinafore dress, blue tights and T-bar shoes. Her hair is still wispy but it's shoulder-length now. Big curls, round cheeks. A sparkly blue slide pins back her fringe on one side. One small hand rests casually on the neck of a black-and-white dog.

Eliza leans closer, gazing through this window into Sam's world. The image has a yellowish, electric-light-bulb tint. Eliza can make out a colourful rug on the floor, an overflowing laundry basket beside the turned leg of a pine table, a distant shelf piled haphazardly with what might be cookery books. Beyond the child another figure is half obscured by shadow.

'Think that's Nicola in the background?'

'Yep, I'd say so. She fits the descriptions.'

The woman is cross-legged, holding a wineglass. Short blonde hair with a long fringe sweeping over one eye. Jeans, a turquoise blouse, bare feet. Slender fingers touch the side of her own head, as if smoothing her hair. She's looking directly at the photographer but there's no hint of a smile.

'The girl in the cupboard,' says Eliza.

'That's right.'

'Sam took this photo. We're looking through his eyes. This is where everything happened.'

THIRTY-TWO

Sam

When he phoned Mum with their baby news, she cried. He wasn't sure they were happy tears.

He hadn't seen her in months. He hardly ever went to London, she never ventured anywhere without Robert anymore, and Robert refused to visit Tyndale Farm. The baby changed all that. Even Robert couldn't keep Mum from being involved in the life of her first grandchild.

'When can I come down?' she asked.

Robert's voice was rumbling in the background. Sam imagined her with the phone jammed into her chest, trying to stand up to him. When she spoke again she sounded triumphant.

'Robert's going to come too! He's dead keen to meet the mother of his step-grandchild.'

No, no, no! 'Hasn't he got a café to run?'

'You're going to be a father,' she said. 'It's time the pair of you mended your fences. Saturday okay with you?'

'I don't want him here.'

'Oh, Sam. Please. *Please.*'

She sounded desperate. It occurred to him that if Robert didn't come, neither would she.

'Okay,' he muttered. 'But it's my house now.'

Rain set in that evening and continued all the rest of the week, but on Saturday morning he woke to a washed blue sky. He was up and out by dawn, trying to fit a day's work into three hours. Toby the puppy snuffled and capered around his feet. Someone had left a gate open on the public footpath again, letting the heifers into a field of beans. Why did they do that? Was it so hard to shut a gate? He had to move the reluctant animals, which was a nightmare. By ten in the morning he'd changed and was pacing around the house, trying to hide piles of washing and other mess. Neither Nicola nor he were what you'd call house proud. He only ever seemed to succeed in making things look worse.

She was standing at the mirror in the kitchen, serenely putting on lipstick, wearing an oversized grey cardigan and jeans. She suffered morning sickness for the first few months but that was all over now and she was glowing. He thought she looked magnificent, like something out of a magazine. He was proud of her. They'd ground fresh coffee beans in their new grinder, even laid on a packet of posh biscuits for the occasion. They were twenty-two years old, playing house.

'Your mum sounds like a real sweetheart,' said Nicola. 'This is all going to be fine.'

'Yeah. *She* is.'

'The wicked stepfather?' She blotted her lipstick on a tissue. 'You're not really scared of him, are you?'

Oh, but he was. He'd spent the past ten minutes scrubbing the sink with a wire brush, for no good reason. The devil in human form was coming for coffee at his kitchen table, to meet the love of his life. Sam had witnessed Robert's charm working its magic. Convolvulus.

'I can handle him,' Nicola assured him. 'I've never been scared of bullies. If he gives you any trouble I'll just tell him to sod right off.'

As she spoke, Sam heard wheels splashing through the puddles in the yard.

'Talk of the devil,' he said.

By the time the engine stopped, Nicola and Toby had already trotted outside to meet them. Nicola was good with people. She had her best lipstick smile on, wide and eager, ready to chummy up and make things easier for everyone. Sam trudged along in her scented wake, arriving just as she and Mum were hugging like old friends—two women who'd never met, but now there was this baby.

Robert had bought himself a flashy little car, a racing-green MG, and had the roof down. He was striding around the long bonnet towards Nicola, greeting her affably in his deep voice. 'Hello! I'm Robert. I'm guessing you're Nicola?' When she put out her hand, he held on to it, and at the same time he laid his other paw on her shoulder. 'I think we can do hugs, can't we? We're family now.'

Sam stood on the doorstep with clenched fists, watching that man pull his beautiful girlfriend into his arms and press his mouth onto her left cheek, then her right, then her left again. Fuck, he wanted to kill him. Spring sunshine glowed on her hair, on his craggy face. They looked glamorous together.

He was all chummy with Sam too, greeting him with a manly slap on the back, demonstrating that he was the adult in the yard while Sam was just a sullen kid. He won every time. *Every time.* Game, set and match.

It turned out that Sam and Nicola didn't need their posh biscuits because Robert produced almond croissants from the café. He spent the morning rolling out a major charm offensive. Mum was wary, the rabbit in the grass, looking to him for approval every time she spoke. She didn't want a croissant—patting her stomach, smiling and muttering *just watching it a bit*—though she was skinny as a twig, pale skin stretched across her cheekbones. Her hair was twisted and pinned back so tightly that it pulled at her face. No curls could escape that torture. She bore no resemblance whatsoever to the bride in Sam's parents' wedding photos. That curly-headed, laughing girl had been airbrushed out of the world forever.

If his wife was faded, Robert glowed in glorious technicolour. His presence filled the room. Sam had forgotten how he could do that. Having him in the house brought it all back—those first days when Dad had died and this interloper somehow managed to take over the universe. He gave Nicola the full blast of his charisma, got her talking about her mother—who sounded like a saint, but then don't all dead people?—and her useless father who was on to his fourth wife, smoked dope like it was going out of fashion, couldn't hold down a job and had never shown the slightest interest in Nicola. Robert listened without ever taking his eyes from her face. Sam recognised his technique: an understanding smile, a way of looking intently into her eyes after she'd finished speaking.

'I bet you didn't expect this,' he said, gesturing around her. 'How old are you? Twenty-two? Stuck in the country with a child on the way.'

Nicola chuckled. She was sitting with her hand on Sam's leg.

'Hell, no! I didn't expect it.' He felt her fingers squeeze his knee and was reassured. 'But it's just fine with me, Robert. Just fine.'

Morning sun was blasting in through the kitchen windows, so Nicola suggested a stroll. Sam found everyone boots to wear and they set out across the yard. The farm was a piece of heaven that morning. A fresh wind made rippling-water patterns in the spring barley; hawthorn blossom danced a jig in the hedges.

'Sam, this place is a picture!' boomed Robert, shaking his head in wonder when Sam showed them a soya crop he'd drilled. 'Heck, you've achieved miracles in a short time. You're really thinking outside the box. Poor old Tim Appleton never had Tyndale looking as good as this.'

But Sam wasn't having it; he wouldn't play the grateful stepson. Robert soon gave up the act, and minutes later he was bragging about his best-ever turnover at Tuckbox. Sam listened in silence until they were crossing Sundance's field. He thought Mum might at least acknowledge the significance of the place, but she never opened her mouth. When they reached the trough by the spinney, he couldn't stand it any longer. He stopped in his tracks.

'Has he been erased from existence?' he asked loudly.

Mum dropped back to take his arm. 'Shh,' she hissed. 'Please.'

'He's my child's grandfather. Do we just pretend he was never here?'

'Sam. Sammy.'

She sounded pathetically anxious, desperate for everyone to get along. She was the only person he was hurting. He whispered, 'Sorry,' and stretched his free hand across to cover hers. They walked on together, Mum holding on to his arm.

'Look,' she murmured, 'bluebells in the spinney. He loved this time of year.'

They made slower progress than the other two, who strode ahead, heads bent together, deep in conversation about God knew what. Nicola's pale blue poncho matched the sky. Sam fretted about what tales Robert might be spinning. He was a magician. He could make anyone fall in love with him.

'He'd be so proud, you know,' said Mum. 'Your dad. I hope he can see what a fine job you're doing.'

'I wish he was here. Every single day I need his advice. Every single day there's some new problem. So much knowledge died with him.'

'I know.' She tilted her head so that it rested on his upper arm. 'I know, Sammy. I feel exactly the same. We used to turn things over and work out what to do. We were a team.'

This was as honest as she'd been in years. Perhaps he should have stopped and looked her in the eye and asked, 'Are you all right, Mum? How are you, really? Blink twice and I'll rescue you.' Perhaps he could have helped. But he didn't want to spoil this moment.

'I've been worrying about you,' she said. 'You're both so young for such a lot of commitment . . . I thought Nicola might be trying to trap you. You're a catch, after all. The farm and everything.'

He was startled into laughter. 'What, you mean by getting knocked up? The boot's on the other foot! Of the two of us, she was the more shocked. I think most people will be saying I'm the lucky one.'

'She's good for you, I can see that. But having a child, and farming life—it's a lot to ask. And people change as they grow through their twenties.'

He glanced up the field towards Nicola, who was stooping to pick up a stick to throw for Toby.

'You know what, Mum? I think I'm actually happy. I wouldn't change a thing.'

She looked at him and smiled, said that was good enough for her, and that she couldn't wait to be a granny.

From then on it was lovely, that hour or so when they wandered together across the landscape they both knew so well. He had a glimpse of Mum's old self. Perhaps she glimpsed it too. He even had her laughing. They made a shortlist of baby names to run by Nicola later: Sophie, Ella, Julia. Or Max, Mark, Jonty. He thought perhaps the baby could be a new beginning for everyone.

'Well! This has been great,' gushed Robert, when he and Mum were getting back in the car. 'Sam, you've got yourself a hell of a girl there.'

Nicola had taken up position beside Sam, her elbow resting casually on his shoulder.

'He knows,' she said, tweaking his ear.

Mum waved as the car turned into the lane. Robert tooted. It was all very matey.

'You were right,' said Nicola. 'He's *much* too smooth, and that car is a mid-life crisis on wheels. But I think everything's going to be okay.'

Suddenly the day seemed brighter than any day ever had. A thrush chirruped from the poplar tree, its song clear and light and hopeful. Sparrows flirted among the chimneys. Blue sky in the puddles, sunshine on the old stone of the house. Sam grabbed Nicola's hand, holding it high over their heads while she spun around. They laughed and danced without music, slipping and sliding on the muddy gravel.

It was all going to be okay.

•

And it *was* okay, at first. Sam grew up fast in the months before Julia's arrival. They were given baby clothes and a cot, and saved for other things. Nicola went to pregnancy yoga classes, slept with a pillow under her bump and developed a waddling-duck walk. Towards the end she got stuck in the bath and he had to help her clamber out again, both of them giggling. Yet she somehow managed to remain graceful. She really did glow.

They turned Sam's old bedroom into the baby's room. He used to stand in there sometimes, looking at the white wooden cot and wondering who was this new person who'd soon be sleeping in it. He tugged the string on the farm-animals mobile to make it play Brahms' Lullaby. Nicola had lined her old teddy bears along the mantelpiece where the Santa Claus devil had sat leering at him all those years ago. He began to hope that the blue flashing ghosts had been exorcised at last.

Summer merged with autumn. One lush evening Nicola and he sat in the garden by the pond, watching the swallows gathering. An hour later they were on their way to the hospital, down the lanes, but this time there were no blue lights.

It was 12 September: the day everything changed. Everything, forever.

The midwives called it a normal delivery, which made him wonder what on earth an abnormal one looked like. Sam had helped plenty of newborn animals into the world but that was no preparation at all. All the back-rubbing and special breathing they'd learned in birthing classes seemed pathetic, like trying to put a sticking plaster on someone who's been decapitated. To the midwives Sam was just another gibbering father, and a young one to boot. He felt like a gatecrasher in an all-female secret society.

'Try not to scream, petal,' one of them nagged Nicola. 'You'll get a sore throat.'

Nicola nearly throttled her. 'Sore throat? *Sore throat?* Are you kidding? I'm in frigging agony here. Gimme a frigging epidural! Then her eyes widened and she yelled for the frigging gas mask. Sam pressed it over her face, wishing he could have some too.

Julia arrived in a slippery rush just before midnight, alive and miraculous and more beautiful than Sam had thought possible. The midwives got on with their checklists and tasks but he simply stood and gazed at his daughter. Eventually someone sat him down and put her into his arms. He'd never felt anything like the love he felt at that moment. It knocked him right down. She was so perfect, so unimaginably precious, staring into his eyes. He sat and held her and talked nonsense to her and felt as though he might burst. He was shattered. The midwives said *aw* when they saw him crying. One of them gave him a hug, which made him cry more.

From that moment everything else faded into irrelevance. Everything, including his own life. And he was truly terrified, because from now on there was someone he couldn't bear to lose.

THIRTY-THREE

Eliza

Sam sounds different when she finally calls him. The anger is gone, for now at least. There's just the sadness.

'Sorry,' he says. 'I expect you've all got homes to go to.'

Eliza smiles. 'This is our job.'

'Robert's mother tried to phone his mobile a while ago. We didn't answer. Haven't you told her yet?'

'That will be happening about now.'

'She's lost a son.' A pause. 'Couldn't I at least talk to Julia?'

'She's not here, Sam. I'm sorry.'

'Oh.' He sighs. He sounds defeated. 'So you've got nothing to offer.'

'You and I need to work out a way to bring this situation to an end. I think it's time to start doing that. I'll help you.'

Eliza hears a woman's voice in the background, and Sam thanks somebody. Then he's back.

'Mutesi just brought me some dinner.'

'That's nice. I wish she'd bring me some.'

Eliza listens to the silence, counts to ten. Twenty. She doesn't want to lose him again.

'I've been looking at photos of Julia on Facebook,' she says. 'What a cutie.'

'You've seen photos?' There's a lift in his voice. Tears too. 'Isn't she beautiful?'

'She is.'

'And clever.'

'Tell me about your daughter. What does she like to do?'

'She loves coming out on the farm with me. She's been doing that all her life, even before she could walk. I used to get up early and Julia would be standing in her cot, holding out her arms for me to pick her up. Big smile! She'd lean forwards in her backpack and pull my ears. It was a game we played, her pulling my ears and me pretending I didn't know she was there, and I couldn't work out what was wrong with my ears. She loves riding on the tractor, feeding the calves, all the things I used to do when I was a kid. Tim Appleton reckons she's a real daddy's girl. He thought Nicola might be jealous, but she seemed happy to get a sleep-in every morning. We'd take her coffee in bed when we got back.'

'Wow. Lucky woman.'

'That's what she used to say.'

'But there were arguments, Sam?'

'Yeah . . . well, you get ups and downs with farming. I was paying a ridiculous amount of rent to Mum and Robert. Tyndale's not big enough to support two families let alone carry Robert's massive debts. Money needed spending on the place and I wasn't able to borrow much working capital. I tried everything: new crops, different rotations and methods. I stopped using contractors, rebuilt Dad's tractor, even resurrected his Land Rover. Productivity and profit margins went way up—*way* up. If Robert hadn't lumbered us with extra borrowing for Jackson's Lodge and Tuckbox and all his batshit-crazy ideas I wouldn't have been lying awake at night worrying about money. It's an awful feeling when you've got a child to think about. I wanted the world for Julia but I felt like I couldn't provide for her. D'you know what I mean?'

'I *do* know what you mean.'

'You got kids, Eliza?'

'Two.'

'You never stop worrying about them, do you?'

'Isn't that the truth?' She's imagining a young father, sleeplessly fretting about how to make ends meet. 'Didn't you have anyone on your side?'

'Tim Appleton was around a bit to start with, but he's nearly eighty and he's old-fashioned. Farming can be lonely. It's a way of life; it's twenty-four seven not nine to five. Nicola had never lived that life, that's the thing. Turned out she despised it. I think she'd imagined it would be romantic and would look good on Instagram and we'd be rolling in cash—the county set, hunt balls and brand-new Range Rovers. She couldn't see why we didn't go out much or take holidays. I'd explain—there's stock, there's jobs to do every day, there's no spare cash. The best we managed was a weekend in a caravan in Cornwall. It rained for forty-eight hours straight.'

'Oh no.'

'Yeah, I couldn't believe it. We'd promised Julia the beach but it just poured. Mum and Robert used to invite Nicola and Julia up to London. They did exciting things like going to the aquarium. Julia always came home with a big grin and a new outfit.'

'Ouch. While you were working to pay them rent.'

'I wanted her to have a nice time and get to know her granny—but I didn't like the way Robert carried on with Nicola. He called her "Rosie" and she called him "Robbie", for God's sake!'

'Ugh, that's a bit twee. Rosie and Robbie.'

'Mm, and he gave her little presents. One time it was a pendant, a dewdrop pearl, way out of our price range. She said it was from both of them but it had Robert written all over it.'

'You really think your stepdad was coming on to your girlfriend?'

'I think he was laying the groundwork. His old tricks. He used to whisper in her ear, and it worked because when she came back from London she saw nothing but faults in me. She was always rolling her eyes, every time I said anything. *You've got ADHD, you're chaotic, you're making a pig's ear of this farm*—it was all coming from him. It's really hard to counter someone who lies like a flatfish—just lies and lies, says whatever suits him. He was like an alien; he could worm his way into people's minds. He was getting ready to pull the rug out from under me.'

'How did he pull the rug?'

'Easy. He rang and very calmly informed me that I had to be off the farm by Christmas. Said they needed the cash because he'd signed up for yet another wacky scheme—a boutique chocolate factory, whatever the fuck that is. I had to pack up and leave the land that's been in my family forever. My past, my future, my livelihood. My home. My boots have walked on every inch of that place, and my dad's, and his dad's, and his dad's too. None of that counted for anything. *You're out. I want you gone. I've already got a buyer.*'

Eliza glances again through Nicola's statement. It tells the same story, yet somehow it's a completely different story.

Sam was given notice that Tyndale Farm is to be sold . . . unable to earn enough to pay a commercial rent . . . Once Sam knew that he was losing the farm, he became untethered.

'You must have been gutted,' she says, and hears him laugh. She's often heard people laughing at their own despair. It's a desolate sound.

'Yeah. Gutted doesn't really describe . . . doesn't really get close. It was fucking heartbreaking. Things were beginning to turn around. I'd just negotiated to sublet twenty acres to a riding school and livery and to provide all their hay—that would have been a game-changer! I'd finally got on top of the grassweed problem I'd inherited from Mr Appleton. The place was in fantastic shape. We were having perfect weather, looking at record yields. Nicola was going to start working as a teacher's aide at Holdsworth Primary. Is she telling you I went nuts when I got my notice?'

'She's not here.'

'I did go a bit nuts maybe—but who wouldn't? A solicitor's letter arrived the next day, making it official. A massive farming syndicate has bought my farm and Mr Appleton's. They're not farmers, they're bankers. They don't want my stock or machinery. They'll take out the hedgerows—well, they will if they think they can get away with it—and farm on an industrial scale. Tyndale was always teeming with insects and birds. Could be a desert by next summer.'

'Oh, Sam.'

'My solicitor was disgusted but he said he couldn't advise me to spend a fortune I didn't have, trying to fight it. The lease was informal, nothing in writing except a few emails, and Robert had sneaked in a bit about it being a month-to-month agreement. My dad did *not* foresee this. Not at all. He should have left Tyndale in trust or something, but he left it to Mum because he loved her and trusted her—and, anyway, he didn't expect to keel over before he even reached forty. Mum had, of her own free will and with independent legal advice, made Robert a joint owner. She'd signed on the dotted line every time he remortgaged Tyndale, and was now of her own free will selling up. I reckon she had Stockholm syndrome.'

'Really?' Eliza writes down the phrase. 'What makes you say that?'

'After years and years of total immersion in Robert World, she could only see what he showed her. She'd bought into the propaganda peddled by the Robert Bureau of Alternative Facts and Misinformation. She believed I was mentally unstable, incompetent, that it would be better for everyone if I got a job washing dishes in the Wheatsheaf. I mean . . . my mum. Fuck, that hurt. I drove up to their place to beg and plead but it just made things worse. Robert threw me out. I'd lost everything. It was too much, it was too hard. I felt devastated for Julia. She loved the farm—it was her inheritance and I'd lost it forever.

I'd let her down. The old darkness came rolling back; I couldn't even get out of bed some mornings. Nicola told me to stop moping over spilled milk. Whenever I mentioned Robert she'd sigh and walk out of the room.'

'Wasn't she upset about the farm?'

'She seemed relieved to be getting out. She didn't love the place; she'd begun to see it as a prison. Tim Appleton had this theory that all she'd ever wanted was the status, and she wouldn't stick around now I'd lost it. I don't like to think he was right, but maybe he was, you know? Because one night—one night . . .'

There it is again, the despairing *ohh*. Eliza waits out his anguish, resisting her instinct to trot out anodyne emptiness: *It's okay, don't worry*. He's off the air for over a minute, and again there's a murmur of other voices in the background. Paul meets Eliza's eye, blinking as he listens.

Sam is back. He sounds as though he's in pain.

'You still there, Eliza?'

'Still here.'

'Thanks. Sorry. I want someone to know what's happened. I want to put it out there. This is my side of the story, okay? My side. I don't think I'll be around to tell it myself.'

'Why not? Why not, Sam?'

'So, um, how do I describe . . . It was in July, Robert's birthday. We were in the kitchen. I remember Julia was building towers and knocking them down and I was slumped at the table with my head in my hands, trying to get my head around the farm accounts. But I couldn't block out the sound of Nicola flirting with Robert down the phone. She sang "Happy Birthday", Marilyn Monroe-style. Sexy. Really sexy. She looked at me—*Hang on, Robbie, walls have ears*—then got up and left, and as soon as she was out of the room I heard her burst out laughing. It seemed like she was doing it on purpose. She *wanted* me to think the worst—which is exactly what Robert used to do to Mum. He'd wind her up so she'd have no idea when he actually *was* playing away.'

Eliza tuts, to let him know she's still listening. 'Doesn't sound good.'

'Yeah. I gave Julia her bath, got her all settled. We read a story, I'll never forget—*The Tiger Who Came to Tea*—and once she was asleep I came down and asked Nicola straight out if she was sleeping with Robert. She bit my head off. *Not this again! What a disgusting suggestion, you're sick*. She yelled at me, and I yelled back, but we made up—at least I thought we had. I ended up apologising for being a jealous twat. We even had a drink together out on the kitchen steps, and talked about having another child one day. It was a lovely evening. Then I went to bed because I had an early start the next day. Nicola said she'd be up later. I had this kind of foreboding. I hate arguments, and summer nights always make me . . . so I, um, so I didn't sleep really. And much later I heard Toby bark and . . . sorry. I can't . . .'

'Sam?

'Sorry. Jesus.' She hears his despairing laugh. 'I'm pathetic.'

'Take your time. What did you hear?'

'Julia's voice. Julia, talking—yabbiting on, I used to call it. She was always yabbiting on. And it sounded like she was *outside* the house, down in the yard. What the heck was a little person doing out in the middle of the night—lost, or sleepwalking, being abducted by some weirdo? I ran over to the window and there was Nicola, putting Julia into her car seat. Toby was hopping in too. There were suitcases. I yelled out the window, asked Nicola what the bloody hell she was doing. She seemed pissed that I'd caught her. *What does it look like I'm doing?* I got down to the kitchen just as she came back in. She wanted her phone, I think. I was standing in my boxer shorts literally begging her not to go, not to take Julia away from me—*Please don't leave me, stay for a cup of coffee, stay for one more night, I'll take the day off tomorrow and we'll talk*—but the more I begged the more she seemed to despise me. She said nope, sorry, she was leaving me, and as long as I didn't make any trouble I'd still see Julia sometimes. *Sometimes.* My own daughter! The pair of us were yowling like cats. I'm not proud of it. I remember shouting *over my dead body do you take her, over my dead body*—and she was threatening that if I made any trouble she'd stop me seeing Julia ever again. *I'm her mother, you've got no rights.*'

'No rights?' Eliza glances at Nicola's statement. 'I think she's mistaken motherhood for dictatorship.'

'Well, but she's turned out to be bang on, hasn't she?'

'Maybe.'

'She grabbed her phone and sprinted outside like I was Jack the Ripper. Julia was in that car, and they were leaving me, and I panicked. I lost it. I said I'd kill them both, Nicola and Robert. Stupid thing to say. I didn't mean it. I tried to open the door to get Julia back out again, but it was locked. She was smiling out at me, saying, *Daddy!* She thought I was coming too. I ran around to Nicola's door and yanked it open just as she got the engine started. I think I grabbed her by the shoulders; I was just trying to stop her from taking Julia away. It was all a mess. I know she says I bruised her—I don't think I did, but maybe I did, and if so I'm sorry. She set off with gravel flaring everywhere. I was dragged along halfway to the gate until I fell over. The back window slid past under my hands. I can see it now, you know? Julia wailing, Toby barking. And that's the last time I ever saw Julia. That's the last time she'll ever see me.'

His voice collapses yet again, and again Eliza hears people speaking to him. She strains her ears to catch their tone. There's no hint of fear; no hyperventilating or crying from anyone except Sam. She clearly hears a male voice saying, *Okay, mate?* She raises her eyebrows at Paul, and from his incredulous frown she gathers he's heard it too.

'I tried phoning Nicola,' whispers Sam, 'but she blocked my calls. Messenger, WhatsApp, everything blocked. I soon worked out she'd run to Mum and Robert. They blocked me too. I phoned my solicitor. He doesn't do family law but he put me on to someone who does. She sent me an email with her fees and I could nowhere near afford it but she gave me an hour's free advice. She told me how to make an application. After that I was on my own. It's all dragged on and on. Every single morning I imagine Julia waking up without me. She's my whole life. There's this massive Julia-shaped hole, and without her I just don't see the point.'

'Why's the court taking so long?'

'We had to go to mediation, which took ages to set up and got us nowhere. Nicola wouldn't even be in a room with me. She said Julia has a recurring nightmare about how Daddy tried to drag Mummy out of the car, and it would be child abuse to make her see me. I think it's child abuse to *stop* her seeing me. So I was going through the court process and then . . . well, then I had the call from Mum. I was really happy for the first few seconds, pleased she was speaking to me, but then she said she was phoning to let me know she'd had a diagnosis. A cancer diagnosis.'

'That must have been an awful moment.'

'I couldn't take it in. I really couldn't. I asked her, *But it's not serious, is it? You're not worried?* I hoped she'd put my mind to rest. I expected to hear, *No, I'm not worried! It'll be fine, they got it early.* But what she said was: *Sam, I've never been so scared in my life.* Poor Mum. I wanted to drive up to London that minute but she asked me please to stay away. She said she couldn't face another fight. She was tired, I think. Just tired.'

'Poor lady.'

'I didn't know what to do. I didn't sleep all that night, and next day I turned up on their doorstep and leaned on the bell. I never saw her. Robert threatened to call the police on me. I mean why? Why keep Mum and me apart? I don't get it. Actually—yeah, I do. Like everything else, her illness was all about *him*. He had to be the centre of attention. He was the loyal husband, keeping the barking-mad foaming-at-the-mouth son at bay. She probably died thinking I didn't love her.'

'But you did love her.'

'Which is why I wasn't going to put her through a court battle while she was fighting cancer. I had no solicitor, remember. I was making decisions as best I could. Meanwhile, I still had a farm to manage. I've had to sell up all the equipment and stock and get ready to hand over everything to the new owners. I felt as though I was drowning. So I let Nicola have all her adjournments.'

Eliza is trying to imagine how it would feel, to be so young and lose so much.

'And all this time your mum was having treatment?' she asks.

'I think so. They wouldn't tell me. I kidded myself she'd be okay. I thought we had plenty of time to make things right, plenty of time . . . she'd have chemo or whatever and go into remission. People do, don't they? Stupid, I had my head buried in the sand. Nobody told me the oncologist had given her about three months. Six if she was lucky. Which she wasn't.'

'She wasn't lucky?'

'She wasn't lucky.'

THIRTY-FOUR

Sam

No, she wasn't lucky.

It's choking him. He can't get any more words out.

When was it? Friday. Three days ago now. He'd just come in from seeing the old mower being removed by a haulage contractor. Dad's mower, which he'd fixed in the hours before he died. The stock was gone from the fields, the machinery had been auctioned. Nicola, Julia, even Toby—all gone. Tyndale felt like a ghost farm.

It was already dark at five o'clock. He wandered into the house, poured half a tumbler of whisky, knocked it straight back, poured another one. That was when the phone rang.

It was a man's voice. Very precise, very polite. He asked if he was speaking to Sam Ballard and then introduced himself as David May, solicitor to Harriet Lacey.

'That's my mother,' said Sam. 'Harriet Ballard.'

'Yes. Is this a good moment? I've just a few loose ends to tidy up, since Mrs Lacey has sadly passed.'

'Sadly . . . what? No. You've made a mistake. You've got the wrong file. Perhaps you mean my grandmother, Patricia Ballard. She died in India a few years ago.'

'Harriet Lacey,' the solicitor repeated. 'The lady who recently passed away at St Columba's Hospice in South London.'

'You've definitely got the wrong Mrs Lacey.'

But David May insisted that he had the right person. Sam could hear him sounding more and more embarrassed as it dawned on him that he'd put his foot right in the middle of a landmine.

'When?' Sam croaked.

Ten days ago, the solicitor said. He'd understood that her close family was with her at the time.

'They weren't,' whispered Sam. 'I wasn't.'

The poor guy was obviously mortified. He stammered something about how this perhaps wasn't a good time, and how sorry he was, and rang off sharpish.

Sam walked around and around the kitchen table, trying to think how this mistake could have been made. Perhaps it was *Robert's* mother who'd died? Mrs Sheila Lacey? In the end he looked online, found St Columba's Hospice and dialled the number. The receptionist said they'd call him back, which they did half an hour later. By that time he was sitting with his head in his hands and another glass of whisky in his stomach. The world was spinning and swinging, spinning and swinging.

His caller was a woman with a gentle Irish voice. She introduced herself as Kathleen, the nurse who'd primarily looked after Harriet, both at home and in the five final days when she'd been in the hospice itself.

'I came to know Harriet very well,' she said. 'It was my privilege.'

'She's really dead?' asked Sam. He was digging his nails into the back of his hand, trying to wake up. This must be a dream.

'You didn't know?'

No, he said, he didn't know. Why did nobody tell him?

At this stage Kathleen began to sound wary. She beat around the bush, talking about what a lady Mum was, how the staff had all come to love her. Sam listened through a haze as she explained what the oncologist had said about Harriet's prognosis. The hospice had been involved since then. Apparently his mother had been lucid until the last day or so, and had never been in great pain. That was something, he supposed. Kathleen talked about Nicola and Julia, who were frequent visitors.

'Your Julia's a darling,' she said with a chuckle. 'I wish I had half her energy! Your mum's face would light up whenever she came into the room. And she behaved like an angel at the funeral, carrying a wreath almost as big as herself.'

'Funeral?'

'A lovely, very simple service at the crematorium. I always go if I can. It's a part of the journey for me too.'

'When was my mum's funeral?'

'Um, Monday I think. Let me just double-check the calendar. Yes, Monday. I had the morning off to go.'

Sam imagined a row of people in some faceless chapel: Julia, Nicola, Robert. Probably Oma and the dreaded Aunt Monique. Nurse Kathleen. Perhaps other friends of Robert's. But not Sam, not her only child.

Monday. Where was I on Monday? Selling up my home.

'Was she cremated?' he asked.

'Cremated, yes. That was her wish. She told me her ashes were going to be scattered on a farm where she lived for all the happiest years of her life. Does that ring any bells? It was a comfort to her, the notion of ending up on the farm with her first husband. She mentioned it several times in her last days.'

'Is Robert going to respect her wishes?'

Kathleen assumed so, because Robert was utterly devoted to Harriet. Nothing was too much trouble. He used to bring her a gift every day. A CD he'd made with a medley of her favourite music, so she could just lie and listen. Lip salve for her dry mouth. Flowers. At the end he sat by her bedside for thirty hours straight, holding her hand and talking to her even when she couldn't respond. The staff were all very touched by his devotion.

'Actually, though . . .' She hesitated, then seemed to come to a decision. 'Well, look, tell you the truth, I'm quite happy you've called,' she confided, with a conspiratorial lowering of her voice. 'Harriet had you on her mind. She wanted to know when you would be coming. It was quite a theme.'

'Nobody told me. I didn't know.'

He couldn't think of anything else. Just that. *I didn't know.*

'Robert explained that you and Harriet were estranged, that the last time you saw anyone in the family you were threatening to kill people, that the courts had been involved. He felt he couldn't risk a visit from you. He was afraid there would be a terrible scene and Harriet would be devastated. Robert was always very—' she searches for the word '—protective. And, you know, we have rules. He was her husband. He had the final say. Family disagreements are very common here, sadly enough, and we can't have loud conflict in the hospice. We do our best, but we have to stick to the rules.'

She sounded uneasy. Sam had obviously been on her conscience.

'She died on the Tuesday night,' she said. 'On the Sunday before, when I was bathing her, she only wanted to talk about you. *My Sammy.* She was a little bit confused by then, she kept drifting off to sleep. I think she was getting ready for her journey. She told me you were the greatest joy of her life.'

'Is that what she said?'

'Her exact words. *Greatest joy of my life.* She looked so happy when she talked about you. She told me that when you were a small boy, you had a dog named Bouncer. You and Bouncer grew up together.'

'We did,' he whispered.

'She said you used to be your Dad's shadow. Wherever he went, you were trotting beside him. If your dad wore overalls, you wanted your own pair. If he wore gloves, you ran to put on your mittens. You loved an old, lame horse called Sundance. You hated school but you lived and breathed the farm.'

'I did.'

'You were in your mum's heart, Sam. Right up to the end. She hadn't forgotten you. She hadn't forgotten you for a single moment.'

He thanked Kathleen, and she said she was so sorry, so sorry, losing a mother was a terrible thing. Then she went back to her work. Other families, other lives. Other deaths.

He dropped the phone as his world caved in. Mum was asking when he'd be coming! She must have been bewildered. She must have thought he'd turned his back. Now she was gone and there was nothing he could do for her, ever again. He couldn't tell her how much he loved her. He couldn't tell her she was the best mother in the world. He would never hug her again.

He has a vivid, nightmarish memory of staggering into the December night, his breath freezing into pale plumes, and smashing his forehead into the crumbling bricks of his home. The pain made him do it more. *Once. Twice.* Again and again, trying to escape the darkness.

Kathleen was his last human contact until he walked into Tuckbox three days later. His mangled forehead throbbed for a while before blending into all the other pain. He hasn't slept since. How could he sleep? What is the point of sleep, really? For those three days he didn't eat. He didn't wash. He didn't do anything normal. He disintegrated. The act of squeezing toothpaste onto the brush seemed mundane and ludicrous, and there was Julia's special baby toilet seat and her shampoo and her towel and her bath toys. There was Nicola's make-up bag, her bathrobe on the back of the door. He chucked brush and paste over his shoulder and walked away. The kitchen tap was dripping—he began to fix it out of habit but gave up when the pointlessness of the exercise overwhelmed him.

His mind chattered and screamed all day and all night, but he didn't hear another voice. Not a real one, anyway. He didn't see any living human being except the occasional car rumbling down the lane. The tap dripped, mice scurried in the kitchen, the Rayburn went out, the temperature plummeted. Sometimes he tried to find comfort by lying on Julia's bed, on the dinosaur duvet that still smelled of her, just a little bit. *The Tiger Who Came to Tea* lay on top of the pile of books on her chest of drawers. But there was no comfort for him. Within minutes he'd be up again, roaming outside, clutching at memories with numb fingers. The grain dryer was silent, the barns and kennels and stable were cold and empty. He wept at the sight of Julia's tricycle, her miniature wellies still parked side by side at the kitchen door. One night he climbed onto the stable roof and stood, precarious on the icy tiles, shouting for Mum. His cries will have carried on the crystalline air, probably as far as Holdsworth. People will have hoped it was just a dog howling, pulled pillows over their ears and gone back to sleep.

During those days the outside air temperature never rose above freezing. The air was like smoky glass. Frost grew on the drooping brown remnants of Mum's roses, on Julia's swing, on every strand of the washing line. Drifts of leaves turned to crackling layers of ice. He pictured a curly-headed toddler skipping beside him, rugged up in her jacket and mittens and bright blue hat. He felt the warmth of her hand tugging him along. He heard her giggle as she slid along the ice. He actually—physically—heard Julia's laughter, several times. Logic tells him this was hallucination, but he clearly heard her, as clear as the chirruping of the robin that kept flitting around his head. Funny thing: that robin even followed him into the house, perched on a lampshade and watched him with beady eyes. It wasn't until the crazy bird started flying right through walls like a ghost that Sam began to suspect he wasn't real. That's when he began taking the Ritalin. Insanely, he thought it might keep him sane.

Last night he'd found himself in Sundance's field. No horses anymore. When he got to the spot where they scattered Dad, he stretched himself out on the ground, facing the starless sky. After all these years of struggle, the darkness had finally beaten him. He'd come to the end. He hadn't bothered to put on a jacket or even a jersey. He had no intention of ever getting up again. He heard the church clock striking midnight down in Holdsworth, but it wasn't striking for him. Time was for other people.

He heard his own voice, calling out: *Mum? Dad? You here? Hello?*

They weren't. Of course they weren't. The cold rose up from the earth and wrapped itself around his body. He might as well have been lying in a freezer. His fingers and feet ached until they disappeared. This was emptier than loneliness. This was nothingness. He wishes now he'd never moved again. Hypothermia should have got him.

Hours later, one of the owls hooted in the dark mass of the spinney. He opened his eyes and saw that the sky had cleared, and so had his mind. Stars blazed from one horizon to another. The clock was striking again. *One, two, three strikes and you're out.*

In the final echo of the last of the chimes, he heard Dad's voice. It was perfectly clear and coming from very close by. He sounded just like his old self. Sam wasn't even surprised. He'd lost touch with any kind of reality by then.

Bring her home, Sam. Bring her back to me.

Just those words, then silence again.

Sam lay and looked up at the stars, and it all made perfect sense. There *was* something he could do—something for both his parents! Together, Mum and he would stand up to Robert for the first and last time. It would be their rebellion.

The creak of the Land Rover's rusted door was like a screech of agony. He used a credit card to scrape ice from the windscreen. The poplar tree lowered over him as he laid his shotgun on the back seat. *What the hell do you think you're doing with that?*

He stood for a final moment outside his home, feeling the

solidity of the land under his boots, inhaling the brilliance of the stars. This was where he was born. This was where everything happened. The next moment he'd swung into the driver's seat, shattering the night with the cough of the old engine. He was rocking through the potholes in the yard, turning out of the gate. Turning into nothing.

•

They're all listening as he tries to describe those last three days. Mutesi hasn't moved from her armchair. Buddy has crawled half onto Neil's lap, rumbling and crooning with pleasure, and Neil's arms are wrapped around his beloved friend. Abi is still the restless one. She's been prowling around the place, turning the radio on and off, stretching, messing with things.

Down the phone, he hears the negotiator sigh.

'I see,' she murmurs. 'I see. I *see.* So when you said to Robert, *I've come to get her*, and, *What have you done with her?* you were asking for . . .?'

'Mum. Well, her ashes. They were the only thing left of her. Maybe it seems like a mad obsession to you, but all the way to London I was promising her—*promising* her—I'd bring her home to be with Dad in Sundance's field, like she wanted. I've failed as a son. I wasn't there for her when she was dying. But there was this one thing left I could do for her and for my dad. It was all that mattered.'

'You took a gun with you, Sam. Why?'

'Stupid, I know. At four o'clock this morning I imagined threatening Robert if he wouldn't give me Mum's ashes. By the time I'd got to London I'd thought better of it. I left it in the truck when I first came in. I honestly never intended to get it out at all.'

'And you confronted Robert?'

'I asked him why he didn't tell me she was dying.'

'What did he say?'

'He said I'd have destroyed her peace. He told me to stop making a fool of myself. I'd just seen Nicola running to avoid me, and there he was, being a twat. I tried to stand up to him. I said I'd come for her ashes. He said—fuck, he was pleased with himself—he said, *Whoops, you're a bit too late!* He delighted in telling me what he'd done with her . . . what *they'd* done with her. It was both of them. Nicola was in on it too.'

'Which was?'

'They'd chucked her into the Thames.'

'The *Thames*?'

'Yep, just lobbed the whole urn into the water at high tide, somewhere near Battersea. They didn't even bother taking the lid off. That was the *last* thing Mum would have wanted. She was never a townie; she was a gardener, a country woman. She had a real horror of deep water. She didn't even like swimming, so the idea of her being shut in an urn, sinking into that muddy river . . . and Robert was grinning from ear to ear—fuck, he was pleased with himself. *Good luck getting your mum back from Old Father Thames.* I looked into his face, and you know what I saw? I saw the devil puppet grinning back at me. He'd done it to hurt me and hurt her and hurt Dad. That's the only reason! And everything hit me at once. All the years of Robert World. They all came together in those few seconds. I remember these pulses of something . . . I don't know how to describe it . . . um, a bit like electricity, like holding on to an electric fence. I felt like I couldn't breathe, couldn't speak, no coordination, no proper thoughts, just this jolting. It took me over, it switched off my . . . I stopped thinking. I couldn't even see properly; I was looking down a tunnel. People talk about being out of their mind, and now I know what that means.'

'You must remember going to get the gun from your vehicle?'

'Not really—well, yes, I remember grabbing it out of the case, and a handful of ammunition. Felt like a dream.'

'How did it come to be loaded?'

'I dunno. I must have done that, but the next thing I remember is running back into Tuckbox. I was holding it. Robert looked up and saw me and said, *You again?* Smiling. Still smiling! And I wanted to stop him smiling, and he'd thrown my mum into the river, and I shot him. Once. Twice. I'm surprised I hit him 'cos my whole body was shaking. Fuck, I wish I'd missed.'

He's looking over towards the far corner by the swinging door, where Robert's body is somehow seeming less and less human. So much blood. What was he even thinking? Julia can't come in here, there's a dead body! And, anyway, what kind of a last memory of her dad would she have, filthy and crazy in a blood-spattered café? Much better if she remembers a happy half-hour snuggling up with bedtime stories.

Emmanuel's crayons are still scattered across the table in the booth. He chooses a dark blue one. Julia likes blue. It's her favourite colour: blue slides in her hair, blue pyjamas, blue everything. Of course, in the future she might prefer red, or green, but he has to start somewhere.

'Eliza,' he says. 'I just want to do something. Can you call back in five minutes?'

She sounds worried, but she says she will. She's really got no choice.

He takes a seat at the table and unfolds a serviette, thinking about what he wants to say. If he had time to write a million words it wouldn't be enough. He has no idea who Julia will be when—if—she reads this. He doesn't know what worries she'll have, or what dreams. The chances are, she'll have been told nothing but horror stories about her father. She might have no memory of him at all, or of the farm, or the happy times they've spent together.

He crumples up the first three attempts. His handwriting's embarrassing, his spelling is worse. Autocorrect has been his saviour but a blue crayon doesn't have that. Everything he writes looks lame, or childish, or just plain stupid. He imagines Nicola rolling her eyes and throwing his letter in the bin. Julia will probably never see it and, if she does, she'll think her dad was an illiterate fool.

He doesn't even notice he's crying, until the tears blur his vision.

Eliza

Sam's words drag along behind him like a weighted chain.

'I've written a letter to Julia,' he says. 'Just a short one. Wish I could spell. Will you see Nicola gets it? Ask her to give it to Julia when she's old enough?'

Eliza catches Paul's eye. They both grimace.

'Please?' persists Sam.

'You don't need to write to Julia. You'll see her yourself one day soon.'

'Can I trust you to do this for me, Eliza? I can trust you, can't I? Promise me.'

'I promise to do my best. It might depend on the content of the letter. Julia's only two.'

'Three. She turned three in September. I bought a present for her: a really flash silver pedal car. It's in the back of the Landy. I brought it with me in case I got to see her today. She'll love it! Tell Nicola, will you? Make sure she gets her pedal car.'

Eliza's frantically thinking of reasons for him to live.

'She's very small, Sam.'

'She is.'

'She needs her dad.'

He doesn't reply. Something has changed, something has gone very wrong. His next words are a shout of fury but it's not aimed at Eliza.

'You've got to be fucking kidding me! That was Nicola, wasn't it? Where is she?'

Eliza's stomach clenches. She can hear a cacophony of rage and fear—a shriek, protests from the hostages, bellowing from Sam.

You're imagining things, Sam. Too much bloody Ritalin! You're hallucinating, mate.

'Where the fuck is she? Where is she? Get out of my fucking way, Abi!'

It's happening, it's happening—the worst-case scenario, the unthinkable. Ashwin's clutching at his hair, mouthing *shit, shit*, he's on his phone and alerting the boss to this disaster. This negotiation is hurtling out of the sky, the ground is rushing up to meet it, and there is definitely no parachute.

Someone must have turned on the speakerphone at Sam's end, because the voices are suddenly amplified into Eliza's headset. She can hear every word. A woman seems to be trying to take control of the situation. Not Mutesi—this voice isn't nearly so mellow. She's crisply telling Sam to stop being an idiot and put that frigging gun down unless he wants the fucking SAS smashing in through the plate-glass windows and blowing his head off—which they will, she assures him.

Ashwin's still muttering into his phone. He listens, glances at Eliza.

'The boss wants your urgent assessment: are we looking at immediate loss of life?'

She takes a breath, forcing her mind to straighten out of its tailspin. She can't afford the luxury of panic. If she gives the word, the negotiation will be over. Tuckbox will turn into a battleground within seconds.

'We're out of time,' groans Ashwin, who is listening to the boss through one ear, the café through the other. He's lost his cool. 'For God's sake, Eliza! He's about to find her and when he does—'

'Tell the boss to hold on,' she says, interrupting him. 'We've finally got a listening device. We can hear, we're monitoring. Hold on. Tell him.'

Ashwin looks aghast. 'You sure?'

Of course she isn't sure.

At that moment, the shouting stops abruptly. There's nothing. No noise, no voices. Eliza listens with her whole being, pressing the headset to her ears. She may have just made a catastrophic blunder. Every nerve, every thought, every breath is focused on what's happening in that café.

The silence is menacing. It has undertow, like the swell of a breaking wave.

She shuts her eyes. If the next sound she hears is the report of a shotgun, she'll have to live with the guilt forever.

THIRTY-FIVE

Sam

If the others hadn't been dead quiet at that precise moment. If the radio hadn't been turned off. If a dodgy hinge hadn't caused the swinging door into the storeroom to stick, leaving it just a little bit open.

If, if. If any of those things hadn't happened, he would probably never have known she was there. She sneezed three times in quick succession, each one louder than the last. He's loved that girl. He lived with her for over three years. He knows her sneezes when he hears them.

It all makes sense! Now he knows why Neil and Abi have been so keen to keep nipping out to the back kitchen. Now he knows why the police have spent all day insisting they can't find her.

Everyone's been lying to him.

They try to stop him. They're all yelling. Neil flails out and even manages to grab his arm, but Neil's no athlete. It's easy to barge past him and into the back kitchen. The most obvious place to hide is the staff toilet—no, it's empty. He emerges to find Abi blocking his way with a stubborn pout and her arms held out wide, as though heading off a raging bull. She's demanding that he put his frigging gun down unless he wants the fucking SAS smashing in here and blowing his head off—which they certainly will, she declares triumphantly, because *they're listening to you, Sam! They're listening to all this on speakerphone! See?* She's holding up the café phone to prove her point.

Now Mutesi has joined her, while Neil and Buddy are limping into position on her other side. A cuddly grandmother, a tactless lawyer, an arthritic gambler and his dog. A stubborn wall of oddballs. Sam's about to try and shoulder his way through them when he hears a familiar voice yelling his name. They all look round as Nicola half tumbles, half crawls out of the cupboard under the sink.

'Stop, Sam!' She sounds panicked. She's on her hands and knees. 'Stop. Stop.'

The three of them gather around, helping her to her feet while shielding her from him.

He's silenced. He's stunned. The love of his life has changed so much, but not as he expected. In his bitter moments he's imagined her drinking champagne or shopping for designer clothes, prosperous and smug after months of secretly banging Robert. He couldn't have been more wrong. She looks half-starved. He can see the bones of her elbows and hips, mauve shadows under her eyes. Her face is chalk-white, streaked with running mascara and smudged lipstick. A clown's face. He's built her up in his mind as the cold-hearted, unassailable bitch who stomped on his heart. The Nicola he knew was never frightened of anyone but she's scared witless right now. Her whole body is trembling. She seems horrified by the sight of the gun in his hand. He's ashamed.

'Sorry.' He turns away from her, laying it on a benchtop. It's the first time he's put it down since this whole thing began. 'Sorry, Nicola. See? I'll leave it here. I've put it down, okay?'

She shifts her gaze to his face. She's never looked at him so intently—at least not since those early days when she thought she was in love with him. Her voice is hoarse.

'Where's Robert?' she asks.

Nobody speaks. Mutesi lays a consoling hand on her arm.

Nicola is still staring into Sam's face. 'Did you kill him? Is he dead?'

When he nods, her eyes close for a second. She lets out a long breath.

'Good,' she says.

Good?

'I was caught between the devil and the deep blue sea. Robert was the devil.'

Of all the conversations he's imagined having with Nicola, this isn't one of them.

'See these?' She's twisting her left arm, holding it up to the light. When he looks more closely, he sees what she's pointing out: dark blotches, spread all the way from her wrists to her shoulders. What are they—bruises? They look like purplish fruit, dropping from the leaves of her vine tattoo.

'Robert,' she declares furiously. 'Bloody Robert Lacey. He turned out to be a piece of work! I said it was wrong—him and me—I told him it was immoral and we had to end it. I tried to kick him out of my flat. Well, he didn't like that. He showed his true colours. Look. These—' she lays her own fingers over the marks '—are where he grabbed me. See? Same on the other arm.' She turns to show those ones too. 'You know how easily I bruise, Sam. He said Julia and I owed him. Our home, our income, our security, everything was down to him. He lied to me right from the beginning. He lied about you, he lied about Harriet. By the time I worked out what he really was, it was too late. He owned me.'

Up is down, day is night. Sam has no idea what to believe. It occurs to him that lying is a game for people like Robert and Nicola. To them the truth is just a football, to be kicked and passed around.

Abi seems to have appointed herself chair of this strange meeting.

'Okay,' she says, holding up both hands. Sam's sure she uses that booming voice in court. 'Okay, okay. Sam—you've been demanding to talk to Nicola all day. Right? Right. Well, here she is! Your wish is granted. So get talking. What exactly d'you want to discuss?'

'The truth,' he says.

'Truth.' Abi narrows her eyes. 'You're going to have to be a bit more specific.'

'I've lived through years of Robert World, followed by years of Nicola World, and I feel like I've gone crazy. I want to know what really happened between you and Robert. I want to understand why my life got destroyed. Then I'll say goodbye and you can all walk out of here. Five minutes of truth, and after that you'll never hear from me again.'

'Is that a promise?' asks Nicola.

'Hope to die.'

'No matter what I tell you?'

'No matter what, as long as it's real. No more twisting, no more spin.'

She wraps her bruised arms around herself. She looks lonely.

'Go on then,' she says. 'You ask, I'll answer.'

He can't think. He doesn't know where to begin. He didn't expect it to happen like this. It's so sudden—after all the months of silence, of meaningless solicitors' letters and being blocked from phoning and lying awake hour after hour, imagining what he'd say to her if only he had the chance.

'Start with Robert,' he says in the end. 'You and him were sleeping together?'

She nods.

'Even when my mother was dying?'

She hesitates, glancing towards the shotgun before she nods again.

'You visited her in the hospice, dutiful daughter-in-law, and all the time you were shagging her husband?'

'I didn't want to by then. Robert told me—way, way back, not long after I first met him—he made out their marriage had been pretty much a fiction for years. He told me Harriet had never got over the loss of her first husband, and Robert felt like a third party in someone else's love affair. He was about to leave her when she got her diagnosis. Then he couldn't. He couldn't leave a dying woman. That's what he told me, and I believed him. Now I'm not so sure.'

'When did it begin, this thing with you and him?'

'Sam, don't do this.'

'When?'

'Okay. Okay. He made a beeline for me the very first time we met. Remember we walked ahead across the farm that morning when they visited? We got on like a house on fire. Later he told me he'd never connected with anyone like he did with me. He said it was our star signs that were in alignment.'

'Ugh, spare me,' mutters Abi.

'But nothing happened while you and me were together, Sam. I promise. Robert acted very loving, very generous—and, yes, there was a spark. He pressured me all the time to leave you, he said their door would be open to me, and in the end I did. That's when . . . well, you know. He waited until your mum was out, we shared a bottle of wine and he came into my room and announced he was violently in love with me, that you have to seize what you want in life. He . . . one thing led to another. He was just so overwhelming. He made me feel amazing. It didn't feel wrong. It—'

'It was betraying my mother! An innocent woman who trusted you—and with the grandfather of your child, for God's sake!'

'Step-grandfather.'

'It was totally fucked up.'

'I know. I know.' There are tears now. She wipes one eye, sniffing. Maybe she's genuinely remorseful, but he doubts it. 'I know it was fucked up. But he promised me their marriage had been over for a long time, he swore they'd be getting divorced. In the end I started to hate what he and I were doing. I started to hate him too.'

So it's true. He wasn't paranoid to suspect them; it wasn't all in his mind. His stepfather *was* sleeping with his girlfriend. It's like having a reliable compass for the first time ever. Up is up. Down is down. Night and day are in their ordered places.

'I kept trying to end it,' she says. 'He always persuaded me to stay. The day of the funeral I told him no more, it's over. That's when I got these.' Her fingertips caress the bruises on her arms. 'Shoved me against a door, tore my clothes. What Robert wanted, he got. And what choice did I have? I've got nobody else. He's my boss, he pays my rent, he organises every little thing about my life. The flat belongs to a shady mate of his who would have thrown Julia and me onto the street at a single word from Robert. So I gave in, yet again. Does that make me a whore?'

Sam laughs shortly. 'If the cap fits.'

'I felt like one. I kept coming to work every day, kept letting him into my bed and into my mind. I began to think I'd never be free of him.'

'You could have come back to Tyndale.'

'Yeah.' She rolls her eyes. 'Yeah, Sam, you'd have made me so welcome. *Not*.'

'I'd have been happy to see you. Happy to have Julia home.'

'No! Don't you dare minimise your part in all this. I left in the middle of the night because when you lose your temper you're like a different person. You can't control your anger, Sam. You tried to drag me out of my car. You threatened me, you bruised me, you terrified your baby daughter. These things happened. They *happened*. You can't deny it. Robert was the devil but, in your own way, you were the deep blue sea.'

She's getting back some of her chutzpah. Her eyes have taken on their slate-grey gleam. She's got her hands jammed into the back pockets of her jeans.

'That's it,' she says, staring him down. 'That's the truth. The whole truth, and nothing but. And I'm sorry, Sam. I really am. I wish we could have the time over again. Robert was a big mistake. He seemed to be offering the earth, and I was taken in by him. I was dazzled. Despite everything, you're the one I really loved.'

She has no idea how empty and stupid those words sound now. He could laugh. He could cry. Perhaps she even believes her own lies.

'How was Mum?' he asks. 'How was she in the end?'

At last there's something honest, a softening. Her shoulders drop. Her voice loses its defensive brassiness.

'Peaceful,' she says. 'She wasn't in pain, especially not in the last few days. I was there. She was asleep for a while, and then she was gone. They were wonderful in the hospice.'

'Why didn't you tell me she was dying?'

'Robert said no. I asked him, and the nurse asked him. He was sure you'd cause a scene and upset her.'

'Why did you throw her ashes away?'

She blinks. Her gaze darts to a spot somewhere behind him, and then back to his face.

'What?'

'Her ashes.'

'Why did I . . .' She's frowning. 'What about her ashes?'

'Robert told me what the pair of you did with her. He told me this morning. Why? Hadn't you humiliated her enough?'

Nicola's gaping at him as though he's speaking Klingon. Silently, she repeats his words: *Robert told me*. Her brow is crinkled, one corner of her lip curled upwards. He knows that expression. She's genuinely perplexed.

'Oh my God,' she breathes, as realisation dawns. 'Oh my God. What the fuck did he tell you? Did he say we flushed her down a toilet or something?'

'Into the Thames, off Battersea Bridge.'

'I don't believe this!' She puts her hand to her face, smothering a whooping kind of shriek. 'Robert Lacey! You've got to be kidding me. What a knob. He couldn't tell the truth to save his life—literally! If he'd told the truth he'd still be alive. Look.'

Suddenly she's broken away from her trio of bodyguards. She marches past Sam to a corner of the storeroom, stretches her graceful body to lift something down from a high shelf.

'Here,' she says, turning around. 'Is this what you're looking for?'

It's a cardboard tube, about a foot high and six inches across, covered in pictures of red roses.

Abi takes a step closer, obviously fascinated. 'Is that what I think it is?'

'Harriet's ashes,' declares Nicola. 'They've been in this room—on this shelf—since Saturday afternoon, which is when Robert collected them from the funeral director. He hadn't decided what to do with them. All he had to do when you arrived this morning was walk in here, pick this up, hand it over to you. Job done. He'd still be alive. None of this would have happened.'

'Why on earth would he say he threw it in the river?' asks Abi.

Nicola shrugs. 'Probably because he liked to lie. Because he liked to wind Sam up. Because he didn't want Harriet's ashes going back to Tyndale, back to Sam's dad. He'd never have expected you to turn up with a shotgun, Sam.'

Sam is barely listening. He can't take his eyes off the rose-covered tube. It's what he came here for. He watches as Nicola lays it on the benchtop beside his gun, and then dusts off her hands. It's an unconscious movement; she's brushing non-existent dust from her palms with long, slow strokes.

'I'd like to go now.' She speaks smoothly, as though she's accidentally fallen into the tiger enclosure at the safari park and is trying to keep the prowling animal calm while she climbs out again. 'Okay, Sam? I've told the truth like you said. I need to collect Julia. Social services had to step in 'cos I've got no family in London. She's with strangers, she'll be beside herself. You don't want that, do you?'

He doesn't want that. He picks up the gun in his right hand, the cardboard tube of ashes in his left.

'Okay,' he says. 'It's time for everybody to leave.'

Nicola leads the way out of the storeroom. The scene in the kitchen makes her stop dead in the doorway for a moment. She has to step around Robert's body, and over the trail of blood, muttering, 'God save me,' under her breath.

The brightly lit café feels like home, as though they've lived here for weeks. Their mugs and plates and teapots are still scattered around the tables. It's warm, it smells of tea. Not much point in doing the washing-up; he doesn't imagine Tuckbox will be open for business again any time soon. Neil helps Nicola to drag the barricade away from the street door.

Meanwhile Abi is on the silver café phone, keeping the negotiator in the loop.

'We're all coming out,' she says. 'All of us. Yes, Sam too. I think Nicola will be first.'

The tables are out of the way now. Nicola unbolts the street door, top and bottom, and turns the key.

'This is for Julia,' Sam says, handing her the message he wrote on a serviette. 'For when she's older.'

'How much older?'

'I don't know. I'll leave that to your judgement. Please give it to her.'

She nods, slipping the folded serviette into the pocket of her jeans. She doesn't seem frightened of him anymore. He's pleased about that. After all, she's got rid of both the devil and the deep blue sea. Two birds with one stone.

'How is she?' he asks.

'Julia's great! She's talking even more, loads of new words, she's so funny. She's going to nursery school.'

'Will she be all right?'

'She'll be fine.'

He wishes they had longer. There's so much more he wants to say; so much more he wants to know.

'Look after her, will you?'

She smiles at him as she opens the door.

'You know I will, Sam. Give me that, at least. I may have been a shitty girlfriend but I'm a good mum.'

'Give her my love. Please. D'you promise?'

'I promise.'

'Read her a story tonight. *The Tiger Who Came to Tea.*'

She has one foot over the threshold when she turns back. She takes his face in her two hands, kisses him on the mouth.

'Sorry, Sam,' she murmurs. 'Good luck.'

The next moment she's dashing out into the street. She's gone. The door is standing open, letting in the icy wind.

The three hostages are getting ready to follow her. Neil's threading a piece of string under Buddy's collar. Mutesi has shrugged into her anorak and is zipping it up. Abi's still talking to the negotiator, who seems to be giving instructions.

'Eliza says to remind you to put your gun down now,' she tells Sam. 'It'll be like the O.K. Corral in Wilton Street if you step outside carrying that bloody thing.'

'All right.' He slides into the booth, puts the box of ashes on the table. 'You lot go on. I'll follow you.'

'Why?'

'I just want to do a couple of things before I leave.'

The stock of his shotgun is resting on the floor; he has a leg each side of the barrel. He picks up the last mug of tea Mutesi made him and swigs it straight down. It's lukewarm. Better than nothing. For some reason he was craving that little bit of comfort.

The three of them are standing by the door, watching him.

'Coming now?' asks Abi.

'In a minute.'

They seem nonplussed, glancing at one another. Mutesi jerks her chin towards the door.

'We will step outside together, Sam. You and me. It's time to face the rest of your life.'

When he shakes his head, she sighs. She slips out of her anorak, folds it neatly and drapes it across a chair. Neil's locking the door again. Abi is whispering into the phone. *We've got a problem*. After a moment, she hands it to Sam.

'Eliza wants to talk to you,' she says.

Eliza

'Nicola Rosedale has just left Tuckbox,' announces Ashwin. 'She's unhurt.'

Paul gives a breathy whistle of relief. 'That's very good news.'

Abi Garcia has been keeping up a running commentary over the café phone. 'Nicola's out . . . we're on our way.'

'Has he put the gun down?' asks Eliza. 'Tell him he must put it down now. He must not on any account emerge with it. Okay? Make sure his hands are empty when he steps outside. There's a fair bit of firepower lined up beyond that door.'

'Okay.'

The negotiators listen as Abigail passes on the message in her own words. *It'll be like the O.K. Corral in Wilton Street.*

'Are you coming out now?' asks Eliza.

'Any second.'

'Walk slowly, clearly showing that your hands are empty, just to avoid any misunderstanding. Leave the café phone behind. Leave everything behind. The whole place is a crime scene. Okay?'

'Okay.'

Eliza's drawing a mass of heavy bars on her notepad. Ashwin is blinking compulsively behind his glasses. Even Paul seems to keep forgetting to breathe. The end of a siege is one of the most dangerous moments for hostages. A mistake, a change of heart, a last-minute cock-up—there's plenty of scope for carnage. A minute crawls by. The hostages seem to be taking a long time to appear, but then people don't always sprint joyfully into the arms of the police. Sometimes they need time to adjust.

Abigail's voice is on the line again.

'We've got a problem.'

'What's happening?'

'Sam's not coming with us after all. I don't know what he's planning but I don't think it's good.'

'Is he still threatening you?'

'No.'

'Let me talk to him,' says Eliza. 'You three need to leave now. You hear me? *Right now*. I want you, Neil and Mutesi out of that building. Give Sam the phone and then leave.'

When Sam comes on the line, he sounds calm, almost jolly.

'Hi, Eliza.'

'Hi, Sam. You found Nicola?'

'I did. Pretty funny really. You were a bit fucked, weren't you, when I kept asking where she was and you knew full well she was under that sink the whole time.'

'I'll see you in a minute, okay? I'll be waiting at the cordon when you come out. They'll bring you to me. I'll stay with you for a while, make sure you're looked after.'

'Yeah . . . maybe not.'

'Come on, Sam.'

'It's the right time for me to go. I've decided. Just need the courage now. I've had this darkness inside me ever since I was a kid. It's never going to leave me. I've tried to fight it but there's no point anymore.'

'You think that now, but—'

'I've nothing left, you see? Everything's gone. My home, my family. I've killed a man. I'll never get past that. And I think I'd rather die than end up in prison. I've got a bit of a phobia. Something my aunt once told me.'

'It wouldn't be forever.'

'It'd be years. I might be an old man when I come out. Listen, though, 'cos there's a couple of things I'd like you to do.' He sounds like someone in a business meeting, ticking off things on his to-do list. 'Mutesi, Abi, Neil. You know why they got caught up in this? Because they're heroes. The only reason they didn't run away with all the others is because they were trying to help. They should get medals. Also, Neil and his dog need somewhere to live.'

'I can't promise that.'

'Please. He and Buddy have got to stay together.'

He's making plans for his own departure, tidying up as best he can. All Eliza can do is find some reason for him to be ambivalent about his death.

'Can you imagine Julia growing up?' she asks. 'Leaving school, maybe going to university? Getting married one day? Imagine! She'll be a clever, lovely young woman. You'll walk her up the aisle . . . Sam? Are you there? Sam?'

'I'm not much good to Julia now.'

'You're her dad.'

'Thanks for listening to me today,' he says. 'Believe it or not, I feel a lot better for being listened to. You're good at your job. I feel ready now.'

'Sam—'

'Over and out.'

'Wait! Sam, wait—'

But he's gone.

She dreads the next sound. It will arrive in stereo, travelling simultaneously through the air and down the line. She's heard it before: a single shot. She knows the horrible finality of that sound.

Flying a jet down a canyon. One mistake and you're embedded in the cliffs. Or someone else is.

THIRTY-SIX

Sam

He drops the phone onto the table. He can hear Eliza's voice—*Sam, wait*—as he lowers his head until the barrel is pressing under his chin. His forefinger is stretching to release the safety catch.

This darkness is his childhood friend. This is the same inky emptiness that led him to make a noose in the boys' changing room. It's been biding its time all these years. He feels relief now that he's finally giving in to it. He's surprised: it was so hard to make the decision to die, but now that the moment has arrived, it seems a lot easier than making the decision to live.

The passing seconds are heavy, stretched by the massiveness of this thing he is about to do. There'll be an inquest for him, another one for Robert. The incident at Tuckbox will be all over the news. People will keep press cuttings and one day Julia will read them. What will she think of him?

'Sam? Mate?'

He opens his eyes to see Neil crouching down, his bearded face close to Sam's.

'Mate. I'm serious now. Do me a favour and take your finger away from that trigger, will you?'

Sam manages a bit of a smile—not easy when you've got a barrel digging into your chin.

'You'll have to see yourselves out,' he says. 'Go on. All of you. Get lost.'

Neil exchanges glances with the two women. His face is mobile, creased by life—once you've noticed that in him, the dirt and tangled hair are irrelevant. Sam wishes he'd known him before now. He wishes he'd known all of them. The strangers we pass on the street.

'Actually, I'd rather stay in this nice warm café,' says Neil.

'I don't think I'll be off just yet either,' says Abi. 'I think I'll hang about right here, if it's all the same with you.'

'Mm.' That's Mutesi. He hears her footsteps, a contented sigh as she sinks heavily into an armchair. 'We are all very comfortable.'

He doesn't want them to see. This isn't their darkness. They shouldn't be drenched in it.

'Please will you all fuck off,' he begs them. 'Please. I mean it.'

Nobody moves. Buddy's tail swishes the floor.

He's not scared anymore. He feels giddy with his impending liberation. He doesn't have to *be* any longer. The coldness of metal, the familiar smell of gun oil. This trigger doesn't take much pressure to fire. It's always been on the light side. Dad used to complain about that.

The clock on the wall has a loud tick. He hasn't even noticed that until now.

Tick-tick, tick-tick. Five. Four.

He hears Abi draw in a sharp breath.

'Sam! Sam, hang on a minute. Tell us about Julia. Maybe we could meet her after this is all over. I'd like to meet her.'

She's playing for time. Nice of her. She could be gone by now. She could be skipping down the street, back to normality, back to her baby-shaking client and that guy half the nation heard on the radio—the one who obviously worships her, who offered to take her place. He hopes they'll be happy.

He shuts his eyes. *Three. Two.*

'There was a nightwatchman,' says Mutesi.

They all look around at her. Even Sam. There's something in her voice that compels it. She nods slowly, as though giving herself permission.

'The nightwatchman. Sometimes he and I sat on wooden chairs under a tree outside the hospital and chatted about our children. When I was working on the ward at night, I'd see his light and know that he was patrolling. I was happy to think that we were safe in his care.'

She covers her eyelids with both her hands.

'I can see him now. Yes, there he is. Holding his kerosene lamp.'

Mutesi

Shadowy behind the oily plumes of smoke: a tall figure in a yellow cotton shirt. Thin shoulders, a bony face.

His name was Philippe. His name *is* Philippe. He wasn't especially handsome nor especially clever; nor, she honestly believes, was he especially wicked before the hate crawled into his mind. He was like her, just an ordinary person doing an ordinary job. When he talked about his children, his smile was very bright. Elegant hands—she remembers those, especially. She can still hear his reedy voice, chuckling about that baby son of his.

You could taste the approach of the madness. Eddies of hatred on the wind. Propaganda on the radio. The neighbour whose child you helped to deliver begins to avoid you, she won't meet your eye. Colleagues huddling in corners; sidelong glances when you walk down the street. Rumours. She thinks sadly of whispered discussions with her husband, the plans they made to save their children if the worst should happen. Then the president's plane came down and a monster was unleashed.

'My country lost its mind,' she says. 'In one hundred days about a million people were slaughtered. Can you even take that in?

I can't. I can't at all, and I was there. Babies, grandparents, young teenagers—killed like animals, killed in horrible ways, piled up like rubbish. Every one of them has their own story. People nowadays are so fond of their crime dramas, their serial killer Sunday night miniseries. Well, I am not fond of those because I've seen serial killing on an industrial scale. I know an ordinary person can get out of bed in the morning and get dressed and think of new ways to murder innocent children.'

Nobody speaks. She takes a long breath while she orders her thoughts.

'They used the radio to plant seeds. We like to think of the radio as a friendly thing, don't we? We've been listening today to the traffic and travel and the news. The chat. The music. But in those days in Rwanda it spilled out hatred all day long, saying the Tutsi were cockroaches, that we were a dirty race who must be exterminated. Again and again the country was told this. If you tell lies often enough, people begin to believe them. That is brainwashing.'

She can hear it now, the voice of the presenter on Radio Mille Collines. The chirpy song.

Let us rejoice, friends
Cockroaches have been exterminated.
Let us rejoice, friends
God is never wrong.

'They broadcast lists of names, described exactly where people could be found. So the militia—the Interahamwe—took up every weapon they could find, even homemade ones, machetes and spears and clubs, or sometimes guns and grenades that were provided to them. They went from house to house. There was nowhere for anyone to hide. People ran to us because my husband was a pastor. He tried to offer sanctuary in our church but it was no fortress, it was small, made of mud bricks and with a tin roof, and packed with frightened people. When the militia came, they had no respect for God. The altar became a place of execution. Everyone was murdered, including my husband. They locked the doors and burned down the building to make sure nobody survived. My three elder sons were killed as they hid in their classroom at school. One of their killers was their own teacher. Some were other children.'

Horrified silence from her listeners. Mutesi is barely aware of them now. The film is running, the dreaded film. She has no choice but to watch it.

'My two youngest were with me at home. Giselle was three years old, Isaac was seven. I took their hands and we ran to the hospital. I hoped Philippe would be there, and that he'd hide us. But when he saw me come running up with my children, he laughed. I begged him to hide us but instead he cried out to the gang. He shouted in a loud voice—*Cockroaches are here! Cockroaches are here!* And so they came, with such hatred in their eyes. Straight away they dragged Giselle from my hands. I tried to hold on but they brought down a machete, here.' She touches her arm just below the elbow, where the long scar is hidden by her sleeve. 'How could they hate a little girl so much? I think it was a collective insanity. They believed we were vermin, because they had been taught that we were. They all descended on Giselle with their machetes and their—'

'My God,' mutters Neil. 'Mutesi, no. Stop. Stop.'

She shuts her eyes again, covers them with her hands, but she can never blot out her child's screams nor the workmanlike determination on the faces of those killers. For a quarter of a century she's been forced to watch the same piece of footage. She smells the burning, hears the screaming, is overwhelmed by the same grief and terror. She's found no way to stop the film from running.

'You don't have to tell us,' says Neil. 'We know what happened. It was on the news.'

'The news!' Mutesi opens her eyes. 'Yes, it was in your living room. But we couldn't turn off the television and walk away. After they had finished with Giselle they threw her body into a pit. I held Isaac close and told him to close his eyes. We crouched down together and waited for our turn, for the blows of the machetes and the clubs. I didn't even have time to pray. I hoped it would be quick for us, and that they wouldn't rape me as they had thousands of other women. But then the gang was distracted by some other people who came out of the hospital, and in those few seconds we ran. We crawled into a garden full of cassava plants. We hid there. It was getting dark, rain began—it was the rainy season. The sun was low. Blood was pouring from my arm so I tied a cloth around it. They came hunting us. We were almost under their feet, but we lay very still among the leaves. I could hear their conversation while they were searching. I heard them calling out to us.'

She's watching their feet pass by, sinking into the mud. She hears their laughter. They are having fun. Isaac's face is pressed against her chest. He's crying. She feels her own bladder give way, soaking her dress. She's praying with all her soul that her last child will die quickly.

'Maybe a guardian angel hid us with his wings,' she says. 'Maybe. But if that's true, why us? There was no angel for the multitude who died. No angel for Giselle, for my husband, my sons, my parents. Why should Isaac and I be spared? Why did we deserve any sheltering wings?'

She looks from one shocked face to another. Sam has taken the barrel away from his chin. He sits upright, pressing his fist against his lips. Abigail is wide-eyed, shaking her head. Neil has been shedding tears as he listens to her story. Even Buddy lies flat, his nose on his paws, his tail still.

'When it was dark, the men went away. They laughed and shouted to me that we couldn't hide forever, they'd come back for us tomorrow and finish the job. We waited an hour in the rain and then we crawled very slowly to the house of a friend, a woman I hoped I could trust. She was a widow. I only asked for food and water but she hid us in a small shed at the back of her house. It was a long-drop toilet, full of flies. We could only lie down if we curled up on the floor one at a time. My friend was risking her own life. I heard she died last year. I hope she will rest in peace and rise in glory.'

Mutesi takes a moment, her head bowed in homage to the woman who saved their lives.

'We hid for five weeks,' she says at last. 'Among a thousand buzzing flies, with just the filthy clothes we were wearing when we ran from our home. We had one book, which my friend brought to us. She found it on the ground outside the ruins of our house. Everything had been burned or stolen but she found this one thing. It was my book on anatomy, from my days at the nursing school. It was a very good book to have. By the end of five weeks we had no strength left and no muscles; we hadn't walked in all that time. But Isaac knew all about anatomy! There were gaps in the wooden walls and sometimes we peeped out. That brave woman smuggled in food when she could, but she had to be very careful. There were spies everywhere. I felt our situation was hopeless—as you feel now, Sam. Every time the sun came up I was sure we would die that day. The worst thing was wondering what method they would choose. They were—' she grimaces '—imaginative. We were saved when some soldiers from the Tutsi army arrived in the area and took us to a camp for displaced persons. I was thin by then! I had almost disappeared—can you imagine me thin?'

She tries to laugh at herself, but her listeners don't smile.

After a long moment, Abigail clears her throat. 'Where did you go?'

'I had an uncle in Uganda. A teacher. We were able to get to him and then we were not homeless anymore. His wife had relatives in London so at last we came here. They didn't recognise my nursing qualification but I was able to work as a carer. Isaac is a scientist now. That book was the start! You met his son.'

'Emmanuel?'

'Emmanuel! Yes! So, Sam. This morning when you pointed your gun at my head, I thought maybe you were just finishing the work that fate began. You were delivering what was intended for me all along.'

Sam draws a hand across his face. 'Sorry.'

'You don't need to be sorry,' says Mutesi. 'It's all over now.'

'How did you manage to keep going?' whispers Neil.

'For Isaac. He lived, so I had to live too. Otherwise I would have wanted to follow my family. You know, to be one of eight kids, to have had five of your own, and to find yourself almost alone in an unfamiliar, cold country, using a language I didn't know very well . . .' She shakes her head. 'Isaac and I were lucky to be alive, but at first it was hard to be a survivor.'

The kind cousins met her at Heathrow, embracing her with tears. She didn't know them; she didn't know anyone in this strange continent. She and Isaac arrived at the start of an especially bleak January, and for the next three months they shivered. Mutesi had never felt so cold in her life. She wouldn't have believed it possible for a city to have such short days, to be smothered in grey skies for weeks at a time. Was there no sun here? She points to the table, where Emmanuel's pencils are still scattered around his artwork.

'But spring came in the end. And look—see that? The picture Emmanuel drew of his daddy. That's what we survived for.'

'And the nightwatchman?' asks Sam. 'The others? Don't tell me those bastards got away with it.'

'Many of them were imprisoned. Not all, but many. Philippe went to prison for a long time, but his wife and children stayed in their same house not far from the hospital. He returned to them. He lives there now. It's a nice place, high on a hillside. I'm told that he has grandchildren, great-grandchildren. I haven't forgiven him. I'm not a saint, I don't want to kiss him and say it's all forgotten. No! I remember it every day. I hated those people for a long time. I used to imagine cutting off their limbs if I ever had the chance. But then I realised that I was wasting my emotion on them, so I made the decision to stop hating. Perhaps God will reward them for what they did, or perhaps he will forgive. It's not for me to decide. Many of them are ashamed—they don't understand how they became such monsters. Many have tried to make reparation.'

'Reparation!' Sam looks incredulous. 'What, with money? Seriously? Do they think they can buy their way out of that kind of guilt?'

'They just want to show their remorse. There are peace clubs where people go and meet. Victims and perpetrators talk to one another.'

'Jesus—they pulled your daughter out of your arms, they . . .' Sam can't say it. He can't put the evil into words. People never can.

'Yes.'

'And your boys too.'

'My boys too. But don't forget, my friend risked her life for us. Perhaps she was the real angel. There are many such angels.'

Sam raises a hand to his forehead, fingering the wound. He seems dazed. His eyes aren't focused.

'When?' he asks. 'When did all this happen?'

'In 1994.'

'I was born in 1994. The tenth of May.'

'Were you?' She smiles at him. 'Good! Then your life began when my children's ended.'

'I don't know what to say.'

No. People never did, and that's why very few have ever heard this story. She has learned from experience that it's not something people want to hear. They avoid her once she's told it, as though the horror of her past taints her. Years ago, Mutesi made a statement to the new authorities in Rwanda, and of course she told her uncle in Kampala what had happened to his family. But ever since then she's kept this thing locked away. It's constantly pacing, snarling, overshadowing her days, but she refuses to open the door of its cage. Even Isaac knows only the bare facts. Mercifully, his memories are patchy. The account she's just given is heavily edited, the atrocities skimmed over. She saw more, heard more, felt more, smelled much more than she's described. The video that replays in her head at night is a thousand times more harrowing.

But today is different. She's told her story in the hope of reaching out to Sam. He's lost. Perhaps she can help him find his way. She wants him to live. She wants him to have a tomorrow. Perhaps this is why the Lord brought her to Tuckbox today.

She leans closer to him. 'Listen, Sam, please. The point is that *your* life doesn't have to end here. That's what I am trying to tell you. People survive. Human beings go on. They have a capacity for love and a capacity for evil, but they go on. Like you, I lost my home and my family, but I had other moments. There will be other moments for you too. Better moments. The law will take its course—' she claps her hands, staring into Sam's face to emphasise the point, forcing him to meet her eye '—and you'll *meet* it, Sam, and you will survive it. Yes?'

'I'll get life for murder. Then there's kidnapping you lot.'

'False imprisonment actually,' says Abigail. 'But I think there's a good chance you could avoid a murder conviction. If they'll accept a guilty plea to manslaughter on the grounds of loss of control, you won't get a mandatory life sentence. You could be looking at, say, twelve years, could be out after about six. Julia will still be a child! You can still be a dad.'

'We'll come and visit you,' says Neil stoutly. 'I'll probably end up in there with you, the way I'm going. And the day you come out, Buddy and I will be waiting at the gates.'

Sam smiles down at the old dog. 'He'd be about three hundred in dog years by then.'

'Come with us,' urges Abigail. 'We'll all stay right beside you so no trigger-happy copper shoots you. Come with us. Do me a favour—make me feel I've done at least something useful with my life.'

Mutesi says nothing more. It's all been said, and she is so very tired now. It's time for action.

Lord, she prays silently, *give strength to my arm and courage to my heart.*

Then she stands up from her chair, reaches both hands towards Sam, takes hold of his gun by that wicked barrel. He loosens his grip as she pulls it from his grasp.

She's never held a gun before. Sam made it look easy to fling the thing around, but it's heavy and cumbersome in her hands. It feels evil, like holding a snake. She'd unload it if she could, but has no idea how. She grips it with extreme care, making sure the barrel is facing the ceiling, and carries it to the counter. Then she lays it down full length, wincing as the metalwork hits the benchtop with a clunk.

'There,' she says, turning around. 'Sam! You look like a very nice boy without that thing.'

He *does* look like a nice boy. A lonely, vulnerable boy. She wants to take him in her arms.

'Can we stay for another few minutes?' he asks. 'Even just five?'

Abigail shrugs. 'What's five minutes? We've been here all day.'

'Tea?' suggests Neil.

THIRTY-SEVEN

Mutesi

In the end, it's half an hour.

While Mutesi and Neil produce one final, ritual cup of tea, Abigail uses the phone to update Eliza.

'We'll be out soon,' she says. 'We've had a hitch, but it's fine . . . yes, really, it's fine . . . don't worry. We'll be out in a few minutes.'

Once she's ended the call, Abigail swings into problem-solving mode. She sits down opposite Sam and delivers a crash course in the differences between murder and manslaughter. Mutesi listens with interest. This girl may not always be the most patient, but she's useful to have around when you're in trouble with the law.

'Are you listening, Sam? Now's the time for some damage limitation. The moment you step outside you'll be arrested. You'll be taken to a police station somewhere and I won't be able to come along with you. First thing to remember: get a solicitor. Okay?'

'Okay.'

'Don't say a single word until you've got one. They'll have a list of solicitors on duty. And they have to make sure you've had enough sleep before you're interviewed.'

Sam is rubbing his eyes with his knuckles.

'Okay,' he repeats wearily. 'Get a solicitor.'

'You're guilty of manslaughter, at least. I can't really see a defence to that. But you've got a run with a defence to murder. If you lost control—' she draws a tick in the air with her forefinger—'*tick*, on your own account you were off the planet—and if that was attributable to things said or done which were really terrible—*tick*, Robert royally fucked you over—and caused you to have . . . um, what's the test? A "justifiable sense of being seriously wronged", or words to that effect. *Tick, tick*. You've told us yourself: years of manipulation, losing your farm, your child, Nicola, your mother, not even knowing about her death or her funeral, then he makes out he's dumped her ashes. I bet most juries would be sympathetic. They'd find your sense of being wronged justifiable. Got that?'

'I think so.'

'Now.' She's tapping the table. 'The fact that you drove all the way to London with a shotgun and ammo in your car is a *really* big problem. Makes it look planned. You can't argue loss of control if it wasn't spontaneous. But you were just intending to threaten him, right?'

'I never thought I'd shoot him.'

'Right. So make that very clear in your interview.'

Sam doesn't seem to be taking in much of this lesson. His arms have crept around the cardboard urn on the table, his gaze straying towards Robert's body.

'I killed him though, didn't I? I did it. I'm guilty.'

She smacks her palm to her nose. 'No! Manslaughter, yes, but maybe not murder. I mean, yes, you carried out the act, but that's not all that matters. Look, here's how it works . . .'

And off she goes again, patiently explaining details of the law to a man who doesn't care at all. It's very obvious that he doesn't care. Mutesi suspects he's not even listening, though he's nodding at random intervals.

'Does that make sense now?' Abi asks, once she's been through it all for the second time.

'Okay.' Sam gives her a thumbs-up, but his face is bloodless. 'Got it. Thanks.'

A pause follows. Nobody seems keen to move.

'I thought I'd be cock-a-hoop to be walking out of here,' says Neil, fingering his tattered bobble cap. 'But I'm not really. Dreading it a bit. Not sure I want to face the outside world. Dunno why.'

'Because the rest of your life awaits you,' says Mutesi.

'You think?'

'Oh yes. You've been given a second chance, and that is a daunting thing.'

Abigail is staring at Neil's sore hands. His finger goes right through a hole in the cap.

'Where are you planning on sleeping tonight?' she asks.

'Mutesi's church.' He winks at Mutesi, who smiles back at him. 'They're very hospitable, they don't put spikes on their bench.'

'Well, that's not happening.' Abigail's tone is brisk. 'You're coming back to my place. We've got two spare bedrooms.'

'Thanks, Abi, but I'd rather say no than have you regret it. It's too much. I know in here, today, we've been in the same boat, but as soon as we're back on that street I'll be the rough sleeper and you'll be the commuter who buys my *Big Issue*. And ne'er the twain shall meet. I'm not meaning to sound bitter, it's just a fact. I smell. I'm a thief with a gambling habit. I've got an old dog who dribbles and eats from bins.'

'I'm sure you'll both scrub up.'

'It's not just the physical mess, it's where I've been in my mind. Trying to get me to reintegrate into the mainstream of life is like trying to put a new patch on an old coat. It doesn't work; the stitching pulls away and the patch falls off.'

'You're not an old coat. You're a Neil.'

He's still fidgeting with his hat. 'I've been in and out of squats, bed and breakfasts, emergency shelters. A couple of years ago a nice family took me in. Born-again evangelicals. They got me a haircut and a trip to the dentist.' He puts a finger to his jaw, wincing at the memory. 'Actually the dentist *was* a lifesaver because I was in bloody agony with a broken tooth. Anyway, this family made me their project. They fed me up, helped me get a job-seeker's allowance, put me on the list for a bedsit. They took me to their church and everyone laid hands on me and spoke in tongues and prayed the gambling demon out of me—*abra-cadabra*—just like that! I didn't enjoy the experience at all, but I could hardly refuse, could I, when they were being so good to me?' He turns the bobble cap inside out. 'Yup. Nope. Took me ten days to answer the siren call of the bookie. I blew the money they'd lent me to buy second-hand clothes for interviews. I knew I'd do it again, and again. I knew I'd do to them what I did to Heather and the kids. So I upped and left. And, Abi, you know how I felt when I was walking away in the middle of the night?'

'Um . . . guilty?'

'Free. I felt *free*. I'm a gambler to my core. If anyone tries to stop me, I just walk away.'

'You ever see those people again?' asks Sam.

'I saw the parents one night near St Paul's, working in a soup kitchen. Nice people. Really nice people. I was in the queue but I put down my plate and left. Too ashamed to face 'em.'

Abigail raises an eyebrow. 'Yeah. Well, I'm not born again, I'm not after a pet atheist to convert and I have never turned the other cheek in my life. I'm offering you—on a very short-term basis—a bath, a bed and some of Charlie's clothes. He won't mind. I don't do the casting-out-of-demons thing, but if you steal from us I'll kick you where it hurts.'

Mutesi chuckles, blowing on her tea. She didn't want yet more tea, she's sure nobody did. But they have all welcomed this lull before the storm. As soon as the four of them step outside, their fragile balance will be shattered. The intensity they have felt within these four walls may never be felt again, by any of them.

Intensity of fear, of comradeship, perhaps even of love. Sam will be taken away and she shudders for him. God knows what he will face. For the hostages there will be police and statements and reporters. There will be life. A soft bed, yes, a shower—lovely—phone calls and visits from family. And then the flat emptiness of escape.

'Go and stay with Abigail, Neil,' says Sam suddenly. 'Don't be a jerk about it.'

Mutesi looks at him, surprised by the cheerfulness in his voice. His shoulders have straightened. There's a new lightness to him.

'I mean it, old man.' He's grinning at Neil. 'She can be your surrogate daughter. Abi, you've scored yourself an extra dad. Be happy.'

Woman behold your son, thinks Mutesi. Behold your mother.

'Deal!' cries Abigail. 'And no matter how long you get, Sam, we'll visit you. Mutesi will smuggle in tea and carrot cake until you're a free man again.'

Sam's staring at Abigail. Such intensity. Mutesi wonders what it is he'd like to tell her.

'Thanks,' he says. 'I'll look forward to it.'

It really is time to go. They all seem to sense the moment. There's a collective sigh, and Neil lays a hand on Sam's arm.

'Ready, mate?'

Sam swallows, and nods.

'Eliza says we're not to bring anything,' says Abigail, placing the café phone on the table. 'No handbags, no nothing. This is a crime scene.'

Everyone begins to shuffle along the booth, standing up, looking apprehensive. Abigail is the first to reach the door.

'You two go first,' says Mutesi. 'I'll walk right behind you, with Sam.'

'Shall we take bets on how many guys in combat gear are waiting out here? I reckon at least ten.'

'Not funny,' says Neil.

Abigail grins, mutters, 'See you on the other side,' then opens the door and steps out, followed by Neil with Buddy. Sam is flexing his fingers, stamping his feet like a man at the starting gates of a marathon.

'I'm scared. I'm scared, Mutesi.'

She takes his hand in hers, tucking it firmly under her arm. Later, she will realise that she's completely misunderstood what it is he fears.

'We'll go out together,' she promises. 'Like this. I will not let go of you.'

A bitter wind swoops on them as they move over the threshold. Spotlights are shining in their faces. It's disorientating. They're blinded. Mutesi hesitates, wondering which way to turn.

Sam has stopped too.

'Oh! Mum's ashes!' he cries. 'I can't leave them—they're what I came for in the first place! You go on, I'll nip back in and grab them.'

She feels his fingers grasping hers for one final moment before he pulls himself away. By the time she's turned around to follow him, the door is slamming in her face. She hears the key turn in the lock. The bolts.

She's banging the palm of her hand on the glass, shouting and rattling the handle as people run from all sides. Heavy boots, loud voices. She's surrounded by rescuers, but they're irrelevant now.

THIRTY-EIGHT

Eliza

An aluminium can clatters down the gutter ahead, leading the way, tumbling faster than she can walk. She hadn't realised quite how cold it is out here.

It's almost ten o'clock. She's a hermit leaving her cell. Stepping out of the negotiation room is like entering another world—a crowded, active world. All day long other units have been rushing around, making decisions and organising practicalities while she has sat in that one small, silent space, building a connection with a disembodied voice.

She's wrapping her scarf around her mouth as she heads towards the inner cordon. A couple of uniformed officers have just got out of a squad car and are moving in the same direction, chatting about something they saw on telly last night. One of them spots her and calls out, 'Well done, ma'am, I hear it's all over bar the shouting.' An ambulance is waiting with its engine running, prepared for any casualties. Hospital staff will be on standby too.

Everything is in place; everyone is ready to do their job. Sam will be arrested as soon as he steps out of Tuckbox. Teams will go in, secure the crime scene and begin the investigation into Robert Lacey's death. Others will deal with the taking of statements, the media, the contacting of Lacey's relatives, the traffic chaos. It's going to be a busy night for a lot of people.

Eliza's task now is to keep her promise to Sam. She'll meet him and stay with him for the first few minutes of his arrest. For a negotiator to break promises is counterproductive. It's amazing how often you find yourself in a crisis negotiation with the same person a year down the track. Lie to them once, or let them down, and it comes back to bite you.

As she passes the ambulance a figure hurries around it, hailing her with a raised hand.

'They said I could wait at the cordon,' he calls out. 'Well . . . at least, they didn't say I *couldn't*. You're the negotiator? You're DI McClean?'

She nods, perplexed. 'And you are . . .?'

She can sense his jitters, though she can't see much of him in the dark. His hands are shoved into the pockets of a rain jacket: a young man, stocky but not heavy. Nervous smile.

'Charles Bowman,' he says. 'Abigail Garcia is my, um, fiancée. Or something.'

'You're engaged?'

'She doesn't approve of marriage as an institution. But I hate the word *partner*. Is it true—she's coming out now?'

'Let's hope so,' mutters Eliza, silently cursing whoever's in charge of families and witnesses. This man shouldn't be here. He should have been kept well back, out of sight and out of range. This isn't over yet.

'Can I tag along with you?' he asks, and falls into step beside her.

They arrive at the inner cordon, waiting at the tape beside a small crowd of police and other personnel. There's an air of relief and expectation. Eliza rubs her cheeks vigorously with her hands. *Come on, Sam, come on.*

'You've got to stay behind the tape,' she tells Charlie. 'No matter what.'

'Will do.' He shivers. 'This has been the worst day of my life.'

She doesn't answer. Her focus is on the street door of Tuckbox, willing it to open. *Come on, Sam. Come on, Sam.*

'I've got to give Abi some upsetting news,' says Charlie. 'We've been trying IVF for ages and I got the latest result today. Negative. I don't want to have to tell her. She was really hopeful this time, I could tell from her internet searches. She's been looking for cots and things.'

'And were you hoping too?'

He's staring towards the café, hands still in his pockets, shoulders hunched.

'I just want her to walk out of that door. That's all I want. I don't really care about anything else.'

'Me too,' says Eliza.

Wilton Street could be a film set: spotlights, ghost-faces, people entering stage right, exiting stage left. There are scripts, there are roles. This is the final scene. It's a wrap.

Come on, Sam.

Ah! Movement down at Tuckbox. A pair of spotlit figures step out of the doorway, hands held high, and walk towards the firearms officers. They have a dog with them.

'It's her!' shouts Charlie. He looks ready to leap over the tape. He reaches out to grab Eliza's arm, doesn't even seem to know he's doing it. 'That's Abi! She's safe! Thank you, thank you.'

A smattering of applause breaks out from the group at the cordon as a third and fourth figure step into the spotlights, holding on to one another. That's it. Four people. That's everyone.

Eliza is about to duck beneath the tape when something seems to go wrong. One of the figures has turned and run back into the café. The other is banging on the street door, shouting.

'What's happening?' asks Charlie.

The negotiation phone begins to vibrate in her pocket. *Tuckbox.*

She fumbles to answer.

'Sam? Hello? Is that you?'

'Eliza.'

'What happened? I saw you come out! I'm here, waiting for you.'

He's panting loudly, as though he's trying to speak while running up a mountain.

'Tell them to take Mum home,' he gasps. '*Take her home*. Tell them, okay? They'll know what it means.'

'Sam, hang on a minute—'

'This isn't your fault. Okay? Okay, Eliza? This isn't your fault.'

'Sam!'

It reaches her in stereo, exactly as she predicted, travelling through the air and down the line. It echoes around and around the street, around and around in her brain. A dog barks. There are groans from the watchers at the inner cordon.

A single shot. The final one.

THIRTY-NINE

Eliza

It's long after midnight by the time she unlocks her front door.

There's bound to be an internal inquiry as well as public inquests. The media will be all over today's events. Eliza has already spoken to the three hostages. They'll be asked for detailed statements tomorrow but tonight they're exhausted. They're also grieving; they seem distraught, as though they've lost a family member.

'He was coming out with us,' Abigail Garcia kept saying. 'He was right behind us. Mutesi was holding his hand, weren't you, Mutesi?'

'I was!' Mutesi screwed up her face, sighing, 'Sam . . . Sam.'

Neil was tearful. 'We were going to help him. We were going to visit him in prison.'

The negotiation team have already begun writing reports, filing their notes and records. The three of them spent another hour in the attic room, pulling everything together. Thank God Paul had done such a meticulous job of noting every decision along the way.

'This was a success, Eliza,' he insisted. 'The hostages all got out unharmed, not a shot fired by police. Fantastic. You kept your nerve. If you hadn't, we'd have had SCO19 storming the café when he found Nicola. That might have led to a far worse tragedy.'

'I failed, though. I lost Sam.'

Ashwin was leaning his forehead against the window.

'You didn't lose him,' he said. 'You walked beside him, you listened to his story.'

'But he still died.'

'That was his decision to make. He's lived with depression for years, and his future wasn't looking bright. You showed him a way out of Tuckbox, you gave him a choice, but there was no escape from what was in his own head. He talked everything through with a person he trusted—you—and he knew what he wanted to do. He chose to speak to you in his last few seconds. *You*. Nobody else.'

The three were quiet for a while, looking out towards the café.

That single shot. Such a lonely sound.

•

On the way back to her car, she looked in through the door of Tuckbox. It was all so familiar, all exactly as she expected it to be. She felt as though she'd spent the day in there alongside Sam and the hostages. It's a crime scene now, brightly lit, sealed off and guarded. SOCO will be taking measurements and samples, photographing everything including what's left of Robert and poor Sam. She doubts whether the place will ever function as a café again, now that the last act of a tragedy has played out there.

Nicola has handed over the message Sam wrote for Julia. She seems shocked about his death—horrified, even—but not grief-stricken. Eliza has a suspicion that she'll be on her feet again in no time. Perhaps she was too young when her pregnancy forced her to try to settle down with Sam; perhaps she wanted things from life that he could never give.

Sam's letter is written on a white serviette, neatly folded into four. The handwriting is childish, each letter individually and carefully formed, all in blue crayon.

My Julia,
The last time I saw you we read The Tiger Who Came to Tea. Do you remember? That was one of my happyest memries ever. All my best memries are of you. You are the most wonderful thing in my world.

I know you will be an amazeing woman by the time you read this. Whatever your doing, whoever you are, I will be prowd of you. Please be happy.

I love you with all my heart and all my soul. Sorry not to be with you but if I can I will be watching over you and cheering you on every step of your life.

LOVE
Dad XXX

She drops her keys into the bowl by the front door before listlessly hanging up her coat and scarf. She feels as though someone's hit her on the back of the head with a mallet, and yet she won't be able to sleep. She'll hear that last shot again. And again. And again. She'll know exactly what it means. She'll hear his voice: *This isn't your fault*. He's putting down the phone, picking up the gun, shutting his eyes. He's all alone.

Yoda appears from nowhere and winds around and around her legs, butting her calves with his solid little head. She stoops to lift him into her arms, carrying him into the kitchen.

Richard has left a note on the table.

Shepherd's pie in fridge. Your mother phoned, no message. Liam ran out of school shirts, I put one in machine can u hang it up? Liam is not wanting to go to school tomorrow. Will need to make some decisions. Am worried.

Well done in Balham, heard on news all hostages released. Proud of you.
R X

She deals with Liam's shirt, tips cat biscuits into Yoda's saucer. She ignores the shepherd's pie in the fridge. After glimpsing the carnage in Tuckbox she can't imagine ever wanting to eat again. She knows from experience that the effect will wear off.

Putting down the phone, picking up the gun, shutting his eyes.

She turns off the kitchen lights and walks quietly upstairs. The third stair creaks when she steps on it. Always has, always will.

Jack's room first: calm in the soft glow of the nightlight. The baby is jammed into one corner of the cot, lying on his front with his bottom sticking up in the air. He's wearing his all-in-one sleep suit. *Julia would be standing in her cot, holding out her arms for me to pick her up.* Blankets and toys are scattered haphazardly all around him. It looks as though he's been having a party in there. She covers him up, leans down and kisses his pudgy cheek.

Liam's room is darker, but there's enough streetlight filtering through his curtains to see his head on the pillow. The teenager is snuffling quietly. She crosses to the bed and sits down on it, close to the curve of his bent knees.

'Mum.' His voice is slurred, half drowned in sleep.

'Shh.' She leans down to tuck the duvet around his chin.

'It was awful.'

'I'm sorry. Dad told me.'

'I'm never going back to school.'

'Park that worry for now. We'll talk about it tomorrow.'

He curls in on himself, burying his face in his pillow.

'I'm never going back. I can't go back. I really can't, Mum.'

She feels his misery. It overwhelms her. She drops down to kneel on the floor, putting both her arms around him.

Picking up the gun, shutting his eyes.

'No school for you tomorrow,' she says. 'That's a decision made. We'll go to the winter ice rink, just you and me. We'll decide what to do.'

'Work?'

'No. Day off.'

'Promise?'

'Promise.'

Little by little his breathing slows. In ten minutes he's snuffling again. She rests her head on the pillow and shuts her eyes. She's still kneeling on his floor when a weak winter sunrise seeps through the curtains.

FORTY

Sam

He's glad to see they've remembered to shut the gate behind them.

They could almost be a walking club: a small girl, a man and three women of different ages and stages of life. They spread across the rich pastureland, looking around as they orientate themselves. There's a dog too, a shining black-and-white collie who goes nuts as soon as he's let out of the car. He remembers this place.

It's a glorious day on Tyndale Farm. Blue sky and sunshine, bright clouds scudding in a steady breeze. The hedgerows are bursting into leaf. The air rings with the songs of nesting birds as they dart and chatter around the spinney. The new owners haven't destroyed it after all—not yet, at least. Until yesterday ewes and lambs were grazing this field, but it's empty now. Probably a good thing because Toby wouldn't have been able to resist trying to round them up.

My Julia! Look at her!

She sticks out her arms and pretends to be an aeroplane, charging down the slope in her new blue wellies, curls flying. He reaches out to touch her head as she skims past. Perhaps she feels him. She stops suddenly, looks around, laughs and gallops on again.

Mutesi and Neil have travelled here in Abi's car. Mutesi looks exactly the same as ever, but Neil could be ten years younger: clean-shaven, short back and sides, plumpness rounding the gaunt cheeks. The limp has gone completely. He's managed to land a job as handyman in Mutesi's nursing home. She swung it for him, just as she found him a bedsit near her own place, just as either she or Abi march him to Gambler's Anonymous twice a week. Nobody else could do it, but they can. Mutesi tried very hard to persuade him to visit her church but there he drew the line.

Abi's pregnant, though she doesn't know it yet. She and Charlie have an adventure ahead of them. They'll be doting parents. It's a brave thing to do, risking so much love. Too brave for Sam. It broke him.

Nicola stands a little apart, wearing her sky-blue poncho.

'We're here,' she tells them. 'You're standing in Sundance's field. That's the spinney. That's the trough.'

He knows she's remembering the night they rode through the midsummer-scented darkness, and sat on that gate, and watched the moon rise. She didn't want to be a part of this gathering today, she didn't want to set foot on Tyndale ever again. Abi pressured her to come, to bring Julia and show them exactly which field they should be in. Nicola agreed because she feels guilty. Guilt can drive a person mad.

'I was a victim too,' she said, when Abi phoned her.

Abi laughed at her. 'You keep telling yourself that.'

Abi is carrying the rose-covered urn. Mutesi has hold of a green plastic tub. It looks exactly like the one they had for Dad.

'Shall we wait for a gust of wind?' asks Abi as they prise off the lids.

'Yes,' says Mutesi. 'A really good, strong gust to give them the best send-off.'

Neil is shielding his eyes with both his hands, looking across the valley towards Holdsworth.

'What a lovely spot,' he says. 'I can see why they wanted to come home.'

Abi wets her finger and holds it up in the air, waiting. She looks very different today. Her hair is bundled messily into a clip. She's wearing jeans and a T-shirt, Converse shoes. She isn't thinking about her work at all, or about the phone call she'll soon be getting from the clinic. She's made all of this happen. She's doing it for Sam.

He senses the gust before it arrives. It stirs the treetops. It plays in the grass, lifting tendrils of hair around Abi's face. Julia runs headlong into it, yelling at the top of her voice. There's so much joy in her. That makes him happy. She'll be all right.

'Now?' asks Abi.

'Now!' cry Mutesi and Neil.

Together the two women tip their urns. Ashes pour out in a cloud of fine dust, mingling and billowing for one last moment before the air lifts them. Then they fly and tumble, swooping across Sundance's field like a swarm of bees.

Acknowledgements

I was in a crowded café with my friend Liz Tovey when I first glimpsed the idea for this book. I interrupted our conversation and began to babble about it. This behaviour must have appeared unhinged but Liz remained—as always—thoughtful and interested. Just days later she learned of her tragic illness. It is a measure of her fundamental generosity that as time passed she continued to encourage me while her health deteriorated, never failing to ask for a progress report on 'the siege story'. Thank you, Liz. I finished the darned thing. I wish you were here to see the result of that day's brainstorming.

I owe heartfelt thanks to Jane Gregory and her team at David Higham Associates, especially Stephanie Glencross; to Annette Barlow and Ali Lavau at Allen & Unwin for their editorial wizardry; and to Angela Handley for keeping the whole show on the road. Thanks also to Clare Drysdale and Kate Ballard in London for their unflagging support.

To Tim Meredith, who has fixed more than one mower and ploughed more than one Sussex field: thank you for knowing about haymaking, hedgerows and ancient Land Rovers; for all those cups of coffee made just right; and for putting up with this whole writing malarkey.

George, Sam and Cora. Thanks for travelling with me.